The Seventh Door
and Other Stories

The Seventh Door
and Other Stories

Intizar Husain

edited and with an introduction by
Muhammad Umar Memon

A Three Continents Book
Lynne Rienner Publishers
Boulder & London

Published in the United States of America in 1998 by
Lynne Rienner Publishers, Inc.
1800 30th Street, Boulder, Colorado 80301

and in the United Kingdom by
Lynne Rienner Publishers, Inc.
3 Henrietta Street, Covent Garden, London WC2E 8LU

Library of Congress Cataloging-in-Publication Data
Intiẓār Ḥusain, 1925–
The seventh door and other stories / edited and with an introduction by Muhammad Umar Memon.
Translated from Urdu.
ISBN 0-89410-821-2
ISBN 0-89410-822-0 (pbk.)
I. Memon, Muhammad Umar, 1939– . II. Title.
PK2200.I57A6 1998
891'.43937—DC20 95-49396
CIP

British Cataloguing in Publication Data
A Cataloguing in Publication record for this book
is available from the British Library.

Printed and bound in the United States of America

The paper used in this publication meets the requirements of the American National Standard for Permanence of Paper for Printed Library Materials Z39.48-1984.

5 4 3 2 1

To

Anis, Asim, Laura

with much affection

Contents

Acknowledgments

All the short stories included in this volume, except "The Seventh Door," have previously appeared in the *Journal of South Asian Literature,* 18:2 (Summer/Fall, 1983), which I guest edited; these are reproduced here with the permission of the *Journal*'s editors. In most cases the earlier translations have been substantially revised. "The Seventh Door" has also appeared previously, in the volume *The Tale of the Old Fisherman: Contemporary Urdu Short Stories,* which I edited for Three Continents Press in 1991; it is here included with the permission of the publisher.

The stories were published originally in Urdu, as follows:

"The Seventh Door" ("Sātvāṅ Dar"), from Intiẓār Ḥusain, *Kaṅkarī* (Lahore: Maktaba-e Jadīd [1955]), pp. 179–195.

"An Unwritten Epic" ("Ēk Bin-likhī Razmiya"), from Intiẓār Ḥusain, *Galī Kūčē* (Lahore: Maktaba-e Kārvāṅ [1952]), pp. 193–224.

"The Stairway" ("Sīṛhiyāṅ"), from Intiẓār Ḥusain, *Shahr-e Afsōs* (Lahore: Maktaba-e Kārvāṅ [1973]), pp. 62–83.

"The Back Room" ("Dehlīz"), from Intiẓār Ḥusain, *Shahr-e Afsōs* (Lahore: Maktaba-e Kārvāṅ [1973]), pp. 44–61.

"A Stranded Railroad Car" ("Kaṭā hū'ā Ḍibbā"), from Intiẓār Ḥusain, *Shahr-e Afsōs* (Lahore: Maktaba-e Kārvāṅ [1973]), pp. 29–43.

"Toward His Fire" ("Apnī Āg kī Ṭaraf"), from Intiẓār Ḥusain, *Shahr-e Afsōs* (Lahore: Maktaba-e Kārvāṅ [1973]), pp. 190–206.

"The Lost Ones" ("Vō Jō Khō'ē Ga'ē"), from Intiẓār Ḥusain, *Shahr-e Afsōs* (Lahore: Maktaba-e Kārvāṅ [1973]), pp. 9–28.

"The Shadow" ("Parčhā'īṅ"), from Intiẓār Ḥusain, *Ākhirī Ādmī* (Lahore: Kitābiyāt [1967]), pp. 37–56.

"Comrades" ("Ham-safar"), from Intiẓār Ḥusain, *Ākhirī Ādmī* (Lahore: Kitābiyāt [1967]), pp. 75–92.

"The Legs" ("Ṭāṅgēṅ"), from Intiẓār Ḥusain, *Ākhirī Ādmī* (Lahore: Kitābiyāt [1967]), pp. 107–132.

"The Yellow Cur" ("Zard Kuttā"), from Intiẓār Ḥusain, *Ākhirī Ādmī* (Lahore: Kitābiyāt [1967]), pp. 14–35.

"The Last Man" ("Ākhirī Ādmī"), from Intiẓār Ḥusain, *Ākhirī Ādmī* (Lahore: Kitābiyāt [1967]), pp. 1–13.

"Metamorphosis" ("Kāyā-kalp"), from Intiẓār Ḥusain, *Ākhirī Ādmī* (Lahore:

Kitābiyāt [1967]), pp. 93–105.
"Prisoner(s)" ("Asīr"), from Intiẓār Ḥusain, *Kačhvē* (Lahore: Maṭ̤bū^cāt [1981]), pp. 46–54.
"The Turtles" ("Kačhvē"), from Intiẓār Ḥusain, *Kačhvē* (Lahore: Maṭ̤bū^cāt [1981]), pp. 73–92.

A Note on Transliteration

Non-English words have not been transliterated in the text of the short stories, but in the critical and expository sections of the book the letters of the Urdu alphabet have been transliterated as follows:

alif	as: a, i, u, ā
bē, pē, tē, ṭē, s̱ē	as: b, p, t, ṭ, s̱
jīm, chē, ḥē, khē	as: j, č, ḥ, kh
dāl, ḍāl, ẕal	as: d, ḍ, ẕ
rē, ṛē, zē, zhē	as: r, ṛ, z, zh
sīn, shīn	as: s, sh
ṣuād, z̤uād	as: ṣ, z̤
t̤ōʾē, ẓōʾē	as: t̤, ẓ
ᶜain, ghain	as: ᶜ, gh
fē, qāf	as: f, q
kāf, gāf	as: k, g
lām, mīm, nūn	as: l, m, n
vāʾo	as: v, ū, o, au

chōṭī hē	as: h
chōṭī yē	as: ī
baṛī yē	as: y, e, ai
nūn-e ghunna	as: ṅ
hamza	as: ʾ
iẓāfat	as: -e

Word-final *h* is indicated only when it is pronounced, e.g., in *nigāh* but not in *ghunna* or *qaṣīda.* The *vāʾo* of the conjunction is written *-o-*.

Perhaps the poet knows, as well as his audience, that the picture presented is not the actual story. Yet while the *ta^c^ziyah majlis* lasts, myth transcends itself; for the moment, it becomes history. For the historian of religion, however, the myth actually becomes part of history; the history not of the event, but of the community's understanding and interiorization of it, the history not of historical facts, but of the way the community has lived them. This interiorization of the drama of Karbalā⁾ is powerfully expressed in the *zīyārah* ritual. Through this ritual the community renews its covenant with and its loyalty to the *imāms,* and in a very personal way renews its own participation in this drama.

—Mahmoud Ayoub, *Redemptive Suffering in Islam*

Introduction

If I hold so firmly to the inheritance of Kafka, if I defend it as my personal inheritance, it is not because I think it useful to imitate the inimitable (and to discover again the Kafkaesque) but because it is such a formidable example of the radical autonomy of the novel (of the poetry that is the novel). Thanks to that autonomy, Franz Kafka (or the great, forgotten Hermann Broch) has told us things about our human condition (as it reveals itself in our age) which no sociological or political reflection will ever be able to tell.

—Milan Kundera, "Somewhere Behind"[1]

I

Imagine a pair of young lovers. Alone—finally. Breathless. But he pulls away. He pulls away not because he is shy. He is wearing "an inelegant and shabby pair of undershorts," which he is reluctant to peel off in her presence. A shabby pair of undershorts? Well, those were the only kind available after the Soviet invasion of Czechoslovakia. No history book will tell us about this sad little tragedy of life. Milan Kundera will.[2]

Or take the delicate young wife Lajvanti. Torn away from her home in the bloody aftermath of the partition of India in 1947, she is finally reunited with her husband, but only after she has been gang-raped by her Muslim abductors. Her silent suffering prompts her husband to treat her with all the tenderness he is capable of—more gently, perhaps, than he would the fragile plant *lājvantī,* whose leaves curl up and fold when touched. Indeed, he looks upon her as a goddess. But with all that, he is unwilling to resume conjugal relations with her, afraid that she might have been—perhaps—defiled. Lajvanti, on the other hand, longs, indeed she passionately yearns to be treated harshly by him, abused, even beaten—as she had been, daily, or almost daily, before her abduction. Not because she is masochistic; rather, because such behavior, however cruel and demeaning, still carried some tactile sensation of living, promised, at the very least, some human contact and warmth, some affirmation of her identity as a physical being, a woman, awaiting fulfillment through love and embrace—yes, quite earthy love. Again, no history book will tell us about this sadness of life. Rajinder Singh Bedi will.[3]

And Pichwa? Ah yes—Pichwa. The stuff epics are made of. Larger than life. A wrestler, an adept club-fighter, who did not allow "his *art* to be tainted by purposiveness." Who thought of the newly created Pakistan not in political, nationalistic, religious terms—as a homeland for disadvantaged Indian Muslims—but purely as an opportunity to perfect his art. A Pichwa treated poorly by Pakistan, humiliated, vanquished. A Pichwa betrayed. Intizar Husain will recount this "unwritten epic," even if no historian would ever know about those myriad, unsung, tragic heroes—forgotten in the commerce of history, in India's "tryst with destiny."[4]

Or, finally, why have the trio in "The City of Sorrow" been divested of all particularizing detail, without personal attributes and names? What robs an individual of all sense of personality?[5] Little did Zulfiqar Ali Bhutto—the ex-premier of Pakistan, hanged in 1978 by General Zia-ul-Haq, who himself one scorching day in August ten years later disintegrated in mid-air aboard his C-130 transport—know the price of his arrogance, his unyielding nature, which, combined with other factors, resulted in the dismemberment of Pakistan. But Intizar Husain, the writer, knew. In fact, he knew all too well. Or, perhaps he did not know, just as Kundera and Bedi did not know; perhaps instead, each in his own way and under some inexorable inner pressure tried to know, to articulate in the process of writing the meaning of it all, to remember, to chronicle the demoralizing, often quite comic, effects of politics on the individual psyche.

So if you want to know how simple, ordinary lives are wasted by politics and history, read a novel, a short story, a poem.

Which is not to suggest some inevitable causality between politics and creative endeavor, or that fictional aesthetics invariably do or should lie in the socio-political reality that in fact inspired a work. Of course something of the empirical will always survive in a fictional piece—however oblique and tenuous its ascription to the times—if only because fiction knows no way wholly to transcend temporality; even the best attempts in the "spatial form" have not accomplished that. But a writer's world is a radically autonomous world. It is equally fictive. An act of the imagination. It will always be different from the sum of its empirical parts. In the final synthesis of the real and the fictive, objective truth will always be subverted, almost of necessity, in favor of a fierce personal vision. Nothing, however, can stop this "personal vision" from providing insights into socio-political reality that are truer than any afforded by even the most objective chronicle of events.

Milan Kundera, in response to a question by Jordan Elgrably, has put the matter quite clearly:

> Recently I asked myself, quite suddenly, Lord, where on earth did you get the character of Lucie from, this Lucie in *The Joke*? . . . Well, where *did* I find her? The answer is that of all the women I have known in my life, Lucie represents the only type which I have not encountered. Never, in reality, have I known a truly simple woman. . . . But because Lucie was precisely the kind of woman I'd never known, something drew me to want to discover her. Lucie is a woman who is at once simple and enigmatic, and enigmatic because she is so simple. Normally you would consider that which is complex to be enigmatic, yet Lucie is so simple that I did not understand her. A positive simplicity, a simplicity adored, Lucie was a kind of counterbalance to my own visceral cynicism; she was an experience beyond my own experiences. Here is the most imaginative and inventive part of *The Joke*. Lucie is true poetry; she is not *Wahrheit* but *Dichtung*. (Elgrably 1987:23)

Poetry—indeed! Not *Truth*!

Intizar Husain articulates the multifaceted character of reality somewhat differently. Trees always fascinated him as a child—they were the object at once of longing and awe. The mangoes, the goutiered fruit of the tamarind, the birds fluttering and twittering in the foliage represented only the visible aspect of a tree's being. He rather wished to know the mystery crowding its invisible core, its impenetrable interior. And so:

> behind the trees were the stories and legends I was told as a child. In a certain tree there lives a headless man whom I never did see. I heard from others that behind another tree there lives a ghost of a woman. Where was the headless man? Where was that ghost? Where was the genie who lives in a tree and who could catch you if you passed under it on a Thursday evening? I longed to see these unknown creatures. Those things I could see and those things

> which lay behind them I couldn't see. . . . All of these things together are for me a *vāridāt,* an almost spiritual experience. (1983:160–161)

Reality is both the visible and the invisible. And more. Sometimes reality is also that which does not as yet exist in either realm—awaiting discovery in the process of writing. Thus it would be counterproductive to depend too closely on sociopolitical reality for the final meaning—rather, the experience—of a fictional work. Kundera, Bedi, and Husain might draw, as indeed they do, upon the external, but once the external is added to the creative amalgam, it is distorted beyond all recognition. And for the better. Fiction is thus a way of deliberately losing the "straight path"—the *ṣirāṭ-e mustaqīm*—for a ride along a tortuous, bumpy dirt road, of divesting oneself of the common truth, of defamiliarizing oneself with the norm.

But neither must one wholly disregard the sociopolitical reality, especially where it could conceivably augment one's potential to experience a work's aesthetic more fully. One must only be aware that the key to a work's mode of being does not lie in the external, but is inherent in the work itself. The fallacy is too apparent to need comment. But if it should, here is one. One may not be quite as lucky in the case of past writers. One may not have enough information about their sociopolitical reality. What then? Must their creative world therefore remain entirely unintelligible? And in the case of contemporary writers, who is to say that the explosion of information that quite overwhelms us is free of all emotive or ideological distortion? That politics does not decide what truth is, or ought to be? Add to it the personal reality of the writer. His or her eccentricities, idiosyncrasies. It could complicate matters further. (Imagine the dilemma of trying to psychoanalyze writers who have read Freud and thus play the same games consciously.)

In the case of a writer like Intizar Husain, some reference to sociopolitical reality is perhaps unavoidable. One of the reasons has to do with the development of modern Urdu fiction and the politicization of the literary scene during the years of Husain's apprenticeship. Premchand (1880–1936), the father of the Urdu short story, refused to see fiction—the novel, the short story—in any but a dialectical relationship with the social and political aspirations of the Indian people. Literature as an instrument of protest, reform, and redress. This conception proved normative—not because there weren't alternative voices, but because Premchand's was the most vigorous. It was also the most sustained. More importantly, it blended so well in the emergent symphony of nationalism.

When the Progressive Writers' Movement got underway in the last year of Premchand's life, when Intizar Husain must have been a child of ten, it took over intact the former's views on the role of literature in society. The Progressives dominated the literary scene entirely right up to the partition of India in 1947, and in a somewhat diminished capacity until the late 1950s. Again, there was no dearth of independent-minded writers during this period (for instance, Ahmed Ali [d. 1994], Saadat Hasan Manto [d. 1955], and Muhammad Hasan Askari [d. 1978], among others), but their individualism was unable to make any but the most diffused impact amid the pervasive influence of the Progressives, who were not only more numerous but also better organized. They could denounce with impunity whoever didn't conform to their notion of literature. In fact, they did indulge in polemics and innuendo. If some of the individualists, averse to utilitarianism, still felt compelled to associate with the Progressives, it was because the Progressives embodied the popular hope of freedom from British subjugation.

These developments, perhaps less important from a literary point of view, command considerable significance as the immediate backdrop against which Husain started his literary career. In fact, he too had come under the Progressives' influence. Soon, however, he broke with them. What alienated him most was their attitude vis-à-vis the partition of India and the formation of Pakistan. He found the literary treatment of the religious riots in the Progressive writing dogmatically liberal, lacking in depth and therefore in art (cf. 1983:160). Since then, consciously or unconsciously, Husain has been haunted by the specter of the Progressives, and has been fighting it in both his creative and critical work, most unequivocally in the latter. The passion and vehemence of the battle might appear somewhat puzzling and anachronistic today—long after the Progressives have made their exit from the scene. Yet Husain's tenacity is not without a certain value: at its root lies an unrestrained belief in the radical autonomy of literature, in a poetics of fiction disengaged from extrinsic criteria and pointed, inexorably, to what is inherent in the work itself.

The other reason for discussing sociopolitical reality stems from the necessity—or the desire—to introduce a literary tradition to a readership little familiar with it. Urdu literature continues to be a neglected field in the West. It is less known than even its other "exotic" sister-literatures—Arabic, Persian, Turkish.[6] Yet it is equally sophisticated, if not more. Some introductory information about its origins and its cultural matrix is indispensable.

To these extraneous reasons may be added a third, vitally important one. Of all the Urdu fiction writers, past and present, only Qurratulain

Hyder[7] and Intizar Husain represent the most cultured—and culturally open—personalities. Husain's memory is phenomenal and his reading, extensive. Which makes it possible for him to draw freely from a variety of sources: memories, beliefs, dreams, visions, legends, and stories from Middle Eastern oral traditions and native South Asian (Hindu and Buddhist) mythology. But this ability also invests his creative work with an allusive richness not easily accessible to a non-native Urdu reader. Practically all of Husain's fictional characters, from the most naïve and uneducated to the most sophisticated and erudite, stand in exact antipodal relationship to the minimalist conception of man fostered by the Progressives—viz., man as an economic being, alive in the present moment, aware only of the most pressing physical needs, indifferent to culture. Husain's characters are inevitably more than the sum of their parts. Each is a cultural microcosm, breathing in an instant of time. Each defies temporality through memory and desire. Hence the need to pursue *memory* and *desire* (allusion) and, of course, *temporality* (the concrete historical situation)—their mortal enemy—which activates them, brings them into play in the creative space of a short story, a novel, if only to attempt to kill them in the end.

While concrete historical situations might possibly have some relevance to Intizar Husain's creative world, they cannot be expected to expose the artistic potential of that world fully. The external is absolutely transcended in Husain's finer work, and only rarely does it threaten seriously the artistic integrity of a piece.[8]

II

In the aftermath of the turmoil of 1857—the "Mutiny," as the British still call it, but the first war of independence to most Indians—the British colonial rule became more firmly entrenched in India. It was there to stay—or so it seemed. The year 1857 was the darkest moment for the Indians, more so for the Indian Muslims. After all, the British had wrested power directly from the Muslims, and it was the latter's emperor whom they had deposed and exiled. The Muslims emerged from the "Mutiny" in a politically weakened state. Their confidence was shattered and their pride severely injured. While most drowned themselves in self-pity, and others plunged into a romantic recital of the days of their former glory, some others, like Sir Saiyad Ahmad Khan (1817–1898), thought more pragmatically. This pragmatism would become the foundation of the efforts that eventually led the British to fold up and leave their prized colony.

However important, the Muslims' share in the eviction of the British was only as large as their numbers. Being a minority—albeit sizeable—they could not have realized their goal without the Hindus—the majority population of India, among whom the process of reformation and national awakening had started even earlier than among the Muslims.

While nationalistic aspirations united the two communities, much else divided them. And even on the nationalistic front, mutual distrust never allowed the two to work together except for brief periods. The British, naturally, stood to gain by the division, which they fueled and fanned, often unabashedly; but they intensified what already existed.

As the exuberant hope of eventual freedom became a distinct possibility, it also shattered the dream of a united India. Hindu-Muslim suspicion intensified. The British departure in 1947 was thus followed by the worst Hindu-Muslim riots and bloodshed India had witnessed in its history. The emergent geometry of the new South Asian map needed all the exuberance of religious imagination to be appreciated. A tri-colored India flanked on its eastern and western borders by the stark Islamic green. In time the religious element, which had provided the rationale for the creation of Pakistan, proved too weak a bond to keep the country united in the face of its linguistic and ethnic divisions. Consequently, in 1971, the eastern wing of Pakistan broke away and, after a bloody civil war, emerged as the sovereign state of Bangladesh.

India, on the other hand, still left with numerous religious and ethnic minorities, opted for secularism. The foresight and commitment of its first leadership helped the country maintain some semblance of unity. But with the manipulation of resurgent Hindu chauvinism by the late Mrs. Indira Gandhi, a crack opened in the fragile crust of secularism. Today it is threatened by the assertion of Sikh religious nationalism.

The turbulent century (1857–1947) and its fiery passions triggered a process of evaluation and change not without impact on literature. Urdu literature of the period bears a visible imprint of the process.

The way out of the dwindling Muslim fortunes was devised by the pragmatic Sir Saiyad according to a flawlessly simple logic. To take on a technologically superior enemy, one must know the sources of the former's strength. It was not a purely reactive logic either, motivated only by the desire to win and vanquish. Sir Saiyad genuinely believed that Muslims stood to gain from Western knowledge, science, and technology, above all from the peculiar brand of Western praxis and rationalism, and that the relationship between the Muslims and British need not be one of hostility and distrust.

In hindsight, although Sir Saiyad had few other options under the circumstances, his program, despite its pragmatism, suffered from the congenital simplicity of its design. Missing from it was the creative synthesis of the new and the old. Whether he intended it or not, his plan polarized the Muslim intelligentsia into two discrete, rival camps, with no middle ground for give and take.

Acceptance of Sir Saiyad's plan meant a conscious rejection of the past. In literature, it meant a repudiation of those very forms and genres and conventions and ways of looking at oneself and the world in which Muslim genius had articulated itself most powerfully for a millennium and more. It also meant an equally conscious espousal of Western modes of thinking and expression. No wonder Maulana Altaf Husain Hali (1837–1914)—a religious Muslim right to the core, but nevertheless an ardent champion of Sir Saiyad's bid for the most thorough Muslim house-cleaning under an elaborate reform plan touching on all aspects of individual and corporate life—revised the aesthetic canon of the poetic tradition of the *ghazal* in favor of Western "naturalism." His *Muqaddima-e Shᶜir-o-Shāᶜirī* (Introduction to Poetry and Poetics; 1893)—a seminal work in which Hali argues for a radically new poetics of literature—thus begins, appropriately, with a profound skepticism about the value of fine arts:

> The farmer toils and provides sustenance for the whole world; and thanks to the builder's efforts, people are protected from the harmful effects of the elements. Thus their respective occupations are regarded and valued by all. But society does not expect anything in the least from the loner who sits atop a hill somewhere in the wilderness and amuses himself with his flute and occasionally perhaps charms the hearts of others as well. (9–10)[9]

Hali's influence proved decisive, if fatal. Henceforward Urdu literature was to serve the nation.

Hali's bid for utilitarianism, Sir Saiyad's for Western rationalism, and that of the British for consolidation of their power all combined to produce a curious—though in retrospect not entirely unwelcome—phenomenon: the rise of written Urdu prose in a simple, direct, and unadorned style that both Sir Saiyad and Hali had taken great pains to cultivate. Proficiency in English opened up the world of Western fiction and its forms for the Urdu writer. Two strains are immediately apparent in the prose literature of the period: romanticism and, under Hali's enduring influence, didacticism. There are, of course, exceptions, among them Mirza Muhammad Hadi Ruswa's (1858–1931) novel

Umrāʾō Jān Adā (the name of a fictitious Lucknow courtesan; 1898)—an isolated achievement midway between the two strains.[10]

There had been a number of attempts at writing fiction already in the nineteenth century. However, the first true professional fiction writer with a plan for social amelioration was Munshi Premchand (1880–1936),[11] referred to above as the precursor of the Progressive Writers. He wrote both novels and short stories. Even if not directly influenced by Hali, he certainly imbibed the literary ambience Hali had helped create. Much of Premchand's social realism is distinctly reminiscent of Hali's utilitarianism, reform, and didacticism. Only to Premchand it was not just the Muslim who needed reform, but India as a whole.

To Premchand, literature had a social and political purpose. The India of his time was groaning under the pressure of two formidable forces: the British, and its own decadence represented by the rapacity of the rich and the religious dogmatism of the upper-caste Hindus. The rich sapped the poor financially, and the upper-caste Hindus taught acquiescence to fate as a religious duty.

Much of Premchand's writing is thus an unrelenting crusade against the sociopolitical reality of his times. It does not even pose, much less answer, the question of literary autonomy.

When the Progressive Literary Movement in Urdu got underway (1936), it took over Premchand's assumptions about literature.[12] What was social realism with the latter became socialist realism with the former. The movement, inasmuch as it represented the literary arm of the Communist Party of India, sought reform along socialist lines. Whatever its literary shortcomings, it at least was passionately committed to Indian independence and religious harmony. This latter aspect of the Progressive mandate—its "anti-imperialist slant," in Rajinder Singh Bedi's characterization (1972:147)—continued to enthrall and fascinate even those writers who found little else to agree with in the literary mind-set of the Progressives, which was now threatening to become increasingly doctrinaire. It also kept them glued to the movement. But not for too long.

Some independent-minded writers, including some of those who had been at the cutting edge of the Progressive Movement, eventually broke away from it. Not that they didn't believe in the sociopolitical reality of their times; rather they found it irrelevant or inadequate as the final arbiter of the value of their creative work.

Something remarkable happened. Quite unexpectedly in Lahore in 1939, without premeditation or retaliatory fanfare, a few literature enthusiasts got together and formed themselves into a loose and informal literary circle. In spite of sporadic minor tremors of disagreement, if the Ḥalqa-e Arbāb-e Z̲auq (Circle of Possessors of Taste) has survived into the 1990s and remains the only literary group of its kind in the world, it is precisely because of its looseness and quite conscious rejection of ideology.[13] It has never had any headquarters, nor even a membership fee. Weekly or fortnightly, people came together informally at somebody's house or at a rented hall and collected the expenses for that day's meeting from those present.

Most of the Circle writers stood for freshness, creativity, and vigor. But even more, they stood for the freedom to experiment in the literary arts. In the earliest period the Circle had no recognizable aims and objectives. A body of goals, however, materialized in time. None of the goals even remotely upheld an ideology.

The Circle's birth has long been interpreted as a direct affront to the Progressive Writers' Association. But it probably came about, as Yunus Javed has persuasively argued, more in response to literary needs than by any desire for a showdown with the Progressives (cf. 1984:38–39). It was not launched deliberately, to counter the literary outlook fostered by the Progressives—who may themselves be blamed for creating this impression. The Circle stood for experimentation with the form and content of literature; the Progressives vociferously promoted the production only of socially aware writing, even if that meant subordinating creativity and imagination to fixed, party-approved formulas.

The Progressives' distaste for the Circle may also have had another source. French symbolists, such as Mallarmé, and late Romantics, such as Baudelaire, were anathema to the Progressives. But these same French writers commanded the respect and admiration of some of the early members of the Circle. It may well be that the Progressives transferred to the Circle as a whole the ideological distaste they felt for a few of its members.

The year 1946, when the British departure from India seemed imminent, may be the Progressives' shining moment. After all, half their battle had been won. But they could not secure the other half of their dream: the interreligious unity of India. India was partitioned along religious lines on August 15th, 1947, amid religious rioting, which resulted in countless dead and homeless on both sides of the Indo-Pakistan border. Many Muslims saw their homes divided: part of the family now living in Pakistan, part in India.

The Progressives, who stood for Indian unity, denounced the creation of Pakistan. When writing about the events of 1947, they quite naturally sought to expose the fallacy of Partition by concentrating chiefly on the religious riots and their outrageously large toll in human lives.

By reducing the epochal event of the Partition to mere religious violence, the Progressives showed a conspicuous lack of realism. Their misty-eyed idealism, the sincerity of which we have little reason to doubt, failed to appreciate that a substantial number of Indian Muslims had looked upon the Partition as the telos of a burgeoning historical expectation. Religion to them meant a lot. Then again, by August 1947, in the highly charged political climate of the subcontinent, with Hindu-Muslim religious tension near the flashpoint, the impracticality of the Progressive position should have been obvious to anyone. Elsewhere I have examined extensively the contradictions inherent in the Progressives' position, and also the tragically limited scope of their writing on the theme of the Partition.[14]

To conclude the historical overview: British domination prompted many Indian Muslims to question the viability of their world view. In literature, this led to a profound skepticism about the value of certain time-honored forms. As a result, a good deal was devalued, or, at any rate, came under heavy scrutiny. At the same time, some new ways of looking at the world also became accessible, chiefly through experimentation with Western fictional forms like the novel and short story. Two tendencies immediately stand out in the writing of the period: literature subordinated to societal regeneration (the didactic impulse) and literature as an autonomous realm (the individualist impulse). The didactic writing is socially oriented. It seeks to reform society by ridding it of its own traditional ills (religious, economic, and sexual exploitation), and by generating strong feelings of patriotism to help put an end to British colonial rule. The individualist strain offers two varieties: romantic and psychological. It is the latter that vehemently preserved the integrity of literature as an autonomous domain, bound only by its own values and laws. If it appears somewhat overshadowed by the utilitarian writing of the Progressives, it is because the latter's ideological commitment to Indian freedom exercised a hypnotic pull on the nationalist aspirations of the people.

It is in this atmosphere of pervasive utilitarianism that Intizar Husain started his literary career. It was also an atmosphere in which the population had become extremely polarized, politically and ideologically, on the twin issues of India's partition and Pakistan's creation, with the specter of religious violence always lurking in the shadows.

III

Intizar Husain, in interview after interview, and not infrequently in his critical essays, has been unusually taciturn about his political thinking as a young man (he must have been about twenty-two years old at the time of the Partition). On the other hand, he has been unusually forthcoming about his childhood days and the general religious milieu of his family. However, the same expositional materials almost never lack some reference to his views on the two seminal issues of his time: Partition and Pakistan.

One meets with a strange paradox in Husain: a passion for the composite Hindu-Muslim culture of pre-Partition India, held dearer than life (after all, his childhood memories are buried there), and an equally ardent love for Pakistan, as the fulfillment of a radiant historical expectation.[15] Both, however, are entirely free of the maudlin desire to turn the wheel backward and long for unity. Or, alternatively, like the Progressives, to suspend the past, blind oneself to the reality of Hindu-Muslim differences, and, lured by distant utopias, impose the idea of interreligious unity from above without infrastructural support. Curiously, it is his love for the Indian Muslim culture that is most readily visible to many critics, who look upon it as something of a crippling limitation, as the dead weight that keeps him hopelessly anchored to a time beyond all possible hope of recovery. Hence the verdict: his creative work is no more than mere "elegies on the fading culture of the Muslim nobility of Uttar Pradesh, . . . because he is in search of 'things that are lost'" (Narang 1973:132). Or that while Qurratulain Hyder "decided to turn her culture into an epic, [Husain] has changed that epic into one continuous dirge" (Akhtar 1981:99). But such critics have not seen that his modernism lies precisely in his ability to see the incompatibility of the noble vision with contemporary times, a truth that cannot be willed away or voided. And his humanism lies in the acceptance of much that was good in the past, even if the sad truth might annoy an ardent Progressive, or make his loyalty to Pakistan suspect for the literary columnist Safdar Mir (cf. Zeno 1984:4, 1984a:4).

How to reconcile Husain's passion for Pakistan with his passion for the composite Hindu-Muslim culture of pre-Partition India? Certainly not in the realm of objective reality. But there is room for both in literature. One might even say the purpose of literature is to gather just such antithetical truths and unite them in art. In their astute revaluation of Cervantes, both Milan Kundera and Carlos Fuentes have forcefully argued for the novel as the meeting ground of contradictions, a space filled with the presence of two or more mutually exclusive entities

(Fuentes 1988:49–71; Kundera 1988:3–20); in Bakhtinian terms, a dialogue of opposites. (This, in a somewhat exaggerated sense, may hold equally well for fiction as a whole.) For the novel as a form does not seek knowledge but wisdom, or a special kind of knowledge that only it can deliver. Because it views man as a complex being and breathes in the twilight shadows of relativities, it cannot survive in the blinding glare of absolutes, certainties, and dogma. And because it "has an inbuilt skepticism in relation to all systems of thought,"[16] it can accommodate them all in its expansive structure.

So there is no contradiction in fictional logic if both the composite Hindu-Muslim culture and the irreversible reality of Pakistan are assigned a common space.

As a young adult, working under the influence of the Progressives, Husain had decided to become a critic. The tragic events of 1947, however, intervened. While still in India, he was paralyzed by the level of religious violence around him. One question preoccupied his thoughts: how can such brutality come out of man? He did not pose the question as a Muslim, but neither did he pose it as a Hindu. And certainly not in political terms. He posed the question in anthropological terms. In the sobering aftermath, his mind was made up. Creative writing, not criticism, offered the only possible way to deal with the experience of the Partition. In his own words:

> But when the process leading to partition began and the series of riots started, I reacted strangely and I felt a sense of anxiety, as if something were slipping through my hands. I hadn't emigrated and saw everything which was going on around me. I tried to put my reactions to all this into writing, into prose. Two short stories resulted: "Qaiyūmā kī dukān" [Qaiyuma's Shop] and "Ustād" [The Teacher/Boss], both of which are included in my collection *Galī kūčē* [Lanes and Alleys]. These works I wrote in Meerut during the time of the riots and I think that it was because of this that I became interested in becoming a short story writer. When I emigrated to Lahore, I left behind any idea of becoming a critic or a poet. (1983:155)

A short story writer, but not of the Progressive kind. For when he turned to the Progressive writing on the subject, he came away thoroughly disillusioned. Their self-righteousness appeared downright brutish to him. And their utopian expectation that no matter what, the sun will also conrise—insufferably vulgar. "They were not describing the truth," he concluded, "but were rather hiding it behind a veil and obscuring it with a layer of politics" (160). He could not have adopted their concept of literature, any more than he could have assumed their literary attitude toward Partition or Pakistan.

The Progressives had little use for history or culture. Consequently, they did not regard Partition as a historical process. In both their creative and critical writing they laid the blame for the division of India squarely on a conspiratorial alliance of the British and the native feudal aristocracy. They conveniently forgot the long history of religious strife that predated the British advent in India. Some Progressive writers, such as Krishan Chandar (1913–1977), the most zealous of them all, treated the riots as merely "a case of some Hindus killing Muslims, some Muslims killing Hindus" (161). He lacked either the will or the sagacity to see the event's tremendous potential for a fresh, if painful, exploration of human possibility. For Husain, on the other hand, the event was not quite so transparent. It was, rather, "a complex and convoluted human tragedy which raised many other kinds of questions and doubts" (161). A retrospective glance at Hindu religious tradition across history convinced him that it upheld the values of constancy, peace, patience, and forbearance. How, then, could this tradition beget the men who produced such horrific events in 1947?—he wondered. The event clearly went far beyond the journalistic marginalization to which Krishan Chandar had reduced it.

> I recollected our ancient traditions and legends, the *Mahābhārata* of the Hindus and the history of the Muslim migration, the *hegira*. It was against this whole background that I was trying to understand and comprehend how it came about that one man was killing another, cities and towns were being destroyed, people were abandoning their homes—how and why did this occur? What is behind it? What historical process gave rise to it? And what has happened to that history which, for example, had produced the Buddha? What new era of history had begun? Or is it that mankind is the type of creature who can build a movement over centuries, can construct diverse philosophies, but when a crisis comes, when some critical moment occurs, his animal [nature] emerges from within to overwhelm him?
>
> But Krishan Chandar was not prepared to view this event against any larger human background or in the wider historical or cultural context of India. In his view, the background was extremely limited—the British Empire, a conspiracy of feudal landlords and the killing of some Muslims by Hindus and the killing of some Hindus by Muslims—equal numbers of each—he had as many Hindus dying as Muslims. So he reduced this catastrophe to a nar-

> rowly defined incident, describing what happened in a very artificial manner. I was hesitant to accept his writing because I felt that he regarded as a trivial incident a great human event which changed the history of India. (161–162)

Why does Husain consider Partition the "great human event which changed the history of India"? The source for this observation is found in what now looks like his outgrown pragmatism.

But first, let us look at his view of Indian religious history up to Partition.

Husain does not deny the reality of religious distrust among Hindus and Muslims; he rather concentrates on those Muslim individuals who imbibed the spirit of liberalism and worked toward bringing the two communities together. These individuals—among them Amir Khusrau (1253–1325); Nizamuddin Auliya (d. 1323); the brothers Abul Fazl (d. 1602) and Faizi (d. 1595); the Mughal prince Dara Shikoh, defeated and killed in 1658 by his brother Aurangzeb, the future Mughal emperor, who represented the puritanical attitude; and Shah Abdul Aziz Dihlavi (d. 1824)—in fact laid the foundation of, and nurtured, what is often described as the *gaṅgā-jamnī* (composite Indian Muslim) culture.[17] Husain again:

> We've used the term Indo-Muslim culture. What a purely Islamic culture would be, I don't have any idea.[18] It is this Indo-Muslim culture of which I am a product and which has shaped the history of which I am a part. The Muslims came to India and formed ties with its soil. Indian Muslim culture is that creative amalgam which came about in response to the intellectual and emotional climate that was here . . . the feel of its seasons . . . these ties with the land. Much in it is Indian and much was brought from outside.
>
> I have already said that Khwaja Nizamuddin Auliya and Amir Khusrau are for me important symbols of this culture. Nizamuddin Auliya said at some point that I listen to the "Song of *Alast*" in *rāga pūrbī*—this for me is Indo-Muslim culture.[19] It was this frame of mind, this attempt to understand the Islamic revelation in terms of our land, this endeavor to merge that revelation with our soil, which yielded a unity that later was shaped into what we know as Indo-Muslim culture. But we did not permit this unity to continue for long, as its progress has been constantly obstructed or halted by that extremely unfortunate frame of mind which may be called the "puritan" attitude.
>
> I believe that there was this on-going cultural process which was brought to a halt in a very unnatural way. Its progress was

> blocked by a few Muslims who were victims of this puritan frame of mind and also by some conservative Hindus. On the one hand, there was the Muslim who tried to erase all of his history and live in some period before Muslims had come to India. On the other hand, there was the conservative Hindu who strove to ignore all this interaction and return to some earlier period before it began.
>
> So these few reactionary Hindus and reactionary Muslims blocked the way of this culture, ushering in those tragic events which have afflicted us ever since. It seems to me that a fundamental cause of all the troubles and miseries which have befallen this subcontinent and its people is the fact that a few powerful figures were able to halt the development and emergence of this culture. (1983:167–168)

It is with this pained consciousness that Husain approaches 1947. The creation of Pakistan is not thus a moment to gloat over.[20] Rather, it is a sad moment whose agony could be lessened—perhaps—by exploiting the event's potential creatively. To salvage whatever one can of that culture, if only by enacting it in literature. To preserve a memory, however fugitive, of that culture before time and history have placed it beyond reach.

Almost suddenly, as it were, Husain becomes aware of a familiar motif from Muslim history and of its creative potential. He hastens to appropriate it. It was the motif of *hijrat* (migration), the principle of creativity and growth, but not without the attendant pain of separation from the familiar.[21] He takes the temporal event of the Prophet Muhammad's migration from Mecca to Medina in 622 C.E. and turns it into a seminal, archetypal event, beyond temporality, renewable, capable of enacting its own myriad epiphanies across time and history, in spite of time and history.

The baggage of pain slung across his shoulders, but his heart full of uplifting hope, Husain entered into the promised land in late 1947 and took up residence in Lahore. Here too the creative writing reproduced more or less faithfully the same attitudes which the Progressives had displayed regarding Partition. He was disappointed—that is, until one day he read a few *ghazal* compositions of the young poet Nasir Kazmi (1925–1972). Suddenly he knew this was the voice he had been waiting for—the voice "which could convey me to the depths of that experience, to its very soul." The kindred spirits soon found each other. Their thinking accorded so well that Husain even "made the announcement that we were completely separate from that generation of Progressives which had been born in 1936 and that we were the first literary generation of

Pakistan and were the representatives of a new consciousness" (1983:164).

IV

In an early article, Husain has captured rather well the general climate of optimism and hope pervading his own thinking as well as that of a few other writers in the decade following the birth of Pakistan (1963; tr. Hanson 1983). In the aggregate of the writing of the decade he discerns three attitudes in relation to Partition: the reductive attitude of the Progressives, who marginalized, indeed trivialized the event and denounced the religious massacres in the name of humanity; that of Saadat Hasan Manto (1912–1955), who used the incident as an exploration of human possibility in a moment of crisis; and that of such poets as Mukhtar Siddiqi (d. 1972), Qaiyum Nazar (d. 1989), and Yusuf Zafar (d. 1981), who systematically avoided any mention of the event lest literature degenerate into journalism.

Among these three a wholly new attitude was slowly making its hesitant but unmistakable appearance. It identified the *hijrat* as the seminal experience of the age, and arose out of the necessity of turning that experience into something creative. This was Husain's own attitude as well.

Roughly a decade and a half later, in response to a question about the above article, Husain admitted to his earlier optimism, adding,

> But today, after our political ups and downs, I find myself in a different mood. Now I feel that sometimes a great experience comes to be lost to a nation; often nations forget their history. I do not mean that a nation does, or has to, keep its history alive in its memory in every period. There also comes a time when a nation completely forgets its past. So, that experience, I mean the experience of migration, is unfortunately lost to us and on us. And the great expectation that we had of making something out of it at a creative level and of exploiting it in developing a new consciousness and sensibility—that bright expectation has now faded and gone.[22]

Husain's weariness is fully plausible in a man robbed of all hope by his country's failure in leadership. Suppression of democracy, annulment of civilian government, inauguration of military dictatorship—all accomplished in one fell swoop by Field Marshal Muhammad Ayub

Khan in 1958; the painful outcome of the 1965 military showdown with India; and, perhaps most humiliating of all, the 1971 civil war, which blew away the fragile unity of Pakistan once and for all—these are but a few sad notes that give his despair a tragic resonance.

How does a writer of the humanism and sensitivity of Intizar Husain look at his country's disaster and breakup?

In a sentence one might say that he sees the period between 1947, when Pakistan was created, and 1971, when it was fragmented, as a process in which the light of conscience is steadily extinguished in the individual. Man's frantic efforts to retain his humanity are subverted every step of the way, until he loses all moral distinction.

In a short but penetrating study Javaid Qazi has examined Husain's creative work up to the 1970s. He divides it into three distinct phases and shows how the underlying literary concerns of the writer, while remaining basically unchanged in each phase, acquire different emphases and employ different techniques. Thus in phase one, the decade of the 1950s, the emphasis is on social, cultural, and religious symbols; in phase two, the decade of the 1960s, on animal imagery and metaphor; and in phase three, the decade of the 1970s, on concepts of self and self-identity. The unifying theme is that of man's effort to keep his humanity, or humanness, intact, and his inability to do so (cf. 1983:187).

This corresponds fairly closely to my own descriptive taxonomy of Husain's work. I see his work, rather, in terms of a metaphor of journey. It starts with the realization that while something has grievously gone wrong, something else, with abundant creative possibilities, has also been gained. I suggest a thematic triad to delineate the three stages of that journey. They are: (1) reclamation of memory, some initial success in this respect, but, ultimately, failure, leading to (2) man's moral perversion and fall, resulting in (3) the extinction of all the creative principle in life.

In an earlier article, I have exhaustively dealt with this thematic triad and have examined a number of short stories to support my argument (1981). Elsewhere I have also warned against too uncritical and rigid an identification of each of the three themes with stories in each of the three phases (1987:14–15). While it is true that each phase has its dominant theme, the latter is not found there to the exclusion of other phases, which may offer still newer variations of that theme, or ramifications hitherto unavailable in the principal phase.

It would be redundant no doubt to reproduce here the totality of the argument from my earlier work; however, it cannot be dispensed with entirely. Briefly, then—

The odyssey begins in 1947. India's partition was followed by a painful dislocation of sizeable numbers of Muslims, Hindus, and Sikhs. Any exodus or dislocation is always a frightening experience. For Muslims, however, it is also filled with grace. Exodus, in Husain, carries within it the germ of unbounded future creativity. It is also a time for renewal and fresh beginnings. Through a bold and imaginative leap backward into the primeval hour, Husain equates—rightly or wrongly—the 1947 exodus of Indian Muslims with the historic migration (*hijrat*) of the Prophet Muhammad to Medina in 622 C.E. In spite of its attendant pain of separation for Muhammad and his companions, the first Muslim exodus turned out to be a stunning moment of creativity for the nascent Muslim community; indeed it is in its wake that the Muslim community came to political power. In a way, the latest Muslim migration in 1947 was simply a reenactment of the seminal Mecca-to-Medina *hijrat*, or a renewal of contact with the archetypal experience of distant antiquity at the very least. It also carried promise and hope.

To exploit the potential of the 1947 *hijrat* creatively, Muslims needed to look back to their past and define their cultural personality. It is exactly at this point that things failed to go the expected way. Hope floundered. The task of regenerating society proved altogether too inhibiting. In spite of some initial success, the effort ultimately met with failure. Loss of memory—the loss, in other words, of identity—spelled disaster, even death, which, however, didn't come soft-footed or unannounced. It was preceded by a state of moral turpitude, when a nation's conscience darkened and lost all power of distinction between right and wrong, good and evil.

Although a temporal event, the *hijrat* as a constitutive experience is not shackled or limited by time. It can be invoked anywhere and at any time when Muslims are forced out of their homes by the determination of history. Thus there is no contradiction if it is identified as the dominant experience of an age even if the aggregate of Muslims of that age in a given area did not physically experience it. Only a part of the population of contemporary Pakistan is made up of Indian immigrants. The rest remained right where they were. But even they, Husain thinks, participated in the dominant experience of their age. Their participation was, however, purely imaginative (cf. 1963:9; 1983:166).

The partition of India rudely interrupted the continuity of Muslim culture. The immigrants, emerging from the vertiginous merry-go-round of events, felt disoriented and cut off from the mainsprings of their identity in their first days in Pakistan. Husain's early stories contained in his first two collections *Galī Kūčē* (Alleys and Bylanes) and *Kaṅkarī* (Pebble) thus project a number of characters who make desperate efforts to reestablish a link somehow between their past and present and thereby make themselves whole again. Because most of these characters happen to be Shīᶜites, the retrieval is made possible by the employment of powerful Shīᶜite symbols and images.

The process of retrieval and regeneration is poignantly displayed, for instance, in the struggle of Saiyid, the protagonist of the short story "Sīṛhiyāṅ" (The Stairs; 1973d).[23] He has arrived in Pakistan without memories, robbed of all sense of past or personality, a plight underscored by the loss of his ability to dream. Dreams in Husain often help activate memory, needed to bridge the past and present. Saiyid continues to live in a state of eerie suspension, until one night the topic of dreams and oneiromancy crops up among his fellow immigrants. As Razi goes over his dreams and begins to recount snatches of his life in pre-Partition India, inadvertently as it were, he activates Saiyid's own memory, which had lain arrested until that point. Images of the past come crowding in. By the end of the story, Saiyid has relived his past. More importantly, he has been made whole, fully rehabilitated to his past. This awareness is powerfully conveyed in the concluding lines of the story: "He opened his sleep-laden eyes and, looking toward Razi, said in a mysterious voice, 'My heart is beating rather fast. It seems I'm going to have a dream after all'" (83).

However disoriented he may be, Saiyid has not abandoned hope. The loss of memory is therefore only temporary in his case and can be restored relatively easily. But as time wears on and the political fortunes of the new country show little sign of improvement, a profound uncertainty sets in as to whether the loss can ever be recovered. Correspondingly, the effort to recollect becomes more intense and urgent. Indeed, it is transformed from a mere desire in Saiyid into a frenzied struggle in the case of the nameless central character of the short story "Apnī Āg kī Ṭaraf" (Toward His Fire; 1973b). This nameless character has just emerged from an apartment building that has caught fire. He runs into a friend, who offers to put him up. But the latter declines the offer and explains: "Shaikh Ali Hujviri once saw a mountain on fire. In the fire he spotted a tormented little mouse running frantically around. Somehow in its mad running about the mouse managed to get away from the erupting volcano. But as soon as it had got away from the fire, it dropped dead!" An uneasy silence ensues. After some time he adds in a very low voice, "You see, *I don't want to die*" (23).

In other words, he is aware that outside the building—which probably stands for an entire cosmos, a self-sufficient and self-sustaining universe—he is irrevocably estranged from his essence. Stretch the metaphor and there is no creative life possible outside one's tradition.

So, even if there is death inside, he must—as do Pichwa in "Ēk Bin-likhī Razmīya" (An Unwritten Epic; 1952a) and Arshad and Naim in "Andhī Galī" (The Dead-End Alley; 1973a)—return to his own element, his own fire, because a more fearsome and painful death awaits him outside.[24]

The second phase of Intizar Husain's writing is guided by the theme of moral fall. *Ākhirī Ādmī* (The Last Man; 1967), his third collection of short stories, is more of a novel in eleven stories, as each piece explores with haunting power the steady erosion of moral conscience and the resulting decline in imaginative cognition, leading to an eventual hollowing out of personality. The stories range from the first hesitant stirrings of evil in the heart, through the advent of doubt, to the inevitable headlong plunge into sin.

Thus in the story "Ṭāṅgēṅ" (The Legs; 1967f), the coachman Yasin's experiences of quotidian Pakistani life underscore the decline in personal morality. A man refreshingly simple, almost childlike in his endearing naïveté, but, above all, guided by an innate morality, Yasin finds himself repeatedly betrayed in the new country. A fellow immigrant from his hometown back in India, whom Yasin has provided with a roof overhead for a whole month, makes off with his, Yasin's, horse.

It seems that even nature has conspired against the country. A violent storm knocks over the minarets of the tomb of the revered tenth- or eleventh-century saint Ali Ibn Usman Jullabi (also known as al-Hujviri, and endearingly among the populace as Data Ganj Bakhsh). To Yasin, religious buildings exude an aura of sanctity and are somehow impervious to the vagaries of time and nature. He finds the incident quite incomprehensible; he observes:

> There have been terrible storms before, Saiyid Sahib, and there have been floods as well. Many times the river has overflowed its banks all the way up to the foot of Data's tomb, but it never climbed past the lower steps.[25]

Yasin wonders: after all, during the riots whipped up by religious passion, the Hindus and Sikhs resorted to stratagem after clever stratagem but failed to set fire to the Jama Masjid (congregational mosque) in Delhi! The knocking over of Data Sahib's minarets—Yasin broods darkly—must surely be the work of the Pakistanis themselves! But why?

The general morality has sunk so low that without graft and "contacts you can never get anything done." And no sooner does a perfectly honest, decent, God-fearing man set foot in Karachi, then the capital of

Pakistan, the economic hub of the country, than he is divested of the smallest moral feeling. Turns into a perfect rogue! "We've fallen on evil times" is Yasin's sad conclusion; "there's no joy left in living these days." Just about everyone has sprouted goat's legs—the metaphor of erosion of personal morality.

While "Parčhāʾīṅ" (The Shadow; 1967d) and "Ham-safar" (The Comrade; literally, a fellow-traveler; 1967b) graphically portray the advent of doubt about self and identity, "Ākhirī Ādmī" (1967a) and "Zard Kuttā" (The Yellow Dog; 1967g) underscore man's desperate attempts to maintain his humanity, or rather his humanness, and his ultimate failure. In "Kāyā-kalp" (Metamorphosis; 1967c), essentially a variation on the latter theme, loss of personality becomes an act of will. Therefore it is the more tragic. It is no longer the rottenness of the times, but the canker on the soul of man himself.

Thus in this story Prince Azad Bakht meets a different end from that reserved for the princes of popular folk-romances. Unlike a true fairy-tale hero, he neither slays the white giant nor rescues the embattled princess, but quietly submits to his considerably eclipsed role of antihero brought on by a steadily declining perception of his humanness. Turned into a fly each evening at the first rumblings of the giant's returning footfalls, and back into human form by a felicitous touch from the princess with the departure of the giant each morning, Prince Azad Bakht is stripped of the last trace of his human identity. The eventual collapse of identity is signaled one fateful evening when the princess does not change him into a fly but nevertheless finds him changed into one of his own accord the next morning. Prince Free Fortune (that's what his name means) has himself abdicated his human attributes for those of a fly! The outer change is only a metaphor for the inner change—a change of perspective on oneself and the world.

The two flagrantly apparent attributes of this new—shall we say, Pakistani—individual are his nonpersonality and his stark cruelty. Only he who has no sense of himself can act toward others without the least bit of restraint or discriminating judgment. No wonder this kind of man produced the unprecedented horror in the former East Pakistan. But he could have done so only by extinguishing the light of conscience first.

The interconnected themes of crass inhumanity and loss of selfhood appear again and again in the stories of Husain's fourth collection *Shahr-e Afsōs* (City of Grief; 1973). However, these stories are deliberately swathed in eerie unreality to discourage any attempt to ascribe them too closely to a specific time and place.

"Vō Jō Khōʾē Gaʾē" (The Lost Ones; 1973e) provides a stark

example of the collapse and death of personality. Here are four people, divested of names to symbolically enhance the sense of loss of personal ego, identified only by their appearance: the bearded man, the youth, the man with the bag, and the man with the wounded head. At some point they begin to suspect that their number is short by one. Since they have no memory at all, they cannot remember the face or even the name of the missing person, or whether, indeed, the missing person is a man or a woman. They count and re-count. Each time, the one who counts fails to include himself. Therefore each thinks that he is, in essence, the missing man. The missing man thus replaces the real man, while the man of flesh and blood, from loss of self-awareness, fades into non-being. The tragicomical paradox implicit in the situation is made tantalizingly explicit when "the man with the wounded head" realizes that his being depends not so much on his thinking and awareness of himself as on the goodwill of others who are willing to testify to that effect. Addressing the "old man," he says, "And suppose you suddenly decided to withhold your testimony—I would right away cease *to be*, wouldn't I?" (23)

In the short story "Shahr-e Afsōs" (1973c), which structurally resembles—or even looks like a sequel to—"The Lost Ones," the two processes of moral fall and consequent death of the personality as a creative principle converge into one. It was written shortly after the political fragmentation of Pakistan in 1971, though it makes no direct reference to that event. The process of moral disintegration and death evident (the former only as a faint suggestion, the latter as the dominant metaphor) in "The Lost Ones" culminates in this story.

Knowledge of the circumstances amid which Bangladesh became a nation can enhance the impact and haunting power of "City of Grief." If 1947 divided the Indian subcontinent on the basis of religion, 1971 left no doubt that religion itself had proved to be the most tenuous of bonds for keeping a people united. The events of 1947 pitted those of one faith against those of another; the events of 1971 pitted Muslim against Muslim. Such inhumanity could be explained only by the weakening and eventual collapse of individual moral sensibility. In the present story, Husain attempts just such an explanation. If the foursome in "The Lost Ones" are lost, the trio in "City of Grief"—also without name or identity—have been reduced to mere corpses. They linger in the city of grief, bearing the burden of their sin and inhumanity, expectantly awaiting burial. They are disfigured beyond recognition. Their present plight is the result of their evil deeds.

The theme of moral death is introduced in the opening line—"I have nothing to say," says the First Man, "because I am dead"—and sustained throughout. What caused his death? During the breakdown of civil order and subsequent utter chaos in what was once East Pakistan, the First Man, by his own admission, forced a young man, most likely a Bengali, to strip his own sister—a scene that he watched with sadistic glee—and then to rape her. This act, which should have caused any man to die of shame, leaves the First Man quite remorseless and unmoved. When the Second Man asks him, "Then you died?" he replies, "No, I lived on," which makes the Third Man wonder, "Lived on?—Well?" (250)

The First Man lives on to witness a whole series of moral crimes, leading up to the most devastating of them all: the rape of his own daughter by no other than himself at the express command of the same Bengali youth who now, by a curious turn of fate, has the upper hand.

The Second Man and the Third Man too have gone through a similar process of dehumanization, except that the latter is not dead but "missing"—a worse fate than being dead. He must first find himself, then die, and only then worry about burial. He looks at the human debris of the other two; lest he too should lapse into inertia before he has found himself, he tries to shake himself free from them. But the other two manage to convince him of the futility of such an act. "So?" asks the Third Man in despair. The Second Man fixes his gaze upon the Third Man for so long that the latter feels he is becoming inert. At last he says: "So you sit down, Missing Man, don't ask where you are, and believe you are dead" (270).

In yet another story, "Asīr" (The Prisoner/s; 1981b), the validity of the Pakistani position vis-à-vis the events of 1971 is called into question. This story is also a subtle indictment of the thoughtless gaiety, total indifference, and crass materialism dominating the national mood in West Pakistan just as momentous and bloody events were occurring in Bangladesh. Javed, who has escaped from the grisly scene in Bangladesh, meets his old friend Anwar in Lahore. Anwar wants to know what exactly happened in East Pakistan. Javed, even though he would like to talk about the horror he has witnessed, is strangely unable to do so; something of the gaiety and indifference around him kills the smallest desire. He rather wants to know more about Mirza, somebody Anwar had mentioned the previous day. Anwar informs him that this fellow, Mirza, ended up being shot as he was coming out of a political rally that had just ended.

Javed is horrified. And truly shocked when he learns that there was no apparent reason for the killing, nor was the killing followed by any protest or event. Even Anwar didn't pay much attention to the incident. The last few sentences of the story follow:

> "Friend," began Anwar in a diffident but probing voice, "you must have seen worse things over there. Isn't that so?"
>
> Javed hesitated a bit, then said with sorrow, "Yes, you're right. But at least we knew what was happening—and why." (54)

In a similar story, "Nīnd" (Sleep; 1981e), on the other hand, when Aslam, Zaidi, and Zafar badger Salman, who has just escaped with his life from East Pakistan, with questions about the horrible scenes he has witnessed, Salman evinces absolutely no desire to go over the painful experience. Instead, he repeatedly dozes off. Finally, he tells them that all he wants is to fall asleep. And he does.

Reminiscent of the experience of many veterans of the war in Vietnam, both Anwar and Salman are painfully aware of the futility of talking about the incident. A visceral feeling informs them that what they have to say is not likely to be understood. The country just doesn't want to know. Then again, the experience is so formidable it can hardly be captured in words or understood by the workings of the conscious mind. The soft, subdued glow at the edge of sleep might prove more hospitable. Sleep, interestingly enough, is rarely the desire to forget in Husain's work. He rather sees it as that reassuring realm of half-light in which the meandering vision quickens, the subconscious spills over and invests fuzzy thoughts with brilliant definition, focus, and intensity. Not surprisingly therefore, Husain says: "It is when I am thinking of writing a story, working out its details that I sleep the most. Morning, noon, and night—all the time!" (1981:86)

That a man could be murdered cold-bloodedly without evoking the slightest response among people is surely a sign of apathy, a crisis of comprehension among a country's inhabitants. A senseless death can only point to a senseless life. The situation at home is thus sharply contrasted with that in East Pakistan, where warring groups have, at least, a clear perception of what it is they are fighting for or against.

What Husain seems to be saying is this: unless the western half of the country is willing to understand itself, it will not be able to understand the eastern half. This is because self-knowledge generates knowledge of *the other*; and self-knowledge, in order to be authentic, must proceed from a healthy self-doubt.

The last four short stories, along with "Hindūstān sē ēk Khaṭ̤" (A Letter from India; 1981c) and "Kačhvē" (The Turtles; 1981d) and the novel *Bastī* (Town; 1979), to be discussed in the following section, make up the corpus of Husain's fiction that could be said to have been inspired by the events of 1971. There is nothing, however, in the stories themselves to pin them down decisively to 1971. This is even more true of the novel. Husain's basic impulse is moral. He is not after historiography, but the reality of man in history. His concerns are anthropological, not historiographic. While conscious subversion of chronological time and almost hermetic exclusion of particularizing detail in the surrealistic atmosphere of some of these stories does create the impression of unrelatedness, attenuation, unreality, and remoteness, this is more than offset by a relentless chronology of inner events of the self and the consequences upon it of external happenings. The eerie, apocalyptic realm of these stories, however, is neither accidental nor arbitrary, but self-conscious and deliberate, almost a choice organically imposed by the subject matter. By distancing himself from the immediate scene of disaster, but not from the moral consequences generated by it, Husain is thus able to create an atmosphere of brooding melancholy and introspective gloom that leaves a more lasting impression of Pakistan's failure to avert national disaster than does most of the other Urdu creative writing on the subject.

V

Although Intizar Husain's forte is the short story, he has had some considerable success as a novelist also. Of his four novels to date, *Bastī* (Town; 1979), the second in order, has generated the most comment, partly because of what I suspect to be its presumed ascription to a national event of disastrous proportions, viz., the fall of Pakistan and the subsequent emergence of its eastern wing as independent Bangladesh.

Personally, I look at *Bastī* as a kind of summation, an ingathering of all those different creative strains that have preoccupied Husain since he began writing. There is the same emphasis on memory as a principle of healing and integration—it restores what time and morality violate and annul—and the same inexorable need to relate to one's deeper self, made more urgent in a world of rapidly declining moral values.

Perhaps then, it is germane to discuss this novel at some length.

Bastī does not replicate familiar reality. Events, otherwise concrete, appear swathed in an eerie half-light hovering at the edge of consciousness. They are recognized not so much by their physical attributes as by their effect on Zakir, whose consciousness is rendered through what may be described as "consonant psycho-narration."[26] Characters, too, appear shorn of physical traits and particularizing detail; only their mental events are given. Evocative speech, rather than dramatic unfolding of a well-constructed plot, moves the story forward. The opening chapter sets the narrative paradigm, flashback and interior monologue being its dominant characteristics. The impression of dramatic immediacy is created by employing a combination of narrative voices. But the transitions between the third-person omniscient narrator and first-person narrator are often so seamless as to be almost unnoticeable. For example:

> With his heart and mind full of memories, he half heard and half didn't hear. He had come back from the zone of memories the way a sleeper might suddenly wake, with sleep still filling his eyes. The sleep-spirit might then come like the touch of a breeze, and he would again be oblivious and dead to the world. Memory-images were floating around him. . . . Then Sabirah was moving in his imagination, when she had come to Vyaspur for a few days. In those days we two had come close to each other. When the engine whistled, she too was drawn up to the open roof, where I still came when I was home from Meerut during the vacations, to sit from evening into night, watching the fields that went on into the distance, beyond the fields the railroad tracks, beyond the railroad tracks the rows of trees. We both stood leaning on the parapet, our heads touching. We watched the whistling, smoke-spitting engine, and the moving, lighted cars that followed. In the day, these cars looked separate, but in the dark of night they were like a row of lamps strung together and moving. The row of lamps was drawn along, it came running along. When it passed, Sabirah would say with delight and wonder, "What a long train it was, car after car. Which train was it?"
>
> "The Delhi train."
>
> She was amazed. "This train goes to Delhi!"
>
> "Yes, of course."
>
> She was silent for a little. "Zakir, you must have seen Delhi? What's it like, Delhi?"
>
> "I've only gone once, but after my exams, I'll go there to live." (Husain 1979:63–64; tr. 1995a:66–67)

In its design *Bastī* resembles an elegant hourglass: two large sections—comprising Chapters One through Six and Eight through Eleven, respectively—held together by a slim waist (Chapter Seven). Chapter One, much the longest, is made up entirely of Zakir's past. It is recalled through a flashback frequently interrupted by events in the narrative present. By the end of Chapter Four the past is fully assimilated to the present. Henceforward, events occur in the narrative present. The slim middle portion is reserved almost entirely for the events of the twelve days of the 1971 war and the thoughts and feelings they generate in the "figural consciousness"[27]—all recounted in diary form. The events of the last section are overwhelmingly psychic. But they occur to Zakir in an indeterminate time following the breakup of Pakistan, symbolized by the fall of Dhaka.

This seemingly simple structure hides a conceptual complexity of some magnitude. The ostensible purpose of the prolonged flashback is to acquaint the reader with Zakir's past. But it is not there merely to evoke a childhood idyll, as some have wrongly assumed. After all, the childhood is recalled through the point of view of an adult Zakir, who both mediates and transforms its events, assigns them value and importance based upon his experiences in the present. The process of remembrance itself is triggered, moreover, by specific events in the present. Rather, the idyll's purpose is to bring into focus some fundamental psychological traits of Zakir's personality that later would provide the rationale for his future conduct and responses to events in the present. The idyll establishes Zakir as a fairly complex character. And the narrative structurally supports this complexity by employing a set of devices chiefly associated with postrealist fiction. Linearity and chronology, if not altogether suspended, are nevertheless kept at bay. Events in the present are juxtaposed with analogous events in the past, some even extending back a millennium or more. The cumulative effect is that of a distorting prism, of a dizzying collage of discontinuities and refractions, of melting images and blurring edges. The narrative structure thus not only supports but also replicates the structure and state of Zakir's mind.

Let us look a bit more closely at the first chapter. The hypnotic idyll, which breaks upon the senses with its immense evocative beauty, underscores the beginnings of a faintly tragic note: the perception that the paradisiacal time and space of Rūpnagar, seemingly impervious to change, have finally succumbed to the corrosive powers of time. Zakir's paradise is a preindustrial town in memory—pristine, whole, full of wonder and harmony between man and nature. Above all, it is a town full of religious accord. The latter aspect of the town's corporate identity is brought out in the largely cordial interaction of its mixed population of Hindus and Muslims, and in the symbiotic existence of two conflicting visions of truth, as embodied in the Hindu and Muslim stories of the creation of the world. Here the parallel worlds of Bhagat-ji, a devout Hindu neighbor, and Abba Jan, an equally devout Muslim, of Hindu mythology and Muslim legend and lore, could coexist in a single novelistic space and time.

Eventually Rūpnagar is pure fiction. Unlike most other cities later in Zakir's life, it has no reality in geographical or cartographical fact. It exists only in cranial space. The very name Rūpnagar ("city of beauty")—just as Ḥusnpūr in his first novel *Čāndgahan* (Lunar Eclipse; 1953), which also means "beautiful town"—represents a yearning for things that might have been. It is a utopia that harks back to Intizar Husain's idealistic vision of what Hindu-Muslim—or, as he prefers to call it, the *gaṅgā-jamnī*—culture was or should have been (see p. 15 above).

Rūpnagar could not survive as a myth. Its purity was sullied. But the discord and destruction that ruptured its harmony already existed within it as a latent possibility. They were not imposed from outside. The rupture is signaled almost within paragraphs of the creation stories. Little Zakir, educated about how the world came to be, wonders what happened to it next. The crumbly, foxed tome in Abba Jan's bookshelf introduces him to that archetypal story of fratricide—Cain's slaying of his brother Abel. That helps some. But it also leaves him confused. He wants to know why Cain slew his own brother. He asks his grandmother. Her explanation grips him with both wonder and fear. (The tragic motif of fratricide will appear as a central metaphor again and again throughout the novel with the regularity of a mournful refrain, for the last time in the dismemberment of Pakistan, when brother killed brother.) The outbreak of plague in Rūpnagar and the ominous appearance of a black cat (which, too, will reappear later in the novel) further intensify the sense of impending doom and disharmony. The destruction of Rūpnagar as a haven of peace is complete with the act of Partition. Scenes of the religious violence of 1947 merge with nightmarish scenes of civil disorder and anomie in the Lahore of late 1971. The chapter thus connects the two aspects of time through Zakir's consciousness. At a subtler level, because the past is recalled from a future point in time, it both provides relief against the present; for instance—

> The rain poured down all night inside him. The dense clouds of memory seemed to come from every direction. Now the sky was washed and soft. Here and there a cloud swam contentedly in it, like a bright face, a soft smile. How deeply self-absorbed he was! For him, the outer world had already lost its meaning. Seated at the breakfast table, he ran an indifferent eye over the headlines and slid the newspaper toward Abba Jan. (1979:53; tr. 1995a:55)

—and confirms the present anomie as inevitably atavistic. The idyll, figuratively speaking, becomes a kind of hell. Creation ends in destruction. The space between the two portrays the events and human conduct that causally explain the inescapability of death and destruction. The harmony of Rūpnagar was already breached with the introduction of electricity and the consequent death of many of the town's monkeys. Nature was held hostage to the onslaught of industrial culture.

I would argue that the opening chapter contains the reduced blueprint of the entire novel. Creation, the immorality of human conduct, and consequent destruction—creation, insubordination, deluge—all three major events are present here. The rest of the novel simply expands on them. For instance, the joy and exuberance of Zakir's first days in Pakistan, the uplifting hope that something positive will emerge from the migration experience (81 ff) can be easily equated with the joy of "creation." The middle part presents the progressive deterioration of Pakistan as a moral ideal, which forces Zakir to withdraw into himself, frantically seeking some untapped inner source of strength. The pace of violence around him increases, Pakistan loses its eastern wing, the country is placed in the path of destruction, and, to compound the tragedy, Zakir's own father dies.

If the above scheme is valid, all the main events of the novel effectively and naturally terminate in Chapter Seven. The fratricidal prophecy of Chapter One has come full circle. The country is thrown into the grip of fear as a result of constant shelling by the Indian Air Force, while its eastern wing irrevocably breaks away. The feeling of uncertainty and fear that has settled over the city is captured in all its haunting power in the diary Zakir has kept during this tumultuous period (Dec. 6th–16th, 1971)[28] when the population was sequestered in their homes by nightly curfews. The entries culminate in a flow of inchoate fragments, but preserve in their rambling and fractured rhythms all the destructive energy of an apocalypse.

The novel is, however, allowed to drag on for four more chapters. Even if some justification could be found for Chapters Eight through Ten, the eleventh stands totally unrelated to the work's basic design and ends on a cryptic note of optimism—the so-called *bashārat* (propitious sign)—at odds with the overpoweringly gloomy vision of the novel. It also ends with what might appear as a flawed sense of closure. I shall discuss these two points more fully a little later. For now, let me mention the controversy that followed the publication of *Bastī*.

Published exactly twenty years after Qurratulain Hyder's *Āg kā Daryā* (River of Fire; 1959), *Bastī* shares with it the distinction of having provoked considerable critical comment. On closer examination, this criticism appears to be ideologically based, in that its motivating force lies in valorizing Pakistani nationalism. It views the novel as a "national allegory," exactly as proposed by Fredric Jameson (1986),[29] except here the text and the critic are both from the third world.

Conspicuously absent here is any regard for the work as an autonomous creation to be understood by reference to an aesthetics inherent in it. One might parenthetically mention here that *Bastī* came at a time when Pakistan was still hurting from the public humiliation of 1971. The breakup of the country had invalidated, retrospectively, the two-nation theory that had created the country in 1947. In that bleak and gloomy national mood, what people needed was a regenerative and revitalizing text, not a novel which could conceivably seal the memory of that humiliation for all time. Thus many critics came to demand from *Bastī* and its protagonist Zakir feats of valor and honor that it was neither Intizar Husain's intention, nor lay within Zakir's power, to deliver. They failed to appreciate Zakir as a novelistic character, and took him for the author's double. His presumed failure was equated with the writer's failure. It is evident from the first chapter, which contains all the vital information about Zakir, that Zakir certainly is not a man of action. He is an introvert, one who sees himself and his world as a cultural continuum. Consequently he reacts to events in ways that may be unexpected, but are in no way contrary to his own nature.

Failure to distinguish between reality and expectation has given rise to a controversy over *Bastī*'s supposed intent. Politically active critics have denounced it for its lack of revolutionary content. Others have found it merely a pale replica of Husain's finer moments. In the confused and frazzled tenor of much critical writing on the work, only the comments of Ja^{c}farī (1984) and Akhtar (1981) show any real insight or perspicacity. In the remaining part of this section, I shall therefore discuss Zakir's character more fully and show that as an artistic creation it is not merely plausible but also entirely consistent with the structure of the novel. I shall first present the substance of Urdu critical comment on the novel and then demonstrate how it has failed to appreciate the character of Zakir by paying little or no attention to his cultural background.

Bastī came out in late 1979. Almost immediately it became the subject of praise and denunciation. Among the more circumspect critics, Muhammad Salim-ur-Rahman felt that the two important areas of personal experience—mythic childhood and urban doubt—which seemingly obsessed Husain, had again come to haunt him in *Bastī*, but with considerably less of his earlier grace, freshness, and artistic finesse. Rahman's conclusion: "Everything that Intizar [Husain] did successfully once is repeated here, with less vigor and noticeable lack of panache" (Rahman 1983:206).

The charge of creative depletion was renewed in another critique by Enver Sajjād, eclipsed in intensity and ire only by his other charge of reactionary sentiments and cowardice.[30] Intizar Husain's characters, even if they are the products of a specific temporality, understand themselves as the products of a cultural continuum. This, inevitably, packs his creative work with an abundance of historical and legendary allusion. *Bastī,* especially, abounds in this sort of reference. Now this historical and mythical material of the novel, Sajjad believes, does not warrant the passivity with which Husain has imbued his characters, most of all Zakir.[31] For instance, medieval Muslim savants and sages such as Imam Ghazali (d. 1111); Ibn Arabi (d. 1240); Ibn Rushd (d. 1198, known to the Latins as Averroes, the commentator of Aristotle's works); and Mansur Hallaj (executed in 922) all resisted both secular and ecclesiastical authority, and Hallaj even laid down his life to preserve the integrity of his own mystical truth. A real mystic did not merely invite others to the mystical path, but entered upon it himself. And the true mystical path, according to Sajjād, lay "in struggle against the declining moral values and the prevalent exploitative system which the oppressive ruling classes and religious groups had both conspired to produce." Now Husain was unwilling to pursue the path of resistance and sacrifice because of the terrifying consequences that might follow.

> When, however, cowardice stings the innards, one way to ease out of one's sense of shame is to become a masochist, to lament, to recall old times and stories of verdant glory in hopes of recovery and dramatic reversal. Undaunted defiance and struggle inevitably produce change. Husain just doesn't want change. Change frightens him. . . . He keeps talking about the advent of the occulted Mahdi (*ẓuhūr*). All right. But doesn't that require that we facilitate the coming of the Mahdi through action against the tyranny of the times? Perhaps Husain does not care about the (*ẓuhūr* after all. What he is waiting for is a savior who would set things right for us without our participation and move along. . . . If Mecca is our dream and Kufa our fate, what significance would Husain then attach to those countless martyrdoms, both great and small, that have occurred since the martyrdom of Imam Husain? You see Husain is a very sneaky fellow. Scared, he shrinks and withdraws into the cocoon of silence, hoping that we would mistake his silence for eloquence. (1983:990–991)

This rather long quotation from Sajjād reveals the tenor of much of the critical writing on Husain by both friend and foe. At the same time, it also presents most graphically some of the errors of understanding which have all along bedeviled most such critiques.[32] First of all, not only do Ghazali, Ibn Arabi, Ibn Rushd, and Hallaj not appear even once in the work, but Sajjād also distorts or misrepresents their true missions.

For example, Ghazali never rebelled against any authority, religious or secular, at least not in the sense of a contemporary revolutionary or utopian socialist. In fact, he taught at the Nizamiyya School in Baghdad, a government-run religious institution set up by the Persian Nizam al-Mulk. If Ghazali later resigned his post at the Nizamiyya, it was dictated more by a harrowing personal crisis than by reasons of conscience triggered by state policies. Ibn Arabi, on the other hand, was the very model of prudent fear and dissimulation. His speculative theories of *vaḥdat al-vujūd* (transcendent unity of being) and *al-aᶜyān as̱-s̱ābita* (fixed prototypes of being) outraged the firmly held beliefs and tenets of exoteric Islam. Rather than die defending those theories, he chose to couch them in the most extravagantly muddled and elliptic language.

Ibn Rushd, too, declined to rise to the eminence Sajjād has lavished upon him. He quietly submitted to the decree of exile given by Abu Yusuf, the Berber Almovhid king of Muslim Spain. The same monarch also ordered Ibn Rushd's books to be burned, and burned they were. Yet the sage did nothing to stop that madness.

Hallaj comes to us filtered through mists of romantic attachment and mystical love that have been steadily accumulating over centuries. But he was not decapitated on account of his so-called blasphemous cry "*Ana 'l-Ḥaqq*" ("I am the Truth/God!"). Instead, he met his end as a result of petty jealousies of state bureaucrats (cf. Massignon and Gardet 1971:101–102).

Yet these men were among the brightest Islam has produced. What is wrong here is that we cannot expect these men to have embraced our contemporary political and social concerns, any more than we can base our judgment of their ultimate success or failure solely upon their espousal or rejection of our own specific cares, concerns, and anxieties. This sort of appropriation is not only dishonest but also bad history.

Worse still, Enver Sajjād, wittingly or otherwise, throughout confuses a novelistic character (Zakir) with the persona of the writer (Intizar Husain), thereby committing an outrage against the most elementary rules of literary criticism. In good fiction characters are rarely human; they are invariably artistic creations.

My purpose in dilating rather at length here on what is merely a peripheral issue within the novel's context is simply to show how Husain's critics have tended to ask the wrong kinds of questions of his fiction. In doing so they have all along betrayed a lack of sensitivity to the religious element in his work. Where, however, they do bring in that element, their perception of it appears generally at odds with reality, whether historical or emotive. On the other hand, if this element is properly discerned, it could conceivably explain what has been viewed as a contradiction in Zakir's character.

To recapitulate: the two main counts on which critics have faulted *Bastī* are: (1) Husain has recycled a lot of old material in it; and (2) Zakir, the novel's protagonist, lacks dynamic will, which presumably reflects Husain's own lack of will. In other words, neither Husain nor Zakir are revolutionaries. The world around them, Pakistan to be more precise, has all but gone to the devil, yet they do nothing to change its fate.

The first question need not detain us here. For Western readers of *Bastī*, who are presumably unacquainted with Husain's other works, this question is perhaps less relevant. However, I do think that *Bastī* unmistakably recalls, both in narrative technique and theme, a number of the author's earlier works. But I would like to discuss fully the charge of lack of dynamic volition leading to apathy and political quietism. In doing so, I hope to take the issue out of the realm of revolution, politics, and ideology and into that of literary aesthetics, where it properly belongs.

I would also argue that in the case of Husain's fictional characters the question is not one of consciously embracing or spurning dynamic will. Rather it is preeminently one of remaining loyal to a greater will that transcends the limitations of time and space. According to the Qur'ān (33:72), God in pre-eternity offered His trust to "the heavens and the earth and the mountains," but they all excused themselves. Only man, though infirm, willingly accepted it. It was a burden that broke his back; worse still, it exposed him to the divine jest: "Verily he was very iniquitous and very ignorant." Why is it that man, otherwise endowed with discursive reason and free will, chose what God had wanted him to? Was there perhaps some inevitability to the choice? Individuals, like nations, sometimes consciously and willingly opt for a course of action—or inaction—that leads to sure annihilation. In their choice they are supported by a unique personal vision of transcendent truth. For instance, in mid-9th-century Muslim Spain, a group of Christian monks, later identified as the Martyrs of Cordova, were so possessed by sublime dementia that they made open scurrilous attacks upon the Prophet of Islam in hopes of speedy martyrdom (cf. Daniel 1975:23–30; Coope 1995:35–54). Such behavior defies conventional logic and might even seem irrational. Is it? I shall return to this question later. For now let me move out of the arena of shadowboxing and give, as briefly as possible, some idea of the novel's contents.[33]

The novel's locale is a city in Pakistan, presumably Lahore; its time, the last few months leading up to the fall of Dhaka; its protagonist, a young professor of history—Zakir, a typically Shīᶜite name. Originally from a small town tucked away somewhere in the mythic landscape of eastern Uttar Pradesh (India), Zakir, along with his parents, moves to Pakistan in 1947, leaving behind not just an idyllic childhood, but also his childhood sweetheart Sabira, a cousin of his. Sabira never comes to Pakistan, even when Muslim life is threatened in India and her own immediate relatives emigrate to what was once East Pakistan. She never marries, nor does Zakir. He is in love with Sabira, but lacks the will to either call or fetch her from India.

Although the novel chronicles only a few months in the life of Zakir, his entire life, and, more importantly, his entire cultural personality extending back through a millennium and a half of Muslim history is recalled via skillfully deployed flashbacks.

Being a professor of history, Zakir is aware (perhaps all too well aware) of the course of Muslim history in the subcontinent; being a Shīᶜite, he is also aware of the course of this history beyond India in the mainlands of Islam. This history has been one of constant internecine feuds among Muslims for political dominance and—as the Hindu freedom fighter Tantiya Topi says at one point in the novel with brutal irony—"for the throne" (186). In fact, for Zakir, it was the advent of the scheming Umaiyads on Islam's political horizon in 661 that inaugurated an interminable era of dissension, strife, and hatred—Islam's dark night of the soul.

There are references to Muslim South Asian history throughout the novel: the 1857 war of independence; the creation of Pakistan in 1947; the 1965 war between India and Pakistan; and finally the 1971 political disintegration of Pakistan with the emergence of Bangladesh as a sovereign nation-state. The novel ends with this last event.

This skeletal account hardly does justice to the rich details of the novel, but I have here all the elements I will need for my discussion.

All the critical fuss about Zakir's inactivity centers around his characteristic lack of emotion regarding the course of political life in Pakistan. The separation of Bangladesh showed in stark detail the failure of religion as a principle of bonding among linguistically and ethnically diverse groups. But the failure of religion itself had been foreshadowed by a morally bankrupt political leadership. In these harrowing circumstances, why is it that neither Zakir nor any of his friends does anything to change the course of life in the country? Why do they sit silently and let the worst happen? They could, at the very least, show verbal disapproval of the situation, rather than rush off to an old, rundown cemetery, as Zakir and Afzal do, and give themselves up to inconsolable torpor and grief.

Critics like Sajjād feel that Zakir, by his silence and failure to act, teaches dastardly acquiescence to an oppressive and corrupt political system. But in my view Zakir's silence, or apparent lack of overt political activism, does not stem from some inherent flaw in his moral fiber. On the contrary: it is the result of a particular view of history shaped in the crucible of Karbalāᵓ.[34] Seen as such, it is not failure. The novel is not about political resistance and activism. If anything, it is about how a personality survives in a morally corrupt universe by drawing on its own inner resources.

Naturally it is significant that the author is a Twelver Shīᶜite, but what is more important for us is that Zakir is a Twelver Shīᶜite. One only has to look at the first chapter to appreciate how thoroughly Zakir is soaked in an environment rich in Shīᶜite ambience. We can best understand the logic of some of his apparent behavior by referring it to Shīᶜite phenomenology.

There is a controversial idea expressed by Freud in *Moses and Monotheism* (1939) and later revived by Norman O. Brown in *Life Against Death* (1959). Freud suggests that traumas—rather, "traumata"—determine not just individual but group psychology as well; indeed they make history possible. Just as traumas received by the individual in early life persist through memory and shape her/his adult life, so too traumas experienced by the group in its infancy may come to determine the behavior of that group.

The hazards of psychoanalytical perspective on religion notwithstanding, one could possibly argue that Karbalāᵓ offers the best example of just such a traumatic event for the Shīᶜites, occurring quite early indeed in their history. Presumably it has in a fundamental way shaped their psyche for all subsequent time. Some important Shīᶜite concepts may have emerged in the aftermath of this event, and may be identified as those of redemptive suffering; the *rajᶜa* or *ẓuhūr* (i.e., the Mahdi or the Savior's eschatological return or manifestation); *taqīya* (i.e., dissimulation or prudent fear); celebration of *via dolorosa*; and the vision of the empirical time between the martyrdom of the Prophet Muhammad's grandson Imam Husain and the return of the Mahdi as inherently corrupt, graceless, oppressive, and immoral.

The details of the martyrdom of Imam Husain at Karbalāᵓ are quite well known and need not detain us here. Suffice it to say that the episode of his slaying is full of pathos and highlights passion and suffering. Outnumbered and "outgunned," abandoned or betrayed by many of his supporters, Imam Husain marched against the Umaiyad forces with all the odds fatally against him. Still more striking is the fact that right from the start he had absolutely no illusions about the outcome of the battle. He did nothing to avert it.

The Shīᶜites believe that from the time Imam Husain left Mecca, he knew of his impending doom. His willing sacrifice therefore underscores the primacy of a certain higher principle. He was not motivated by the desire for personal gain. On the contrary, from beginning to end his strategy seems to have been to look evil in the eye with undaunted self-immolative defiance. He "was planning for a complete revolution in the religious consciousness of the Muslims. All of his actions show that he was aware of the fact that a victory achieved through military strength and might is always temporal . . . But a victory achieved through suffering and sacrifice is everlasting and leaves permanent imprints on man's consciousness" (Jafri 1979:202). On the eve of Ashura (the tenth day of the month of Muharram, according to the Muslim calendar), only hours away from his death, Imam Husain gathered his seventy-odd followers and said:

> I think tomorrow our end will come . . . I ask you to leave me alone and to go away to safety. I free you from your responsibilities for me, and I do not hold you back. Night will provide you a cover; use it as a steed. (189)

It is hard to imagine that these could be the thoughts of a man motivated by political ambition.

At any rate, however small and militarily insignificant, Imam Husain's was still an armed struggle. But with Karbalāᵓ, Shīᶜism would seem to have given up faith in armed struggle as a viable means of achieving essentially spiritual and moral goals. Yet wherever and whenever such a struggle is joined, its moral and religious motivation dominates the Shīᶜite consciousness. Indeed with the advent of the sixth linear Imam, Jaᶜfar as-Sadiq (d. 765), uprising and military struggle were effectively renounced. In interpreting the function of the Imamate (Shīᶜite leadership), Jaᶜfar as-Sadiq "differed categorically from the hitherto dominating view that an Imam [religious/spiritual leader] should be a caliph [political leader] as well, and put forward the idea of dividing the Imamate and the caliphate into two separate institutions until such time as God would make an Imam victorious" (281). Whatever the hope of such "victory" in calendar time, it was effectively dashed with the occultation of the twelfth Imam Muhammad al-Mahdi in 874. Henceforward, Shīᶜite concern with material history and empirical time noticeably declines. Instead, aspirations to victory come to be placed, dramatically, in metahistorical time. Henceforward, Shīᶜite history enters the murky domain of time suspension or, to use a more trendy phrase, "time-lock." This, of course, holds true only for the Twelver or Imami Shīᶜites. The Ismailites (or Seveners) and the Zaidites never renounced the military option.

Now in a dark, sinful world, the only "healing of existence or the fulfillment of human life" is located by the Shīᶜite piety, as Mahmoud Ayoub has poignantly shown, in the "phenomenon of redemption through the suffering and passion of a divine hero or holy martyr," none other than Imam Husain (1978:23 and 7). In order to exist, suffering presupposes continued enactment of the principle of evil. The Shīᶜites look at "trials of affliction [as] more than a mere discipline," as "an active choice made independently of rewards and punishments." "All suffering and martyrdom after [Imam Husain] are only modes of participation in his martyrdom" (26–27), which he voluntarily and unconditionally accepted for the love of God and for the preservation of His religion. The Muharram piety—with its mourning assemblies, memorial services, self-flagellation, and displays of grief (made abundantly familiar throughout in *Bastī*, but especially in the first chapter)—underscores a Shīᶜite desire to share vicariously in the pain of Imam Husain and symbolically connect his "here" and "now" with sacred time and space, with the *karb* (sorrow) and *balāʾ* (calamity; test, trial) experienced by the Imam at Karbalāʾ.[35]

Zakir (*ẕākir*: "one who remembers") walks through his time and space with the graphic memory of Shīᶜite suffering. I think Husain's choice of Zakir as the name of the novel's figuratively martyred central character and of "history" as this character's profession is quite deliberate, though, interestingly enough, it does not appear forced. Not uncharacteristically Zakir says, "I want to remember, to dwell on my pains. . . . The tragedy of this war-infected age is that it stops our pain from becoming our memory" (152).[36] And elsewhere: "One can study the history of another people with indifference, not one's own" (79). The more the world around him crumbles into chaos, the more he withdraws into himself in what appears to be almost a scramble for a very private kind of salvation through the Shīᶜite principle of interiorization of suffering (cf. 14).[37]

Yet the most powerful allusion to "defeat" and "humiliation" as catalyzing agents for a redeemed existence occurs toward the end of the novel. News has just arrived that East Pakistan has fallen. Zakir and Irfan sit sadly in the Shiraz, their favorite hangout. In walk Salamat and Ajmal. In an impassioned outburst of anger, Salamat places the entire responsibility for the humiliating defeat squarely upon Irfan and Zakir.

Later, outside the café, when the accusation of "Traitor!" rises above the din of a scuffling band of young men, Zakir says to Irfan, "You know, Salamat wasn't perhaps all that wrong. *I am* responsible for this defeat." When Irfan looks at him uncomprehendingly, Zakir explains, "The thing is this, Irfan, that *defeat*, too, is a kind of trust. But, today, in this country, everybody is accusing the other, and will still be tomorrow; today everyone is trying to prove his innocence, and will still be tomorrow. Somebody must bear this trust. I thought I might just as well" (178).

Our expectation that a consciousness so deeply immersed in a Shīᶜite ambience would feel outraged over the misconduct of a temporal leadership is, I am afraid, quite illogical. Being the person he is, Zakir is not likely to react openly to such temporal issues as the conduct of the government and the nature of political authority. Where in the Shīᶜite world view have government and authority ever been anything other than corrupt? I am less inclined to attribute Zakir's quietism and so-called lack of will to the more attractive Shīᶜite doctrine of *taqīya* (prudent fear), even when support for *taqīya* is not wanting in the novel itself (see, for instance, Zakir's interior monologue on p. 23). Rather, I strongly feel that a truly Shīᶜite personality, formed in the tragic aftermath of Karbalāᵓ, inherently transcends involvement in issues pertaining to profane time, or articulates them in unmistakable religious terms.

I do not wish to imply that external events, however intrinsically insignificant, are, or can be, quite without impact even on an excessively introverted Shīᶜite personality such as Zakir's. That is hardly the case. But material events, instead of inciting the personality to physical action, can conceivably heighten its sense of suffering. They are, therefore, irreplaceable items in the baggage of redemption. Grief, experienced in all its harrowing intensity, helps the personality rise to sublimity.

Not confined to external events, a similar stunning restraint in the display of raw emotion is evident even in intimately personal areas of Zakir's life. His love for Sabira—another name rich in symbolic connotations (Ṣābira means "one who is patient, is able to endure")—remains unfulfilled, not because of external impediment, but by deliberate choice. Salim-ur-Rahman has demanded:

> May we have another novel, please, Mister, one in which you tell us things you have always held back, like the escapades and attachments of your salad days. . . . Also one in which we can come across women in their prime, not one with sexless kinky grandmas or innocent childhood playmates in it. Give us women

> who talk and think and love, don't just drool over their attractive curves. (1983:207–208)

I am afraid this demand is likely to remain unfulfilled—and for a deeper reason: Zakir is not given to expecting love to blossom in a morally imperfect world. The Shīᶜite "House of Sorrows encompasses not only all human history, but the cosmos in its totality as well" (Ayoub 1978:26). Even physical relationships have to be blessed by a state of moral beatitude, impossible in this life for a post-Karbalāᵓ Shīᶜite. Hence the self-willed denial of the barest creaturely pleasures.

Yet neither Shīᶜite history itself nor Zakir's biography may be assumed to be entirely free of contradiction: both lie between empirical truth and emotive truth, between humiliation and proud, assertive exaltation, between stout will and meek submission, between cruel judgment and compassionate pardon, between existential despair and messianic hope—all of which are located and held in tense equilibrium along a single continuum. Even as he prepared for the fateful encounter, knowing the inevitable end, Imam Husain kept asking his adversaries for understanding and mercy. Left alone, unable to move, he sat on the ground and uttered a pathetic cry for help:

> Is there no one to defend the women of the Apostle of God? Is there not one professing the oneness of God [*muwaḥḥid*] who would fear God for our sake? Is there no one to come to our help, seeking thereby that which God has in store as a reward for those who would aid us? (Ayoub 1978:118–119)

Imam Husain's consciousness is beset with enough agonizing conflicts to thwart even the most liberal attempt of the historian to reach some workable logical resolution of them. Similarly, Zakir too is by no means free of heart-wrenching contradictory feelings. For example, the most obvious instance of conflict is this: in spite of his near-hermetic abstemiousness in his relationship with Sabira, he has known and experienced desire. Although his relationship with Tasnim never came to anything, he did come close to the pleasures of the flesh in his fleeting encounter with the promiscuous Anisa. What is significant here is not that desire for sexual gratification remained only latent, but that he consciously and willingly experienced it. In fact, one could say he virtually burned in it.

A more subtle instance has to do with a raging conflict in Zakir's historical consciousness. This is his ambivalence toward the creation of Bangladesh—yet another incident from temporal and, therefore, spiritually unavailing history. Developments in Pakistan since its creation in 1971 have left Zakir's father in a state of stoic resignation. One day he sums up his dark thoughts for Zakir by narrating a saying of Zain al-^{c}Abidin, the fourth linear Shī^{c}ite Imam, who died in 712 or 713. On being queried by an individual about the state in which he had spent the night, the Imam rejoined with sadness, "By my Creator, I have spent it in the tyranny of the Umaiyads!" After recounting the saying, Zakir's father adds pessimistically, "Son, it's been the same ever since . . . and will continue to be so till the Mahdi's advent [*ẓuhūr*]" (202).

Now Zakir tacitly accepts his father's characterization of Pakistani life and history as tyrannical. The recent events in East Pakistan seem to him an instant replay of the earlier Muslim civil wars. A history in which brother killed brother is being reenacted with inexorable normative force. One would least expect a response of shocked disbelief at these predictable events from a person whose entire consciousness is formed in the crucible of sectarian injustice, tyranny, usurpation, and wrong. Yet there is more than a measure of loss and personal unhappiness in Zakir's attitude toward Pakistan's national disintegration. In his diary entry for December 18th, 1971, he mentions three separate instances of stunning courage from Indian history. Two of the individuals involved are Hindus—the Queen of Jhansi (a small Maratha state in central India) and Tantiya Topi—the third a Muslim, Navab Hazrat Mahal, the woman ruler of the Shī^{c}ite state of Oudh, who rather than surrender to the British forces when they came to annex her state to their Indian dominion, disappeared into the forests of Nepal along with a group of her loyalists. We are thus left to conclude that the surrender of Pakistani forces in East Pakistan and their inability to avert national disaster was a particularly humiliating event. The question arises: why should this sadden a Shī^{c}ite for whom historical time is basically tyrannical time? Why must he agonize over the defeat and humiliation of a country to which he had emigrated not out of ideological preference but out of sheer necessity? More importantly, what possible significance could such purely temporal concepts as national honor and unity have for a person whose entire attention is focused, unwaveringly, on metahistorical time?

There are other examples of Zakir's muted anger at the turn of political events in Pakistan. Their presence suggests, at the very least, more than a whisper of regard for that country.

But these contradictions ought really be seen as attributes of a fairly complex character. They might even be more apparent than real. On closer examination it can be seen that in no pair are the two terms of opposition either fully equal or truly contrastive and comparative. In each case the weaker one seems to have been marshaled only to underscore the incontestable superiority of the other and to bring out, dramatically, its inherent truth. Zakir's sexual desire could have found gratification in Anisa—it didn't; his feelings of outraged honor in the wake of the 1971 debacle could have turned him into an ardent revolutionary—they didn't. Ultimately, we are left with a personality curled back upon itself, seeking salvation through redemptive suffering in the impersonal cruelty of empirical time.

Contradiction, moreover, cannot be rooted out from life. It is perhaps less significant that an individual may consider several options, each essentially different from or even antithetical to the others. What is significant is that the choice ultimately made is the only choice one could have made, the only choice consistent with one's nature. As a human being, Zakir experiences moments of love, pain, desire, anger, and frustration—all prompted by external events, but all ultimately dissolved in an enduring and powerful feeling of suffering. This suffering alone can redeem those other feelings, alone can redeem existence. In my opinion, Zakir's response, described as "cowardly" by Enver Sajjād, is religiously determined and has its origin in the collective experience of the Shīᶜite community, as it stood in the plain of Karbalāᵓ, mourning the cruel murder of its innocent leader. Why else would Zakir's father, the old wistful recluse, remind his son: "Son, it's been the same ever since"? And what is the meaning of the following exchange between Zakir's father and a friend in a Pakistan torn apart by civil strife:

> "Khwaja Sahib, hundred and twenty-four thousand prophets were sent into this world. Did it change?"
>
> "No. It didn't."
>
> "So then, if prophets couldn't change it, what makes you think these brats would?"
>
> "Yes Maulana, you spoke the truth. The world *cannot* change." (69)

Finally, overt activism and passive submission may be interpreted as two modes of resistance, of denial and disapproval. Sunni pragmatism—always unable to comprehend the Shīᶜite response to questions of history, time, and temporal authority—places its confidence in the efficacy of arms. The Shīᶜites, on the other hand, reach a state of grace through suffering: as if truth becomes manifest through the enactment of grief. Ultimately, they too by their self-immolative, but entirely self-willed, forfeiture of conventional modes of salvation, deny the victor the spoils of victory.

It would seem that some Urdu critics, working perhaps under the residual influence of the Progressives, still insist on a socially useful role for literature. If Zakir's character seems fanciful or far-fetched to them, and it certainly does to Enver Sajjād, it is because they have tried to judge him by expectations which either ignore or dismiss the religious element at work in his consciousness. His character and his responses are entirely consistent with the Twelver Shīᶜite world view that is inherent in the structure of the novel. I am not suggesting that a creative work must be ultimately valid in religious terms, or that these terms are the only valid means of approach to its inner life. Rather, I am making a case for greater sensitivity to crucial religious concepts that might be organically present in a work. If properly discerned, these concepts can often enhance our ability to experience its inner world more fully and, thus, deepen our understanding of its poetics. This certainly seems to be the case with Husain's *Bastī*.

It is only proper that I mention here a tentative reservation I have about *Bastī*. Tentative—indeed, for I would like to keep the option of revision open should a future reading of the work warrant it. I mentioned earlier that the novel ends without a true sense of ending. By that I do not mean that closure ought to be an indispensable requirement of a novel. Recent Western theories of narrative argue acutely against it (cf. Martin 1986:83 ff). To end "with a kind of permanent openness or lack of resolution" merely implies possibilities a novel may take if continued (83). My problem with *Bastī* is that it achieves structural integration by Chapter Ten and then takes off on a different tangent. Then midway it breaks off the narrative and leaves it dangling.

If all Zakir wanted was to reiterate for the umpteenth time the blueprint of the world as an inherently tyrannical and graceless place, then this was effectively achieved by Chapter Ten. In my opinion, what follows only manages to distract more than creatively expand the narrative structure.

The optimistic note at the end appears to me at least a non sequitur.[38] Zakir tells Irfan that he wants to write to Sabira after all. "Now?" Irfan asks, as thoroughly nonplussed as the reader. "Yes, now."

> "Now when . . ." God knows what Irfan wanted to say; he fell silent in the middle of his sentence.
>
> "Yes, now when . . ." he [Zakir] hesitated, then drifted off into another direction. "Before . . ." Confused, he fell silent. (228)

What follows is a paragraph of inarticulate fragments reproduced through psycho-narration, during which Zakir sits dazed, like someone possessed, on the verge of a revelation from on high. Irfan prods him to go on, but Afzal tells Irfan to keep quiet, because there is going to be a *bashārat* (a propitious vision).[39]

Though it is not clear who will be the recipient of the propitious vision, let us assume it is Zakir. A propitious sign after the frightening apocalypse? What does it mean? Fulfillment of any kind isn't part of the work's inherent structure. *Bastī* derives its power from a sad and gloomy view of human time. Why weaken it with a cryptic note of optimism? Cynicism or irony might have provided the saving grace, but the tone of the narrative is so neutral that these possibilities cannot even be contemplated. Likewise, we know for a fact that Zakir will never write to Sabira. His character, as Husain has developed it over the last 227 pages, itself guards against such an eventuality. And even if he were to write to her, would Sabira, again as Husain has portrayed her, really join him in Pakistan? Join him, in other words, to consummate their relationship at a physical level? Perhaps not. Her decision to stay on in India is not foisted upon her by the agony of physically unrequited love. It is quite deliberate. She hasn't given up on love. But love's fulfillment in a physical sense is just not part of her ethos. She is deeply in love with Zakir, has been all along, and will always be. Put somewhat differently, hers is an intransitive love.

What significance then could the dubious *bashārat* and Zakir's sudden toying with the possibility of writing to Sabira have in the entirety of the novel? Unfortunately I do not as yet know. Until I do, I am inclined to think that Husain, terrified by the chilling aura of his own prescience, has tagged the work with incipient hope. In doing so, he may have dispelled some of its gloom, but only at the cost of robbing it considerably of its haunting power.

VI

Intizar Husain is one of the most powerful, prolific, and talented writers of Urdu fiction in Pakistan.[40] He was born into an orthodox Shīᶜite family. His father, along with a brother, had been recent converts to Shīᶜism. The rest of the family, however, was overwhelmingly Sunni Muslim. The family history included at least a Sufi or a religious figure in each generation. Open-minded and ecumenical in spirit, these men looked upon their faith as a living and spontaneous experience of the divine, unencumbered by the confining literalism of exoteric precept and text. Husain's own father, by comparison, was "something of a *maulavī*" (a zealot, a preacher) and a "proselytizer." A man who despised modern ways, very much like Zakir's father, he didn't allow his son to be ruined by the "new kind of education." So Husain ended up receiving his early education at home in his native Dibai (a township in the district of Buland Shahr in India) under the watchful eye of his father. This included a study of Arabic and of preponderantly religious texts, though on the sly the inquisitive boy managed to read a number of Urdu books, among them, of course, that fascinating tome "with yellow covers and pictures of magicians and genies" whose name he was to find out only much later. It was *The Arabian Nights*—a book that has left an enduring influence on the greater part of Husain's fiction, especially on its narrative structure.

The family moved to Hapur. Husain was enrolled in a school. Here, as he describes it, the process of his "de-education" began. He made a conscious "attempt to obliterate what I had learned up to then." Hapur was also a small town, but still quite a bit bigger than Dibai. Husain finished high school there and then moved on to Meerut for college education. On August 15th, 1947, the partition of India brought his college career to an abrupt end and he decided, like many other Muslims, to migrate to Pakistan. After arriving in Pakistan in late 1947, he settled permanently in Lahore.

Husain's literary career began almost as soon as he set foot in the new country. He wrote two stories in 1948, "Qaiyūmā kī Dukān" (Qaiyuma's Shop) and "Ustād" (The Teacher/Boss). He read the first before a meeting of the Ḥalqa-e Arbāb-e Z̲auq (see above, p. 10). It received appreciation and was later published in the literary journal *Adab-e Laṭīf*. He also received quite a bit of encouragement for the second story when he presented it at a meeting of the Progressive Writers' Association. Both are included in his first collection *Galī Kūčē* (Alleys and Bylanes).

Since then Intizar Husain has kept up a steady flow of writing. The author of some 125 short stories, all of which have appeared in Urdu periodicals in both Pakistan and India, Husain has also experimented with a number of other forms: novelette, novel, biography, and plays for stage, radio, and television. He has also edited a number of old Urdu *kahāniyāṅ* and *qiṣṣas* (popular tales), translated Russian and American fiction, and compiled a number of selections of what he considers the best Urdu fiction. His conversations with the late poet Nasir Kazmi on various literary issues and problems appeared at one time in the literary journals *Nayā Daur, Savērā,* and *Māh-e Nau*. He is, however, best known to the Urdu readership as a master of the short story. Among his published works are the collections of stories, *Galī Kūčē, Kaṅkarī, Ākhirī Ādmī, Shahr-e Afsōs, Kačhvē, Khaimē sē Dūr,* and *Khālī Pinjrā;*

four novels: *Čāṅdgahan, Bastī* (which has recently appeared in English translation), *Tazkira,* a controversial work about the Bhutto era, and *Āgē Samandar hai,* a fictional portrayal of the tragic civil strife in the city of Karachi; a novelette, *Din aur Dāstān;* a travel account of his three visits to India more than three decades after Partition, *Zamīṅ aur Falak aur*; and a collection of his literary essays and book reviews, *ᶜAlāmatōṅ kā Zavāl.* Sang-e Meel Publishers of Lahore have decided to bring out Husain's entire fiction to date in a complete set, of which two volumes, *Janam Kahāniyāṅ* and *Qiṣṣa Kahāniyāṅ,* have appeared so far.[41]

In 1982, Intizar Husain was offered the Adamjee Literary Award for *Bastī*, but he declined it. In a letter addressed to the secretary general of the Pakistan Writers' Guild, he said: "Thank you for the charity. I do not find myself deserving enough for the distinction. I may please be spared this honor. . . . That will earn you requital [*Sawab*] and provide me relief."[42] In all likelihood, Husain's refusal was prompted by the belated recognition of his talent and contribution. Some lesser writers had preceded him in the award since it was instituted more than two decades ago. He must have noted that fact—not without a feeling of injured pride. On the other hand, he readily and gratefully accepted, in 1993, the first Yatra Award, instituted by Rupa & Co. (a publishing firm), with assistance from HarperCollins, India. He personally went to Calcutta to receive the award and was much honored and widely interviewed throughout India. The same year Indus, an imprint of HarperCollins Publishers of India, brought out in English translation a selection of his short fiction works entitled *Leaves and Other Stories* and, in 1995, a translation of his major novel *Bastī.*

In 1983, the *Journal of South Asian Literature* devoted an entire special issue to Intizar Husain and his writing. This number includes translations of several of his short stories and articles, an interview, critical essays on his art, reviews of his books, and an extensive bibliography of works by and on him.

Intizar Husain is married, has no children, and makes his home in Lahore. After working for nearly three decades as a columnist for the daily Urdu newspaper *Mashriq* (The East), he moved, in 1989, to the English newspaper *The Frontier Post* and, subsequently, to *Dawn*, Pakistan's foremost English-language daily. For some time Husain also edited the two Lahore-based Urdu literary periodicals *Adab-e Laṯīf* and *Khayāl.*

A man of mysterious silences about himself, quiet and reclusive, Intizar Husain must be in his mid-seventies at the time of this writing.

Notes

1. Kundera (1988:117).

2. The allusion is to an episode in Kundera (1974), which he especially mentions in "Dialogue on the Art of the Novel" (1988:37) to underscore his thoughts on the use of history in novels.

3. In his short story "Lājvantī"; tr. by Khushwant Singh, in Mathur and Kulasrestha (1976:126–135). *Lājvantī* means a bashful and chaste woman.

4. In (1952a); tr. by Leslie A. Flemming and Muhammad Umar Memon, in Memon (1987:23–49); for a discussion of this story, see Memon (1980:402–406).

5. In Ḥusain (1973a); tr. by Rahman, in Azim (1977:128–145).

6. Michael Beard, my friend and colleague, whom I would like to thank for reading this introductory essay and for offering insightful comments, feels that I should rather have put Urdu on a level with Turkish, because "The Turks complain constantly that no one reads them." The Turks may very well complain, for reasons of their own, but the fate of Urdu humanities in the West has been, decidedly, far worse.

7. Qurratulain Hyder is among the foremost women Urdu writers of India and Pakistan. She was born into a highly educated family toward the end of the first quarter of this century. Nazar Sajjad Hyder, her mother, was among the early feminists who wrote extensively on women's issues, including a carefully reasoned essay ("Purdah") against their confinement and seclusion behind the "veil." Syed Sajjad Hyder Yaldarim, her father, is counted among Urdu's earliest essayists and fiction writers. She received her M.A. in English literature from the University of Lucknow (India). She has published extensively: seven novels, several collections of short stories, and translations into Urdu of such writers as Henry James, T. S. Eliot, and Truman Capote. In 1968 the Sahitya Akademi (Indian Academy of Letters) awarded her a prize for her collection of short stories *Patjhaṛ kī Āvāz* (The Sound of a Falling Leaf; 1965) and her highly controversial novel *Āg kā Daryā* (River of Fire; 1959), which stands apart from most Urdu novels in its sustained use of stream of consciousness, has been translated into fifteen Indian languages. She was one of the editors of *Imprint* magazine (Bombay); later she worked for many years as a member of the editorial staff of the *Illustrated Weekly of India*. She is widely traveled and in 1979–1980 was a writer-in-residence in the International Writers Program of the University of Iowa. In 1990, she was the recipient of India's highest literary prize, the Bharatiya Jnan Pith Award. She now lives in Delhi.

8. As, for instance, the short story "Saikinḍ Rā°ūnḍ" (The Second Round), for which, see (1967e).

9. For a critical review of Ḥālī and for an analysis of the nature of his

influence, see Salīm Aḥmad (1982:53–88 and 1984:14), and for a summary of a portion of Ḥālī's book, *Muqaddima-e Shᶜir-o-Shāᶜirī,* see Steele (1981:24–42).

10. *The Courtesan of Lucknow, Umrao Jan Ada*, tr. by Khushwant Singh and M.A. Husaini (Delhi: Hind Pocket Books [n.d.]).

11. On his life and works, see Pandey (1989); Rubin (1969:13–17); Sadiq (1964:44–55); and Sharma (1978).

12. On this movement, see Coppola (1975) and Malik (1967).

13. My account of the Circle is based exclusively on Jāvēd (1984); for a review of Jāvēd's work, see Memon (1984).

14. For a critique of Urdu short stories inspired by the Partition, see Memon (1980: 388–395).

15. My impressions are based largely on Ḥusain (1983).

16. Kundera, as quoted in McEwan (1984:34).

17. For a good introduction to the liberalism and syncretism of these individuals, see Ahmad (1964).

18. Ḥusain seems to be particularly fond of making this observation. When the Indian literary critic Alok Bhalla visited Ḥusain at his home in Lahore in October 1992, Ḥusain made it yet again: "I have no idea what a pure Islamic culture is . . ." (Ḥusain 1993:vi).

19. On the day of creation God asked man, *"Alastu bi-rabbikum?"* ("Am I not your Lord?"), and the latter replied, *"Balā"* ("Yes"). This episode is recorded in the Qurʾān (7:171). *Alast* is part of the Muslim mystical (*ṣūfī*) vocabulary and underscores the basic doctrine of Islam, viz., *at-Tauḥīd* (the perfect transcendental *Unity of God*). "Song of *Alast*" would thus mean "the song acknowledging the *Unity of God*"—the ultimate goal of a mystic aspirant.

It has not been possible to ascertain the nature and character of *rāga pūrbī.* Danielou, however, mentions a certain *rāga* called "*puravi*," for which, see (1954:128–132).

20. "He [Ḥusain] said that though he accepted the fact of Pakistan as an irreversible part of the geopolitical reality of this region, he didn't think there was anything either 'historically inevitable' about its creation or 'natural' about its emergence"—Alok Bhalla (see Ḥusain 1993:vi).

21. For a more extensive discussion of the notion of *hijrat* as formulated by Ḥusain, see Memon (1980:377–379 and 1981:73–75); and for a critique of Ḥusain's concept of *hijrat* in the short story "Vō Jō Khōʾē Gaʾē," see Ibn-e Farīd (1981).

22. 1963; this translation is mine.

23. In my analysis of some of the stories in this section I substantially borrow and paraphrase from my earlier articles (1981 and 1983). Some of the stories discussed in this section are available in translation, for which, see Azim (1977) and Memon (1987).

24. This motif occurs frequently in Ḥusain; for instance, in the novel *Bastī*, Afzal relates: "A traveler, passing through a forest, saw that a sandalwood tree was on fire. The birds that used to perch on its branches had already taken wing, but one swan still sat glued to a branch. The traveler asked, 'Oh swan! Don't you see that the sandalwood tree is on fire? Why don't you then fly away? Don't you care about your life?' The swan replied, 'Oh traveler! I've found much comfort under the shade of this tree. Must I now, when it's struck by misfortune, abandon it?'" (1979:144) Elsewhere, Zakir's father tells his wife, "Death is everywhere. Where can one go to escape from it?" He then cites a tradition (*ḥadīs̱*) of the Prophet Muḥammad: "'Those who run from death, run toward death instead!'" (153). Unless otherwise indicated, all translations in this essay are mine.

25. Tr. by Nancy D. Gross, in Memon (1987:153).

26. A psycho-narration in which, according to Cohn, an otherwise effaced narrator "readily fuses with the consciousness she/he narrates" (1978:26).

27. Cohn's terms; see (1978:31).

28. December 16, 1971, was the day the Pakistani military forces surrendered to the Indian army at Dhaka and East Pakistan formally became Bangladesh.

29. For a critique of Jameson's theory, see Aijaz Ahmad (1987).

30. ᶜAlavī (1984:173) also faults Ḥusain for repeating himself ad infinitum.

31. Jaᶜfarī also feels that Zakir is a passive character (1984:541).

32. See, for instance, Jaᶜfarī (1984), Kāmrān (1983), Malik (1983), Munīr (1983), and Qāsimī (1983).

33. For a fuller idea of the plot, theme, and technique of this novel, see Jaᶜfarī (1984) and Wentink (1982).

34. For this incident and for a general introduction to Shīᶜism, see Jafri (1979) and Momen (1985).

35. The pun is borrowed from Ibn Ṯāwūs al-Baghdādī, as quoted in Ayoub (1978:109).

36. Unless otherwise indicated, all translations from this work are mine.

37. Thus I do not agree with Jaᶜfarī's contention (1984:541) that Ḥusain has failed to make use of Zakir's profession and intelligence.

38. Akhtar (cf. 1981:104–105), however, thinks that both Zakir's desire to write to Sabira and the expected *bashārat* at the end reflect positively on the novel. But such a reading, in my opinion, is more romantic, even ideologically motivated, than aesthetic.

39. Platts (1968:157) defines *bashārat* as: "good news, glad tidings, joyful annunciation made to one in sleep or in a vision by some saint; happy dream or vision; divine inspiration, revelation."

40. This account of Ḥusain's life is based on biographical details contained in Ḥusain (1975; tr. 1983).

41. For a select bibliography of works by and on Ḥusain up to 1982, see Wentink (1983:209–218).

42. As quoted in "News and Events," *Annual of Urdu Studies 2* (1982):147.

Works Cited

Ahmad, Aijaz. 1987. "Jameson's Rhetoric of Otherness and the 'National Allegory.'" *Social Text* 17 (Fall):3–25.

Ahmad, Aziz. 1964. *Studies in Islamic Culture in the Indian Environment.* Oxford: Oxford University Press.

Aḥmad, Salīm. 1982. "The Ghazal, a Muffler, and India." Tr. John A. Hanson. *Annual of Urdu Studies* 2:53–83.

———. 1984. "The Future of the Ghazal: A Symposium." Tr. Muhammad Umar Memon. *Annual of Urdu Studies* 4:1–23.

Akhtar, Vaḥīd. 1981. "Sukhan-gustarāna Bāt: Tahẕībī Bāz-yāft kā Mas'ala" [A Protracted Matter: The Problem of Cultural Reclamation]. *Alfāẓ* (Aligarh) 2, nos. 3–4:91–108.

ᶜAlavī, Vāris̱. 1984. "Ākhir-e Shab kē Ham-safar" [Companions of the End of Night]. *Iẓhār* (Bombay) 5:170–200.

Ayoub, Mahmoud. 1978. *Redemptive Suffering in Islam.* The Hague: Mouton Publishers.

Azim, S. Viqar, ed. 1977. *Modern Urdu Short Stories from Pakistan.* Islamabad: Pakistan Branch, R.C.D. Cultural Institute.

Bedi, Rajinder Singh. 1972. "*Mahfil* interviews Rajinder Singh Bedi." *Mahfil* 8, nos. 2–3:139–158.

Brown, Norman O. 1959. *Life Against Death.* Middletown, Connecticut: Wesleyan University Press.

Cohn, Dorrit. 1978. *Transparent Minds, Narrative Modes for Presenting Consciousness in Fiction.* Princeton: Princeton University Press.

Coope, Jessica A. 1995. *The Martyrs of Córdoba: Community and Family Conflict in an Age of Mass Conversion.* Lincoln: University of Nebraska Press.

Coppola, Carlo. 1975. "Urdu Poetry, 1935–1970: The Progressive Episode." Ph.D. Diss., The University of Chicago.

Daniel, Norman. 1975. *The Arabs and Mediaeval Europe.* London: Longman.

Elgrably, Jordon. 1987. "Conversations with Milan Kundera." *Salmagundi* 73 (Winter):3–24.

Freud, Sigmund. 1939. *Moses and Monotheism.* Tr. Katherine Jones. New York: Alfred A. Knopf.

Fuentes, Carlos. 1988. *Myself with Others*. New York: Farrar, Straus & Giroux.
Ḥālī, Alṭāf Ḥusain. 1960. *Muqaddima-e Shᶜir-o-Shāᶜirī* [Introduction to Poetry and Poetics]. Karachi: Urdu Academy Sindh.
Hanson, John A., tr. 1983. "Urdu Literature of Our Times." Pp. 133–143 in Memon 1983a.
Ḥusain, Intiẓār. 1952. *Galī Kūčē* [Alleys and Bylanes]. Lahore: Maktaba-e Kārvāṅ.
———. 1952a. "Ēk Bin-likhī Razmiya" [An Unwritten Epic]. Pp. 193–224 in Ḥusain 1952.
———. 1953. *Čāṅdgahan* [Lunar Eclipse]. Lahore: Maktaba-e Kārvāṅ.
———. 1955. *Kaṅkarī* [Pebble]. Lahore: Maktaba-e Jadīd.
———. 1962. *Din aur Dāstān* [Day and Tale]. Lahore: Idāra-e Adabiyāt-e Nau.
———. 1963. "Hamāre ᶜAhd kā Adab" [Literature of Our Time]. *Savērā* (Lahore) 31:8–17.
———. 1967. *Ākhirī Ādmī* [The Last Man]. Lahore: Kitābiyāt.
———. 1967a. "Ākhirī Ādmī" [The Last Man]. Pp. 1–13 in Ḥusain 1967.
———. 1967b. "Ham-safar" [Fellow-Traveler]. Pp. 75–92 in Ḥusain 1967.
———. 1967c. "Kāyā-kalp" [Metamorphosis]. Pp. 93–105 in Ḥusain 1967.
———. 1967d. "Parčhā'īṅ" [The Shadow]. Pp. 37–56 in Ḥusain 1967.
———. 1967e. "Saikinḍ Rā'ūnḍ" [The Second Round]. Pp. 133–148 in Ḥusain 1967.
———. 1967f. "Ṭāṅgēṅ" [The Legs]. Pp. 107–132 in Ḥusain 1967.
———. 1967g. "Zard Kuttā" [The Yellow Dog]. Pp. 14–35 in Ḥusain 1967.
———. 1973. *Shahr-e Afsōs* [The City of Grief]. Lahore: Maktaba-e Kārvāṅ.
———. 1973a. "Andhī Galī" [The Dead-End Alley]. Pp. 227–248 in Ḥusain 1973.
———. 1973b. "Apnī Āg kī Ṭaraf" [Toward His Fire]. Pp. 190–206 in Ḥusain 1973.
———. 1973c. "Shahr-e Afsōs" [The City of Grief]. Pp. 249–270 in Ḥusain 1973.
———. 1973d. "Sīṛhiyāṅ" [The Stairway]. Pp. 62–83 in Ḥusain 1973.
———. 1973e. "Vō Jō Khō'ē Ga'ē" [The Lost Ones]. Pp. 9–28 in Ḥusain 1973.
———. 1975. "Intiẓār Ḥusain aur Muḥammad ᶜUmar Maiman kē Drmiyān Ēk Bāt-čīt" [A Conversation Between Intiẓār Ḥusain and Muhammad Umar Memon]. *Shab-Khūn* (Allahabad) 8, no. 96 (July–September):3–35.
———. 1979. *Bastī* [Town]. Lahore: Naqsh-e Avval Kitābghar.
———. 1981. "Ḍēṛh Bāt Apnē Afsānē Par" [A Thing or Two About My Short Stories]. *Alfāẓ* (Aligarh) 2, nos. 3–4:85–90.

———. 1981a. *Kačhvē* [The Turtles]. Lahore: Maṯbūᶜāt.
———. 1981b. "Asīr" [The Prisoner/s]. Pp. 46–54 in Ḥusain 1981a.
———. 1981c. "Hindūstān sē Ēk Khaṭ" [A Letter from India]. Pp. 55–66 in Ḥusain 1981a.
———. 1981d. "Kačhvē" [The Turtles]. Pp. 73–92 in Ḥusain 1981a.
———. 1981e. "Nīnd" [Sleep]. Pp. 67–72 in Ḥusain 1981a.
———. 1983. "A Conversation between Intizar Husain and Muhammad Umar Memon." Tr. Bruce R. Pray. *Journal of South Asian Literature* 18, nos. 1–2:153–186.
———. 1983a. *ᶜAlāmatōṅ kā Zavāl* [The Decay of Exponential Signs]. Lahore: Saṅg-e Mīl Publications.
———. 1984. *Zamīṅ aur, Falak aur* [A Different Land, A Different Sky]. Lahore: Saṅg-e Mīl Publications.
———. 1986. *Khaimē sē Dūr* [Far from the Camp]. Lahore: Saṅg-e Mīl Publications.
———. 1987. *Janam Kahāniyāṅ* [Life Stories]. Lahore: Saṅg-e Mīl Publications.
———. 1987a. *Tazkira* [A Telling]. Lahore: Saṅg-e Mīl Publications.
———. 1990. *Qiṣṣa Kahāniyāṅ* [Tales and Stories]. Lahore: Saṅg-e Mīl Publications.
———. 1993. *Khālī Pinjrā* [Empty Cage]. Lahore: Saṅg-e Mīl Publications.
———. 1993a. *Leaves and Other Stories*. Tr. Alok Bhalla and Vishwamitter Adil. New Delhi: Indus.
———. 1995. *Āgē Samandar hai* [Ahead Is the Sea]. Lahore: Saṅg-e Mīl Publications.
———. 1995a. *Bastī*. [Town] Tr. Frances W. Pritchett. New Delhi: Indus.
Ibn-e Farīd. 1981. "Vō Jō Khōʾē Gaʾē—Unkā Almiya" [Those Who Got Lost—Their Tragedy]. *Alfāẓ* 6, nos. 3–4:28–40.
Jaᶜfarī, Fuẓail. 1984. "Intiẓār Ḥusain kē Nāvil 'Bastī' kā Tajziya" [Analysis of Intizar Husain's Novel *Bastī*]. *Iẓhār* (Bombay) 5:520–545.
Jafri, S. Ḥusain M. 1979. *Origins and Early Development of Shīᶜa Islam*. London: Longman.
Jameson, Fredrick. 1986. "Third World Literature in the Era of Multinational Capital." *Social Text* 15 (Fall):65–88.
Jāvēd, Yūnus. 1984. *Ḥalqa-e Arbāb-e Ẕauq* [Circle of Men of Literary Taste]. Lahore: Majlis-e Taraqqī-e Adab.
Kāmrān, Jīlānī. 1983. "Intiẓār Ḥusain—Bastī, Jaṅgal, aur Shahr" [Intiẓār Ḥusain—Town, Jungle, and City]. Pp. 978–986 in Qāsimī 1983.
Kundera, Milan. 1974. *Life Is Elsewhere*. Tr. Peter Kussi. New York: Alfred A. Knopf.
———. 1988. *The Art of the Novel*. Tr. Linda Asher. New York: Grove Press.

Malik, Hafeez. 1967. "Marxist Literary Movement in India and Pakistan." *Journal of Asian Studies* 26, no. 4:649–664.
Malik, Rāḥat Nasīm. 1983. "Makrūh Bastī mēṅ Bashāratōṅ kā Lamḥa" [The Moment of Glad Tiding in an Abominable Town]. Pp. 997–999 in Qāsimī 1983.
Martin, Wallace. 1986. *Recent Theories of Narrative.* Ithaca, New York: Cornell University Press.
Massignon, L., and L. Gardet. 1971. "Al-Ḥallādj." In *The Encyclopaedia of Islam,* vol. 3, ed. Bernard Lewis et al., pp. 99–104. Leiden: E.J. Brill; and London: Luzac & Co.
Mathur, Ramesh, and M. Kulasrestha, eds. 1976. *Writings on India's Partition.* Calcutta: Simant Publications India.
McEwan, Ian. 1984. "An Interview with Milan Kundera." Tr. Ian Patterson. *Granta* 11:21–37.
Memon, Muhammad Umar. 1980. "'The Lost Ones' (A Requiem for the Self) by Intiẓār Ḥusain." *Edebiyāt,* A Journal of Middle Eastern Literatures 3, no. 2:139–156.
———. 1980. "Partition Literature: A Study of Intiẓār Ḥusain." *Modern Asian Studies* 14, pt. 3:377–410.
———. 1981. "Reclamation of Memory, Fall, and the Death of the Creative Self: Three Moments in the Fiction of Intiẓār Ḥusain." *International Journal of Middle East Studies* 13, no. 1:73–91.
———. 1983. "Pakistani Urdu Creative Writing on National Disintegration: The Case of Bangladesh." *Journal of Asian Studies* 43, no. 1:105–127.
———, ed. 1983a. *The Writings of Intiẓār Ḥusain.* Special issue of *Journal of South Asian Literature* 18, no. 2.
———. 1984. "A Storm in a Teacup." *Annual of Urdu Studies* 4:101–106.
———, ed. 1987. *An Unwritten Epic and Other Stories.* Lahore: Sang-e Mīl Publications.
Momen, Moojan. 1985. *An Introduction to Shīᶜa Islam.* New Haven, Connecticut: Yale University Press.
Munīr, Sirāj. 1983. "Bashāratōṅ kā Lamḥa" [The Moment of Glad Tidings]. Pp. 1000–1014 in Qāsimī 1983.
Narang, G. C. 1973. "Major Trends in the Urdu Short Story." *Indian Literature* 16, nos. 1–2:113–132.
"News and Events." 1982 *Annual of Urdu Studies* 2:147–150.
Pandey, Geetanjali. 1989. *Between Two Worlds: An Intellectual Biography of Premchand.* Delhi: Manohar.
Platts, John T. 1968. *A Dictionary of Urdu, Classical Hindi, and English.* Reprint. London: Oxford University Press.
Qāsimī, ᶜAṯāʾu 'l-Ḥaqq, ed. 1983. *Muᶜāṣir.* Lahore: Maktaba-e Muᶜāṣir.

———. 1983a. “Intiẓār Ḥusain aur Unkī Bastī” [Intizar Husain and His Town]. Pp. 1015–1018 in Qāsimī 1983.

Qazi, Javaid. 1983. “The Significance of Being Human in Intizar Husain’s Fictional World.” Pp. 187–191 in Memon 1983a.

Qurʾān Mubīn. Tehran: Sihāmī Offset Co.

Rahman, M. Salim-ur-. 1983. “An Enriched White-Bread Novel.” Pp. 206–208 in Memon 1983a.

Rubin, David. 1969. *The World of Premchand*. Bloomington: Indiana University Press.

Ruswa, Mirza. 1961. *Umrā’ō Jān Adā*. [The Courtesan of Lucknow] Tr. Kushwant Singh and M.A. Husaini. Delhi: Orient Paperbacks.

Sadiq, Muhammad. 1964. *A History of Urdu Literature*. London: Oxford University Press.

Sajjād, Anvar. 1983. “Intiẓār Ḥusain par Čand Nōṭ” [A Few Notes on Intizar Husain]. Pp. 987–996 in Qāsimī 1983.

Sharma, Govind Narain. 1978. *Munshi Prem Chand*. Boston: Twayne Publishers.

Steele, Laurel. 1981. “Hali and His *Muqaddamah:* The Creation of a Literary Attitude in Nineteenth Century India.” *Annual of Urdu Studies* 2:1–45.

Wentink, Linda. 1982. “Curfew in Kufa.” *Annual of Urdu Studies* 2:123–130.

———. 1983. “Intizar Husain: A Selected Bibliography.” Pp. 209–218 in Memon 1983a.

Zeno (pseudonym of Ṣafdar Mīr). 1984. “The World of Intizar Husain.” *Dawn* (Karachi) (17 February):4.

———. 1984a. “India According to Intizar Husain.” *Dawn* (Karachi) (27 April):4.

The Seventh Door and Other Stories

The Seventh Door

My mother looked upon the pigeon as a holy spirit and made sure that she was not harassed by anyone. Once, when my older brother aimed a slingshot at her, Mother got very upset, snatched at his hand, and began to tremble. Her attitude was the result of something that had actually happened to her. One day after she had said her prayers, her eyes closed briefly and she thought she saw a dignified old man, dressed in white, walking casually about the room. She woke up with a start. There was no one in the room except for a pair of small bright eyes shining like stars above the cornice.

Once, I also had a similar experience. Early one morning, I had a dream. I can't remember now what it was about, but it seemed to me that a kind of brilliance, a white glow was leaving the room. I tried to touch it. . . . Just then, I woke up. Mother had unlatched the door and was just stepping out of the room with a jug of water. And just before she crossed the threshold, a bright shadow floated out above her head. All I saw was a ghostly blur and all I heard was the soft flutter of wings.

Mother used to say that in days gone by, there were so many pigeons roosting on this cornice that when they flew out in the morning, they darkened the courtyard as though the sky had clouded over.

Once my uncle fired a gun at them. He only managed to kill one. The others flew away leaving the cornice bare. Mother told us there was a time when our home was full of guests and the kitchen fires burned constantly. But once the pigeons left, misfortune and anxiety wracked our lives and the family scattered to the winds.

Now, all the pigeons are gone. There was only one left. Just one nest on the cornice. Apparently she had decided to desert the flock. She was the mate, perhaps, of the one who had been killed. Her nest was directly across from my bed. The twigs which made up the nest were still there. The cornice was too high for me to reach. Now the nest was empty. But when the pigeon was there, it looked warm and cozy. At night, I would often wake up and hear the soft rustle of feathers in the dark. Then a silence would descend on the room, and I would drift back to sleep. In the morning when I woke up, the room echoed with the gentle cooing of the pigeon. On summer afternoons when I lay beside my mother, the cooing would lull me to sleep. My eyelids became heavy with drowsiness. But in the winter, this soft cooing served to wake me up and I would glance up at the skylight and see the paleness of dawn through the dusty panes of glass. Then the walls seemed to melt away before the rising waves of the musical murmur and light flooded into the room. Mother would begin to stir. She'd rise, pick up a jug of water, and head for the door. As soon as she opened it, the soft, white brilliance spread everywhere. This had a magical effect on the pigeon. She would stretch out her neck, do a little pirouette and then fly out the door with a loud flap-flapping of wings. For a minute or so, she'd perch on the parapet and then she'd be gone, way past the distant rooftops. At dusk, just before the *muezzin* gave the call for evening prayers, she would reappear on the same parapet. She looked tired, as though she had traveled hundreds of miles. She would be carrying a twig in her beak. She would fly into the room very carefully, and in the gathering darkness, one could hear the sound of her cooing which was like the sound of a bubbling brook. And when she settled into her nest, one could hear a muffled rustling like the murmur of leaves in a gentle breeze. And then—silence.

During the day, one almost forgot she was there on the cornice. Once in a while, I would see the glimmer of a pair of bright eyes. She sat quietly on her nest of dried twigs as though mourning for someone.

I believed what mother had told me. This was certainly no pigeon. Perhaps she was a holy spirit. Mother could not possibly have seen a false dream; in fact, what she had seen was not a dream at all.

So when my cousin Munni announced that she didn't think the pigeon was a holy spirit, I was shocked.

My aunt had arrived only a few days earlier. I had no difficulty recognizing her. Mother took me to her house, telling me that I had to greet her since she was my aunt. She made no mention of Munni. It was all a little embarrassing because she was decked out in fancy clothes whereas mine were rather shabby. My pant-cuff was torn and my shirt had ink spots. Even my face was smudged whereas Munni's was very fair. . . . Anyway, I didn't say a word. I just sat there beside my mother for the longest time. Munni seemed tall to me. But then my aunt told us that we had been born in the same year.

That may or may not have been true. She looked tall to me. Anyway, I never spoke to her. Next day when she came to our house, it was she who started the conversation. I showed her my red and blue pencil, my paint box and my collection of cowries. I would have showed her the pigeon's nest, but she spotted it herself.

"Look! A nest!" she cried out happily.

I said, "Yes. It's a pigeon's nest."

The pigeon, fully alert by now, turned about and flew out at once with a loud clapping of wings.

"It flew away!" said Munni excitedly.

In my simplicity, I said to her, "Let her go. She is bound to come back since her nest is here."

"I think we should catch her." She presented a plan.

Alarmed, I timidly said, "No, no. She is a holy spirit."

"A holy spirit!" Munni burst into laughter.

"Yes, a holy spirit," I repeated, a little embarrassed.

"A holy spirit!" She laughed uncontrollably, and a dark curl fell across a rosy cheek.

"Ha, ha, ha . . . holy spirit!"

I was very quiet. "She is a holy spirit, isn't she?"

She stopped laughing and said, "You silly fool. How can a pigeon be a holy spirit? A pigeon is a fairy."

"A fairy?" I said, surprised.

"Yes, a fairy. Haven't you heard the story of King Bahram?"

"What of it?"

"You fool," she said playfully, "there was a prince in the story. And the White Giant gave him the keys to all seven doors of the palace, telling him he could open all of them except the seventh door. Every day, the prince opened six doors, looked in and then closed them. But by and by, he got tired of the six doors. He began to wonder why the White Giant had forbidden him from opening the seventh door. Why, what could be behind it? He had to see. . . . Finally, he did open the seventh door. What he saw took his breath away—there was a huge pool of sparkling water. And pigeons were diving into the ripples and coming out again all changed into fairies."

I had heard this story from my mother, but it seemed as though I were hearing it for the first time.

Munni spoke up again, "And among them, there was the Green Fairy. And the prince hid her clothes. The Green Fairy stood in the pool naked with her long hair all streaming wet and pleaded with the prince to give her back her clothes. But the prince wouldn't listen."

I began to believe Munni's theory. This pigeon was also a fairy, without a doubt. We decided to find out more. Munni thought that the pigeon went from the parapet onto the roof and there she bathed in dust until she turned into a fairy. And then she flew away on a magic throne.

Next day, Munni came and we waited in the courtyard for the pigeon to emerge. We were then going to follow her to the roof to see what she did. When she did not come out for the longest time, I went in and threw pebbles at her till she flew up. We raced out after her, but by the time we got to the roof, she had vanished.

We were very disappointed. The next day, we waited for her on the roof to see what she would do. She came eventually, but we had to wait a long time. My knees had begun to hurt and my right foot had fallen asleep.

In spite of all this, we were not able to discover anything. The pigeon sat on a second-story ledge for a while and then flew over us.

"She must have seen us," Munni said sadly.

Eventually, I gave in to Munni's proposal. We concluded that we would never discover the pigeon's secret until we captured her. One afternoon, we shut the door of the room and I got hold of the long bamboo pole with which I used to catch stray kites. I began to strike the cornice with the pole. This startled the pigeon. She left her nest and ran on her delicate pink feet to the far side of the cornice. When I struck the other side with the pole, she ran back. After a few minutes of this, Munni took the pole in her own hands and began to hit the cornice. To tell you the truth, my heart had begun to beat very fast. I couldn't bring myself to use the pole with such violence. But Munni hit the cornice with utter recklessness. The pigeon was very agitated. It flew from the cornice but then, finding the door shut, circled round the room and returned to its nest. But Munni was not about to let it rest. The pigeon flew to the opposite cornice. Her chest heaved with each breath and she glanced about wildly.

Terrified of the thrashing pole, she flew up again and, circling near the girder, alighted on the fan. But the fan began to move and she couldn't stay there. She rose once again and continued to fly around, eventually landing on the skylight. By now, her little gray-feathered body had begun to tremble. She was panting violently. Munni swung the pole once more and the pigeon, unable to rest, rose again only to sink in utter fatigue. She clung to a wall and hung there with her wings and tail feathers spread out while spasms of terror swept over her. Munni slammed the pole again and the pigeon let go of the wall and began to fall. I was ready and went for her even as she fell. She tried to get away, but then, all of a sudden, she stopped, tucked in her neck and tail, and turned herself into a little bundle of feathers. I made a quick grab and held her in both hands. Munni grinned joyfully. She threw the pole away and quickly opened the door, yelling, "Bring her into the light!" I went toward the door. Something warm quivered in my hands—bright, terrified eyes, a heaving chest, and soft feathers charged with a current of fear. I don't know why, but my heart was so agitated that I relaxed my hold. The pigeon fluttered its wings and flew away.

Munni glared at me with angry eyes. "You let it go?"

I cringed beneath her scolding. I was at fault and I knew it.

The pigeon flew up and sat on the parapet. Perhaps she was catching her breath. I dashed toward the stairs. Munni was right behind me. On the second-story roof, I crouched low and began to move softly toward the parapet. I inched forward till I was very close. I was just about to reach out and grab her when off the pigeon flew with a sudden clapping of wings. I felt awful. I couldn't bring myself to meet Munni's eyes. She gave me the same angry look and left without a word.

I don't know how long I sat near the parapet. The ragged clouds which had been slowly moving across the sky all afternoon had become a solid gray mass. I began to feel cold and went down the stairs in a melancholy mood. When Mother saw me in the courtyard, she called out, "Come in, child. Don't wander about in the cold." When I joined my mother near the glowing charcoal fire, I realized how cold I had been. My teeth were chattering. In a little while, the wind picked up and it began to rain. Mother, my elder brother, and my uncle all gathered in the room. My brother closed the door and threw more coals on the fire. A layer of black covered the glowing embers. But pretty soon, they too caught fire and tiny greenish-red flames came to life.

I must have fallen asleep as I sat next to my mother's knee. Late at night when I woke up, I found myself in bed. At some point, Mother must have put me to bed. When I woke up the next morning, I sensed that the nest was empty and forlorn. Even the room seemed quiet without the soft musical cooing of the pigeon. Mother rose for dawn prayers, opened the door, and stepped out with a jug of water. No gray shadow fluttered past her head. Even then, Mother never suspected that anything was amiss. I lay quietly in bed for the longest time, pondering what had happened. At times, I wondered if the story of the Green Fairy weren't true, if the pigeon hadn't actually turned into one and flown away. I also wondered whether some kid had brought her down with a slingshot. Then I thought that she may have come back but had then gone away again fearful of being harassed.

I could have asked my mother, but I was afraid she should find out what we had done. Until noon, I didn't say a word, acting as if I didn't know anything about the incident. But eventually, I couldn't bear it any longer and questioned my mother. She recalled that the cornice had indeed been quiet that morning and when she had opened the door to go out, no fluttering shadow had gone past her head. And then she remembered that the night before, the door of the room had been closed. For a while, she was lost in deep thought. She was probably wondering if we had shown disrespect to the holy spirit and caused it to go away in anger.

In the afternoon, Munni came back. The anger she had felt the day before had more or less subsided. When she heard that the pigeon had not returned, this changed the whole picture. Immediately, we went up to the parapet to look for her. We searched every ledge and cornice. We even climbed up the second set of stairs to the topmost roof. We looked everywhere, searching the distant roofs, the electricity poles, the nearby *imli* and *neem* trees, but the pigeon was nowhere to be seen.

From where we stood, we could see the temple clearly. It was covered with niches and each niche contained a figurine. As usual, pairs of wild pigeons were sitting in these niches. A few were sunning themselves and dozing on the dome. It seemed as though some of them had no necks or heads. Then, all of a sudden, one would poke out its head and do a little dance. In one niche, a pair was busy kissing. Then the two were locked together and their eyes closed. I was afraid they would fall. But then they separated. Among all these pigeons, we couldn't locate ours.

We wearied of looking. Munni sought my eyes, but I did not have the courage to meet her gaze. I stared at the dense *imli* tree where the pigeons never rested anymore. You could only see an occasional crow or dove. At times, flocks of long-tailed parrots came down in an explosion of screams and then flew away again. Once in a while, a brown-feathered mynah bird landed quietly on a branch and then took off. Suddenly, we'd see a bluebird on the highest branch, looking as though he had been there for ages. When we looked again, the branch would be bare and we'd wonder when the bird had flown away. I stared at the tree for the longest time. Munni sat quietly. At length, she said, "You chased her away."

"Why would I do that?" I said, feeling ashamed as though I really had chased her off.

"Then, do you think I did it?" she snapped angrily.

I did not respond. She didn't say anything else either.

Presently, she spoke up again. "If you think you didn't, then let me hear you swear."

"I won't," I answered irritably.

Munni thought for a second and then said, "Whoever chased the pigeon away is going to burn in Hell."

Hell! This scared me to death. After all, hadn't Munni committed a great sin? I responded quickly, "The person who brought her down with the pole is the one who'll go to Hell."

My answer angered her so much that she hit me with her elbow. "Get away from me," she said.

This made me mad and I grabbed her hair. She tried to pull away but I wasn't about to let her go. After all, she had been the first to strike. We began to wrestle. All of a sudden, my heart began to pound and a tremor ran through my body. . . . Once again, it seemed as though I had something warm and quivering in my hands, a heaving chest, feathers charged with current. . . . I relaxed my hold. She shook me off and went and stood a few feet away. Stray locks clung to her cheeks. She was all disheveled.

She smoothed her hair and glared at me. Then she said, "You don't have any manners," and slowly walked down the stairs. She stopped there briefly. I thought she would look back. She did seem to stop and turn, but then she went down without even a glance.

I sat on the roof for the longest time, dazed. The pigeons sat as usual in the niches of the temple, cooing and kissing. A male with a black ring around his neck circled round a female, cooing loudly. Then when they heard the sudden noise of a bucket dropping into the temple well, off they flew, up and around, swinging in a wide curve, and then settled back in the niches.

A crow sat all by itself in the *imli* tree. Opening his beak, he cawed and cawed. Then growing weary of that, he fell silent. Eventually tiring of just sitting there, he flew away without a sound.

The *imli* tree stood desolate, its dry seedpods hanging still.

I sat there for ages. I don't know what I was thinking about. Perhaps nothing. There wasn't anything to think about. My mind was blank. At last, I got tired of sitting on the roof, just got bored by it. I stood up, yawned, and headed down the stairs sleepily.

In the evening, Mother made a special point of leaving the door open. I watched the ledge for the longest time, thinking that the pigeon would land there any minute. But she never came. Darkness settled everywhere, and I fell asleep. I woke up many times through the night. And every time I saw that the door was open and the cornice bare. Then I had a dream of sorts in which I caught the pigeon and she turned into a Green Fairy. . . . And Munni walked quietly to the stairs, stopped and then went down without looking back. I woke up with a start. It was early in the morning and the room was filled with light. But the cornice was still bare and the nest looked cold and empty.

Translated by Javaid Qazi

The Back Room

The threshold of the back room appeared to her to be a boundary to a dark land. As she stepped across the dust-coated sill, her heart began pounding. She moved slowly and deliberately into the dark room, always apprehensive and on the verge of turning back. Her perception of this room had changed many times. Out there, on the other side of the sill, was another world: dark but comforting and familiar. Often after playing in the scorching sun in the lane or courtyard, she entered the back room to hide behind its doors or slip behind the dirty tarnished cauldron in one of the corners. The cooling darkness quenched her flushed, warm body. Her feet luxuriated in the chill of the soft soil. Mother was alive then. Whenever she saw her going in or out of the back room she chided her, "Hey, you little pack rat! What are you doing rummaging around in all that junk? It's dark in there . . . what if a bug bites you?"

But her childhood had departed, her mother too, and with them, even that comforting darkness. The existence of the back room had become dulled in her memory—besides the house's many rooms, porticos, and courtyards, she rarely even considered any more that it also had a back room.

The back room had remained closed for many years except when the change of seasons required its opening. Sometimes particular seasonal supplies were needed. Occasionally it was also opened to store a broken charpoy or to take out a broken water-pot or a bucket splitting at the seams for repair.

This year with the arrival of summer the back room was opened again. The advent of this summer signaled another change in her perception of the room. She entered and arranged the winter quilts and mattresses on the upper shelf. As she descended she noticed a braided hairpiece hanging on a peg in front of her. She began thinking how oily and soiled her own had become. This one had a much nicer sheen, she was convinced. "Why not take it?"

Suddenly her glance fell to the dusty floor below. God knows how many years had passed since it had been swept last. A broad, undulating line extended in the dirt from one corner where an old dusty chest of pots was stored and disappeared behind the tarnished cauldron in the corner near the door. She stared at it intently. Her feelings balanced between surprise and trepidation. She suspected something and contemplated calling Apaji. Then she noticed the ropes of the charpoy were lying loose and felt she had concluded hastily: "It was probably only the imprint of the open charpoy lacings."

Whenever she passed by the back room while sweeping in the main rooms and courtyard, she thought of its dirt floor, a place where the dust was so deep that if she were to step inside her bare feet were certain to be enveloped by the soft powdery earth. No matter how many times it was swept there would always be more dirt. And that wavy line was there too, undulating across from the big chest to the copper cauldron. Its image billowed up in her mind and she tried to suppress it. But after a while her determination weakened and the coiling tracklike line in the dark soil emerged in her imagination and swayed on into the darkness of the past . . .

"No, daughter, no! Don't ever call it out loud by its name!" Mother admonished Apaji. "It has extra-sensitive ears and hears its name the moment it is spoken. I'll tell you about the experience I had once. I got up after my nap one afternoon and put on my slippers, and right in front of me in the courtyard was the cursed thing lying there looking half-dead. I called for your husband. But curses! As soon as I uttered its name it went slithering off."

Apaji was speechless, huddled up with her chin on her knee, her eyes fixed on mother's face. Mother started again:

"It is a very ancient one. We've heard tales about it ever since we first settled in this house. Our dear old mother-in-law—God rest her soul—used to go into the back room to get things without ever bothering to take a lamp. The poor old woman was nearsighted and tottered haphazardly into the room. There were a few times when it heard her footsteps and quickly slithered under the chest. But once she escaped by just a hair's breadth. She entered the room and began mumbling, 'Hey, who threw this hairpiece on the ground?' She reached down to pick it up and, God preserve us!, it was that snake!"

Apaji sat motionless. A shiver ran through her. "Personally," she said, "I'd have never thought of such a thing. But now I remember a similar thing happened to your son. One day at high noon I went into the room to get the cot with the canvas strappings which I knew were grimy and needed washing. I didn't realize it at the time but he had followed in behind me. I was busy tugging at the cot when I heard him begin to mutter, 'Who threw this cane on the ground? It was ordered special from Naini Tal and they're hard to come by. Once it's broken that'll be the end of it.' He was about to put his hand on it when, I tell you, it suddenly recoiled and slithered instantly out of sight."

Mother confirmed, "It's true. One moment he shows himself and the next he's disappeared . . . I pray to Allah that we be spared from all evil spirits."

Apaji drifted off into her thoughts. Shuddering, she returned to her senses. "Yes, may Allah protect us from every evil, and especially from that dreadful thing whose very name gives me gooseflesh."

"But, daughter," Mother responded, "each has his own fate. Those destined with good fortune will receive it even from their enemies. God bless our mother-in-law, she used to tell us this story: Once a prince was tricked by the family of his bride-to-be. They put a common old hag in the marriage palanquin instead of the princess. She was toothless and gray-headed. Her body was listless and her skin was as wrinkled as a prune. On the wedding night she sat waiting on the nuptial bed covered with a beautiful red mantle. She trembled, fearing the prince's arrival and the disastrous moment when he would lift her veil. Then suddenly a very strange thing happened. A black snake hung by his tail from the rafters just over her head. His mouth was gaping. He glided down, and then a little more until his mouth touched her hair. The poor thing froze stiff with fear. Then the most bizarre thing happened. He drew a strand of her hair into his mouth and then dropped it. The strand had turned completely black and was so long that it extended all the way down to her waist. He took another and another until her whole head of hair had turned completely black and was so long that it extended all the way down to her waist. When the prince entered he was overwhelmed. He thought he had entered the boudoir of a fairy princess rather than an ordinary bridal suite. The fairy princess was his bride; her face shone like the moon, her body was supple and fair as flour, her tresses were luxuriant and serpentine. His heart and soul were captured by her beauty."

Apaji fixed her gaze on Mother's face. She was astounded by the story.

"Mother," she asked, "how could she turn into a princess?"

"My dear, when fate is set in motion, even the physical body can change."

"But Mother, a change like that?" Apaji exclaimed incredulously.

Wrinkles formed on Mother's brow. "Do you think I would tell you a lie and wager my chances for heaven?" she said. "If it's a lie, then the punishment goes to the one who first told the story. I told you just what I heard. But, daughter, the important point is that every person lives according to the decrees of his fate. Normally that creature wouldn't hesitate to harm anyone. Snakes are poisonous enemies of mankind. They are such stubborn things that neither disease nor death can subdue them."

"Oh, mother! What are you saying?" Apaji couldn't contain her words of wonder and disbelief.

"Girl, you doubt everything. You may not believe this either, but it's said that snakes only begin to age after a thousand years. He sheds his skin a hundred times and just like that he's rejuvenated. He never dies a natural death. If someone were to bash his head in, well, that's a different matter."

Apaji thought for a while, then asked, "Mother, why doesn't he die?"

"Because he's eaten a charmed herb, that's why," Mother replied and went on. "Long, long ago—and you may doubt this too, if you like—there lived a king in Babylonia. He had a minister—a very chivalrous minister it is said. Together the king and his minister conquered one territory after another. Then one day the minister died unexpectedly. That shook the king's spirit but he bore the loss courageously and solemnly pledged to conquer death itself. A wise old dervish told him about one of the Seven Seas which contained a special herb. The king followed his directions and journeyed heedlessly, without thought of food or water, until at last he reached his destination. As soon as he arrived at the spot he plunged into the water and brought the charmed herb up from the bottom. Had he but eaten it, he would have rid himself of death, once for all. But as luck would have it, on his return journey, the king came upon a river. He was exhausted and decided to bathe and cool his body in the river. Leaving his clothes on the bank he splashed into the river. Meanwhile, back on the bank a snake snatched the herb into his mouth and slithered quickly away. The king dashed out of the water and ran after the snake. He trampled the whole jungle, turning it upside down, searching every tree, examining every cave. But, girl, the creature had completely vanished."

Again and again things appeared and vanished; lightning would flash before her eyes, then darkness. This elusiveness of things was a constant source of bewilderment. She recalled her childhood and her playmate Battu. They played together untroubled by the time of day or concerns outside of their own amusement. And Battu—so accomplished in his ability to disappear at any instant from her sight! Those days were merely a dream to her now. How he could hide in the back room when they played cops-and-robbers! The corner where the big cauldron was stored, the big chest of cooking pots, the charpoy standing up on end—all those things slowly, slowly began to emerge in the darkness . . . everything but Battu. "Oh God, where's he disappeared to? Which cave is he hiding in? Has he been swallowed up by the earth or eaten by the sky?" And just then, as she would be thinking all that, a dark, black head would begin inching its way up from behind the chest of pots. She would spring forward and grab him. "Ah hah! The thief is caught!"

Sometimes when they played hide-and-seek the back room offered the ideal hiding place. They would both enter it and hide themselves in a corner. A long time would pass while they stood silently. Slowly, very slowly the darkness would begin its work. It seeped into their bodies and then departed, establishing a new relationship between the inner and the outer worlds. The world of sound and sight seemed to remain far in the distance as the world of darkness began. A journey of infinite leagues. No signs, no stopping points. With the sound of footsteps in the courtyard the world of darkness contracted . . .

Or when they played blindman's buff. Battu, the blindman, entered the back room with such confidence, as if everything were visible to him. He neared the cauldron and suddenly clamped his hands on her, catching her braid so forcefully that she had to let out a scream.

Only recently she had started using a hairpiece. There was a time when her hair was so long that it was actually a nuisance to care for. It was long, lustrous hair that braided into a thick black whip. It waved over her back far below her waist. Before taking a bath she used to sit on the small bath stool and loosen her hair to wash it with soap-nut powder she had prepared. The tresses bobbed against the wet floor. But a sudden, violent attack of cerebral meningitis had left her hair dull and spotty. During the worst part of the illness she was in a coma for three days. She lost all sense of who or where she was. Now she thought about those three days as a long journey into darkness. She passed from one black boundary to another, each opening into a new, dark land. And finally, into the ultimate black kingdom. Again and again she approached the limits and turned back, returning to the world of sound and light. The effects of that long, fearful journey were apparent: her body had deteriorated and her hair had become thin and short, its luster dulled. Now, only with the addition of the hairpiece could her braid assume its former length.

While passing through the courtyard her feet often led her in the direction of the back room. She remembered the oily, matted hairpiece. God knows how many years it has hung there on the peg. "Would it be worth the bother to weave it into my own braid?"

Repeatedly she abandoned the impulse to go in and take it down from the peg. But unconsciously her glance returned to the back room, spurring thoughts of the hairpiece and the impulse to go there. She approached the door, halted, and retraced her steps. The thread of her imagination began to lengthen and wind into the nooks and corners of days past . . .

"Mother, there was plenty of oil! I shook the lantern at bedtime and checked it myself. I think the wick must have fallen inside."

"Well then, why did you turn it down so low?" Mother demanded. "These are uncertain times; God knows what may come up. The lantern must never be extinguished! Poor me, I didn't know what to do. It was so dark in here I couldn't tell one hand from the other. I heard a rustling sound but couldn't make out what it was. I thought maybe it was a snake but wasn't sure if I was just imagining things. All of a sudden the chickens in the coop began cackling. As soon as I looked toward the coop I saw it . . . you can't imagine how long it was! I almost dropped dead. I couldn't utter a sound. Finally I managed enough courage to call you."

"Mother, I don't remember you calling me."

"My dear girl, you sleep like a log. Even if this house were filled with the tumult of Judgment Day or kettle-drums played right in your ear, they still wouldn't wake you up. A sleeping man's like a dead man; woe to such a sleep! Anyway, I then called Naseeban. I kept calling her but she seemed to have dropped dead too. What could I do? I sat stone-still the whole night and kept reciting verses from the Qurʾan. I was afraid lest I should fall asleep and someone might get up to go to the toilet and . . . especially Safia—she has this terrible habit of getting up out of bed and sleepwalking barefooted to the outhouse. I was in this predicament when the sun finally arose and it gradually became lighter . . ."

"Safia! what are you doing?" Apaji's voice shot up from the kitchen. Safia mumbled something and instantly her thoughts vanished. Then she became so immersed in her household chores that she lost consciousness of her mind and body. She spread the brassware and kitchen utensils out in front of her and taking fistfuls of ash from the plate she dropped some into each vessel. She scrubbed each one so vigorously with the jute pad that when she rinsed them in the tapwater and lined them up on the brick platform they reflected the sunlight like mirrors. They appeared gilded rather than scoured. When her ash-covered hands brushed against the running water the light blue glass bangles on her wrists made delicate tinkling sounds. Her fair fingers and wrists glistened with the water and a ray of light danced across her forearm.

Soon afterward her glimmering fingers became covered with dough and the breadboard began ringing unceasingly from the steady motion of her fists. The moist dough stuck to her wrists and even one or two of her bracelets. Safia kneaded it to the perfect consistency. She rolled out paper-thin *rotis* and put them on the griddle. Then she placed each one on the open coals to puff them up and stacked them in the breadbasket.

In the dusky light of evening when she removed the griddle from the hearth and turned it upside down, the countless flying red sparks looked like so many stars floating in the black soot.

"Apaji, the griddle's laughing!"

"The laughing of a griddle is not a good omen," Apaji answered in a concerned tone. "Put some ash on it."

Even while performing these household tasks her thoughts would stray elsewhere. Sweeping the courtyard or tightening the straps on the canvas-laced cot, or unknotting the skeins of silken thread, the cellar of her imagination would open into its own world, independently of the motion of her hands. The wavy line began to reach into the darkness of forgotten days. The thought of mother brought with it the memory of her gossip sessions and stories. She remembered how calmly she could pass over the most astounding things and yet be so shocked at banal matters. Once when she was cleaning a cauldron stored in a corner of the back room, she uncovered a snakeskin with her hand. She picked it up nonchalantly and tucked it carefully away, saying, "Basheeran could use it to prepare a syrup for her daughter who's ill with whooping cough." There was another time too when the stiff carcass of a white pigeon found in the pigeonhole one morning made Mother suddenly remember the hissing sound she had heard come from the vicinity of the dovecote in the middle of the night.

She envied Mother, a person to whom invisible things revealed themselves. As for herself, ever since childhood her path had been covered by markings and clues of the phenomenal world, but the substance always eluded her. Shadows crossed her path at every turn, but never the figure that cast the shadow. Sometimes the traces appeared so fresh she thought a step or two more and she would catch up. Such a thought invariably set her heart pounding and made her body tremble and her feet too heavy to move.

It rained that day when she and Battu arose at early dawn and left the house in search of rain bugs. At the edge of the black mango orchard a drenched *neem* tree lay fallen on the soggy earth. It was long, serpentlike, and its trunk was jet black. It looked like someone had just flayed it with an axe and the white fat lay scattered everywhere around. The scene froze them.

"Lightning struck last night."

"Lightning?"

"Don't you know," Battu began, "it rained all night and the lightning struck real hard. It seemed like it landed right on our roof . . ." He babbled on, "A black snake used to live in the hollow of this tree. He was a very ancient one. He must have come out in the night. Lightning strikes dark, black things, you know."

"Where did he go then?" she asked fearfully.

"Where did he go!" He laughed at her ignorance. "The lightning ripped him to pieces."

Contemplation of these things elicited an overwhelming longing for those days to return; that someone might seize the spotted snake of the past by its head and reverse the direction of the meandering procession of names and relics. To again hear Mother tell stories and pontificate, but to ignore all that and dart out early at dawn, barefooted, in pelting rain, toward the jungle to search out rain bugs. If there were no rain bugs, there were always cuckoos; and if there were no cuckoos, then at least there were always toadstools.

The awning overhanging the front of the balcony was so old its wood had rotted and turned dark; when it rained it looked darker still. After a few showers a white pulplike substance pushed through its cracks and joints. Gradually black and white umbrella-cap mushrooms began to unfold. Some mushrooms were chalky white, some were black speckled, and others were striped. Picking them was an inviting challenge. The toadstools growing on the awning were within the reach of both of them, but the big fat ones growing directly below it on the wall even Battu could not reach, let alone she. Once, however, supporting himself with the lattice and bracing his foot on the ledge, Battu did manage to raise himself high enough to just touch the awning—the most giant ones remaining still beyond his reach. That did not bother him, for no matter how far a thing was from his grasp, Battu was sure to make a daring attempt, once at least.

On the path to the mango orchard lay an old abandoned well. It was so shaded over by the dense foliage of a sprawling banyan tree that unless she bent over and peered hard she scarcely believed it had any water at all. Battu would crawl out on one of the branches directly above the well and announce audaciously, "I'm going to jump . . ."

The ground seemed to slip from underneath her feet and she would find herself entreating, "No, Battu, no!" From Battu's expression it was evident that her ardent pleadings made no impression on him at all and that he would jump into the well any moment. But he would not; instead, he would slide down the trunk of the tree to the ground. One day he jumped, though—jumped or fell or what, she could never know. He had gone there alone that day. She only heard the commotion afterward. Shabrati, the water-carrier, came running and began pounding on the door of Battu's house. Battu's father ran out, looking stunned and worried, and made straight for the well, followed by many other people from the neighborhood. Those who stayed behind stood about in small groups, dumbfounded.

"Who? Battu?"

"He fell into the old well—how?"

"My God, that child's really wild!"

Apaji was saying, "That boy's a real daredevil. Whenever he came here, all he did was hang from the awning or the edge of the roof. He'd make my heart flip. I scolded him a thousand times for performing his acrobatics here. I even spanked Safia once for being crazy right along with him. But, I'm sure the ghouls ride that boy's back. He never listened to a word I said, nor anyone else's for that matter."

"He's the only son of his poor parents," interjected Mother. "May Allah have mercy on them."

Apaji's tone of voice changed, "Yes, may Allah have mercy on them. I pray that he be spared, but I want to make it perfectly clear that whatever happens our girl will never become his. How can one trust such a youngster? Who knows what he might do!"

"Well, this is a problem for another time." Mother heaved a sigh. "Right now, God have mercy on the poor fellow. There's evil in that dark well. Every year someone's sacrificed to it."

Evening came and some people brought him home stretched out on a cot. His clothes were drenched from the water, his hair was matted, face pale and sallow, and body limp. He was lying unconscious. For some time deathly silence settled over the lane—the same silence which was to return once again many years later and, again, on account of Battu: the day the telegram came. God knows what had gotten into Battu's head that, without telling a word to anybody at home, he enlisted in the army and volunteered for front-line duty. For a year or two there was no news of him. When finally it did arrive, it came in the form of the announcement of his death while serving in a foreign country.

"Good Lord, a telegram about Battu!"

"A telegram about Battu? Allah, be merciful!"

Apaji, who was making *rotis*, suddenly turned the griddle over and snuffed out the fire. For a short time the lane was hushed. People stood about in small groups, stunned, only communicating through their eyes. As Battu's father read the telegram his hands began to shake and without raising his head he went inside.

She shuddered back into the present. She had put soap-nuts in a bowl to soak and placed the bowl itself outside in the sun on the brick ledge; the soap-nuts had ballooned up by now. Hastily she loosened her hair. The gray suds in her hair made it look even more off-color. She finished bathing and went out into the mid-afternoon sun and stood a moment near the brick ledge. She tossed her hair from side to side a couple of times and then walked into the room and stood before the mirror. Some of the body and softness had doubtless been revived, but the qualities it once had when it waved over her shoulders or when she made a bun which swung freely like a shining platter were gone. For hours mother combed it, arranged it, and braided it. Ritually she used to pull it back into coiled strands and blow on them while reciting auspicious Qurʾanic verses. Then taking a small hank of hair she would tuck it away in a chink of the brick wall. Now—now her hair is lifeless and thin. Mother's comb and skillful fingers are gone too. She turned her focus from her hair to her face, a face which used to radiate the essence of beauty. The previous glow of her body had begun ebbing also. She remembered hearing the whispers exchanged between an elderly woman and Apaji in a gossip session just a few days ago.

"Apaji, how long do you people intend to keep this girl at your hearth? She is already past the age. She'll get impatient if you aren't careful."

"Do you think I want to keep her around at home any longer? It's hardly the time for her to be sitting around here . . . but what can I do?"

"As soon as someone comes along, marry her off, I'd say."

She shook herself again and began combing her hair somewhat energetically. Arranging her hair with her fingers she noticed that it was dry and brittle despite all of the oil she applied. Dullness had overshadowed its lustrous shine. While braiding it she picked up the hairpiece. It appeared thinner than her real hair, matted and greasier. She put it down and went out into the courtyard toward the back room. She walked hypnotically, as if in a dream, as if someone had caught her in a magic spell. She put her foot on the door sill and opened the latch. She gave the door panels a slight jerk and shoved them open. As she entered the back room she suddenly became aware that she was stepping into that realm of darkness. She recalled the wavy line coiling from the large chest to the cauldron. Her heartbeat quickened. She moved further into the darkness, as if descending below where the earth beckoned. Another wave of delirium rushed her senses. A state of intoxication, a vague fear that some great trial might confront her—the mystery unknown. Moving on into the darkness she felt the soft earth beneath her feet, the same powdery earth which she had walked on many times before, where the details of her footprints would appear as etchings in the dust. She looked at the floor coated with fine dust beneath her feet; where was that wavy line? Had it been rubbed out or had it never really been here? She reached toward the peg and took the hairpiece down. It was oily, matted, coated with dust. She put it back. As she came out of the back room, the intoxication which had flooded her mind had already vanished.

And a dullness like that of her dry pallid hair began settling over her body like a fine mist.

Translated by Caroline J. Beeson and Muhammad Umar Memon

A Stranded Railroad Car

"All of this, brother, means nothing. To tell you the truth, travel isn't enjoyable anymore."

Bundu Miyan's story was heard with absorbing interest. But Shujaat Ali somehow didn't care for this concluding remark and said, "Well now, I wouldn't go that far. Travel must have meant quite a lot to our elders. Why else would they have stirred out of doors? They weren't crazies. You're too young and inexperienced to jump to conclusions. All you had was a single trip, which ended somewhat badly for you. And right away you decide there's no fun and adventure left in travel. As I look at it, you never did any traveling—I mean any real traveling, which is something else again. Well, Mirza Sahib, what do you think?"

Mirza Sahib gently removed the spout of the hookah from his lips, opened his drowsy eyes, cleared his throat, and said, "Shujaat Ali, you shouldn't argue with these modern boys. What do these kids know about traveling! Especially the train—it's taken all enjoyment out of journeying. You blink your eye and you've arrived at your destination. But there was a time when kingdoms fell and governments toppled by the time you reached where you were going; and the toddlers you'd left crawling naked on all fours—you returned to find them fathers worrying their heads over a suitable match for their marriageable daughters."

The idea of political upheavals caught Bundu Miyan's fancy. He couldn't resist remarking, "Mirza Sahib, even entire governments fall today in less time than it takes to blink an eye. You go to the booking-counter, purchase your ticket, hop on the train, and at the very next stop you can already hear the hawker yelling of a coup somewhere."

"Oh, yes, just a coup. Nothing more and nothing less," Mirza Sahib was quick to remark. "But in the past," he continued, "a change of government invariably meant a change of coinage too. New monarch, new coins. That was a real journey, one hell of a journey. One went on traveling hundreds and hundreds of miles, back and forth, with the destination nowhere in sight and all traces of the starting point irretrievably obscured. Each journey seemed to be the last. Just imagine the hazards attending a journey in the past: the fear of tigers, of snake-bites, of highwaymen and, yes, of ghosts too. You had neither clocks nor electricity in those days. You traveled by the dim star-lit sky overhead and the burning torches below. A torch suddenly blown out by the wind and your heart dropped between your feet; a meteor shot through the sky leaving behind a blazing bright trail, and your heart pounded fitfully, and you prayed, 'Lord God! Take care of us and don't let us wayfarers down!' And now—the night's over before you know it. Back then, though, it took ages to pass a single night in travel; a night then meant the span of a century."

Mirza Sahib was left speechless. So were Bundu Miyan and Manzur Husain. The mouthpiece of the hookah just froze between Shujaat Ali's lips; only the pipe's gurgle, rising in an incessant monotone, fell gently upon the darkening patio where it blended with the tranquil silence of nightfall.

Mirza Sahib resumed his chatter in a manner as though he had strayed away too far and was now back to the point. "No horse-drawn carts, no journey. Today the train is in fashion. I just don't feel like traveling anymore. By God, only one journey's left now. But come to think of it, who needs a carriage for that one? Off I shall go when my time's come . . ." He sighed and became silent.

The spout was still stuck as before under Shujaat Ali's gray moustache, and the gurgling went on as a matter of course. Then Sharfu, the servant, emerged from the house, holding a lantern. The darkening portico lit up dimly and there was a slight stir. Sharfu pulled up a stool near the chairs, set the lantern upon it, and raised the wick a little. Shujaat Ali gently passed the spout to Mirza Sahib, who tried a puff or two, then quickly let go of it, peering at the *chilam*—the clay bowl atop the hookah. "It's gone cold," he murmured. Then raising his voice he called the servant, "Sharfu! Put some fresh tobacco in. A few burning coals too."

Shujaat Ali pushed his chair back for no apparent reason. He yawned languidly, passed his palms over his wrinkled cheeks, and spoke in a measured tone, "You could not be more right, Mirza Sahib. Traveling really has changed a lot these days. But . . . but a journey, after all, is a journey, whether you travel by horse-drawn cart or by train."

"But even in a train journey . . ." Manzur Husain wanted to say something, God knows what, but Shujaat Ali grabbed the thread instead and went on, "Yes, even in a train journey you witness the most bizarre things and encounter strange sorts of people . . ."

". . . and you maybe get to see a face which, in its infinite charm, becomes etched on your heart forever; it stays with you and you are never quite able to forget it," said Manzur Husain, suddenly remembering a long-forgotten incident, feeling the overwhelming urge to narrate it. And why not, if Bundu Miyan could tell such a long yarn? The incident had occurred an eternity ago, and yet how is it, Manzur Husain wondered, that he hadn't told a soul about it? Suppose he told them—what could he possibly lose? At his age who would suspect him of anything unseemly or foul?

Manzur Husain was about to speak when Bundu Miyan burst out, "Look at him. He fancies meeting charming faces. God, I never could believe there are people who travel just looking for love and romance!"

"Miyan, you've got it all wrong," Shujaat Ali interrupted. "A train is a whole city in miniature. Hundreds of people get on or get off at every stop. You're bound to rub shoulders with all sorts of people in the crowd."

"If you rub shoulders, inevitably you may meet the eyes too. Listen, I would like to tell you something." Manzur Husain was at it at last. Bundu Miyan's offending attitude had warmed him up.

But it was Shujaat Ali who cut him short this time. "Eyes meeting eyes—what's so unusual about that? You could be at home and still exchange glances with the woman in the balcony across the street. Why set out on a journey when you could accomplish as much right here at home? Well, stunning things happen while traveling. At times, the very history of a country takes on a new turn." Shujaat Ali had warmed up now. "Well, Mirza Sahib," he said, "you would scarcely remember the time when the railway first came here. We were mere kids then, weren't we? My late father used to tell us about it."

Manzur Husain waited for Shujaat Ali to finish recounting his tale so that he might begin his. But the latter seemed bent on spinning a fresh and longer yarn. In time Manzur Husain's restiveness began to lessen of its own accord. He persuaded himself in different ways: that it ill-behooved a middle-aged man like himself to cackle about such matters, that he didn't seem to remember the whole story anyway, that some links were missing, that it was like an incoherent dream, neither fully remembered, nor totally forgotten either. The dream appeared very hazy to begin with, except for a single bright spot which by the minute grew brighter still. It was a tawny face—full of charm. The spot of light began to expand and illuminated a foggy corner of his memory: a bunch of weary passengers who sat half-awake, half-asleep inside a dimly lit waiting room. He was himself ensconced in a chair, drowsing. Then he dozed off, but the clatter of wheels outside woke him up. The train was late, yet he somehow felt it had steamed in. He darted out to make sure, and found a freight train chugging along. He remained on the platform a while, pacing up and down, and then returned to the waiting room, where from time to time he furtively glanced at the bench opposite him. It was occupied by a heavy, squat man with salt-and-pepper hair, clad in a white *dhoti* and a long coat that came all the way to his knees, and a slim young woman of a delightfully tawny complexion huddled beside him. She too was drowsing. Whenever her onion-colored sari slipped off her head, her long, luxuriant jet-black hair flashed in the light and a pair of delicate, pale earrings, dangling from her lobes, emitted sparks. . . .

Shujaat Ali was narrating his story with gusto: "Both Hindus and Muslims kicked up quite a fuss. They said their holy saints were buried there, so no railroad tracks were going to be laid there. But the British were in no mood for such pious insanities. Why would they be? They were the rulers. And they were drunk with power. The track was laid down anyway. It was then that my father was obliged to take a trip to Delhi." Shujaat Ali paused for a moment. In a tone swelling with pride, he continued, "My father was the first in this city to ride the train. Even the big shots hadn't seen a train until then—why, a lot of them hadn't even heard of it . . ."

Manzur Husain was not listening to the words, but only to the voice of the narrator, staring hard at him, desperately hoping for him to stop at some point. Gradually the narrator's face grew hazy and his voice dimmed. The bright spot became exceedingly luminous . . . those illuminated corners and crannies, flashing bright lines . . . It was a long railroad track along one side of which ran an interminable line of lampposts quietly shedding the gentle glow of their light bulbs. The bright cone of light around a lamppost, the darkness beyond it, the black iron tracks vanishing into the distance. He had unrolled his bed in an upper berth; in the lower berths some passengers were comfortably stretched out and sleeping; others were uncomfortably stuffed in narrow spaces and simply drowsing, their heads resting against windows. From time to time somebody would wake up, turn over onto his side, glance casually at the sleeping passengers, and doze off again. Many stations passed by; many times the train slowed down and came to a halt. The dark car suddenly lit up, followed by a din as the passengers jostled to climb aboard or jump down and peddlers barged in to sell their wares. The whistle, the jerk, and once again the incessant clatter of wheels. As the train picked up speed, the same familiar feeling assaulted him: as if the car he was riding in had come unhitched and stood stranded in the middle of nowhere while the rest of the train, whistling and clattering, had steamed far away. Sometimes he felt as if the train had started running backward, pulling time along with it, and that the night would never end. Half the span of a century had passed and the other half was yet to pass, the train wasn't really going forward—it was merely moving in circles, spinning, as it were, on a pivot; that when it stopped it seemed it would remain standing all night long, and when it moved, it seemed like it would go on racing with the night, competing with it but never quite outpacing it. And then the train would slow down again, as if its wheels had become too tired to turn any more; the same flood of light in the dark car; the din of motley passengers, porters, peddlers; people suddenly waking from their sleep and inquiring, "Is this a junction?"; a semiarticulate expression sinking into the depths of sleep, "No, it's only some small station"; whistles, more whistles; the familiar jerk; the same heavy clatter of lazy wheels. He looked at his watch. "Only one-thirty!"—he was surprised. Many times he had dozed off and many times been awakened; still the night seemed to have barely waned—on the contrary, it seemed to have become even longer. He got up wearily, climbed down from his berth, and made for the toilet. In the lower berth, the squat man in the white, flowing *dhoti* and long coat had dozed off and was snoring away heavily. The young woman beside him with the delightful tawny complexion, with sleep strung in her eyes, her head propped up against the window, looked inebriated. A sudden gust of wind blew her dark, lustrous curls and scattered them all over her face. The hem of her sari too had slipped off her chest, revealing the contours of a pair of beautifully firm, round breasts. The sheer beauty of her blossoming youth enthralled him for a moment or two. It was absolutely quiet inside the compartment; the passengers were asleep, and the only sound came from the incessant clatter of wheels. It was so hot that the man sitting in the opposite corner had even peeled off his undershirt. Suddenly he got up and blurted out, "The black river's just ahead." With an ever-increasing clatter of wheels the train entered a tunnel. He stood where he was as the train emerged from one darkness and plunged into another. It grew pitch dark inside the car . . . his thoughts abruptly derailed.

"No sooner had the train reached the bank of the River Jamuna than it ground to halt smack in the middle of the jungle." Shujaat Ali returned to his narrative. "Midnight! What to do? The times were especially bad. Highwaymen roamed about freely throughout the country. Even in Delhi one dared not go past the banks of the Jamuna without putting one's life in grave danger. Well anyway, they thoroughly checked the engine but found nothing wrong with it. Still, it just wouldn't budge. An endless night, the jungle with its myriad sounds, each more frightening than the next, and no habitation near or far in which to look for shelter—it was some experience. The night came to an end eventually. At the crack of dawn, in that first, hesitant light, people saw a saintly looking gray-bearded man quietly saying his prayers huddled in the corner of one of the cars. Having said his prayers, the hoary old man looked at the people and said, "Have the railroad track dug up!"

Bundu Miyan found himself gawking at Shujaat Ali. Mirza Sahib, wishing to draw on the hookah, felt unable to raise the spout to his mouth. His hand froze, and his grip around the pipe tightened. Manzur Husain, however, was busy retrieving the missing links.

After a pause Shujaat Ali looked up intently at Mirza Sahib and resumed, "People went and reported this bizarre incident to the British officer. He flew into a rage. But there was little he could do. The train simply wouldn't budge. He relented. He agreed to have the track dug out—his hands were tied. A whole slew of laborers was called in and the digging got underway. They had barely dug down a few feet when they discovered an underground vault . . ." Shujaat Ali paused to look briefly at Mirza Sahib,

Bundu Miyan, and Manzur Husain, who all sat perfectly motionless, like images cast in stone. He resumed: "My father used to tell us how three armed men, mustering all their courage and repeating the name of the Lord, descended into the vault. And what did they see but a magnificent hall. A brand-new clay pot of fresh water—filled, as if only moments ago—standing in a corner, its top covered by an upturned silver bowl. Nearby on the floor an aged, saintly figure in white clothes, with a lily-white beard and eyebrows, sat on a mat quietly telling his beads . . ."

Shujaat Ali's voice seemed to be receding. Manzur Husain's mind was changing tracks again. A string of irregularly illumined dots whirred round and round before him. The illumined dots magnified themselves into bright, scintillating images of remarkable clarity . . . The train rushed through the tunnel with a piercing din and reckless speed. The dark water below rose up in gentle waves to kiss the tracks. His lips quivered, his fingers throbbed with sweet warmth. The young woman's disquietingly lovely face, her warm fleshy body—that bright and sparkling image left a ray in his eyes—a ray which penetrated many dark corners and flooded them with light. Early next morning when he got down from his berth his eyes met with hers for a mere second and then traveled through the window to the comfort of the cool and refreshing dawn outside. Their eyes met one more time, when she and the man in the white *dhoti* got down to change trains. The other train stood along the platform nearby. Clouds of smoke billowed out from the locomotive, dissipated in the fresh morning air, and eventually dissolved. There was a whistle. The stationary wheels hissed a little and then set into motion. The locomotive sent up curls of black smoke. Immediately there was another whistle, and his train too began to pull out. The two trains ran parallel for a little way, then the distance between them widened and they drifted apart gathering speed. Her train moved farther and faster away. The cars in her train, jammed with passengers, moved past him like images in a movie. Finally, even that car went past him in which her face, despite its tawny complexion, somehow appeared the sharpest, the brightest. Her train became lost into the distant woods; only the baggage car trailing behind it remained visible for a while longer; then it too vanished into the lush, green space beyond . . .

"When they looked a second time, there was absolutely nobody on the mat." That was Shujaat Ali, still busy narrating his story.

"And the saintly figure—where did he go?" Bundu Miyan asked with surprise.

"God knows," Shujaat Ali replied. "Only the clay pot still stood in its place, but it was empty."

"You mean the water too had vanished?" Bundu Miyan's surprise knew no bounds.

"Yes, it had." Shujaat Ali's voice was now a mere whisper. "My father used to say that the Sepoy Mutiny broke out the very next year; the Jamuna turned into a river of fire, and Delhi was razed to the ground."

Shujaat Ali became silent. Mirza Sahib too sat in wordless immobility. Bundu Miyan went on gazing at Shujaat Ali. Manzur Husain yawned wearily and pulled the hookah toward himself. A minute later he said, poking into the *chilam*, "It's cold again."

Mirza Sahib drew a deep sigh, "Nobody knows the mysteries of God." He then yelled, "Sharfu, put some tobacco in!"

The dim corners and crevices had now assumed a soft, bright translucence, allowing those random images to coalesce into a coherent scene, perfectly intact, lacking in none of its details. Manzur Husain felt excited. The long-forgotten incident had returned to him as a vibrant reality. He was dying to recount it, the whole of it, to the others, withholding nothing, with brio and magnificence. He repeatedly looked at Mirza Sahib, Bundu Miyan, and Shujaat Ali, impatiently waiting for the spell created by Shujaat Ali's story to wear off, so that he could get on with his own tale. When the hookah was brought back, he drew a few puffs and passed it on to Shujaat Ali, saying, "Have a few puffs—it is fresh now." Shujaat Ali took the pipe and started to smoke.

Manzur Husain began impatiently, "Something happened to me too—something truly bizarre."

An indifferent Shujaat Ali kept himself busy smoking, but Bundu Miyan evinced a genuine interest: "Oh, what?"

Mirza Sahib didn't demonstrate anything by his looks; all the same, his eyes had become riveted on Manzur Husain's face.

Manzur Husain was suddenly feeling very tense, at the end of his wits. He didn't know quite where or how to begin. Shujaat Ali pushed the hookah away and started to cough. Manzur Husain grabbed the hookah with nervous alacrity and drew impatiently on it a few times.

"Well?" Bundu Miyan urged.

"It happened when I was very young. Now it all seems so very odd." Manzur Husain fell into thought again.

By now Shujaat Ali too had become fully attentive. Manzur Husain took a few more puffs on the hookah and coughed for no reason at all. "It happened that . . ." He faltered. He was about to start again when, unexpectedly, the sight of several flickering lanterns, followed by the rising, dull sound of light footfalls, came from the alley up ahead. Manzur Husain looked at the approaching lanterns inquisitively and then asked, "Mirza Sahib, who could that . . ." He could not finish his sentence.

In the meantime Sharfu, feeling alarmed, had come out of the house. Mirza Sahib instructed him, "Go find out and let us know!"

Sharfu was soon back, panting. "Nothing in our lane," he informed. "These men are from the hucksters' lane . . . the son of Shammas the huckster . . ."

"The son of Shammas the huckster?" Bundu Miyan was visibly shaken. "But I myself saw him minding his shop this morning—he was quite all right then."

"Yes, yes. He was quite all right until this afternoon," said Sharfu. "He had his lunch, then felt some pain in his chest. By the time the doctor arrived . . ."

"Good heavens!" exclaimed Mirza Sahib. "This cardiac arrest is almost a racket these days. Never heard of this sickness while we were young. Isn't that right Shujaat Ali?"

Shujaat Ali took a deep sigh and nodded absent-mindedly. Mirza Sahib too drifted off into thought. Bundu Miyan and Manzur Husain were also silent. Sharfu remained standing, hoping that they would start talking again and allow him the opportunity to provide some more information. But after a while, feeling disappointed, he decided to go back inside. Then, abruptly, he turned, raised the wick in the flickering lantern, and poked at the *chilam* in hopes of somehow stirring the silent men. They could not be moved. So Sharfu went inside.

After a long pause Shujaat Ali broke the silence, sighing, "Well, that's the way of the world. People are born and people die. There's no escaping the inevitable. Manzur Husain, you were going to tell us something—weren't you?"

"Sure you were," Bundu Miyan chimed in, returning from his silence.

Manzur Husain shuddered, pulled himself up to speak but soon drifted off into thought again. "The whole thing's left my mind," he mumbled. Those luminescent spots in his mind had again plunged into darkness. The railroad car had come unhitched and stood alone on the tracks, stranded in the middle of nowhere, while the rest of the train had steamed away—far, far away.

"What a pity!" Mirza Sahib exclaimed, promptly falling back into his thoughts.

Shujaat Ali pulled the hookah to himself. He drew on the spout a few times, coughed, then began puffing with some regularity.

Manzur Husain's mind had gone completely blank. He was still struggling to dredge out of it whatever he could when his son suddenly appeared and announced, "Abbaji, dinner is ready."

Manzur Husain took it as a godsend. He got up, climbed down the few steps of the portico, and hurried off to his home. It had begun to get dark in the alley. The lamppost at the corner had been lit, quietly shedding a cone of light, beyond which was darkness. A blind beggar finding his way in the darkness with his staff, the sound of dim footfalls coming from a casual pedestrian, a door slamming shut somewhere . . . By the time Manzur Husain reached home the dim spots had assumed renewed brilliance, and the same oppressive urge to tell his story was nagging at him once again—to rescue that dazzling ray from the darkness and expose it in its full glory to the world. He abruptly turned around and said, "Son, you go in. I'll be along soon." He was going back to Mirza Sahib's portico.

The street had become darker still in the meantime. The neighborhood children, who had raised such a racket until a little while ago, had all gone home. Only a couple of daredevils still remained. They stood near the bathroom of the mosque where a firelight had been burning in a small niche in the wall. They had scraped enough soot to roll it into a few black marbles to play with. The fuel had all burned out; merely smoldering embers remained. The soot on the wall was getting harder to scrape. Manzur Husain went past the mosque, entered the side lane, and made for Mirza Sahib's. He found the chairs empty on the portico, but the hookah and the lantern were still there.

"Where is Mirza Sahib, Sharfu?"

"At the mosque—to perform his evening prayer; he'll be back any minute. Do sit down, please."

Manzur Husain flopped back down in his old chair. He sat there for quite a long while and drew a few times on the hookah but it had gone cold.

"Shall I get some fresh fire and tobacco?" Sharfu asked.

"No, never mind. I think I will go home."

Manzur Husain got up and went home the way he had come.

Translated by Muhammad Umar Memon

An Unwritten Epic

In Qadirpur, too, such a battle broke out that people put their hands over their ears in denial when they heard it. Confusion was rampant. Human lives everywhere went for a penny a pound, give or take a few ounces. One person was killed taking two steps back, another taking four steps forward. One was hit in the back, another the chest. How could Qadirpur, insignificant as it was, have stemmed the tide that had shaken even the roots of mountains? But thanks to Pichwa's presence, Qadirpur became the scene of a memorable feat. Knowing they were facing death, friends put on their shrouds, asked their mothers' blessings, committed their wives to God, and marched into battle with such valor and majesty that they revived the memory of wars fought in ancient times. A fierce battle broke out, with incredible bloodshed—heaps of corpses everywhere. Nor were the Jats wanting in character and ceremony. They came out mounted on caparisoned elephants, lighting up the night with their torches. Qadirpur's entire fame rested on Pichwa, so the bravest of the Jats were gathered from far and near. The elephants were lined up, the cannon, gunpowder, arrows, and swords arranged, and the Jat army, weighed down with equipment, set off to conquer Qadirpur. In the branches of the banyan tree near the *ᶜidgah*, Majid sat guard. Seeing light beyond the trees further away, he pricked up his ears and very carefully studied the situation. Listening attentively to all the noises and focusing his eyes, he tried to analyze the light. Finally certain that the expected moment had at last arrived, he thundered out the news on his drum. As soon as the drum was struck, chaos broke out in the houses of Qadirpur. Asleep on the roof, Naim Miyan's two sons, Owais and Azhar, lost their senses when they heard the slogans and drumbeats. Owais was speechless. Azhar, unable to do anything else, got up and leapt headlong over the roofs coming at last to the roof of the Weavers' Mosque. There was a gap between the roofs here, and Azhar was stopped in his tracks. He had no idea what he should do next. Keeping guard below, Rahmat now thumped his club and challenged, "Who's there?" Azhar pulled himself together with great difficulty and somehow or other managed to identify himself. Rahmat laughed and said, "*Miyan*, you have disgraced the name of Aligarh College."[1] Despite Rahmat's opinion, both Azhar and Owais were alumni of Aligarh, and in pre-Partition days whenever they participated in political rallies and enthusiastically shouted the slogan, *India will be divided; Pakistan will be created*, their voices resounded with an unusual note of determination. After the partition of India, however, they had begun to talk senselessly and extravagantly.

When Naim Miyan woke up, Azhar's cot was empty and Owais was standing speechless. Confused, he grabbed his rifle and cartridge case, but the people at the meeting-place suddenly raised the cry "*Allahu Akbar!*" with such gusto that the cartridge case fell from his hand. There had been a vigil at the meeting-place. People were now coming out, each one holding up his weapons.

Straightening his turban, Jafar put his javelin in position and started to draw on the hookah as he went out. Behind him Pichwa straightened his waistcloth and called out, "This is no time for the hookah, my friend!" Jafar put down the hookah and went out thumping his javelin on the ground. Pichwa tightened and knotted his waistcloth with great satisfaction and arranged the silver-covered amulet on his neck. Then he rolled up his shirt-sleeves, spat on his palms, and weighed his club in hand. On his way out he called for Mammad. Annoyed at getting no answer, he called out again, "Hey Mammad, you son of a bitch, where the hell are you?"

Throwing his vest around his neck, Mammad leapt out of a corner. "Here I am, *ustad*."

"Hey, you son of an *ustad*, are you coming out or not?" Reaching him, Pichwa's tone softened, "Now look, you hang on in the Weavers' Mosque trench, and I'll take care of everything here."

After he had instructed Mammad, he left the meeting-place followed by a few of his young wrestlers. As he came out, he glanced at the *haveli*. Kalwa was leading the unit posted there. As soon as he saw Pichwa, he came to attention and shouted, "Don't worry, *ustad*, I'll break anyone who comes here in half."

Pichwa was most worried about the *haveli* entrenchment. And he had reason to be. All the women of the Qadirpur settlement were collected inside it. Although there was a dark well inside the *haveli* and each woman had been clearly told what her duty required in the eventuality, a few nooses had also been set up for good measure. Pichwa had stationed several of his brave young men at the *haveli* and had told them, "I'll roast anyone of you bastards alive who shows the slightest weakness." Confident of Kalwa's bravery and satisfied with what he had said, he went on, weighing his club. A feeling of urgency had now become noticeable in the drumbeats, and far into the distance the conch shells had begun to sound as well. Pichwa quickened his steps. People were beginning to pour out of the other houses. Qurban Ali came out of his house brandishing the siderail of a cot. When the noise arose he hurriedly searched everywhere in the house but could not find even an ordinary piece of wood, let alone a regular weapon. First anger, then the pressure exerted by man's instinctive inventiveness, he fell upon a cot and tore it apart in a flash. Although Saiyid Hamid Hasan had several beautiful walking sticks brought from Naini Tal and Dehra Dun as gifts, he had nothing resembling a club. Hurriedly scrambling around, however, he and his wife finally managed to unearth a rotten, old sword stick. Munshi Sanaullah did not have to face this problem at all. In the front courtyard lay a piece of bamboo used to clear out cobwebs from the rooms; he picked it up as he rushed out. Nor did the Subedar Sahib have to worry about a club. He had a matchlock gun which he always kept clean. In the crowd of clubs, the raised barrels of a few other rifles were also visible. His vest pocket loaded with pellets, Hamid held in his hand a shiny black slingshot of *shisham* wood. A few steps behind Pichwa stood Rasula and Bhallan carrying on their shoulders an entire arsenal, including fireworks shaped like pomegranates, horns, and swords. Allah Razi's party came behind them, dragging an odd-looking cannon. Now this cannon had been fired once before, unfortunately in the direction of Allah Razi's companions. Allah Razi had not had the foggiest idea how the damned thing worked. So, several men were badly wounded and a few others were arrested by the police in connection with the incident. Now, however, Allah Razi was sure that it would not be his companions but his enemies who would be beaten to a pulp. Normally armed with clubs, Pichwa's companions, responding to the demands of time, had made a small modification to their weapons. No longer plain clubs, theirs now had short spears attached to them. Pichwa's, however, was the same as it had always been, except that, having soaked it in oil for three days, it was a little more slippery than usual. So what? The slipperiness that comes from oil makes a club shinier; it does not, however, affect its clubness. It is the spear that destroys the clubness of a club. With a spear attached to a club, it is no longer a club but a spear. Mammad's, Kalwa's, Rahmat's, and Jafar's clubs had thus been reborn as spears. Pichwa's, however, was still just a plain old club—to modify it would have meant for him to change his whole mode of thinking. This club had become an inextricable part of his being. In a way it had given up its separate existence and become an indissoluble part of his own personality. Pichwa's club, consequently, was not merely a club; it was Pichwa's club. Nor was it like the staff of Moses, for that staff had a power of its own apart from Moses; and in a sense, although Moses needed the staff, the staff had no need of him. Pichwa's club was, at any rate, Pichwa's club. And although it too had performed many miracles, the miraculous power was in Pichwa's arms, not in the club itself. The best proof of this was the time Pichwa was accidentally forced to fight without his club. Seeing him unarmed, Tidda the wrestler's companions thought they could at last finish him off. Without hesitating a moment, Pichwa immediately took off his headcloth, tied a coin up in it, and started showing his skill. Within five minutes he had three of them lay their clubs down in sheer helplessness—the many wrists he broke may be considered extra. And then he let them have it, banging their heads with their own clubs. Tidda's companions were not so brave that they could stare down an opponent: a few cracked heads and off they went.

Tidda's poor young men, of course, were small potatoes. Pichwa was always ready to take on an entire village. It so happened that Pichwa was there when the people of Luchmanpura had angrily surrounded the Subedar Sahib. No doubt he had enraged them by firing at peacocks when he could not find any ducks. Anyway, a commotion broke out everywhere. Luchmanpura was nearby and country bumpkins rushed up carrying cudgels. Hardly one to stand around at such a time, Naim Miyan was off like a shot as soon as he heard all the noise. Hamida, at his wits' end, darted off into a nearby cornfield. Only Allah Razi had apparently escaped unharmed, but as luck would have it, he landed in a field where a farmer was plowing. The peasant whacked him in the face first and asked questions later. Saiyid Hamid Hasan's slowness proved his undoing. Lacking any other alternative, he tried to sweet-talk them into letting him go, but his peasant captors knew better than that. The Subedar Sahib just stood there—utterly befuddled, unable to think or do anything. Pichwa was incensed. With a "*Ya Ali,*" he took up his club and beat them mercilessly, killing several peasants, smashing countless wrists, and spraining many more. And when the Subedar Sahib and Pichwa arrived back in Qadirpur, they brought along, in addition to the slaughtered peacocks, a whole pile of very fine, heavy clubs.

It was only a coincidence that Pichwa and Tidda were at odds then over the hillwoman Billo. Although Pichwa was not averse to female company once in a while, he was not particularly one for running after women, as his real interests lay elsewhere. He and Tidda had already locked horns before over the affair with Nasira. Nasira had been legitimately accepted as a member of Tidda's wrestling group, although other people were not willing to accord him that status. Pichwa was never one to hold his tongue, and when he sat at Allah Razi's *pan* shop, put the *pan* in his mouth, and took a puff of his *biri*, he became even more boastful.

As he sat there one day, seeing Nasira he lost control of himself and shouted out, "Pay attention to me, not others!" Nasira was very embarrassed. When Tidda found out about it, his blood began to boil. Anyone else he would have crucified, but here it was a case of a camel against a mountain. Still he was so incensed that he took this boldness of Pichwa's as an act of war. The quarrel festered for several months; several skirmishes took place, but Tidda ended up humiliated every time. Not just this one quarrel; Tidda and Pichwa could never get along with each other.

Although Tidda was proud of his expertise, Pichwa refused to admit he had any. Whenever anyone mentioned Tidda, Pichwa would blow up. "Bah, that son of a barber, that bastard, what does he know about expertise? *Miyan*, his party always puts up the poorest show in the wrestling matches at the *taziyas*."

"But, Khalifa," Allah Razi replied mischievously, for the sake of continuing the argument, "now he's training very hard."

Pichwa grew even more heated, "Oh, to hell with his training; what'll it get him anyway? It's razors he's worked with. What does he know about wielding a club?"

Mammad was now warmed up. "*Ustad*, this son of a barber must really want to get beaten up again. He thinks he's the great Gama, but one slap and all the stuffing will come out of him."[2]

"*Miyan*, I've already beaten that jerk's brains in, but just look, the stupid fool still comes back for more."

Mammad was not the kind to be content with great deeds of the past. He immediately retorted, "*Ustad*, that was a long time ago, and soon it'll be forgotten. I swear to you, *ustad*, I'll beat those jerks till they can't stand up."

"Now wait a minute, boy. I'm itching for a fight with him myself. I'd clip the jerk's wings, but he keeps avoiding me."

Pichwa's excuse was partially correct. Although Tidda's group was not all that weak nor were they short of words when it came to talking big, the fact is that whenever the chance to confront Pichwa presented itself, Tidda always managed somehow to skirt the disaster.

People with common sense in Qadirpur knew that Pichwa was a master of the art of *banaut*, but the superstitious kind circulated all sorts of stories about him. They would say that Pichwa knew magic. And Bhallan suspected this more than most. He had openly expressed his feelings several times: "*Miyan*, whatever it is, Pichwa must have some thing in his power."

Rasula not only vehemently confirmed this, but also provided the proof: "By God, the thing that baffles me is that Pichwa once threw a jinn down to the ground. Now, I've seen a lot of *banaut* in my time, but, *Miyan*, I don't care what you know about moving the stick, no one can win against a jinn. You take it from me, he knows some spell!"

Allah Razi's suspicions were aroused by the amulet Pichwa wore around his neck, but Hamida swore up and down saying, "I saw it with my own eyes. Behind the *ᶜidgah*, in a broken-down grave, Pichwa was standing on one foot reciting something. There's no question that some fakir has given him a charm, and that charm is where his power comes from."

Jafar's story, however, was different. He would say, "*Miyan*, the thing is that Pichwa showed such great courage when those bloody Hindus wanted to tear down the Weavers' Mosque. *Miyan*, you should've seen the way he moved his stick; he made the fools lose their wits. Well, that night what did Pichwa see in a dream but that Maula Ali was patting his back. So you see, this is all through the grace of Maula Ali's feet; otherwise poor Pichwa and his *banaut* would not mean much."[3]

But these were all differences of opinion about cause and effect. That Pichwa was brave had been eminently proven. Pichwa never gave people sufficient time to have doubts about his bravery. Every now and then he would pick a fight with some group on some pretext or other and thus show off his powers. Never concerned about how things would turn out, Pichwa fought without any stab of fear or of thoughts of loss or gain. Moreover, purposiveness had never stained his art. Rather, it was the fight itself that mattered to him, and his club fighting was free of any self-serving. Consequently, when the storm of communal riots began, Pichwa put all other considerations out of his mind and concentrated on the fact that he would now have a chance to display publicly his skill with the club. With both authority and excitement, he ordered his band, "Tighten your belts, lads. After a long time dear Almighty God has finally heard us. We're going to have the time of our lives—God be praised!"

When the members of the group heard this, they could not contain their happiness. Mammad burst out with, "I swear by the Master if Qadirpur doesn't win, Mammad is not his father's son."

Kalwa boasted, "It's true, my club has seen better days. But now I'll dye it red again and bring out its true color."

Pichwa's companions made the same elegant and showy preparations for the coming fighting and bloodshed that people make for *ᶜId*. But all the elegance was wasted, for the tide of the fight turned before their very eyes. Then it was a question not of Qadirpur conquering, but of remaining undefeated. It took Pichwa a long time to feel the change in the wind. Offensive campaigns were all he had ever known, but what defensive action meant he came to learn the hard way only then. When he heard about the creation of Pakistan, he received the news with a feeling of immense chill. He wrung his hands in disappointment and said with deep regret, "*Miyan*, while we sat here rotting, they won the battle over there."

Then he got angry and roundly cursed himself and all the people of Qadirpur for having been unaware. Certainly Pichwa was glad that the battle had been won, but he was also grieved that it was not his blood that had helped buy this empire. After he had lamented enough, he said, "*Miyan*, what was to be has happened. Come on, let's go to the *peepul* tree by the *ᶜidgah* and at least put up a Pakistani flag." The other people of Qadirpur fainted when they heard Pichwa's idea. They tried hard to reason with him and explained where Pakistan actually was. Pichwa was flabbergasted. He could not understand how Qadirpur, where he lived, could be outside of Pakistan. After hearing what people said, he gave up the idea of flying the Pakistani flag, but then, on the urging of Mammad and Kalwa, he decided that, as Pakistan had excluded them from its brotherhood, they would make their own separate Pakistan. Consequently, they decided to fly on the banyan tree by the *ᶜidgah* an Islamic flag representing Pichwa's group, and not the flag of Pakistan. People were even more upset when they heard this. Already in bad shape, poor Naim Miyan lost his senses altogether when he heard Pichwa's idea. He explained up and down to Pichwa and tried in every way to dissuade him. All Pichwa answered was, "Now you listen to me, *Miyan*, no Congress flag is going to fly in Qadirpur; we're going to put up the flag of Pichwa's wrestling group." Naim Miyan was extremely worried and upset, but what could he do? Pichwa was no longer under his control. He had been very obedient and respectful before, but for several days now Pichwa had begun to complain about him, announcing his rebellion openly. Actually, even Naim Miyan was no longer what he had been before. Although he was still called the leader of the Muslim League, he no longer had anything to do with it. He had been very proud before and would get very irritated if anyone so much as mentioned the Congress. He felt it beneath his dignity to talk to a Hindu.

As soon as the partition was announced, however, there was a shift in his behavior. With the creation of Pakistan, poor Naim Miyan was suddenly terribly confused and started to avoid even the mention of the Muslim League and Pakistan. But, anyway, what he did in the end saved him. Before August was over, he had gone to Pakistan. As they were leaving Qadirpur he said, "We're just going to Delhi," but about a fortnight later, the Subedar Sahib received a letter from him from Lahore. He had written: "Brother, all the higher-ups I met in Delhi told me that the lives and fortunes of Muslims are no longer safe in India, and that we must go to Pakistan. We had a very hard time getting here, but, thanks be to God, we reached our country safe and sound. Azhar Miyan got a job in the Rehabilitation Department. God willing, Owais Miyan will also find a job soon. There's nothing left there now in Qadirpur. You should try to come too. By God's grace, I have some influence here, and we can work something out."

When Pichwa heard the contents of the letter, he got up at Allah Razi's store and roundly cursed Naim Miyan. But what good was it to beat the trail when the snake had already slunk away? Perhaps Naim Miyan may have lingered on a few more days, but, in fact, it had been Pichwa himself who had given him the push. Although Naim Miyan had explained the situation over and over to him, once he had taken it into his head, he had to go and put his flag on the *peepul* tree. Although the invasion would eventually have taken place, initially the Jats had hesitated because of Pichwa. But this action of his was especially provoking, and, as the Jats acted on the principle of not putting off for tomorrow what could be done today, they attacked Qadirpur. Now it is true that Pichwa's companions had beaten the hell out of the Jats in the fight, but Naim Miyan was not so stupid that he could not see what was brewing. He knew that the calamity had been averted—but only for a while longer.

Panic broke out in Qadirpur as a result of Naim Miyan's letter. Three days later Munshi Sanaullah folded up and left for good. On market day that week people found good bargains in household goods at the second-hand dealer's shop. Especially noticeable were Saiyid Ale Husain's Naini Tal walking sticks, Qurban Ali's *shisham* wood cots, and Munshi Sanaullah's china.

April 3rd, 1950

How could I have known several months ago when I started writing this story that it would be ruined? If I had, I would have finished it immediately. As I wrote the story, I realized that the character of Pichwa could not be contained in a short story. Justice could only be done to him in a full-length novel. Moreover, I thought, no epic poem has yet been written on the riots. Now, I am no poet—so let me try writing a prose epic. And then, this is not the time for writing great poetry. Now, when we have no great epic heroes, I am surely very fortunate to have a character like Pichwa fall right into my lap. But how could I have known then that after the first riot was over, another would break out and Pichwa would come to Pakistan? How could that same Pichwa, who confronted the riot with his own body, have staggered and been pushed out? What terrible thing happened to Qadirpur? Where did Kalwa and Mammad drift off to? I have no idea. How could I have had the nerve to ask Pichwa about all this? I'm just sorry that the design of my novel is ruined. Pichwa and I are both unlucky. He was not fortunate enough to become the hero of an epic, and I am fated to treat the lives of insignificant people in worthless two-penny stories. People may look down their noses at this. It's true that Pichwa wasn't a great general or a splendid and glorious king; nevertheless, he had a certain dignity and greatness. And I never said my novel had to be called a *Shahnama*. An epic can also be called *Jumhurnama*.[4] Anyway, there's no use arguing about it; it's all just a thought now.

April 7th, 1950

I can't figure out how to write about living things. I write about dead things. How can one possibly write about living things? There's a certain amount of definiteness about them. They don't have hidden corners and evocative shadows. You can write reportage or political poetry about living things, but not short stories or lyric poetry. I feel very nervous when I see living things. The critic who said that a writer should always keep a window open while writing is a fool. Who said you should keep a window open during a windstorm? I'm just amazed at how people can write with their eyes open. I have to write with my eyes closed. I take up the pen only after the subject comes to permeate my mind totally. The trouble is, though, as long as I can still see it, it doesn't settle down in my mind. As long as I lived in Qadirpur, it never occurred to me that Pichwa had it in him to become the subject of a story. When I came to Pakistan, my ties with Qadirpur were broken, and its life and people became a story for me. I didn't care whether Pichwa was alive or dead. As far as I am concerned, he was dead. Out of sight, out of mind. I started to write thinking him dead, but here he is, a living, breathing picture, moving around in front of me, and consequently, the character that had settled down in my mind has vanished like horns off a donkey's head. Down with *real* life: it's stolen from me the hero of my novel.

April 12th, 1950

Day and night I've been haunted by the question of whether I should write my novel. Sometimes I decide to start writing. After all, people do write about living subjects. Everyone is naked in this bath; if I take off my clothes, will a riot break out? Still, I just go on thinking. My head is with me, but my heart is on strike. To hell with writing—the character I had constructed with so much care and difficulty is no longer intact, to say nothing of the living personality. In Qadirpur Pichwa's living personality looked more like a character in a short story, but now that he's come to Pakistan, new twists are coming out. I thought of Pichwa as experiencing unrequited love, and this is the way I imagined the hero of my novel. Now I see more than unrequited love, he's experiencing an unrequited desire for employment. When I met Pichwa this morning, he said, "*Miyan*, get me some kind of work. I have no damned place even to put my feet in. *Babu*, if I can't get any work, at least get me allotted a house."

I was greatly astonished when I heard these words from Pichwa's mouth. He was never worried about daily necessities in Qadirpur. Here he begs for food and wants a roof to cover his head. Where and how can I get him a house and job? All I can do is make him the hero of my novel. Originally I thought I would cast him as a twentieth-century Tipu Sultan, but now that he's come to Pakistan and wants a place to put his feet and something to fill his belly, all the height and grandeur of his character are destroyed.[5]

Pichwa is wandering around looking for work. Today he went to see Naim Miyan about this problem, but he is scarcely the Naim Miyan he was—he won't give a black man the time of day now. He scolded Pichwa, "Everyone just marches to Pakistan expecting to get something, as if his old man had buried a treasure here. They just don't realize that there isn't that much room in Pakistan."

Pichwa complains that Naim Miyan has put on airs now that he's come to Pakistan. What's he complaining about? Naim Miyan is at the top of the heap—if he can't boast, who can? Obviously, in Qadirpur, Pichwa would never have stood for such harsh words, nor would Naim Miyan have had the nerve to look askance at Pichwa. He was always tongue-tied in front of Pichwa. In its own home, however, even the ant becomes a tiger. Clearly Pakistan is Naim Miyan's home and not Pichwa's.

April 20th, 1950

You can't teach an old dog new tricks. Pichwa may have lost everything he had but he still has poetic temperament. Even in his unrequited desire for work, he looks like he's feeling unrequited love. His eyes burst out of his head when he saw the farmland of Pakistan. He told me, "*Miyan*, if I could just get a *bigha* of land, what a change you'd see in Pichwa. Now, I'd put in a mango grove and I'd have a wrestling arena dug on one side where we'd have tests of strength. If you came here in the rainy season, *Miyan*, I'd give you such mangoes that you'd forget Malihabad."

I answered, "Look, you day-dreaming fool, who's going to give you a *bigha* of land? This land doesn't belong to you or me—it belongs to the *zamindars*."

But when Pichwa is caught up in what he's saying, his feet don't stay on the ground. He answered, "The *zamindars*, too, are our Muslim brothers. You just watch: whoever I'll beseech in the name of Allah and the Prophet Muhammad will not hesitate to give me a morsel of land."

You see Pichwa's strange logic—that *zamindars* too must start to be Hindus and Muslims.

April 22nd, 1950

I feel as if the desire to create is decreasing in me. Sometimes I blame myself for this and sometimes external events. Every time I take up my pen, the slogan, "Long Live Pakistan," goes up with such force that I drop the pen. The cry goes up everywhere for "constructive literature." I can't hear anything else in this noise. What is this animal called "constructive literature?" Things are recognized by their opposites. I've never yet seen anything destructive in literature. If literature isn't destructive, how can it be constructive? Literature is neither constructive nor destructive; it's just literature.

After one of my friends had gone on and on and talked my head off about constructive literature, I was just broiling, and I said in no uncertain terms that I wanted to write about homosexual love. He was incensed and said, "That's a very sick love."

"Okay, you give me a healthy subject," I replied angrily.

"Write about Pakistan," he said.

I can't figure out what I should write about Pakistan or how I should write it. Pakistan is a living reality, a fact—and I don't have the power to turn fact into fiction. Pakistan is a reality, while Qadirpur has become a story, a story I can tell. I don't have the power to paint the land of Pakistan, but Qadirpur doesn't need to be painted: it's a story in itself. Its earth is reddened with the blood of its devoted sons. The reddened earth there, the air full of cries for help, the charred houses, the demolished mosque, the ruined wrestling arena—all these things are telling a story eight hundred years old. I can tell this story with all the pain and sorrow that's in it, and I can describe with full feeling the deeds of the vanquished Arjuna of this *Mahabharata*, but this Arjuna—he's the real problem now. How can I write the *Mahabharata* of Qadirpur? The Arjuna of this *Mahabharata* is now the picture of failure and he wanders around the streets and lanes of Pakistan looking for a house and a job. He doesn't get these two things and he continues falling from his true place.

May 2nd, 1950

"*Miyan*, what kind of order is this?" Pichwa was becoming ferocious, and I felt as if he could take a bite out of me. I shuddered. Then it entered my head that this wasn't Qadirpur but Pakistan, and that Pichwa didn't have the same power here.

Surprised, I asked, "What order?"

Pichwa spat out the words. "The order that any refugees that have come here can damn well go back to India."

I didn't know what to tell him. I calmed him down with difficulty, explaining, "Brother, let go of your anger. It's just that Pakistan is full to the rafters now. Where will these new refugees fit? Moreover, some higher-ups went to Delhi and they say all the Muslims in India are doing fine."

At this Pichwa was even more incensed, "*Miyan*, would I lie to you, I, who've come from Qadirpur?"

I know Pichwa is not a liar. He may have a thousand faults, but lying isn't one of them. So what if I know that; the world believes only what the big-shots say.

May 3rd, 1950

How the land shrinks, how food becomes scarce—the reason is simple enough, but I can't help it if Pichwa is too thick-skulled to understand it. They say there was once a king. He went a great distance hunting. He began to pant, and crust formed on his lips. Then he saw an orchard. He stopped in the garden to catch his breath and asked the gardener for water. The gardener's daughter picked a pomegranate and brought it to him. She squeezed half of it into a glass, and the glass was full to the brim. The king drank the pomegranate juice and was refreshed. Then he set off again to hunt. On the way he thought, "Not only are so many pomegranates produced in this orchard, but only half of one fills a glass. Why not tax them?"

By and by the king came back to this orchard and asked the gardener for water. The gardener's daughter squeezed a whole pomegranate into a glass, and then another, but still the glass wasn't full to the brim. She involuntarily cried out, "Father, our king intends evil!"

Surprised, the king asked, "Just how do you know the king intends evil?"

The gardener replied, "*Maharaj*, when the king intends evil the crops begin to fail."

You don't need a great brain to understand a simple thing like this. Both the ignorant gardener and his daughter understood it, but Pichwa—his head is full of cow dung.

Pichwa says, "*Miyan*, make me the king of Pakistan for just one day and then I'll show you how I make those friends who own lots of land, big houses, and several factories jump up and down. I'd beat them black and blue and give a share to every one of the refugees." Snapping his fingers, he says, "Look, *Miyan*, I'd take care of everything just like that."

But I don't believe him—he's always boasting. What he doesn't seem to understand is that if he really were made king of Pakistan, he too would change. The only people with a sense of responsibility are those without it. It is too many responsibilities that produce what is called irresponsibility. What's irresponsible is not a person, but a chair.

May 5th, 1950

The farther I run from politics the more it pursues me. Until Pichwa came to Pakistan he was a genuine fictional character. But now that he's here, he's become an important political issue. Now whenever I think about him I end up in a political morass. Why isn't he allotted a house? Why can't he get a job? Why is he being sent back to India? In short, I get caught in a maze of politics however I think about him. It's not that I can't talk about politics. I can say quite a lot about things like refugee rehabilitation, minority agreements, and abandoned property arrangements. Nor have I kept my mouth shut out of politeness. But why should I poke my nose into politics? Although I feel strongly that my creative talents are being ruined, that doesn't mean I should hold my nose and dive into the cesspool of politics. A frustrated singer should stay a frustrated singer; he has no business becoming a reciter of elegies. I wouldn't interfere even if someone sprinkled this whole terrestrial ball with kerosene and set it on fire.

I'm afraid of external life, the most disgusting aspect of which is politics. Politics makes me tremble just as the butcher makes the cow tremble, and, in fact, politics brings the same doomsday for the writer as the butcher does for the cow. The joke is that politics not only slaughters both literature and the writer, it's the one that eventually gets all the plaudits as well.

May 6th, 1950

My creative desire continues to cool, and whatever magic there was in the fictional potential of Pichwa's personality ebbs away. He no longer seems like a person at all; he seems more like a chess piece. First he's in this square, then he goes to that one, then he's shoved back again to the first one. The characters of a novel are supposed to be human beings—how can I make someone like him the hero of my novel? If I really sweated and ground out a novel with chess pieces for characters, would anyone respect it? Could a novel about chess pieces be called anything but a chess game?

May 7th, 1950

I thought it was just so much bravado, but he did really go back for good. What men call conscience is really a shameless thing. It never dies completely but remains half-dead or pretends to be dead, and can come to life any time at all. Pichwa asked me with some heat, "Will the leaders go with us too?"

I laughed and answered, "If they went, who would lead in Pakistan?"

This made him angrier and he cursed Naim Miyan up and down.

I had told Pichwa to take it easy if he really had to leave and not to be in a hurry, that the government itself would take care of all the arrangements for the trip. This made him furious. "Should I take money for a shroud here and make my grave in India? I don't want a charity shroud."

May 8th, 1950

Pichwa's departure has revived the plan for my novel. But who knows, he might suddenly come back and mess up the plan. Is it inconceivable that death might take him? After all, human life doesn't endure for long. A person can die in a split second. It is entirely conceivable that the heat of Sind might finish off this man from the Doab, or that someone might throw him off the train, or that the train he's riding in might be attacked. In short, death just needs an excuse. What couldn't happen if God willed it, and slaughtering people is certainly an amusing sport, but . . . but why would He ride the horse at the bidding of others?

May 20th, 1950

It's been nearly a fortnight since Pichwa left. I don't know who else is left now in Qadirpur, but I've heard that the Subedar Sahib is still hanging on there. I fired off a letter to him but there's no answer yet. I have no idea where that person ended up after gulping down the sands of Sind. I'd hesitate to say he even got across the border. I wouldn't be surprised if he took a liking to the dust of Sind. Or perhaps the land of Pakistan was offended and hugged the departing guest to her bosom. Isn't it so that the earthly heart of a country throbs for its people even if the hearts of fellow countrymen do not? Both this new country and its uninvited guests are fantastic: the uninvited guests gripe about the indifference of their former compatriots, the latter complain that the former lack foresight and have no feeling for the hosts' difficulties. Regardless of whether there's room in the country, Pichwa left because there's no longer any in the hearts of the people here. And Pichwa left defiantly. He said it was dishonorable to stay any longer. Where has the truthful watchman of his false honor wandered off to? I have no idea. How much he preferred individualism too, this person, how concerned he was about guarding his personal honor. I don't know if he was able to guard his personal honor or not. All I say is this: when the whole nation is being disgraced, does the honor of an individual count for anything? What difference does it make?

May 21st, 1950

I wait for the mailman every day. I keep looking at the door. When the mailman comes, he brings several letters at a time but not the one I'm waiting for. What's happened to the Subedar Sahib that he doesn't answer? Has he also passed away? A person's breath is fragile to start with, and the Subedar Sahib was even then sitting with one foot in the grave. And what happened to that daring fellow Pichwa? Did the earth swallow him, or the sky devour him? Did the winds carry him off, or the snake bite him? Man is no more than a bubble but proud Pichwa went to fight the wind with a lamp.

May 23rd, 1950

This round of the cup, this sorrowful world, this night.
Where do the people light the lamp, O Cup-Bearer?[6]

So that person has gone for good and not only that, he has ended up miles from Pakistan. He has crossed the borders of both Pakistan and India and has entered the country which isn't marked by any borders, where countless refugees arrive every day and are settled in no time at all. The Subedar Sahib's letter—should I call it a letter or an elegy—has come. I didn't realize the Subedar Sahib, in between hunting geese and deer, would start writing elegies. He writes:

Your letter arrived late, but I am thankful it came. It was late in coming for two reasons. First because the address was written in a language that everyone else here except me denies knowing, and second, because Qadirpur is no longer Qadirpur. Now its new residents call it Jatunagar.

You have fired off questions one after another. Which ones should I answer and how? The times you talk about, brother! Where is Qadirpur now? As the poet says, "*Ek dhup thi jo sath ga'i aftab ke!*"[7]

Here there is no longer a Tidda, nor an Allah Razi, nor people flying their own flag on the *peepul* tree by the *ᶜidgah*. When the land of Qadirpur became too narrow for its people, some sank into it, and the rest were driven off. You ask what condition the wrestling arena behind the Weavers' Mosque is in, and I doubt there is even a mosque any more. The mosques would gladly mourn the loss of their worshippers and the wrestling arenas the loss of their young men—but where is there a mosque or an arena today? Allah Razi's store? Your asking brought it to mind—Hindu butchers sell unkoshered meat there now.

Your country had no room for Pichwa, but the earth of his former country clasped him to her bosom. I was not able to meet this fortunate person, but, yes, one day the whole village got excited, and I saw on the same branch of the *peepul* tree by the *ᶜidgah* where Kalwa and Mammad had flown the flag of their party, their master's head was now hanging.

I felt very strange reading your letter. Whatever the reason, you remembered us. Now then continue to remember us with scraps of letters. We are not strangers:

Why do you think us strangers?
We are from the same place you are.[8]

I am getting old and pretty soon the lamp of my life will be snuffed out. Who will you write to then in Qadirpur? Do remember the two things I said about the address.

What a strange letter the Subedar Sahib has written. Is it a letter or the concluding sentences of some epic tale? I think I'll end the novel I'm writing, i.e., my Qadirpur *Mahabharata*, with this letter. And what a death indeed this crazy Pichwa found! His life was a drama, and so was his death. The one undramatic event in his life was his flight to Pakistan. If only he hadn't come to Pakistan. Pichwa disgraced himself coming to Pakistan and threw a monkey wrench into the work of my novel.

May 25th, 1950

Pichwa is dead, but my novel is still not coming together. My hands start to shake whenever I take up my pen. Sometimes I feel as if I murdered Pichwa. What devil got into my head that wanted him dead? If novels and stories got written this way, writers would be tried for murder every day.

May 27th, 1950

Every day I resolve to, but I haven't started to write the novel yet. I picked up my pen and put it back down. I wonder why I'm writing this novel. People don't care about human emotions here—the mention of human emotions is still an afterthought. Appreciation of literature comes from concern for humanity. My nation doesn't value a human being; how can it care about literature? Why should I debase my creative talent and disgrace my pen?

I have definitely decided not to write my novel. But how long can I just sit at home and do nothing? I thought I ought to start moving around. I'm so disinclined to shocking people that I wouldn't want to do anything spectacular. I would be content even to go into the despicable slave trade, but it's not permitted privately now—the governments have taken it over. Naim Miyan says, if it hadn't taken me such a long time to come to my senses, he would have had me allotted some big factory. Now he has promised to have a flour mill allotted. I have to work somehow—if not a factory, let it be a flour mill.

May 29th, 1950

Naim Miyan has sure turned out to be a useful person to have around. Somehow he had a flour mill allotted to me. As the owner of a flour mill, I see a strange kind of change in myself. As long as I was stuck in the web of literature, I felt cut off from my nation. Remaining wedded to literature would have meant being neither here nor there: I wouldn't have written the novel, nor could I have done any other kind of work. Now, however, I consider myself a responsible citizen—a dutiful member of a rising nation.

June 1st, 1950

I'm writing in my diary for the last time today. From tomorrow on I won't have enough time for it. Keeping a diary is something to do when you're unemployed. The arrangements for the mill have been taken care of. God willing, it will start up tomorrow. Since the going price in the city for grinding flour is five *paisas* for five *sers*, I thought at my place I would charge only four *paisas* so that people would patronize the new mill right away.

Translated by Leslie A. Flemming and Muhammad Umar Memon

Notes

1. Aligarh College: refers to the Muhammadan Anglo-Oriental College (also the Madrasatu 'l-ᶜUlūm Musalmānān) which was founded by Sir Saiyid Ahmad Khan (1817–1908) at Aligarh, India, in 1875, for the political revival and cultural regeneration of Indian Muslims. In 1920 it was raised to the status of a university, the Aligarh Muslim University. A considerable number of the intellectual and political leaders of Muslim India in the last decades of the nineteenth and the first half of the twentieth century were educated at Aligarh.

2. Gama: Gāmā Pahlavān, a famous Indian wrestler.

3. Maula Ali: stands for ᶜAlī Ibn Abī Ṭālib, cousin and son-in-law of the Prophet Muḥammad. He is held in great esteem and venerated by the Shīᶜite Muslims.

4. *Shāhnāma* (Epic of the Kings) and *Jumhūrnāma* (Epic of the Common People): The nearest analogy would be Arthur Miller's play *Death of a Salesman*. Tragedy need not have for its subject the fall of an illustrious individual; an ordinary life can just as well be its subject. Likewise, just as there are epics devoted to kings, there ought to be epics portraying the feats of the common people.

5. Tipu Sultan: Ṭīpū Sulṭān was the ruler of the state of Mysore. He is famous in Indian history for his efforts to check the growing power of the British East India company and, possibly, oust the British altogether from India. He was killed in 1799 fighting the British armies at Seringapatam. For an interesting novel based on Ṭīpū Sulṭān's life, see Bhagwan S. Gidwani, *The Sword of Tipu* (Bombay: Allied Publishers Private Limited, 1978). He is also the subject of a book by Praxy Fernandes, *The Tigers of Mysore: A Biography of Tipu Sultan and Hyder Ali* (Delhi: Viking, 1991).

6. *"This round of the cup, . . ."*: The original Urdu couplet is: *Ye daur-e jām ye ghamkhāna-e jahāṅ ye rāt / kahāṅ čirāgh jalātē haiṅ lōg aē sāqī.*

7. *"Ēk dhūp thī jō sāth gaʾī āftāb kē"*: a line from an Urdu couplet, mean ing: "The sunlight has vanished with the sun."

8. *"Why do you think us strangers? . . ."*: translation of the Urdu couplet: *Vajh-e bēgāngī nahīṅ maᶜlūm / tum jahāṅ kē hō vāṅ kē ham bhī haiṅ.*

The Stairway

Bashir Bhai drifted into silence for a minute or two. This made Akhtar restless, even a bit worried. Finally when Bashir Bhai heaved a sigh and stirred, Akhtar felt relieved, but still apprehensive of what Bashir Bhai might say next.

"What time was it?"

"Time?" Akhtar fell into thought, "I can't seem to remember."

"One ought to, though. One must always keep track of the time," observed Bashir Bhai in the same reflective vein. "Without knowing what time it was, it won't make much sense. No worry if it occurs in the earlier part of the night, for then one can dismiss it as the devil's whispering; but not if that happens toward the end of the night. Then, one must give alms."

Akhtar's heart started to race. But Razi still sat silent; only the wonder in his eyes became a shade stronger.

"It is my habit," began Bashir Bhai in his now awakened voice, "to mind the time—always. Then again, as it goes with me, I'm allowed a vision of things before they actually happen—usually a little before dawn. My eyes snap open and I feel I've just seen something wide-awake . . . now take this one time: after arriving here I kept tramping around everywhere for months looking for a job. Oh, was I worried! It seemed all doors to betterment had been slammed shut. Anyway, I had this dream one night. And what did I see? My late grandfather. He seemed to have just stepped out of the mosque, holding a basket made of fresh green leaves. He picked out a *pera* from the basket and held it out to me . . . just then I woke up. . . . The call for the dawn prayer came sailing in. I got up, did my ablutions, and stood up to perform the prayer. . . . Three days later I got a job."

Both Razi and Akhtar were listening with rapt attention, but Saiyid, who had his back turned toward the cots on which the others were stretched out, was trying hard to fall asleep. His eyes were closed tight.

"Bashir Bhai," said Akhtar, "I keep seeing these corpses all the time, a lot of them. What do you make of this?"

"It's a blessing to see a corpse. It means the one who saw it is going to live long."

"But . . . but this one . . .?" Akhtar stopped short.

"Yes, I suppose you could say it's a bit unusual," replied Bashir Bhai, his voice suggesting that the matter wasn't too serious after all. "But if you see a corpse eating with you—now that, for sure, I wouldn't call a good omen . . . it may mean there is going to be a famine." He was about to leave it at that but decided otherwise, saying in a louder voice, "But you don't even remember the time. One mustn't trust *untimely* dreams anyway. Give alms—just to be on the safe side."

Irritated, Saiyid turned over in his bed and sat up. "Damn it, you're incredible, all of you! And you, Akhtar, in particular. I guess you never go to sleep, do you? You keep telling us your dreams till midnight, then start dreaming all over again. Do you ever get time to sleep?"

That irked Akhtar. He snapped, "You're a strange man. You take everything as a joke."

"You're a strange man yourself. You have dreams every night. How about me—why don't I have dreams?"

"It's man's nature to dream," said Bashir Bhai. "Everybody does, only some dream more than others."

"Where has my nature taken off to then? I don't dream at all."

"Not at all?" asked Akhtar, confused.

"At least not since I've set foot in this place. I don't recall having ever dreamt here."

"Then there is something the matter with you . . . did you hear that, Bashir Bhai?"

"On the contrary, something is the matter with *you*," said Saiyid. "I can't imagine how anyone can possibly see so many dreams sleeping on this tiny roof. And what a roof! Four cots and the damn thing is jammed from end to end. Every time I get out of bed at night I feel I'm going to fall into the alley below . . . but the roof of our house," he stopped midway, then continued slowly, "why mourn the lost. There wouldn't be anything left of it now—not even burnt bricks."

Saiyid walked over to the low wall at the edge, and poured himself some water from the clay pot. "The water is warm," he remarked. "When was this pot filled?"

"Why, in the afternoon, of course. But the pot is too old," said Bashir Bhai. "We'll get a new one tomorrow."

"Shall I lower the wick in the lantern?" asked Saiyid. "The light's bothering my eyes."

"Go ahead, set it down over in the corner. The moon will be out in a little while anyway," answered Bashir Bhai.

Saiyid shook the lantern as he lowered the wick, then muttered to himself, "Only a little kerosene left—it might not last the whole night." He raised the flickering wick a little and set the lantern on the ground by the low wall. The weak dim light of the lantern pooled in the small corner, leaving most of the roof in darkness.

Though the cots of Razi and Akhtar boasted of regular bedding, it was Saiyid's that showed in the moonlight. Bashir Bhai only had a lightweight sheet which, for the time being, he had rolled up and stuck under his head as a pillow. Earlier in the evening while sprinkling water on the scorched roof to cool it off, he had also thrown a tumblerful on the coarse, grassy matting of his own cot, so that now not only was his bare back kept cool and moist but also the fragrance, like fresh raw soil, rising from the wet fiber inundated his sense of smell.

Razi, who had been sitting mute for a while, suddenly coughed, cleared his throat, and began, "Bashir Bhai, what would you say if one dreamt of the big *alam*?"

"An auspicious sign—I would say," remarked Bashir Bhai reflectively. "But describe your dream first."

Akhtar turned his attention to Razi. Saiyid rolled over and turned his face away from the rest. He had closed his eyes and was once again trying to fall asleep.

"Do you remember the morning, Bashir Bhai, when you had just gotten up to perform the prayer and asked me why I was up so early?—well, that night I just couldn't fall asleep. God knows what happened. The whole night I kept tossing and turning. All kinds of thoughts went through my head. But I must have dozed off a bit just before dawn. And I dreamt . . ." Razi's voice quaked, so did his body. "I dreamt of our *imam-bara* and saw the big *alam* rising from it . . . the big *alam*, the same *alam*, with the same waving green sash and the swaying silvery *panja* . . . it shone forth so intensely it nearly blinded me. Just then I woke up."

Bashir Bhai sat up with a start and closed his eyes. Akhtar was so over-awed his body was motionless. And there was still a trace of shiver lingering on in Razi. Saiyid too turned in his bed and faced them. His eyes were fully open, a tiny aperture slowly forming in the darkness of his mind. A streak of light filtered in through the aperture. In the fragrant darkness of the mourning chamber he could see arrays of glittering *alams*, silver and gold *panjas* that gave off streams of light, green and red sashes of brocade with their lustrous silver borders, and the crystal chandelier that hung from the ceiling in the center of the chamber with its countless shimmering glass pendants. God knows how, he himself had come to possess one of these glass lusters—it was broken though, almost completely colorless on the outside, but like a rainbow inside if you looked through it with one eye closed.

"A very strange dream," mumbled Akhtar.

"No, I wouldn't call it a dream," Bashir Bhai said slowly.

Both Akhtar and Razi stared at him.

"Were you asleep or . . .?" asked Bashir Bhai.

"No, not completely. I just dozed off."

Bashir Bhai fell into thinking, then said in a low but decisive voice, "It wasn't a dream. Instead, you have received good tidings."

Razi kept staring at him in silence. The wonder in his eyes changed into a bright wave of joy. But it subsided soon, giving way to a sense of deep anxiety.

"That year," he began in a low, solicitous voice, "the big *alam* was not carried out of our *imam-bara* in the procession."

"Why not?"

Both Akhtar and Bashir Bhai became anxious.

"Well, all the members of our family had already migrated here; only mother stayed behind. She vowed that she'd never abandon the *imam-bara* as long as she lived. Every year she herself made all the arrangements for the celebration of Muharram and personally saw to it that the big *alam* was borne out in a procession with great pomp and ceremony just as it had always been."

"Then?"

"She'd grown very old and weak. No matter how hard I tried, I still couldn't get there in time . . ." Razi's voice became hoarse and tears rolled down from his brimming eyes.

Bashir Bhai's head dropped; so did Akhtar's. Saiyid had in the meantime sat up straight. Bashir Bhai heaved a sigh, and after a brief and uneasy silence Akhtar remarked, "You have been living here with us for quite some time now but you never told us that before. How strange."

"What was there to tell?"

Bashir Bhai and Akhtar again felt stupefied, their heads strangely empty of thought. But a peephole had suddenly opened up in Saiyid's memory through which a meandering ray of light made its way down in the darkness . . .

The mourning chamber remained locked throughout the year, except during the ten days of Muharram and a few days on the occasion of *Chihlam*. When the desire to unravel the unknown proved irresistible, young Saiyid would steal his way toward the door and peek through the cracks in it. Seeing nothing, he would step on the door joints and hoist himself up holding on tight to the iron fastenings and peek in through the grating above the door. He would strain his eyes until they became accustomed to darkness and could travel unhindered inside. Suddenly the crystal chandelier would flash. He would stare for a long time but see nothing; his heart, overawed, would begin to pound nervously. Then he would climb down and leave.

Darker still was the underground vault. One of its windows opened into the black stairway. The darkness of the vault never overwhelmed him, though it did frighten him. Even though, as mother used to say, the spotted snake that lived there never bothered anyone unless provoked—once her own hand accidentally fell on something slippery as she was climbing the stairway one night but it simply slithered by, disappearing behind the window without hissing at her once—he could never muster enough courage to climb up to the window and let his eyes probe the darkness beyond. He never caught a glimpse of the spotted snake, but Bundi would swear she saw it with her own eyes.

"You're a liar."

"All right, I'm a liar. Don't believe me."

"I will, if you swear to it."

"By God. It's true."

But he still would not believe her. "Tell me, what did it look like?"

"Jet-black, dotted all over with white spots . . . when I peeked in, it was crawling on the wall. Right away I slammed the window shut."

His heart sank. They both stared at each other. With fear in their eyes and hearts pounding, they suddenly got up from where they had been sitting huddled together on the stairs and rushed down all the way to the courtyard where they perched themselves on the edge of the well.

Soon they were looking down into the well where the light slowly dimmed to a faint shade which little by little thickened and finally became altogether dark. At the bottom of the darkness water rose first in tiny ripples, sending sudden flashes—like lightning—to the surface, then fell to a darker hue. Two reflections fast disintegrating on the lustrous, black, ripply surface.

"Genies!"

"Don't be crazy. Whoever heard of genies inhabiting wells."

"Then who are these?"

"Nobody," he said, sounding like an experienced old man. "You're absolutely crazy. Okay, watch; I'll call out." He stuck his head into the well and shouted, "Who's there?" The darkness echoed back, "Who's there?" A wave of fear ran down their spines. Scared, they instantaneously pulled back their heads.

"Is there somebody down there?" Bundi's heart froze.

"No one—I told you," he replied, absolutely unaffected, as if fear could never enter his heart.

They just sat there in inviolate silence. Slowly the fear began to dissipate. Still perched on the rim of the well, Bundi asked a question: "Saiyid, tell me, where does all this water in the well come from?"

He laughed at her ignorance. "Don't you know even that? Well, there's nothing but water below the ground. That's why the well never dries up."

"If there's nothing except water," she began, thinking hard, "then where do snakes live?"

Yes, where do snakes live?—now, he too fell to thinking. The snake, he speculated, is not the king of water, that's for sure; it is the earth he rules over. But if there is just water below the earth, then where does he live? And how did Raja Basath's palace ever get built?

Saiyid had not quite figured that out when Bundi asked another question: "Saiyid," she said, "is it true that the snake first lived in paradise?"

"Yes, that's true."

"If he lived in paradise then how did he get down here on earth?"

"He sinned. So God punished him. His legs were broken off and that's why he's down here on the earth."

Sin. Fear flashed in Bundi's eyes, and their hearts began to pound.

Bundi got up with a start. "I'm thirsty," she announced, "I'm going home."

With a quick movement of his hand, he grabbed the big water bucket that lay at the rim of the well. "Let's drink from the well," he said. "The water's very refreshing and cool." He quickly lowered the bucket down into the well. The rope raced through his hands, rubbing against his palms and almost burning them. Then came the gentle sound of the bucket hitting the water, a sound which sent a sweet ripple of sensation through his body. Together they began to pull the rope up, aware of a mysterious pleasure slowly emerging in their hearts. When the bucket bearing the delightfully cool water emerged, Bundi first held it while Saiyid cupped his hand and drank his fill. Then he held it and poured the water into the delicate cup of Bundi's hands. The gradually deepening cup of fair hands, pearl-like water, thin, gentle lips—he let the water stream down with such force that it not only splashed on her clothes but also made her choke . . .

"Actually," Razi was saying, "it was a votive *alam*. You see, my mother hadn't been able to bear children. So she went to Karbala-e-Mu^{c}alla. Just about anybody can go and petition at the tomb of the Imam—he is known to be patient after all—but . . . but my mother used to say that such radiance, such grandeur fell on the grave of the Younger Hazrat that as soon as you entered the chamber, you were overwhelmed by reverential awe and began to shake. Not a day passed without a new miracle. When my mother had just arrived there, something strange happened. A man was stepping out of the sanctuary when, all of a sudden, the door grabbed him. He tried, but he just wasn't able to break himself loose from the clutches of the door—unable to go out or in. His body burned red, as if it had just been struck by lightning . . . the man's mother kept crying. Finally, after a long time, one of the keepers of the sanctuary came and said to the woman,

'Lady, your son seems to have offended His Younger Eminence by his rudeness. Now go to the sanctuary of the Imam and beg him to do something about it, for only he can appease His Younger Eminence.' So the poor woman, wailing and weeping, went all the way to the Imam's tomb and clung to his grave . . ." Razi's voice sunk to a whisper. "All of a sudden a radiance broke out everywhere in the sanctuary and the suffering man returned to normal."

"That's really something!" exclaimed Akhtar under his breath.

Bashir Bhai yawned, then drifted off into silence once again.

"What really happened is that the man had taken a false oath," Razi added slowly. Taking advantage of Bashir Bhai's and Akhtar's silence, he continued: "At any rate, my mother said, 'Come what may, I am not going to budge an inch from here without the promise of a child.' The whole night she kept weeping and entreating the Imam, her hands touching his grave all this time. At dawn she dozed off and saw a lion entering the sanctuary. She woke up with a start. Her eyes fell directly on the *alam*, the *panja* emitting flaming rays. Just then a fresh jasmine flower dropped right into her lap . . ."

"Yes," exclaimed Bashir Bhai in a somewhat raised voice, "there can be no doubt about his greatness!"

"That *alam*," a strange dreamy grandeur came over Razi's voice as he began, "is the true *alam*. It's the one that emerged from the Euphrates and still stands at the head of the grave, all wrapped in a green sash, in all its awe-inspiring majesty, so brilliant you can hardly look at it . . . just like the sun."

Saiyid actually felt the strong rays blinding his eyes and filtering wavily through them into the dark interior of the cellar of his mind. The cellar suddenly lit up as the rays penetrated its every nook and corner. Lustrous darkness, bright dreams, a glowing face, the radiant *alam*, and flaming kites—the kite which, when it swooped, suddenly severed from its string in mid-air, brought with it the memory of Bundi drifting farther and farther away from him after a moment of unhappiness . . . the dream that kept climbing an endless flight of stairs, the bed-tapes that rolled out into infinity, the loose end of the kite-string which a gentle breeze had blown almost into the hand but which bobbed and fell out of reach just the instant the hand tried to close on it. He kept climbing the stairs that once led through a tunnel and next rose high into the air . . . higher and higher he rose amid his heart's mad throbbing, his fear mounting that he might trip and fall, feeling at times that he actually was falling into a dark, bottomless pit, ever so slowly: he would try to balance himself, to rise as he fell, only to wake up with a start, filled with horror and shaking all over.

"Ammanji," he would say, "I dreamt I was climbing a flight of stairs."

"A prophetic dream, son. It means you will go far—you *will* become an officer."

"Ammanji, what would you say if one saw a flying kite in a dream?"

"Oh, no, son. No. One mustn't dream such dreams. It is not a good omen to see a kite. It can only be a premonition of vagrancy and homelessness."

"Ammanji, I dreamt that there was this staircase I was climbing. I kept climbing up and up. Finally a roof appeared and the staircase vanished . . . and I found myself standing all alone on top of the roof, and a kite . . ."

"No son, no," his mother cut him short. "It is not a dream. All day long you keep hopping from roof to roof, and that's what you saw in your sleep . . . You mustn't dream such dreams."

"Ammanji, I dreamt about our roof, and a monkey was perched on one of its walls . . ."

His mother again cut him mid-sentence, a little sternly this time. "That's enough, son. Now go back to sleep."

"I will, but first you must finish the story."

"All right. God bless you, where did we stop?"

"The princess asked, 'Who are you?'"

"Oh, yes. The princess kept insisting that he must reveal his identity, but he tried to talk her out of it, saying, 'O lucky one! don't ask me that or you will have to endure great suffering.' But the princess would not give in. 'You must tell me who you are,' she insisted, 'and until you tell me that, I won't talk to you.' So the man reluctantly gave in. 'All right, if that's what you want. Let's go to the river and I will tell you about myself there.' So they both started out for the river. Once there, he again begged her, 'Please don't ask that.' But she just wouldn't listen to him. 'On the contrary,' she said, 'I insist that you tell me that.' The man walked into the water. When the water reached up to his chest he implored her again. 'Please don't ask.' But she remained adamant. 'I *will*,' she said firmly. And when water rose up to his neck, he begged her once again and she once again refused. The water reached all the way up to his face and he beseeched her the last time, 'Listen, there is still time; give up the idea or you will be sorry for the rest of your life.' But she said, 'I *will* ask you!' So the man immersed himself completely. A black serpent's hood emerged from the water and dived back to be lost forever . . ."

"So she had an *alam* made from some silver which had been blessed by a touch from that jasmine flower. And you know what? I was born the same year."

"One must consider that auspicious," observed Bashir Bhai.

"But . . ." Razi's voice trailed off and his body shivered. "But . . ."

"But what?" asked Bashir Bhai.

"It disappeared!"

"It disappeared—how?" both Bashir Bhai and Akhtar were mystified.

"It's like this," began Razi, his body still shaking. "The procession did not take place that year . . . we had a neighbor. He used to say that no one kindled even a single lamp that night in the *imam-bara*, but when he woke up the next morning to offer the prayer, he saw that the whole *imam-bara* was so brightly lit up that for a moment he thought all the light came from gas lamps . . . anyway, when he went there in the morning he saw this strange sight: all the other *alams* were intact, but somehow the big *alam* had vanished . . . "

The darkness that was deepening and had obscured everything suddenly changed into brightness. Still sitting on the rim of the well they saw a shadow glide by in the bright sunshine. "A kite." Like a bullet both shot forward, chasing after it. They went into the stairway, frantically climbing up the flight of stairs and out on to the open roof.

"Where did it go?" he gave a searching look all around.

"I saw it fall right here on this roof," Bundi said with certainty.

"But if it did, then where has it disappeared to now?"

All of a sudden Bundi's hand grabbed his sleeve, and then her grip tightened around his arm. "Saiyid . . ." she whispered, scared stiff, "look . . . a monkey."

He, too, was scared still. "Wh . . . where?" he managed with difficulty.

"There!" she pointed toward the wall with her eyes.

A big, fat monkey sat dozing serenely on the wall. When it saw them it got up abruptly and the hair on its body stood erect like so many quills of a porcupine. They both froze. The monkey stood there for a while, screeched at them menacingly, then, walking leisurely along the wall, climbed down into the alley and disappeared.

When they finally made it to the stairway, their hearts were still pounding and their bodies were dripping with sweat. Bundi rubbed her face dry with her shirt, wiped her neck, and rearranged her dishevelled hair. Then they flopped down on the stairs. He looked at Bundi with fright in his eyes, seeing that her own terror-stricken eyes appeared even more horrified in the half-light of the stairway. By now he was totally overcome by fear. "Let's get out of here," he said, standing up. They began to bolt down the stairs, and he, on their way down, stopped briefly at the first bend to look through the ventilator shaft behind which the field and the trees beyond the field appeared like an altogether different world.

"Don't ever look there," Bundi cautioned him.

"Why not?"

"Because a sorceress lives there," she replied, her terror-filled eyes gleaming. "And she has a mirror. Anyone who looks into that mirror is bewitched and follows her along timidly."

"You're just making that up."

"I swear it's true."

Full of dread he again sneaked a look through the ventilator shaft. "I don't see her anywhere," he said.

"Really?" she couldn't believe it. "Let me have a look." She walked up to the shaft.

She tried hard but was unable to hoist herself up far enough. She implored, "Saiyid, please, please help me see through the shaft!"

He raised her to where her face came level with the shaft . . . and he had the pleasant feeling of holding a bucket of sweet, refreshing water.

The ray of light descending in the darkness got entangled and broke. He rolled over in the bed and sat up. Akhtar, Bashir Bhai, Razi—all three seemed to be sound asleep; Bashir Bhai was even snoring. The moon was slowly climbing up and by now the moonlight had reached all the way to the foot of his bed. He got out of bed and walked to the small drainage pipe at the base of the low wall, which was enveloped in utter darkness. During the rains the pipe served as an outlet for excess water and through the rest of the year as a convenient urinal. After a while he got up and poured a glass of water from the clay pot and downed it in one big, hurried gulp. The water had now become quite cool. He glanced at the lantern in the corner. It had gone out. As he was lying down again his eyes fell on Razi and he had the feeling that Razi was not yet quite asleep.

"Razi!"

"Yes," Razi replied, opening his eyes wide.

"You're still awake?"

"No, I was just falling asleep, but the noise of your shuffling around woke me up."

They fell silent. Razi's groggy eyes once again began to close. Akhtar and Bashir Bhai were still sound asleep. Now Akhtar too had started snoring.

Saiyid yawned, turned over in the bed, patted Razi on the shoulder, and said, "Are you asleep, Razi?"

Razi threw open his eyes again. "No, I'm awake," he replied in a voice heavy with sleep.

"Razi, why is it that I don't ever have any dreams at all?" he asked in a voice which blended innocence with a trace of profound suffering.

Razi laughed. "But why should everyone have to have a dream every night?"

Both of them fell silent again. Sleep was afloat in Razi's eyes and he desperately wanted to turn over in the bed and close his eyes, but Saiyid spoke up again: "When I was a child I once had a dream that . . . that I was climbing up a landing chasing after a loose kite and the stairs just . . ."

"You call it a *dream*, eh?" Razi gave out a laugh. "Those are just vagrant thoughts that cross the mind during sleep."

Saiyid began thinking: Was it not a dream then? And must he therefore assume that his whole life is devoid of dreams? And that he has never in his life seen a real dream? His imagination tried to close in on many a shimmering snowflake adrift in the expanse of memory, only to wake up to the painful realization that these were not dreams but actual events. He cast a probing look at his past life, the whole of it, and saw a dreamy quality in each event, in each corner, and yet he could not find a single dream. He felt that dreams had somehow become inextricably fused with his past so that it was impossible to isolate dream from reality, very much like the *gulal* mixed with mica—shimmering, but from which those sparkling particles could not be neatly separated; or one of those pendants hanging from the crystal chandelier in the *imam-bara*—almost entirely colorless on the outside but full of rainbow colors trapped inside, colors impossible to extricate; or water in the depth of the well—at once bright and dark, one could not tell them apart.

"Are you awake, Razi?"

"Yes." Razi's voice was drowsy.

"After such a long dream," he muttered to himself, "what is left for anyone to dream about? To me even our old house looks like a dream. Climbing up in the half-lit landing you had this strange sensation of walking in a tunnel: one bend leading to another, the second to a third, as if all your life you would be zig-zagging along a never-ending series of twists and turns, with stairs unfolding into infinity, but then, unexpectedly, the bright open roof appeared and you felt you were entering an altogether unknown country . . . and there were times when our roof was invaded by a strange desolation: a monkey, snug and comfortably settled on the wall of the tallest roof, lolled and then fell asleep—inert, you felt it would never wake up again, but then it perked up, shook its body, got up, hopped down onto the roof below, and walked leisurely toward the landing . . . both our hearts cringed with fright. It started descending the stairs, taking all its time to stop on this stair or that. We were afraid of it, and we hid ourselves behind one of the columns in the outer hall. It walked languidly toward the well and settled on the rim . . . it sat there for a while . . . then vanished . . . or maybe went down into the well, who knows . . ."

Sleep began to drift away from Razi's tired eyelids. He gave Saiyid a deep, probing look. Saiyid rambled on undaunted: "We peeked down into the well, then we shouted, 'Who's there?' The well was filled with an immense resonance and an undulating beam of light rising from the water and spiraling upward in the dark, poured out everywhere in the courtyard, as if someone had set the heart of darkness ablaze with sudden fireworks. A shadow was floating on the bright surface of the water. 'It's a kite!' I cried out, pulling myself back and throwing my face up toward the sky. A huge black-and-white kite was loose in the sky, the bit of string still attached to it sparkling against a bright sun. From the wall it swooped down and tumbled into the courtyard where it hovered above my head. I reached for it but it slipped away. I dashed into the dark stairway . . . as I came close to the window of the underground vault my heart skipped a beat. I closed my eyes and threw myself forward, climbing the stairs, cutting one corner, then another, then stairs, more stairs, still more stairs . . . a whole century passed and I was still climbing up and up . . . finally I emerged on the open roof, but then I was once again trapped in a never-ending maze of stairs . . ."

"Friend," said Razi, giving him a look full of wonder, "you are talking dreams."

Saiyid fell silent.

The moon had in the meantime climbed some more and the moonlight which had been at the foot of his cot was now touching the side of the wall in front. The glass sitting next to the clay pot was sparkling in places as if a few beams of light had been trapped inside it. Bashir Bhai and Akhtar were still sound asleep. Because of the cold, Bashir Bhai had removed the light-weight sheet from under his pillow and thrown it over his body, while the quilted blanket that was earlier lying on Akhtar's legs now lay all crumpled and bunched up on his chest.

For a few minutes Razi lay with his eyes closed but soon got bored and threw them wide open.

"Saiyid!"

"Yes," Saiyid's voice was drowsy.

"Are you sleeping? My sleep's gone."

He opened his sleep-laden eyes and, looking toward Razi, he said in a mysterious voice, "My heart's pounding. It seems I'm going to see a dream after all."

His eyes began to close again.

Translated by Muhammad Umar Memon

Toward His Fire

I recognized him in the light of the flames. I walked up to him and tapped him on the shoulder. He looked at me but said nothing; instead he fixed his gaze on the conflagration. I too stood silently and watched. The heat from the flames was roasting us; I tried to drag him away, saying, "Let's get out of here."

But he looked at me indifferently and said, "Where do we go?" I didn't have an answer; it seemed there was none.

Then he pointed to the smoke-filled room on the third floor from which big chips of paint, ripped from the walls by the raging fire, came flying down. "You know," he said, "I used to live in that room."

"I know."

A man draped in a *dhoti*, a big pitcher of milk tied to the back of his bicycle, sped up to us and dismounted. Who in the stupefied crowd had the wits either to listen or to answer? The man saw us standing there silently and approached. He asked my friend, "*Babu*, how did the fire break out?" My friend stared for a moment at the man with the bike, then turned back to watch the burning, collapsing building. The man had gotten his answer, or maybe by then the question had itself become unnecessary. He gawked at the gutted building for a while, then got on his bike and pedaled away.

A tonga driver suddenly reined his animal, pulled up to the curb, jumped out, and leaving the tonga unattended dashed into the building to join the rescuers.

"Were you able to save your things?"

"No. I wasn't. I didn't want to."

"Why?"

"Why?—You see, things have a way of taking root inside houses. Once that has happened, it's difficult to uproot them—you feel you are trying to pull out a tree." He sank into silence for a while, then said, "Don't you know I've been living here for a long, long time?"

"Yes, I do."

"Still you ask that." He looked at me as if he had completely overwhelmed me with his response.

He wasn't wrong, either. As a matter of fact, he had lived in that room since his school days. He never lived in a dorm. He just got himself that room, the same room in which we had spent many sleepless nights before exams. I had gradually come to look upon him and his room as two inseparable parts of a single self. Time rolled on: he finished high school, got his B.A., then his master's. Then came a long and weary period of unemployment which ended when he found a job (for all it was worth)—but he continued to live in that room. It was here again that we shaved our beards for the first time with the razor blade I'd swiped from my father's shaving kit. And now his temples had turned completely gray, and so had mine.

Not that the other tenants of the sprawling building were newcomers. The building, with its many floors and apartments, housed every kind of person you could imagine—natives, immigrants, white-collar workers, college professors, family men who'd stick it out there in a little room with yearly additions to their families, bachelors who would fool around during the day and come in late at night to crash, pensioners—just about anybody. Some of the occupants owned small businesses in the city, others stayed right there, renting one of the building's street-level shops in which they skillfully displayed their wares. These shops were something else again. Some were bright and shiny, where display merchandise was rearranged every now and then. But there were others in which a canister, a box, a burlap sack never moved from the spot it was first placed in, as if it had lain there from the beginning of time and would lie there till eternity—as if it were not merchandise but the very mildew that had stuck to the building and stuck there for good, impervious to any effort to dislodge it. And it wasn't only the merchandise—indeed, some of the old men living in that sprawling complex appeared hardly any different than the mildew in it.

As I look at him, then at myself, I cannot help feeling the inexorable flight of time. How fleeting youth is! It's gone before you know it. But these hoary old men, who looked old even back when we were in our prime, make me feel that old age does not deteriorate—it is durable, restful, steady. Perhaps there comes a point when age itself stands still.

But at that moment almost everybody was in a state of turmoil. People from their rooms and merchandise from shops kept pouring out into the open, like hornets buzzing out of a nest into which somebody had poked a burning torch. Screams, people yelling at one another, voices—angry, nervous, panicky; men, women, and children stumbling over one another as they stampeded out; personal effects, household objects, and furniture flying out of apartments; and hurried footsteps as people came dashing in to help in that pre-dawn hour—some carrying along buckets of water, others wearing improvised masks round their faces and plunging in, trying to get through the wall of fire and salvage whatever they could.

"Brother," somebody shouted across the pandemonium, "does Mukhtar Sahib know what's happened?"

"Don't you worry, he *will*—after the whole damn thing's burnt to the ground!" replied somebody else angrily.

"He'll have to be told though."

Two water carriers dropped in from God knows where, filled their waterskins from the tap by the road, and scurried off into the building.

"Has somebody notified the fire department?"

"God knows."

"Then somebody will have to. Quick!"

"But what's the phone number of the fire department?"

"Phone number . . .? Does anybody know the phone number?"

By then the flames and smoke had completely hemmed in the apartment in one of the corners of the third floor, ripping fair-sized chunks of plaster off the wall facing us. That bothered him a little. "It's spreading everywhere."

"It's spread pretty far already." I too felt rather worried.

"You see," he began anxiously, "the ceiling in my room doesn't seem to be strong enough. Last year it leaked a lot during the rains." He stopped briefly, then said, "I'm afraid it might cave in completely." He suddenly grabbed my hand and said, "Let's go."

We slipped away quietly. People were still coming and the din rose to a roar behind us, but we began drifting away from its deafening impact.

Dawn had already broken and Barkat's tea shop was now open for business. Water bubbled in a kettle on the stove. Haji Sahib and Munshi Ahmad Din, who habitually stopped at Barkat's on their way home from the mosque, were already there. Haji Sahib's lips quivered faintly as his fingers told the beads. We took our places on wicker stools a little distance from Haji Sahib and sat at a broken table waiting for tea. Barkat put the milk pan on another burner, then got busy washing teacups. The cups washed, he addressed Munshi Ahmad Din as he dried one. "Munshi Sahib-ji!"

The Munshi gave Barkat a questioning look, upon which the latter revealed what was bothering him. "Munshi Sahib-ji, when the fire broke out in the market, didn't *they* say that the crowd had set it? How about this one? Now ask *them* who started this one."

Munshi Ahmad Din replied in a sad voice, "Lots of things are happening these days. I feel confused. I don't know how or why they're happening." Then turning to the Haji, "What do you say, Haji Sahib?"

The Haji took a deep breath as his fingers jumped up and down along the rosary: "May God take pity on us!"

"Why expect God to take pity on us when we ourselves don't take pity on one another?" remarked the Munshi.

"True, quite true," Barkat affirmed in earnest. "There is a fire just about every day—God, it's gone far enough."

"Sure, it's gone far enough," replied the Munshi. "I've lived to be as old as I am and have seen a lot of ups and downs, but never so many fires."

"What do you think—are *they* going to spare anything at all or stop only after *they*'ve razed everything?"

The Haji, his fingers still rolling across the beads, asked, "Munshi Sahib, I suppose you remember the day when a fire broke out in the Yellow Manor?"

"Oh, I do, I do," answered the Munshi trembling. "God, that was some fire! Never saw anything quite so fierce in all my life. It looked as though it were going to bring every single house in the settlement crashing down."

"Yes—that's right," the Haji heaved a deep sigh. "Not just the manor house, the whole settlement was swept away along with it. Some buildings have a way of dying—when they die they turn a whole settlement into a pile of dust and ashes. May God be merciful!" He heaved another deep sigh and then lapsed into silence.

The way Haji Sahib had voiced his thoughts left both Barkat and the Munshi with a strong melancholy, and the latter was also suddenly overcome by silence. Then growing somewhat apprehensive of the brooding silence, the Munshi broke in. "Wouldn't you say, Haji Sahib, that the Yellow Manor dated from the time of the *ghadar*?"

"I'd say so. Hazrat Muhajir Makki had sojourned in that manor for three nights."

"Really?"

"Yes, that's right. But something very strange happened on the third day. It was near sundown. Hazrat Sahib was in the stable making his ablutions from a *chauki*."

"Inside the stable?"

"Yes—inside the stable! You see, he was staying there without the British knowing it. He thought a stable would be the last place anyone'd think of. But some ungodly crook squealed on him to the CID. Soon the British Collector himself came galloping in on his horse just when the call for sunset prayer was being made from the mosque. 'Well, Nawab Sab,' he demanded of the local Nawab sternly, 'we want to inspect your horses, so open up the stable!' The Nawab—he froze stiff, he was scared. But what could he do? He had to obey the order. So he had the door opened."

The Haji stopped in the middle of his narration; suspense choked both Barkat and the Munshi. "What happened then?" they asked impatiently.

"What happened? Nothing! The Collector charged right in, but what did he see? Well he saw lots of water on the floor as if somebody'd just finished making ablutions. The empty water jar stood there too and the prayer-rug all spread out—that's all. As for Hazrat Sahib—well, he'd vanished."

"Vanished? Just like that?" asked Barkat, completely mystified.

"Yes—just like that!" the Haji replied, undisturbed.

"But where did he vanish to?"

"He?" smiled the Haji, "You mean Hazrat Sahib? Well, by then Hazrat Sahib had already flown to Madina Munawwara."

"Bravo!" cried the Munshi. "God be praised!"

"That's really something!" exclaimed Barkat, turning his attention to the kettle in which the water had come to a boil and whose lid seemed just about ready to fly off. He quickly removed the kettle from the stove, put the tea leaves in, waited awhile, then poured the tea into cups.

"This Hazrat Sahib of yours sure sounds like some great man!" remarked the Munshi.

"Brother," the Haji began, "it's all due to the blessing of his feet that, although blood flowed like water during the *ghadar*, the Yellow Manor emerged unscathed from the holocaust." He stopped for a moment, laughed, and continued, "Just look at the ways of Providence—the building which even the *Farangis* didn't dare harm finally came to be pulled down by *these people*."

"But we heard that it was the British who had it sacked, as they had so many others," observed the Munshi.

"You're right there. Of course it was the British, but think of the hands that actually put the torch to it. Weren't those the hands of our own brethren?"

"Absolutely true," the Munshi agreed right away.

Barkat had fixed the tea in the meantime. He brought two cups and set them before the Haji and Munshi Ahmad Din, then he brought two more and put them in front of us. The Munshi moved his cup a little closer, took a sip, then set the cup back onto the saucer and remarked, "But you would agree these British are one hell of a people—wouldn't you?"

Barkat heard that. He felt strangely uneasy, as a sudden thought touched off a wave of tremors throughout his body. He seemed to have remembered something all of a sudden. "Munshi-ji," he said, "you remember that white man, the one who lives in the cornermost apartment on the second floor—now that I think of it, I haven't seen him around for quite a while now."

"You mean Mr. James?"

"Yes, yes—Mr. James. Anyway, when the fire broke out I saw everyone who lived there standing lined up on the street, but not him. God knows where he was. I didn't see him." Then he turned to us, "Sahib-ji, did you see him?"

My friend kept quiet. I answered, "No. I guess I did not."

"That's just what I'm saying. I certainly didn't see him, you didn't either, I guess nobody did—so where did he go?"

In the meantime Mumtaz walked in, exhausted, dripping with sweat, face and clothes smeared with soot. He pulled the beat-up, one-armed chair close to the Munshi and slumped over, feeling terribly fed up. A little later he yanked a handkerchief out of his pocket and began wiping his neck.

"Did it let up?" asked the Munshi rather hesitantly.

"Let up? You must be joking. It's getting worse." Mumtaz became quiet. After a while he muttered, "Seems the whole building's going to crash any minute."

The Haji, still absorbed in his rosary, gave Mumtaz a deep, probing look, then asked, "I guess Mukhtar Sahib's been told about the fire?"

Mumtaz made an ugly face. "Haji Sahib, you know better than that. You've spoiled my whole day mentioning that man's name."

"Listen, boy," the Haji said firmly, "I'm asking you a question. Now tell me whether Mukhtar Sahib has arrived on the scene or not."

"Oh, he arrived all right, but played innocent, as if he didn't know anything about it."

"Nobody knew about it or the fire wouldn't have broken out in the first place," said Munshi Ahmad Din.

"Now come on. He knew about it. He *did*."

"Mukhtar Sahib knew about it? No. That's nonsense. Just plain slander." The Munshi gave Mumtaz an angry look.

Mumtaz didn't bother to contradict the Munshi but turned to Barkat and said, "Barkat, won't you give me some tea to drink?"

"Sure." Barkat promptly began fixing a cup.

Just then a newspaper hawker rode in frantically pedaling his bike, tossed an Urdu paper that landed right on the table, and vanished. The Munshi picked up the newspaper, gave one page to the Haji, took one himself, spread it out carefully on the table, and began reading.

When Barkat brought the tea, Mumtaz propped himself up a little, grabbed the cup, took a few sips, and set it on the table. The Munshi read some news items to the last word, read others only halfway through, and with others still he merely sniffed at the headlines and never got beyond that. Finally he turned his page over to the Haji, saying, "Haji Sahib, the situation is getting worse in the Middle East. It's my guess that war's going to break out again."

"And again the Arabs are going to take a beating," Mumtaz butted in, feeling terribly grouchy and irascible as he took another sip.

"I say: let Pakistan get into the action," Barkat contributed his share to the discussion. "Then you'll see how these dirty Jews'll get it."

Haji Sahib put the newspaper aside and said with a bitter, barely perceptible smile, "Let Pakistan straighten out the mess she's in first."

The remark left a deep impression on Barkat. "Haji Sahib-ji," he began, overcome by a feeling of immense sadness, "Why is it that the Muslims are fighting among themselves everywhere? That will be their undoing."

The Haji reflected briefly and said, "Time is against the Muslims nowadays."

"Nowadays time is on the side of America!" the Munshi cut in sharply.

But Barkat lost no time in contradicting him just as sharply. "America—what America, Munshi-ji? It's all over with *your* America. Time is on Russia's side these days."

"So what's the difference?" snapped Mumtaz, again in the same bitter, hurt voice.

"Haji Sahib-ji, when are the Muslims going to have time come over to their side?"

"Time—eh? Time's as good as dead for the Muslims," Mumtaz blurted out in the same vein.

"Easy now, it *will* change and come over to the Muslims' side. You just watch," Barkat declared with unshakable conviction.

"Just as it has for the Muslims in Pakistan?"

This, Mumtaz's last assault, ruthlessly took the initiative away from Barkat. Completely disarmed, he turned his attention instead to the burner with the milk pan. Mumtaz turned to the Munshi, "Munshi Sahib, this Mukhtar—what was he before?"

"A pauper—what else!" said Barkat, warming up, leaving the burner to itself. "But as luck would have it, he made himself quite a fortune, right before your eyes and mine."

"He's an extremely hard-working man," the Munshi tried to explain.

"Of course!" Mumtaz smiled bitterly.

"Munshi Sahib-ji," began Barkat, "you are lucky if you can manage to scrape up two square meals a day out of your honest hard work, but you don't expect to build fortunes out of it—or do you?"

Face flushed from the intense heat of the fire, smeared all over with soot, clothes partly burnt, partly stained by smoke, sopping with sweat—Ramzan walked in so beat up and battered that they forgot all about their discussion.

"Shall I fix you some tea, Ramzan?"

"No. I'll have a Coke instead."

Barkat quickly popped the cap off a Coke and stuck the bottle into Ramzan's hand. After he had taken a few mouthfuls of the cold drink, Ramzan loosened up a bit. "You know what?" he volunteered. "The Prof's wife got out of the fire all right but left the baby boy inside. I had a hell of a time pulling him out of the flames."

"But the child wasn't hurt, was he?" asked the Munshi in a suddenly solicitous voice.

"No, no. He's okay. You can say God just wanted him to be saved. When I finally got in, the fire was almost up to the cradle, and the room was filled with thick smoke." Ramzan stopped, then said, "But the child was amazing. He just lay there sucking his pacifier without getting upset or anything. He didn't even cry."

Mumtaz grated his teeth in indignation and muttered to himself, "Son of a bitch!"

Ramzan stared at Mumtaz, then informed him, "Mark my words, this Mukhtar—he's going to get it this time."

"Really?"

"Yes—really. Rahman has already been apprehended."

"I warned Mukhtar Sahib about that man," Munshi Ahmad Din said regretfully. "I told him that one day that man was going to earn him a very bad name—that's just what seems to've happened."

"But Ramzan," said Barkat, "I suspect something else."

"What?"

"You see, that white fellow, who lived in the cornermost apartment on the second floor . . ."

"Yes, yes—James."

"How is it that he's dropped out of sight—completely?"

"That is surely very odd." Ramzan thought for a while, muttering to himself a little later, "Yes, where did he disappear to?"

"A bunch of dirty crooks—that's what they are, all of them," Mumtaz murmured with some heat.

All of a sudden the Munshi sprang to his feet. "Haji Sahib," he said, "I guess I'll go and have a look myself."

The Haji, still telling his beads, raised his head a little, said good-bye to the Munshi with his eyes, and got busy again with his beads.

Mumtaz gave a long look, rich in suggestion, to Ramzan, then said, "You remember what I'd told you about the Munshi?"

"All right, Mumtaz Sahib, you were right all along."

"Did you see, Barkat," Mumtaz now turned to Barkat, "how that Munshi lost his bearing when I mentioned all that?" Then, still quite angry, he said under his breath, "Stinking bastards!"

My friend got up abruptly. "Let's go," he said.

"Where to?"

"Just anywhere."

We both got up and set out, walking in silence. It was morning now. The sun had risen and one could see its rays as they fell brilliantly on the tall fences. Here and there one could also spot a pedestrian or two, and quite a few carriages were already on the street. We moseyed on. At some point he asked me abruptly, "I suppose you remember how we once used to spend our summer afternoons in the city?"

"Oh, yes. I remember very well," I responded as the memory of the countless scorching afternoons began to come back to me. We would spend those afternoons together, sometimes under shady trees, sometimes walking aimlessly along shadeless, sun-baked sidewalks, still other times inside sultry tea shops without air conditioning. But why was he thinking about that now?

"You know," he continued, "there were afternoons when I'd get dog-tired walking endlessly in the sun, and I'd go home to rest, but that room of mine, without even the comfort of a ceiling fan, got so hot in the afternoons that it was like being in an oven, roasting. I could never take a nap in there—not one, absolutely never."

What could I say to that? I just walked on with him and patiently heard him out. "You know," he reminisced, "I had no particular arrangement for getting my meals either; so there would be nights, a lot of them in fact, when I'd have to sleep under that roof without anything to eat. And when your stomach is empty, you're lucky if you can fall asleep." He stopped, and a moment later said, "I've endured a lot of pain and sorrow under that roof; so it mustn't cave in—it really mustn't."

"What sort of logic is that?" I blurted out.

He thought for a while then recounted, "Shaikh Ali Hujwiri once saw a mountain on fire. In the fire he spotted a tormented little mouse frantically scurrying around. Somehow in its mad running the mouse managed to get away from the erupting volcano. But as soon as it got away, it dropped dead!" He fell silent. After some time he added in a very low voice, "You see, *I don't want to die*."

A fire engine passed and its harsh, ear-splitting siren nearly deafened us. I felt rather strange. Why in the world is the fire engine going there now? So late? Then I thought, maybe they're sending in reinforcements. The fire engine zoomed past us with a deafening wail. Within seconds a huge crowd materialized, standing in small scattered bands—panicked, guessing, whispering apprehensively, "Is there a fire someplace?" "Where did it hit this time?" "Is it going to spare anything at all or let up only after it's leveled everything?" then a sigh, a long sigh, "God, take pity on us!" another long and cold sigh, and a final, "We've been hit by evil times."

"What do you think, will they be able to put out the fire?" I asked with no particular reason.

"What fire?" he gave me a long, inquisitive look.

"This one, of course—the one that's broken out in the building."

"That one—oh, I see." He lapsed into thought. "What do you think?"

"They just might—who knows? At any rate, the fire engine's arrived."

"Yes, the fire engine's arrived," he repeated with a bitter smile.

We were walking again, in dead silence. "But suppose," he said abruptly, "they're unable to contain the fire—what then? Where will all these people go?"

With horror I thought of the panicked mass of humanity I'd seen standing outside their homes and said, "Let's hope, let's pray that they will contain it."

He kept quiet. So did I. We walked on and on, still without exchanging a word. Finally I said, rather hesitantly, "Why don't you come over to my house?"

"To your house?" he laughed in a strange way that made me feel terribly embarrassed.

Once again we walked on in silence. I thought maybe the fire was worrying him. In an effort to distract him from his thoughts, I said something to him. In turn he said something. One thing led to another, then to another, and our minds traveled far and wide. The day was hot, the sun quite strong, as we ambled along like a pair of city tramps, reviving, as it were, an old tradition of vagrancy. In these days we almost never got together as we had done so often in the past, to knock around on sultry, broiling afternoons and desolate wintry nights. We had our different lives now, and separate jobs. Today, after a long time, we'd gotten together again, and in a way that had revived our dormant yearning for wandering.

We kept strolling around all day long and through most of the night, from one tea shop to the next, and still to another. When, finally, the night began to wane and we were just about ready to drop from fatigue, he announced abruptly, "Well, I must go home now."

"Home!" I looked at him, absolutely mystified.

"Yes—home," he answered. "I've suffered a lot under that roof. It really mustn't cave in."

"But . . ." I tried to say something but faltered.

"What you are thinking is absolutely right," he said in a deep, dispassionate voice, "but, you see, *I don't want to die!*"

I just stood there, rooted to the ground, and watched him return to his home, toward his fire.

Translated by Muhammad Umar Memon

Comrades

Boda realized too late that he had climbed aboard the wrong bus. The slender boy with the little suitcase, who had hopped on the bus at the same stop and who was now sitting on the seat in front of him, seemed to be a bit upset. With anxious looks the boy kept asking passengers in front of him and behind if this bus would go to Model Town.

"Yes, it will," replied somebody. "Where do you want to go?"

"Block G, Model Town—will it go there?"

"Yeah, yeah," replied his neighbor, a middle-aged gentleman, rather serious-looking with graying hair. He said it most casually, straightened his glasses, and turned back to his newspaper.

So this was the Model Town bus. Then why had he climbed in? Partly in the rush, partly because of the darkness, he had not bothered to look at its route number. From a distance he saw it waiting and raced forward, but just before he got there the conductor closed the door and blew his whistle. But when the door of the moving bus fell open, he had sprung onto the footboard and with great effort and determination forced his way inside. At the next stop, when a man got off, he had grabbed his seat. And now he was to find out that he had boarded the wrong bus. "Oh well, it's just a seven-*paisa* loss. I'll get off at the next stop." But he did feel irritated about having to get off like that and wait all over again for the right bus. He remembered other bitter experiences like this one. Always, it seemed, buses on all sorts of other routes would come and go, but not the one he wanted. Strangely, when he had to go from home to town, buses returning from town would be stopping across the street at very short intervals, but when he wanted to go home, buses would be lining up for passengers going toward town. On his side the stop would be desolate, without the prospect of any bus appearing even in the distance. Yes, often his bus would rush by while he was still far off, make its stop, and then, just as he caught up to it, it would speed away. Then would follow that same long wait, standing beyond endurance, pacing. . . . Today, catching the bus right away, his spirits had soared. But now he was to find out that he was on the wrong bus.

At the next stop he became embroiled in the struggle of deciding whether or not to get off. It occurred to him that now he was even on a different road. How could he catch the bus on his own route? His only recourse would be to march back to the previous stop and begin the endless wait. He stood up. He sat down. "But why am I letting myself be carried on? I'll be even farther out of my way!" He again determined to get off. But no sooner had he decided this than the bus pulled out. He sank back down, and as the bus picked up speed he was increasingly bothered by the awareness that he was being carried farther and farther away from his own route. "Where will this bus take me?" He remembered Khalid, who once used to live in Model Town. With Khalid there he would have had no problem. The night would pass delightfully at his home. Khalid, Naim Patthar, Sharif Kalia—he began musing over their now-dispersed band.

Khalid was the last to go. He was jealous of Naim Patthar and Sharif Kalia for months because, in spite of getting C grades, they had gotten to America on scholarships. "Look, even if I don't get a full scholarship, if I could just get a little money I'd escape to London. I have really suffered here. Even if I had nothing, I could wash dishes in some restaurant. Just let me get out of here." Boda had not really understood what it was that set Khalid's mind on getting away. But now he was thinking that Khalid had certainly done the right thing. Even traveling in a bus is torture here. The bus was unbearably crowded, and near the doors were so many people there was a constant grappling for even a minimum amount of space. Bumping shoulders with everyone, drenched with sweat and with odor rising from bodies like yeast. The serious-looking man made a determined effort to read his newspaper but he finally folded it up and began to fan himself with it.

The slender boy was still worried. At each stop he asked, "Is this Model Town?" and upon receiving a reply in the negative, would sit down quietly for a few moments. But as the next stop approached his anxiety would return. The man in the filthy clothes beside Boda, who had been dozing for a long time, had now fallen asleep. Boda was impressed by how comfortably he seemed to be sleeping in spite of all the clamor and jostling.

Now the bus was moving faster—partly in fact but partly too in his imagination. They passed up several stops. No passengers to be picked up? As it passed the next one he looked out with a start to observe a mob in the light beside the lamppost: a camp of homeless, desperate people with their eyes fixed on the bus. The bus had seemed about to stop, but at the conductor's "Keep going!" it sped up again. Peering out the window he noticed how quickly the spirit of hope came over the sea of faces and then how quickly it disappeared; how quickly despair took its place on some and anger on others. A few in resignation began to walk. One person had jumped onto the footboard and hung on. Forcing the door open, he began to climb in. The packed-in passengers became furious. They began to push and shove. The conductor blew his whistle and the bus came to a halt. "Sir!

Get off! I say, get off!" The new man gave an indignant look at the conductor, then he looked at the passengers and, biting his lips in anger, climbed down.

Boda began to think that he should get off too. He really had taken the wrong bus. But the bus had started off again. At the door men were falling over each other. Beside his seat people were massed in a solid wall. An abhorrence for them all began to boil inside him. These dirty people with their pushing and shoving, their incredible noise, their stinking sweat, began to seem to him like creatures fallen beneath humanness. He became so repulsed by them that, had he possessed the will power, he would have thrown open the door and leapt out. The lolling head of the sleeping man had come to rest firmly against his shoulder. Looking with contemptuous eyes at that grimy head and sweat-soaked neck, he pushed it up and sat back, firmly upright. But very soon those eyes began to close again. He became wary of that bouncing head with its closed eyes, which seemed about to fall back against him, so with a resigned smile he moved clear against the window. The wall of standing people seemed about to topple over onto him as a unit. Just the thought of it was suffocating. They were indeed fortunate, those friends of his who had escaped from here.

He enviously remembered Khalid, Naim Patthar, and Sharif Kalia. They had all boarded that special train together.[1] They had all passed through that same terror and arrived in Pakistan in the same condition, but now how far apart their separate paths had gone. He likened his own condition to that of a rickety bus, which might at any moment collapse, crawling, in the middle of the road, leaving the passengers to get off, catch whatever form of transportation they could, and make their various ways to the different destinations.

"Is this Model Town?"

"No." The serious-looking man answered the slender boy again in his detached way.

They started off again. "The conductor is strange. He never comes over this way." Boda wanted to call out and get his attention, but then he decided that it was the conductor's own responsibility to go around and write all the tickets. The conductor kept moving about the crowd, passing right by him into the women's section, where he wrote tickets for a long time. Boda's view of the tall girl with the rounded buttocks, whose blouse fitted tightly all the way down, had been spoiled because she found room to sit down in front of the slender boy. It never pleased him to have a girl obtain a seat if he had a good view of her standing. Now only her pale neck was visible to him. But the slender boy kept looking all around in his anxiety, ruining even that sight, which made him very angry. But at the conductor's arrival nearby he forgot for a while the slender boy and the full-bottomed girl.

He suddenly thought that if he wanted to, he could easily save seven *paisas*. After a little while the idea began to gain strength in him again. "Why not?" He became ambivalent. Greed and righteousness had placed him in a moral dilemma. Seven *paisas* could be saved. He remembered he was without a job and thought of his pocketbook. Then he thought that seven *paisas* could be very useful. But an opposing current came, "No, I will not do wrong. Evil eclipses the noble spirit."

And while he was going through this great moral crisis, the conductor came and stood over him. Putting his hand in his pocket, he grabbed the change, which came to eighteen *paisas* only. Leaving the change aside, he took out a rupee bill and gave it to the conductor, who asked, "Model Town?"

"Yes."

The conductor wrote a twelve-*paisa* ticket and gave it to him with the change. Hesitatingly he somehow managed to take the ticket and the change. He had not even been asked about where he got on. He cast a stealthy glance around the neighboring passengers and, after looking at the sleeping one, took a relieved breath and put the ticket and money in his pocket.

The sleeping man's head was again resting against his shoulder, making him feel very irritated; however, he found himself getting angrier with the slender youth who kept getting upset as each stop drew near and would not settle down until he was assured that it was not Model Town.

"Sir, today there was a great crowd at Data Darbar."[2] Nearby a slender-bodied person in a dirty coat was addressing the serious-looking man, and Boda remembered that today was Thursday, which explained why there was such a rush on this last bus. These folk were returning from Data Darbar.[3]

"I was not able to go," said the serious-looking man in a voice tinged with shame. "There is always so much work that I cannot go regularly. Occasionally I go on the first Thursday of the month."

"No matter what," said the man in the dirty coat, "whether there be a dust or a rain storm, I never miss visiting the Data on the first Thursday of every month." The man paused a little, then said, "Khan Sahib, last month a miraculous thing happened. Just think that all night long . . ." His voice faded away. "Sahib, a cat . . . it was a big, black cat with burning eyes . . . I got scared. It went behind the tomb-chamber . . . what a relief . . . But after a little while it came back. My heart skipped a beat! After weaving its way between people's legs it again went behind the chamber and I breathed another sigh of relief. But you know, sir, it was back in a moment. I said to myself, 'What is going on?' I watched it closely. Well, sir, it was circumambulating the tomb! This realization absolutely stunned me. I watched on as it continued circling the shrine. Meanwhile dawn broke and in came the sound of the call to prayer. I shivered. Do you know what happened? The cat was nowhere. It had simply vanished."

"Really!" said the serious-looking man with a start.

"Yes! It was gone!"

The passengers close to that man began staring at him, while the serious-looking man just closed his eyes.

"Well, the thing of it is," the man in the dirty coat began slowly, "on Thursdays the genies come to pay their respects to the Data."

Amazement flashed in the eyes of the silent passengers. A muscular man with a long moustache took a deep breath and said, "That is a great feat of Data Sahib!" and bowed his head out of respect.

"I don't believe it," came a voice from the corner seat, and immediately everyone's eyes were fixed on the man in a business suit.

"You don't believe in Data Sahib?" the muscular man asked angrily in his deep voice.

"I believe in Data Sahib all right, but . . ."

"But?"

"But it's like this, that . . ."

"I won't accept any more *buts*! I asked you straight whether you believe in Data Sahib or do not believe in Data Sahib."

"Brother, these are enlightened people; they don't accept anything which is contrary to reason," said the serious-looking man in a conciliatory tone. Then he addressed the suited man, "But, mister, you did say just now that you believed in Data Sahib."

"Yes, I believe in him. He was a venerable person."

"If you honor him as a venerable person, then you must also grant that he cannot tell lies. Well then, sir, you should read his book. In it he himself records many such incidents." While saying this the serious-looking man looked around at the passengers nearby and the tone of his voice changed from a persuasive to a descriptive one. "Data Sahib once had to take a journey in which he wandered from place to place. As he was passing through an area, what should he see but a burning mountain, one which contained ammonium chloride, in which there lived a mouse. That mouse was alive and was scrambling about inside that erupting volcano. The mouse became very restless and managed to come out of the fire. And just as soon as it came out, it died." The serious-looking man became silent, then said, "Now what do you say to that? Reason cannot accept it."

"Data Sahib's story is true," a bearded man remarked confidently. Then his voice began to break. "Data Sahib's story is true. Man is an insignificant creature and this world . . . a mountain engulfed in flames . . . how true . . . how true!" Tears welled up in his eyes.

Disturbed by this whole episode, Boda thought, "Won't the stop ever come?" Immediately it occurred to him, "So what?" He was on the wrong bus. And then he remembered that he had purchased a ticket to Model Town, so he was committed to going there. But why? . . . The bus roared on. Because of the speed the bus was clattering so much that he began to feel uneasy. He looked at the passengers. Those same travelers who had just been scrambling for the smallest space to plant their feet were now silent—their faces colorless. His own feelings of irritation had given way to passionate feelings of sympathy. He longed to stand up and tell them, "Friends, we've gotten on the wrong bus!" But then he realized how stupid he would look making such an announcement. He had indeed gotten on the wrong bus, but the others were on the right one. "Can the same bus be going on both the right and the wrong route at the same time?" This situation seemed peculiar to him and assumed the form of a metaphysical question. He unraveled the tangle by concluding that no bus is wrong. The routes, stops, and terminals of buses are fixed. All buses ply their respective routes. It is the passengers who are wrong or right. . . . And his shoulder had begun to ache under the weight of the sleeping man's head. But this time he viewed him with sympathy and, with a twinge of envy, thought, "My sleeping companion is comfortable." "What? Companion?" he reminded himself that it was he who was on the wrong bus, so how could the sleeping man be his *companion*? Looking around at all the passengers, he asked himself, "Don't I have any companions at all?"

He began to look out the window. Near a lamppost, partly lighted, partly in the dark, was an empty bus with its front smashed in, resting half-on and half-off the road. Nearby was an empty, unharnessed tonga with its rails pointed to the sky. There must have been an accident. With neck still extended, he turned to look backward. A cloud of black smoke was billowing from the back of his bus. "What if the bus caught on fire? . . . but it *is* on fire!" With this thought he turned his attention to the window labeled "Open only in emergency." The feeling of horror grew as he looked here and there inside the bus. In the light of the discolored bulbs all the faces had turned distinctly pale. They were packed together, silent, like cattle huddled closely together when overtaken by darkness in the jungle. The bearded man's eyes were closed. The serious-looking man was sitting motionless, glued to his seat. The muscular man, holding firmly to the handlebar, was lost in some dream or other. The man in the dirty coat had turned away and was addressing some other people now. And what of the sleeping man, who had become a permanent burden anchored to his aching shoulder? Now he was snoring. He gazed at the arm pinned beneath that head with detachment, as if it were separate from the rest of his body. Only the sleeping man was really comfortable.

"What stop is this?" he wondered as he watched people frantically getting out. They clambered off, tripping and falling over each other in such confusion that one would think they were fleeing some fierce fire. Why, the whole bus was becoming empty! After they had gotten off, a few others got on, but the bus still looked nearly empty. He began to marvel at how many had gotten off at just one stop. And if at the next stop all the rest got off, what then? Well, he would be left alone. What a frightening thought! In order to calm himself he began to seek out the faces of those he had been observing since the beginning of the trip, feeling as if he had known them for many years. He had noticed the suited man getting off, but the man in the dirty coat was still present; he had claimed a whole seat to himself and was comfortably spread out on it. The serious-looking man had again opened his newspaper and plunged into it with a feeling of great contentment. And the slender boy—where had he gone? Had he gotten off already? Amazing! He was surely a strange, mixed-up boy to have jumped off before reaching Model Town. Boda began to feel guilty for having been groundlessly repulsed by the boy's anxiety. If only he had explained to the boy how far Model Town was and which street came before it, then perhaps he would not have made this mistake. The feeling of guilt, however, quickly left him. The girl with the round bottom was still sitting there, her sparkling neck clearly in view, the wall that had once been between them now gone. He took a deep, contented breath.

"Stop! Stop!" a man shouted and stood up.

The conductor scolded him, "Mister, were you sleeping? We will not halt till the next stop," and sat down on the very front seat. The confused man quickly sat down. Suddenly agitation had come over him like an earthquake and just as suddenly this despair, so that he collapsed onto his seat like a sack of flour. His sudden alarm and equally sudden despair struck Boda as remarkable and set him thinking about that thin boy who had gotten off before reaching Model Town. One had gotten off too soon, the other too late. Then there was he himself, who had gotten on the wrong bus, and the one who could not even find room to plant his feet, who had climbed on and been forced back off. Bus riders always get fouled up in some way or other. "But where am I going?" He realized that the bus had now almost reached Model Town. Just see how one impulse had taken him so far from his path! How troublesome it will be to go to Model Town and then return so late at night. He was again reminded of Khalid. All of this would be absolutely no trouble had only Khalid been still here. Khalid, Naim Patthar, and Sharif Kalia—those night-long euphoric meetings in their company. Those nights were bright as days when, far from home, free from all thoughts of having to return home, they would ramble aimlessly around the alleys and marketplaces. How quickly their gang had fallen apart. How many separate places they have now gone! Now the night was like a mountain, where to stray slightly from the path seemed like a disaster.

"Chaudhri-ji, what is that building going to be?" the man in the dirty coat asked the muscular man as he watched out the window.

"A factory."

"Sahib, many large buildings have sprung up along this road," began the serious-looking man. "Earlier this whole area lay empty."

"Khan Sahib-ji, you didn't see this place before the creation of Pakistan," said the muscular man. "It used to be a jungle. Caravans got raided in broad daylight. But once two Englishmen came to hunt. They had been shooting for a long time but the animals kept evading their bullets and getting away. Two boys were standing by. They became impatient, took the guns from the men, and in two shots downed two deer. Then you know what they did? In the capriciousness of youth, they pointed the guns at the Englishmen, who fled, tails between their legs."

"Marvelous, brother!" said the man in the dirty coat, admiration in his voice.

"It was not marvelous, Hazrat-ji," said the muscular man. "Those Englishmen were important people. Next day the foreign regiment came marching in. They scoured the jungle but could not find those boys. In anger they set fire to it. For three days it burned. Whatever stayed there got burned up. Whatever came out got riddled with bullets. It was a very dense jungle. There were many old, old trees. Everything was razed to the ground."

The man in the dirty coat sighed, "It's not good to burn old trees."

"So it was not good! For a long time afterward, the area remained barren. Even a person coming there in the daylight felt fearful."

The man in the dirty coat asked, "Have you seen Delhi?"

"No."

"I've seen it. Those incestuous English burned it badly too. There's the tomb of Hazrat Auliya Sahib.[4] It is so deserted and spooky around the tomb that everybody fears to pass by it alone at night. But, brother, I . . . yes, that gentleman Sahib has gone." He looked at the empty seat where the suited man had been sitting. "Having studied English they catch the disease of attaching *but* to everything, and I am sure he would have also said *but* to this . . . Now what was I saying? Yes, it was a Thursday, the time was past midnight, and the street was deserted. What should I see but a goat moving along ahead of me—a speckled goat with full teats. For a moment I thought I might catch it and take it home. Well, sir, the goat took a big leap like a deer and when I looked at it again it had changed into a huge dog—altogether like a bulldog. My spirit fled like a shot, but, sir, I didn't give up. I kept advancing. Then what should I see but that it had become a speckled rabbit, which ran on ahead of me for a while. Then suddenly—gone! But then it seemed as if something were following me and I said to myself, 'Buddy, that's the end of you!' But I kept on advancing as before, thinking,

'Well, friend, let's find out what will happen. Let's see who it is.' I began to look out of the corner of my eyes and what should I see but the same one following me."

"Who?"

"The same goat, Sahib!"

"The goat?"

"By God, the goat! Exactly that same speckled goat . . . hey, good prince! Stop a second at this bus stand!"

At the sound of the whistle, the bus stopped and the man in the dirty coat got off.

"Brother, next stop, too," the serious-looking man said.

Everyone was getting off. Boda ran his eyes around the bus. The muscular man, the serious-looking man, the sleeping man—indeed, the bus had become empty. What had happened to all those folk who had been fighting one another, pushing each other for just the tiniest bit of space? And the girl with the full buttocks? Her seat was empty. The bus seemed abandoned, desolate. "How short a bus trip is!" His heart cried out for all those people to come back, all those shoving, scuffling people. He remembered those anger-filled but despondent eyes of the traveler who, having climbed aboard the bus, had had to get back down. Where would he be now? Where are those folk who have gotten off, those who could never get on, and that one who was unable to find room for even his feet and had been forced off? A swarm of faces began to hover in his imagination. He had to laugh at his own inconsistent feelings—how he got upset at a crowded bus but even more so as it became empty. "But where am I going now?"

"Say, brother, can I catch a return bus?"

"You might or you might not, one can't be sure. It's well past the time for the last bus."

So it was too late! His heart began to sink. Then a dread began to envelop him and he resolved to get off at the next stop behind the serious-looking man and wait for a return bus. It was pitch black outside. The buildings stood as silently as the trees. Timidly he pulled his head inside.

When the muscular man got off at the next stop he remained visible for a little way in the light of the street lamp. Then he was lost in the darkness. At the next stop the bearded man got off and, in the same way, after being visible for a short distance in the lamplight, he too disappeared. Travelers at desolate, deserted stops individually getting down and going their separate ways. And his thoughts turned to those earlier stops where passengers got off in groups and parted like alleys from a street. Now the bus was empty and at a stop here or there a lone passenger would get off, go a short way, and be lost in the crowding darkness like a stray lamb. When a stop is deserted and passengers have to get off alone and their vacated seats are not occupied by some new people, that is the time when you know the bus is nearing the end of the line. And . . . and he looked at the empty bus and at his aching shoulder where the sleeping man's head was still resting, and for the first time he wondered where this man was going. Then a kind of suspicion flickered in his mind that perhaps this man too had gotten onto the wrong bus. He looked at the dirty head, the sweat-soaked neck, and knew that the sleeping man was a part of his aching shoulder. And he told himself, "I'll go all the way to the terminal."

Translated by Richard R. Smith

Notes

Translator's Note: I am indebted to Mr. Chima and Mrs. Marguerite Jones for their patient help in the later stages of this work.

Editor's Note: The original Urdu title, *"Ham-safar,"* rendered here as "Comrades," is more correctly, though perhaps less idiomatically, translated as "fellow traveler(s)." For greater clarity and to avoid serious confusion, Mr. Smith, the translator, has conferred a name, Boda, upon the protagonist of the story who in the original is nameless. Intizar Husain keeps him anonymous throughout, using the third-person pronoun *"vo"* instead.

1. Special train: Following the partition of India and the creation of Pakistan in 1947, special trains were run between the two countries to help transport Muslims to Pakistan and Hindus and Sikhs to India.

2. Dātā Darbār: refers to the tomb of Dātā Ganj Bakhsh in Lahore. See note on Data Sahib in "The Legs," p. 163.

3. "Boda remembered that today was Thursday." Besides participating in anniversary celebrations of saints, devotees also visit their tomb-sanctuaries regularly every Thursday, especially on the first Thursday of the month.

4. Hazrat Auliya Sahib: refers to Niẓāmu 'd-Dīn Auliyāʾ, the famous Čishtī saint who died in 1325.

The Shadow

He must be imagining, he thought, for one never heard of such a thing ever happening. He adjusted his glasses and wiped his neck dry with a handkerchief. He was already drenched in sweat and his heart pounded away, though the interval between heartbeats had become somewhat longer. He now felt ashamed of his behavior a little while ago, of how he had panicked and scuttled away—and all that because of mere doubt. Why did he have to scurry away like that? No one was after him—or was there somebody? He had committed no crime, had killed nobody—wasn't that true? Why not go back and make sure, he finally decided, to forestall any doubts.

By the time he reentered the restaurant he had overcome his trepidation, though his heart pounded a little faster and his feet felt a bit heavier. He overcame his uneasiness and walked in feeling confident. Once inside, he threw a glance at the table where he had left the man sitting a few minutes ago. But he wasn't there. Where did he vanish to? Hadn't the man just finished ordering his meal before introducing himself? In those few minutes how was it that the man had time not only to receive his food, but to finish it and leave as well? That simply was not possible. But he might also just have walked into the restroom.

He carefully chose a place next to the table and picked up the newspaper. But he was not reading it; instead, all his attention was focused on the door of the restroom, which drew sidelong glances from him every now and again. The door opened, and out came a man in a great hurry, drying his hands with a handkerchief as he walked to a table where some men sat drinking tea.

Where did that man go? He was truly perplexed. Was he a man or a shadow? He dropped the newspaper on the table and got up. As he passed by the cash register, an idea suddenly crossed his mind: Why not ask the manager? But he decided against it, thinking that he couldn't reasonably expect the manager to remember every single customer and, besides, it was hardly proper to ask about such things. God knows what he might think! He stepped out of the restaurant in a rush.

Outside at the cycle stand he let his traveling gaze hurriedly probe every single person who held a bike; then, taking a good look at the street, he set off for home, his mind totally fogged over by bewilderment.

Aren't there two people in the world with identical names?—he tried to reason with himself. Of course there are. Not just two, there can be many people with the same name. But could there be two people with the same face? That threw him into utter confusion. Once again his mind briefly stopped working. Once again the same face floated before his eyes. He had been so absorbed reading the newspaper between sips of tea that he did not have the chance to take a good look at the man. He hated nothing more than introducing himself to strangers, even when he traveled by train or sat idle in a restaurant. But when the fellow introduced himself, his ears perked up at once, for that was his own name as well. With a start he looked up at the man and went into a daze: why—even the man's face, right down to the last detail . . . his pupils began to dilate . . . he felt a cold tingle run down his spine. He shivered and walked on, taking long hurried strides. He was almost running. A thought seemed to be chasing him, although he was trying his hardest to escape it somehow.

What in the world am I running from? I haven't broken out of prison, have I? Or am I guilty of committing murder?

He slowed down a bit—by now he had begun to overcome his earlier trepidation—and thought with a cool head that maybe it was the fact of identical names that had in some bizarre way given rise to the enigma of identical faces. After all, it was not entirely impossible to conceive of two people with the same face. One man does bear resemblance to another man! At any rate, he decided with cool finality that the man certainly was not his double. If anything, his imagination was playing tricks on him.

He reached the porch and made straight for his room. Suddenly he remembered that while he was out yesterday somebody had come looking for him. He turned around midway, crossed the big room, and proceeded into the courtyard.

"Ammanji," he addressed his mother, "did someone come looking for me?"

"No."

"Who was it that came yesterday?"

"I don't know. How would I? He didn't leave his name."

"Didn't leave his name . . . all right . . ." He hesitated a bit, then asked, "What did he look like?"

"How would I know what he looked like? I didn't go out to look at him."

He became ill at ease, realizing how awkward his question sounded.

Who was he? What had he come for? Maybe he was one of his friends. But he met his friends almost every day. When he saw them yesterday, none of them said he had come to his house looking for him. Some old acquaintance then—maybe! But if all the man wanted was to see him, then it did not make much sense that he would come knocking at the door in his absence and then drop out of sight altogether. Was it a man or a shadow? He had not quite figured that out yet when it occurred to him that Misbahuddin had told him that somebody had, in fact, been looking for him all over campus two days ago. He felt inquisitive: who is this fellow anyway? And why does he keep looking for me where I'm not?

Instead of continuing toward his room, he turned and walked out of the house heading toward Misbahuddin's.

"Friend Misbahuddin! Who was looking for me the day before yesterday?"

"I don't know who; but whoever he was, he was at it for quite a while."

"Did he say what his name was?"

"Name? No, he didn't."

"Maybe you remember his face?"

"Face?" Misbahuddin looked puzzled.

"To tell you the truth, I didn't see him myself," said Misbahuddin, trying to avoid the question altogether. "You see, it happened like this: I saw Sami talking to a stranger. I didn't pay much attention. Later Sami came to me and said, 'Somebody's looking for Hasan.' I told Sami that you hadn't come to college at all that day. We searched around for the man but couldn't find him anywhere. So we went to class."

This reply didn't satisfy him at all; indeed, it only further increased his restlessness. He stood there thinking for a while and then said suddenly, "I must go now."

"What do you mean 'must go now'? You've barely arrived."

"No. I really must go. I must ask Sami."

"You are unbelievable! Look, if this man needs you, he'll find you. I wouldn't worry if I were you. I couldn't care less if someone came looking for me. My principle: if he's after you, then it is his business to find you."

"No. God knows who he is. What if there is something urgent?"

He left Misbahuddin and came straight to Sami's. "Sami Sahib!" he called out, rapping hard at the door.

From behind the door came the sound of approaching footsteps and Sami emerged.

"Oh, hi. Come on in."

He dropped all formalities and proceeded straight to the business: "I didn't come to campus the day before yesterday. Misbah told me somebody had come looking for me. Any idea who he was?"

"Yes, yes. There was this man. He looked and looked for you, but you couldn't be found. Later we heard that you hadn't turned up at all that day."

"What was the man's name?"

"Name? . . . I don't believe he gave his name."

"What did he look like?"

"What did he look like?" Sami appeared to be thinking hard.

"Was he lean and thin—like me?"

"Now that you mention it—he did look like you," Sami confirmed hurriedly.

"Did he wear glasses?"

"Glasses?" Sami, who had thought a moment ago that the matter was as good as settled, was taken off guard with this fresh inquiry. "Maybe he did, maybe not—I don't know." Then he thought of a way out. "Listen, I'm sorry. I don't remember. But I'm sure he'll come and see you at home."

"Somebody did call on me at home yesterday but I was at college. What a strange person, always looking for me when I'm not there."

"By the way, he's staying at Edward Hostel."

"Edward Hostel! You know the room number?"

The question took Sami by surprise. He didn't know what to do. "He didn't say what room he was in. You see, it's like this: I went to Misbahuddin and asked him where you were, but he said you weren't in that day, so I thought I should go and tell that man that you weren't in and ask him where he could be reached. But in the meantime he simply vanished. Anyway, during our conversation he happened to mention that he was staying in Edward Hostel. Top floor."

"Top floor! Then there is a chance . . ."

"I think he'll come to your house again soon," said Sami. "He must, if he really wants to see you."

"Yes. That's what one would think. Well, I must be getting along now." He said it with an abruptness that left Sami speechless.

By the time he left Sami he had made up his mind to go home. Whoever it was that wanted to see him would decide himself where and when. But as he walked by the bus station, he saw the bus to Edward Hostel ready to leave and he changed his mind. The bus is ready, he thought. Besides, it won't take too long. Without further thought, he dashed onto the bus.

Inside, his eyes accidentally fell on the conductor and he was a trifle surprised to notice that he had met the same conductor on his morning ride as well. Such coincidences—he rationalized, benefiting from his long experience of bus riding—were indeed common: you ran into the same conductor in the same bus in the evening as in the morning when you had started. So what is there to be surprised at? But if you saw the same passenger twice in the span of a single day riding the same bus—now that's different. The thought brought back the memory of the trip he had taken just last month. There was a man sitting next to him in the lorry. The next day he saw him again coming out of a hotel in the market. And the third day, on the ride back home, he saw him yet again, sitting comfortably in the seat behind him.

Fellow travelers come in different types, he decided. There are those whom you have never seen before and are unlikely to ever see again, but with whom you become very intimate in the course of a ride and then they are gone. But some others—you keep bumping into them all the time; still, the ice is never broken and you remain strangers. A fellow traveler has all the elements of a mystery, whether he disappears after your initial ride together or whether he appears along your path again and again.

With this thought he became aware of a profound wonderment slowly coming to life in him. Meanwhile, the bus pulled up to the Edward Hostel and he was distracted. He got off hurriedly and darted into the red brick dormitory.

He climbed up the dim stairs, thinking that the building looked quite new from the outside, but one look inside and you knew it had stood there since the time of Adam. Lost in his thoughts, he kept climbing the stairs and, absent-mindedly, got to the top of the staircase. He found himself on what appeared to be a long, wide, dark roof. His initial reaction was one of complete shock, but in just the next instant he realized his mistake. Damn it! I should have taken the first exit into the curve leading to the corridor. He hurriedly stepped back onto the stairs and began climbing down. At the first curve he got off the landing and headed down into the long corridor, which seemed strangely silent and deserted. At the other end he caught a glimpse of someone who had just cut around the curve and swiftly turned down another corridor. All he could see of the other man was his fast-disappearing back.

He began to walk the corridor, probing each door with a careful glance. The presence of so many rooms puzzled him. What room could his be? Whom shall I ask? All doors were closed. Either a room was sunk in darkness with a padlock hanging from the door, or, if not dark, its glass panes looked dim and pale as inside light filtered meekly through them; but in each case the door was shut. There was just this one room whose door stood slightly ajar. He gingerly peeked inside but couldn't see anyone as far as his eyes were able to reach.

Walking along the crossword-puzzle row of rooms, some bright, some dark, he finally came upon a room with doors fully open. The lights were on inside. A bed occupied the space near a corner with an empty chair set beside it. No one seemed to be inside. Who lives in this room? Where has he gone, leaving the doors so carelessly open? Following the curve, he suddenly thought about the man who had turned around the same curve and dropped out of sight minutes ago. Where had he gone?

He went down another corridor, as hauntingly silent and deserted as the first, with a row of rooms, some bright and bolted from inside, some dark with padlocks hanging outside their doors, rolling out into the distance. He walked the entire length of the corridor, came to its end, and stopped short before a dark stairway. It is very dark in here! And then myriad questions suddenly rattled inside his brain. Why is there no light in the stairway? Is it never used? But if it isn't, why has it been left open? Where does it lead to anyway? He spun around and walked back.

He came to the curve and turned with it, again entering the first corridor, where his eyes once more fell on the same room with its open door and its bed and empty chair. Passing beside another room that was bolted from inside he suddenly thought he heard people talking. He slowed down, and though he was unable to hear anything, he did feel that the people inside had suddenly lowered their voices, almost to an undertone. That made him walk faster. And for a moment he even felt a door was opening behind him and someone was peeking out at his receding back.

He decided his present activity was futile. He quickened his pace. A strange feeling came over him and he felt as if somebody were pursuing him, while he was frantically trying to hide himself in one room or another . . . ("The one who's after you will find you.")

Who's searching for me anyway? Who? Who is he? And who am I? . . . and that man approached the shrine and began knocking on the door. Whereupon Saint Bayazid cried out from inside, "Who are you and who is it you are looking for?" The man replied that he was looking for Bayazid.[1] "What Bayazid?" asked Saint Bayazid. "Where does he live and what does he do?" The man rapped at the door even harder as he said, "I am looking for Bayazid." And Saint Bayazid cried out with the man, "I, too, am looking for Bayazid, but I haven't found him yet." . . . He almost stumbled over the threshold of the stairway, then climbed down the stairs in a great hurry.

At some point along his downward flight he felt that all doors upstairs had been suddenly flung open, disgorging a crowd of people into the long corridor where they milled and talked at the top of their voices. The distant, vague noise arising upstairs behind him entered dimly into his mind where it spiraled and gradually became part of a fog in which lurked stories of princes who, having plucked the enchanted fruit to which they had been guided by a holy mendicant, would hear a din arising behind them and would involuntarily look back and be instantaneously transformed into stones. Can a man be turned into stone? He immediately rid himself of the insane thought.

An even greater mystery, a more profound wonder, awaited him outside the residence hall. What—night already, and so far gone? Most amazing of all was that it was still day when he had arrived at Misbahuddin's. With Misbah he had a brief, quick conversation and then he had hurried on to Sami's and had spoken fleetingly with him, rushing right away from there to the hostel. In the hostel again he had hardly spent any time at all;

he was out of it almost in an instant, but now it looked as though he had been wandering around inside for hours. How in the world did so much time pass? Why was it already so late? Did he lose his way? Where? Why was it nighttime? Or was he imagining—imagining that it was nighttime?

He took a long searching look around. There was no sign of traffic anywhere on the street as it rolled out languidly under the bright light of the lampposts into the distance. Up ahead was the bus station, its shelter plunged into darkness. Somebody inside the shelter—a suspicion arose in his heart and subsided almost as soon as his eyes penetrated the desolate darkness inside. He began to walk, thinking that it was long past the time for even the last bus and that he would have to walk back home.

A dark empty bus zoomed past him. Was it a bus—really? He was surprised. Buses usually rattled so hard and loud that you could almost hear them coming from miles away. But this one sneaked past so he could not even hear it coming. How incredibly mysterious a known, familiar bus looked with a dark interior!

That was true with most things, wasn't it? Objects—familiar and tested and seen so often—had a way of assuming a distant mysterious look in the dark. But now in the light they looked no less mysterious. He wondered how when he had stepped into the street all its lights appeared to run into one another, almost as if the light bulbs had been strung on a cord in an unbroken chain; but now as he had started to walk it was really amazing how terribly long the distance from one lamppost to the next seemed and how he had to traverse the distance between two lampposts through a veritable pool of darkness.

Then again, the distance itself from one lamppost to the next was so uneven, interspersed with so many ups and downs that the shadow moving ahead of him suddenly became darker and nearer till it came right next to him and walked along beside him all the way to the next lamppost where it suddenly dissolved into thin air to appear again soon, quite as suddenly, as he moved on to the next lamppost. Once again two dark shadows stretched out at an acute angle while he walked on, sandwiched between them from one lamppost to the other.

This second shadow—whom did it belong to? The initial surprise instantly gave way to a vague fear that ran in a wave across his whole body. A sudden, almost uncontrollable impulse made him want to look back, but he stopped short . . .

"So, *Miyan*, I set out on my own, all by myself. It must have been midnight, half the night this way and the other half that way, and the deserted street rose up to me eerily. My heart throbbed away like that." He joined his five fingers, fluttered them, and continued. "The moment I got out from under the tamarind tree, I had this feeling that somebody was following me. I looked back with a start, and lo and behold there was this man . . ."

"You don't mean that—do you?"

"By God! My heart skipped a beat and I felt I'd drop dead right there. 'Bundu boy,' I told myself, 'you're finished today.' But he came from behind and walked past me and got ahead of me, taking giant-size strides, and then, you know what? He began to stretch himself up, taller and taller and taller, until he reached all the way up to the tip of the tamarind. Oh, brother, was I scared! Right away I began to recite the *Qul* in my heart;[2] repeated it three times over and, lo and behold, the lout was gone, just like that. Believe me, he simply vanished. Such is the power of the *Qul*!" . . .

A car coming ahead of him caught him off guard. The street brightened up for a moment as the car zipped past him frantically honking the horn. Its speed irritated him and spoiled his earlier mood. Damn it! What's this, driving like a madman? Then his thoughts turned to the driver. Who was he? Despite great effort, he couldn't conjure up the driver's face. And how could he? The other man had come and gone like a shadow. An insane thought crossed his mind: maybe he drove that fast on purpose. Maybe he was afraid somebody would recognize him. Yes, that's right, he didn't want to be recognized.

Coming up to the restaurant, he took a good look at it. It was still open, though hardly any people in it. The tangled mass of bicycles he had seen earlier in the day at the stand was now gone; instead, only a single, solitary bike stood there. Oh, at least one person inside the restaurant! This thought brought a number of questions in its wake. Why is the restaurant open to serve just one customer? Who is this man in the restaurant this late at night? Does this restaurant stay open all night? He began to walk toward the restaurant but changed his mind by the time he reached the bike stand. It's late at night, he must return home. He quickly turned back.

He was once again walking, trapped between two elongated shadows. Is there a way of getting rid of these shadows? He stepped out of the street and walked on its raw, soft shoulder well beyond the lampposts. I shall walk in the darkness, for in the darkness man's shadow keeps away from him. But he could not quite rid himself of the shadows as the light from the lampposts on the opposite side still reached out to him.

Is there absolutely no way of getting away from the shadows? He thought of the body that cast no shadow at all;[3] a fragment of cloud always kept it shaded on the ground and no fly could ever alight on it. The thought had a strange influence on him: all his doubts and misgivings instantaneously vanished, leaving him very light and at ease. He perceived the sound of his own footfalls to be coming from another world, as if he had turned onto a fresh path, and his ears reverberated with the gentle music of a deep, reverential voice that chanted:

Ae khasa-e khasan-e rusul waqt-e du^c^a hai[4]

In a heron-white shirt of fine muslin, bright, fair-faced, sporting a Turkish cap—his grandfather's image sailed before his eyes. Soon after the dawn prayer, when grandfather finally began to chant hymns, his lips would quiver and his eyes would brim over, leaving his beard all drenched in tears.

This thought eased his heart somewhat. The deep, soulful cadence of his grandfather's voice returned to him, gently permeating his entire being. He lapsed into a state of religious transport, filled with an urgent desire to recite the hymn:

Ae khasa-e khasan-e rusul waqt-e duᶜa hai
saᵓe ki tarah ham pe ᶜajab waqt para hai[5]

But he checked his enthusiasm, thinking that chanting hymns so late at night would indeed be quite odd. Instead, he began to wonder about the incident that had impelled his grandfather to take up singing hymns again with such a richness of heart after so long a time. However much he strained his memory, he could not locate the incident exactly, though he did seem to remember this much—his grandfather used to recite the second line of the verse somewhat differently.[6] How differently?—he couldn't tell.

The state of religious transport he was experiencing soon faded under the conscious effort to remember. All that was left of it now was a painful awareness that pinched his heart inexorably: there was that body . . . beyond any shadow . . . and here was his own . . . nothing but a shadow, swarmed upon by countless flies, shaded by not even a shred of cloud. Shadows that we are—what body do we eventually belong to? Caravan—that has long since hurtled along its way; shadows—that still hover, dazed. What caravan could it be that has left us behind and has itself moved forward? I—a lost shadow from a caravan of lost shadows; a wave of some dark, nagging doubt—what doubt?

Of course, I *am*, but then again, I am not . . . listen, my dear, said the wise man, behind you there is a cave ablaze with fire beyond which there is a wall; a still greater and taller wall stands in front of you. Bondsmen, their hands fettered, walk on the wall that is in front of the cave ablaze with fire, while their shadows move along on the wall that is in front of you. Oh, my dear one, you are caught up in a strange predicament: you simply *cannot* turn around to see either the blazing fire or the shackled bondsmen. All you are fated to see for the rest of your life is merely the reflection of the fire and in the reflection, the shadows . . .

Seeing the bus that was coming up to him from the front, he quickly moved over to the shoulder of the street and walked on along the lampposts. As the bus, one of its headlights shattered, rolled past, he saw that the interior of the bus was pitch dark. A vague feeling that there was somebody sitting in the rear seat right by the window darted through his consciousness. Maybe it was the conductor—but why would he hide himself so? He walked some more, his mind still busy trying to unravel the mystery of the darkish lump on the rear seat. No, he decided quickly, the bus was altogether empty. And if he did see somebody, then he could be sure it was his own mind playing tricks. He was seeing things. A sudden urge made him want to turn around and see how far the bus had gone and whether it had stopped. Midway he stopped abruptly and once again continued onward, taking long, hurried strides.

Before he could enter the gate of the house himself, his shadow jumped forward and went in ahead of him. From inside the yard a dog, its tail stuck between its legs, dashed out toward the gate. Its darting shadow cut sharply across his own advancing shadow.

Coming to the veranda, he wondered if mother was still awake. If she was, he could well expect a plethora of questions. Where were you all this time? What were you doing? Have you had your supper?—and so forth.

He moved gingerly toward his room, unfastened the latch, and ducked inside without making the slightest sound.

There he found everything in quite the same mess he had left it, except for a novel that was earlier in the bookcase but now lay open, face down on the table. He itched to know who had rummaged through his books in his absence. He looked at the novel and thought of Shamim, who had a nasty habit of poking around in his books at least once a day in search of some novel. Invariably she would find one. So she had been up to it again today!

He took a look at the mirror above the fireplace. He could not see his own reflection, though he did see a few ants comfortably stuck to its bright, shiny surface. Thinking that they would mess it up with their filth, he quickly lowered the cover over it.

He changed his clothes, turned off the light, and slipped into bed. But he could not fall asleep, even though he tried very hard. He kept tossing and turning, opened his eyes, closed them, opened them a second time, closed them again, and went on until they burned, his drooping eyelids aching terribly. He opened his eyes once more. All he could see was the glass panes in the door. They rose up to him in the swooping darkness like a pair of large, dim, off-white figures. He stared at them, stared at them a second time, again a third time, thinking, wondering about what might lie behind them. Suddenly he felt he was perspiring heavily, suffocating. He got out of bed and turned on the light. The sudden change in the atmosphere of the room calmed his tired senses a bit, but he soon realized that his heart was pounding fitfully as he choked in the bright light.

On an impulse, he left the bed, changed, arranged his hair, decided there was absolutely no need to look nice, turned off the light, and slipped out of the room, closing the door behind him. He rushed to the street outside as if he had just broken out of prison. The street lay silent and deserted amid a tangled network of crisscrossing beams of light. Beyond the street lamps, straight ahead, under a tree where it was still somewhat dark, he saw a policeman standing motionless over his long bamboo club. He continued onward, feeling quite bold and confident. The cop, like a wooden toy soldier, didn't budge; in his display of confidence he walked past him with an air of supreme indifference. After he had safely crossed this hurdle, he realized to his sudden amazement that he was once again trapped between two shadows, one ahead, the other moving along behind him. He left the street and came over to the soft shoulder. I shall walk in the darkness, he thought, for it's only in darkness that one can rid oneself of shadows. In the darkness one man cannot even recognize another man. Coming into the dark he heaved a sigh of relief, feeling a strange affinity with the shadow, a strange brotherhood.

The shadow, after all, is my neighbor. But when he had made it up to the bridge, a dog jumped out from under an unharnessed carriage that stood buried in the darkness and barked ferociously at him. Right away he changed his mind about the brotherhood idea and felt that the neighbor was instead his enemy. He gave up the idea of walking in the darkness. From the whirlpool of darkness he walked straight into the whirlwind of light. But the dog kept coming after him even in the light. It simply would not stop barking, which made him move briskly onto the bright street. The dog barked even louder. Furious, he picked up a brick, spun abruptly, and hurled it at the dog, which turned around and fled into the fold of darkness. He chased the dog to the edge of light, but the dog crossed over and vanished into the other side—the dark side.

He started off again on his way, taking long strides. Just then the image of the cave spitting fire and flame came back to his mind and he felt that the shackled bondsman who went after the dog had remained behind, while he, a mere shadow of the bondsman, had come forward.

Translated by Muhammad Umar Memon

Notes

1. Saint Bayazid: He was Abū Yazīd (Bāyazīd) Ṭaifūr Ibn ᶜĪsā Ibn Surūshān al-Bisṭāmī, a celebrated Persian Ṣūfī (mystic), who died in 874.

2. *Qul* ("Say!"): There are a number of short Qur᾿ānic chapters that begin with this imperative phrase; the one intended here, however, is Chapter 112, which begins: "*Qul huva 'l-Lāhu aḥad*" ("Say! 'He is God, One'").

3. "He thought of the body that cast no shadow at all; . . .": It is

recorded in Islamic hagiographical literature that when the Prophet Muḥammad walked, his body was always shaded by a cloud overhead. Also, in the Shīᶜite tradition, an Imam should cast no shadow (see Ayoub 1978:66).

4. *Aē khāṣa-e khāṣān-e rusul waqt-e duᶜā hai*: Translation: "O the Most Elect among prophets [Muḥammad], this is the time for you to intercede [with God on behalf of the Muslims]." This is a line from the famous Urdu poem, *The Musaddas*, of Alṭāf Ḥusain Ḥālī (d. 1914).

5. *Aē khāṣa-e khāṣān-e rusul waqt-e duᶜā hai / sāʾē kī ṭaraḥ ham pe ᶜajab waqt paṛā hai:* Translation: "O the Most Elect among prophets, this is the time for you to intercede; / For strange times have come upon us like a shadow." The second line is different from the one found in the original, for which see the following note.

6. "His grandfather used to recite the second line of the verse somewhat differently": The second line reads in the original: "*ummat pe terī ā-kē ᶜajab waqt paṛā hai*" ("trying circumstances have befallen your community").

The Legs

Chuang Tzu dreamt that his form had changed. When he woke up the next morning he kept wondering if he was in fact no longer a human being. No matter how hard he tried he just could not figure out whether he was a human being or not . . .

Yasin set his whip to one side and said, "Saiyid Sahib, he was from my hometown and, that bastard, he did this to me. The rotten human race . . . how can you trust anyone nowadays?"

Saiyid Sahib could not decide what answer he should give to this question, but Yasin was not expecting one either, for he started right in again. "Sir, no matter how much and how well this mare will be trained, she still won't be the equal of my horse. Saiyid Sahib, he was one hell of a horse. Why, you could say he wasn't a horse; he was a man. So faithful." He paused and then said, "Now I'm in a fix. I told everyone that this man was from my hometown, so be nice to him. If I should accuse him of making off with my horse—how embarrassing! If I start a lawsuit, then everyone will throw dung in my face, saying, 'Yasin had his own buddy arrested.'"

The mare stopped again but this time she was not just acting up. A large tree lay fallen across the road. Yasin got down and grabbed the reins, led the animal along the shoulder of the road, and then took it back onto the pavement. Getting back into the tonga, he said, "Saiyid Sahib, that was some storm—it sure knocked down a lot of trees."

"Yes, there was much damage."

"But Saiyid Sahib," his voice dropped suddenly as though he were in awe, "the minarets of the Data Sahib also fell over. How could such a thing happen?"[1]

"Well, it was a terrible storm," he replied casually.

"There have been terrible storms before, Saiyid Sahib, and there have been floods as well. Many times the river has overflowed its banks all the way up to the foot of Data's tomb, but it never climbed past the lower steps." Yasin remained silent for a while and then said, "It's mind-boggling. I'm really confounded. Very well, O Lord," he heaved a deep sigh, "only You know the mystery of Your ways."

Yasin fell silent. Saiyid Sahib's mind began to wander . . . Data Darbar

. . . Ali ibn Usman Jullabi . . . *Kashf al-Mahjub*[2] . . . And the fakir who went to the imam, who was corrupted by worldly power and rank, and declared, "Hey, so-and-so, now is the time to die!" The imam listened and remained silent. The next day the fakir returned. The imam glowered at him and spoke up before the fakir could say anything. "Hey, so-and-so, now is the time to die!" whereupon the fakir spread his prayer rug, stretched out on it, and announced, "Here I die," and gave up the ghost.

Strange sort of fakirs they were. In crowded marketplaces they raised the cry, "I die," and they stood up and died. They died resting their heads against cobblestones, they died standing up, and they died sitting down.

"Brother, please take a passenger to Icchra," pleaded a woman.

"No." He replied with supreme indifference.

"Why not?" asked Saiyid Sahib. "You should have taken her."

"No, Saiyid Sahib." Yasin fell silent. Then he whipped the mare. The tonga sped up. "Saiyid Sahib, absolutely no female passengers in my tonga at night." He again became silent and the tonga kept racing along. "Well," he began again, "let me tell you what happened to me this one time. It was about ten at night. I was hanging around at Chauburji. I had just dozed off when the sound of anklets reached my ears. 'Where in the world can she be?' I wondered. The horse was eating its fodder when all of a sudden it raised its head and neighed loudly. Then the dogs started barking and I perked up my ears. You know Miani Sahib Road—well, the sound was coming from over there. And in the wink of an eye, with a *chum*, she was standing right in front of me. 'Let's go, coachman.' She was so beautiful, Saiyid Sahib, my heart just melted. Then all of a sudden, I glanced at her feet. Well, sir, my breath left me with a hiss. I said to myself, 'Yasin boy, you are done for!' Then I thought, 'Let God do what He will, at least I'll put up a fight.' Advancing, I grabbed her pigtail and tore off a hank of hair. Then she fell at my feet. Saiyid Sahib, you should always grab the hair of a witch in your fist. Then she becomes your slave. I buried her hair in the ground and she was completely in my power. I made great sport with her." Yasin became amused at the thought and, taking a deep breath, urged the horse vigorously. "But I made one mistake and you know what that was? What man can resist when a woman puts her head in his lap and starts to cry? So, I gave in and gave her back her hair. As soon as she got it, she vanished in the twinkling of an eye. I called out after her repeatedly, but she got clean away."

"Hey, brother, I have got to go to Icchra," a pedestrian called out as he walked along the side of the road.

"Saiyid Sahib, should I take on another passenger? It wouldn't be any bother?"

"Go ahead, take him on."

Yasin stopped the tonga, but no sooner had he stopped than he jerked the reins once again, "No, sir."

"What's the matter? Why don't you take that passenger?"

"No, sir, he'll only interrupt our conversation."

"Whatever you say."

"Saiyid Sahib, I've seen a lot of things in my time," Yasin started in again. "You see that dome in front of us? Look at it carefully sometime during the daylight. It's like a watermelon that's been opened and can be squashed with just a snap of the fingers. I've placed my *salamalaikum* upon it."

"You have placed your *salamalaikum* upon it? What does that mean?" He was very puzzled.

"Well, the matter *is* a bit confusing—indeed. It was like this, Saiyid Sahib. The passenger I had was going past the Ravi Road. Anyway, I dropped him off but en route it had started to rain. I pulled my tonga to one side and parked it under a dense tree. Lo and behold, I had no sooner gotten under that tree than a tough guy jumped down from above and landed with a thud. I said to myself, 'Yasin boy, you've run into a mugger today. Give him a run for his money.' In those days I was in the prime of my life. Jumping down from my tonga, I tangled with him. After a while I realized that he was getting taller. I was dumbfounded; he became so tall that his head towered over the treetops. I was left there wrapped around his legs, which were like a goat's."

"Goat's legs?" he asked in astonishment.

"Yes, sir, he had goat's legs. So I said to myself, 'Yasin boy, you're a goner today.' But in those days I was in great shape. Saying 'God help me,' I took him on. Neither one of us gave any ground. Finally morning came and his strength began to wane. I said to myself, 'Now is the time to finish him off.' But that tricky bastard sued for peace. 'Look, man,' he warned, 'you don't invade my turf and I won't trespass on yours.' I agreed to his terms. But when I got home and lay down on my bed, every bone in my body felt like it was ground to powder. For three days and nights I burned up with fever. And when I finally got up and hitched up my tonga again, I met a man in this very street. It was afternoon. The street was totally deserted. He said, 'Brother, I went to Ravi Road. The boss of that place sends you his *salamalaikum*.' Well, I thought for a second and then said, 'Put his *salamalaikum* on the dome of that building in front of us.' He did so and hundreds of cracks broke out on its surface with a rumbling noise. Then the man turned and took off towards Miani Sahib Road. Well, I barely escaped by the skin of my teeth. If I had accepted such a *salamalaikum*, I would have been torn to pieces."

Saiyid Sahib said nothing but he stared at Yasin from head to toe with an incredulous gaze. Still Yasin remained adamant. "Saiyid Sahib, why are you looking at me like this? That was only one of my many adventures. Why, one time I had a wrestling match with a goblin. I sure put that son-of-a-bitch in his place."

He laughed out loud at Yasin's prattling.

"You don't believe what I am saying. The thing is that in those days I was very strong and had good reason. I used to eat a pound of ground almonds every morning and exercised a lot. These days how can anyone afford to keep up his strength? Flour is selling at sixteen and a half rupees a *maund*." He paused and then said, "Saiyid Sahib, inflation has become terrible nowadays. Gram is selling at the price of wheat and wheat is selling at the price of pearls. You're on a newspaper. Why don't you write anything against it?"

"Sure we do write," he said haltingly, "but nothing ever comes of writing."

"Not even of writing?" Yasin was very surprised.

The Saiyid Sahib began to wonder himself. Nothing comes even of writing. If nothing comes of writing, then why is so much written? And if nothing were written . . .? Imagine, if absolutely nothing were written? Then what . . .?

"Saiyid Sahib, there's no joy left in living these days."

And that fakir who knocked on the door of the imam and said, "Hey, so-and-so, now is the time to die."

"Saiyid Sahib, this fellow who says all these things, is he your friend?"

"Yes."

"Is he a poet?"

"Yes, he's a very big poet, very well-known."

"But it doesn't seem like it."

"Why not?"

"Well, he assured the fellow from Jullunder that the government was his friend and that he would have them issue him a taxi license. He just keeps stringing him along but he still hasn't been granted the license. That poor wretch keeps running around after your poet friend. You must have seen him, that fellow from Jullunder. He's very poor, the wretch."

The emaciated, pathetic face of a tonga driver began to take shape in Saiyid Sahib's imagination. Disgusted with his occupation, drowning in worries about his livelihood. "Saiyid Sahib, I'm learning how to drive a taxi."

"Really?"

"Yes, I've already spoken to a taxi driver. He's going to teach me to drive in a week. Shah Sahib is friendly with the government. He'll get me a license tomorrow. The thing is this, Saiyid Sahib, there's no money in driving tongas anymore. Taxis do very well . . . these days rich passengers don't ride in tongas."

"Saiyid Sahib," Yasin raised the question once more, "is this friend of yours really on good terms with the government?"

"Yes, he must be."

"But it doesn't seem like it." He paused and spoke up again. "But if he is on good terms with them, then he would have gotten that poor fellow a license. Without contracts you can never get anything done, right? Saiyid Sahib, this fellow used to live in Jullunder. He came here on the special train during partition.[3] His whole family was slaughtered. He alone escaped. Well, since then he feels sort of lost. He tried his hand at many things, but nothing worked."

At the mention of the special train, Saiyid Sahib's mind wandered back to the days when the cities had become deserted and the clans were being dispersed. The desolate, deserted cities. The tales of the settlement and destruction of the cities of the Old Testament. The lament of the prophet Jeremiah both for those who were slain by the sword and those who died of hunger. Those who are murdered by the sword are better off than those who are murdered by starvation, who shrivel up and die because they are denied even the fruits of the earth. O Lord, remember what befell us, that only after buying our own water did we drink it.

"Saiyid Sahib, are you from Delhi?"

"No."

"Well neither am I. But I used to visit there a lot. I'm a local boy. The Great Mosque in Delhi is as strong and sturdy as an iron pillar. During the riots fanatic Sikhs tried to set fire to it. But the Mosque didn't catch fire. There was just a scar left on it. After coming here, I went to Delhi once and when I saw that scar, I started crying." Yasin's voice became hoarse. He fell silent and then asked softly, "Saiyid Sahib, can I ask you one thing? The Sikhs set fire to the Great Mosque in Delhi but who knocked down the minarets of the Data Sahib?"

Who knocked down the minarets of the Data Sahib? Strange question, that. How superstitious these people still are. While Saiyid Sahib was thinking this, the tonga circled around the Mozang checkpoint, came to a halt in front of the gaudy stalls of the *pan* sellers, and waited.

"Contractor Sahib, I've got to go, so come on!" After yelling this to the contractor, he looked in Saiyid Sahib's direction. "He's our kind of guy. Should I seat him?"

"Yes, yes, seat him."

The contractor quickly had a betel leaf prepared and popped it in his mouth, bounding into the tonga. He sat down in the front seat. The tonga was about to move when a person wearing an overcoat approached stealthily. "Icchra."

"Yes sir." The person wearing the overcoat lifted his feet self-assuredly and sat down next to Saiyid Sahib on the back seat.

"Contractor Sahib, what will Pakistan do now?" Yasin broached the question as he urged the tonga.

"What will Pakistan do? What's it doing now?"

"Sir, I would say that America has let us down. Now what will Pakistan do?"

"Well, yes." The contractor paused and cleared his throat a bit but Yasin did not wait very long for his reply.

Yasin immediately turned and addressed Saiyid Sahib. "Saiyid Sahib, you've worked on a newspaper. Please explain this. If there is a scrap between America and Russia, who would lose?"

The contractor took the responsibility of answering this question on his shoulders and said, "America would beat the hell out of them."

"Still, it makes you stop and think," Yasin said in a pessimistic way.

"Sir, I've given this a lot of thought, too. These English bastards deceive us all so cleverly that they spread dissension, and they're supposed to be on America's side."

"Contractor Sahib," Yasin voiced his own opinion with profound gravity, "I have come to realize that it is all a matter of stumbling blocks. If Russia happens upon one of America's stumbling blocks, then America will beat them to a pulp. And if . . ." Yasin cleared his throat, "America happens upon a stumbling block of Russia's, then you can be sure, Contractor Sahib, after grinding America to dust she'll blow it clean away."

It's all a matter of stumbling blocks—he thought. No one is weak, no one is strong. The question is this: who will happen upon whose stumbling block? And in whose clutches are we caught?

The mare balked as she was moving along. Yasin beat her, but instead of advancing she held her ground and began to jump as though she would soon rear up on her hind legs. Then Yasin got out of the tonga, grabbed the rein, and walked her for a short distance. Then, springing up and sitting on the shaft of the tonga, he gave her one last whipping. And the mare began to move along at her previous pace.

"Boy," the contractor said in an annoyed tone, "your horse is sure acting up a lot today."

"Sir, this is not *my* horse. My horse never acted up. This is a new mare."

"What happened to your horse?"

"What horse?" He laughed a bitter laugh. "What can I say? There was a bastard who came from Karachi, my hometown. He stayed with me for a month and then disappeared, taking my horse with him."

"That's appalling!"

"These days everything is appalling." He heaved a deep sigh. "I went to Karachi. All of my friends and relatives were there with me. I told them that back home they weren't like that, but after coming to Karachi they had fallen into the wrong way of life. They just slapped me on the head and said, 'Boy, this is Karachi, this is the Big City . . .' Contractor Sahib, I wonder what happens to people once they go to Karachi?"

The contractor stroked his beard confidently. "Don't talk of Karachi. There, anything goes."

"But Contractor Sahib," Yasin raised his now-forgotten question once again, cutting off the talk of Karachi, "let me just ask you this, who knocked down the Data Sahib's minarets?"

The contractor heaved an audible sigh and fell silent; then he bowed his head. He was reciting something to himself and a slight tremor ran through his body. Then his voice became louder, but still subdued. He was humming in a quavering, trembling voice:

Ganj Bakhsh, the benefactor of the world, the manifestation of the light of God,
The Perfect saint of the unperfected ones; the leader of the perfected ones.

And as he was humming his voice swelled in excitement. Then he became quiet again.

The tonga had passed far beyond the Mozang octroi post. Stillness and darkness pervaded all around. Here and there policemen stood, some moving slowly as though sleepwalking, others standing still and silent as though they had fallen asleep while walking. Yasin took full advantage of the quiet surroundings. Or perhaps he felt suffocated by the stillness. He thrust his whip into the rapidly turning spokes of the wheel and made a sharp clicking noise. Then, all of a sudden, he burst out singing:

The lover who has remained unloved, must, however, pray:
God, do well unto the one who has given me such heartache.[4]

The Contractor Sahib, lost in thought, perked up hearing this tune. "Hey, that's a very old record you've put on!"

Yasin bristled. "Even Lata won't be able to sing this *ghazal*, I bet.[5] If she could, I'd become her slave for life."

"Beat it!—this idle talk about Lata-Wata. You remember the Kajjan? . . ."

"Kajjan Bai?" Yasin recovered his high spirits. He got up from the shaft of the tonga and sat down on the seat alongside the contractor. "She sure was one hell of a woman. How can this Lata—the slut—compare with her? No, sir, not a chance!"

The contractor started to discuss the voice of Kajjan Bai as if he were beginning some very long story. But no sooner had he finished his first sentence than the turn-off to Icchra appeared. He quickly got out of the tonga and headed straight for the tea stall in front of them without casting a glance back at Yasin.

After dropping off the contractor, Yasin gave an inquiring look to the man clad in the overcoat, but the man just replied, "Further" and buried his face in the overcoat. Yasin picked up the reins and urged the tonga on.

Passing beyond the turn-off to Icchra, Yasin became absolutely quiet. He and the passenger wearing the overcoat had remained uncommunicative from the very start. The chill became quite pronounced and the fog, rising like cold smoke, filled the street for quite a distance.

When they had passed the Icchra police station, the man in the overcoat said in a low but commanding voice, "Stop."

As soon as the tonga stopped, he took some money out of his pocket, put it in Yasin's hand, and got down quietly. He walked a little along the road and then descended to the unpaved shoulder where it was particularly dark. He was visible walking in the darkness for a short distance and then he vanished from sight.

"Saiyid Sahib," Yasin said pensively.

"Yes?"

"Who was that man?"

"How should I know? You must know."

"I'm a bit suspicious of . . ."

"Of what?"

Yasin didn't answer the question, but raised a fresh one instead. "Saiyid Sahib, did you see his face?"

"No."

"I didn't see it either, you know."

Yasin became quiet again. The mare was moving along at a good clip. There was no need to whip her. He inquired again, "Sir, you didn't see his face at all?"

"Well, I must have seen it. But I didn't pay any attention to it."

"Neither did I. Throughout the ride he said nothing. I wonder who he was." Yasin began after a pause, "Saiyid Sahib, when he gave me the fare I saw his hand—it was as big as an elephant's ear. I was scared." His voice dropped down to a whisper, "God knows who he was." He remained silent for a long while, took a deep breath, and then said, "Saiyid Sahib, one can't trust people. One doesn't know who is what. That's why I never take on a total stranger." He paused again, then said, "I didn't pick up that woman passenger—right? The thing is, Saiyid Sahib, I absolutely never take woman passengers at night."

"Why?"

"No, Saiyid Sahib," he paused and began again, "we've fallen on evil times. Last evening, you know, I was at Macleod Road when this *sooted-*

booted gentulman came up to me. I thought to myself, 'Well, Yasin boy, you've finally got yourself a passenger.' But he asked me furtively, 'Where can I get some action around here?' At any rate, he went away. In a little while, a dead-drunk Babu Sahib came sauntering over and plopped himself down in my tonga. When I asked, 'Where to?' he just laughed and said, 'Wherever you like, buddy.' I was furious. I told him then and there, 'I don't do that kind of work. So bug off!' That bastard got down shouting obscenities at me and walked away." He fell silent, then whipped the mare hard and mumbled, "Damned rotten times we've fallen on, Saiyid Sahib. There's no fun left in driving a tonga anymore. No respect, no money, either. By God, I would never hook up my tonga again, but what else can I do? I have to feed my animal somehow. I can't let her starve."

The last sentence shook Saiyid Sahib up. His mind began to wander again: Kufa. *Kashf al-Mahjub*. Ali ibn Usman Jullabi . . . I, Ali ibn Usman Jullabi, once saw a venerable man who was among the great Sufis. Hunger had driven him out of his hermetic cell in the forest to the marketplace of Kufa. He held a bird in his hand and called out, "Is anyone there who would give me something for the sake of this bird?"

Someone asked, "Venerable old man, why do you say this?"

He sighed and answered, "O man, this is the city of Kufa.[6] How can one ask here to be given something for the sake of God?"

Yasin whipped the mare, forcefully, and began to sing again:

The lover who has remained unloved, must, however, pray:
God, do well unto the one who has given me such heartache.

Icchra with its bustling shops was left far behind. The street was deserted and rather dark. The light from the lampposts filtered dimly through the fog. A pedicab noisily pulled in from behind, moved alongside the tonga for a distance, and then left it far behind. Yasin stopped in mid-song and, facing him, said, "You know, the fourteenth century has arrived. How so? you may ask. Well, it's like this: my mother used to tell us that the sign of the fourteenth century is that cows will eat their own dung and daughters will shamelessly pick their own husbands. But nowadays matters have gotten even more out-of-hand. The other evening I was at the Bedan tonga stop. I saw a girl sitting in that no-good Bundi's tonga. What that bastard Bundi does for a living is a secret to no one. I recognized her right away. I had dropped her off at the college many times. And there she was, sitting in that bastard Bundi's tonga. I could have died, Saiyid Sahib . . ."

And that fakir lay down upon his prayer mat, closed his eyes, and proclaimed, "I have died," and he stood up and died.

"Evil days have come, Saiyid Sahib." He took a deep breath and resumed, "You can trust no one—man or woman. Any woman you see is a witch, and all those bastards out there have goat-legs."

Ignoring altogether the coachman's harangue, Saiyid Sahib asked, "Yasin Khan, you are sure that passenger on Macleod Road really asked you where he could find some action?"

"Yes, sir, I can recognize those bastards right off the bat."

"And you threw him off your tonga?"

"Absolutely."

"And, say, if . . ." he cleared his throat, laughed a bit and queried teasingly, "if I asked you the same question?"

Yasin whirled around at once and gazed at him intently. He was dumbfounded. The thought immediately occurred to Saiyid Sahib that he had really asked the question in jest and he started to laugh, but Yasin ignored his laughter and said, "Saiyid Sahib, you?"

Yasin fell silent, which made Saiyid Sahib feel as if he had put the question in all seriousness. Perspiration broke out on his forehead and neck.

"No, Saiyid Sahib," Yasin said, taking a breath, "you will never ask me that." After a pause, he continued, "No, Saiyid Sahib, please don't talk to me like that again."

A taxi emerged from the emptiness and passed alongside the tonga. Several dark, tawny complexions and one fair face came into view for an instant and then disappeared. The taxi had gone far ahead but the red taillights remained visible for a long time. The street was deserted and totally dark again. Power had just gone out, leaving the bright street lamps dead all of a sudden.

"Saiyid Sahib," Yasin spoke softly, pensively, "I'm going to sell my tonga."

"You're selling your tonga? Why?"

"I'm fed up with this line of work."

"Didn't I hear you complain about that guy from Jullunder for giving up too easily?"

"So I'm giving up too easily. That's all right. But I won't run around after a taxi license."

"Then what will you do?"

"Anything—but I won't go for tonga business again. There is no money in it these days, Saiyid Sahib." And instead of dragging out the discussion any longer, he thumped the mare and began to sing again:

The lover who has remained unloved, must, however, pray:
God, do well unto the one who has given me such heartache.

He stopped singing abruptly and asked, "Saiyid Sahib, who was that man?"

"The man in the overcoat. I just can't figure out who he was."

"He must be somebody."

"But *who*?" He wondered again, perplexed. "Men are big bastards. We don't know and haven't any idea who is what. How do you know who I really am and how do I know who you really are?"

The mare balked and halted. Yasin whipped her and cursed her but she would not budge. "Saiyid Sahib," he said, feeling fed up, "this mare just won't go any further. And I am feeling pretty down myself."

"Never mind," he said, getting off. "I can easily walk from here."

Yasin turned the tonga around and took off in the direction of Rahmanpura.

Saiyid Sahib walked on without thinking anything. Yasin's words reverberated through his head riotously, like the clatter of a rickety tonga moving along the unpaved shoulder of the road, kicking up clouds of dust that obscured the entire street. Gradually the dust settled down. Every now and then he recalled a phrase. *No, Saiyid Sahib, you will never ask me that.* And he remembered how terribly grave Yasin looked when he said that. Had he really asked Yasin this question in earnest? He began to think. Perhaps he did; why else would such a thing come to his lips? Perhaps it was just a coincidence that those words had rolled out of his mouth. For some time he puzzled over whether he had, in fact, asked that question in all seriousness or not, then decided that he had asked it purely in jest, and, becoming weary of the whole matter, he banished it from his mind.

But the thought returned in human forms: the man who asked about *the action* and went away, the drunk who got into the tonga and got down hurling insults. He wondered who these men were, and while he was thinking about them, he suddenly remembered the man in the overcoat. Who was he? The question overwhelmed him. When Yasin had raised that question, he had remained altogether unconcerned; but now it hemmed him in on all four sides.

Who was he? Saiyid Sahib tried very hard but all he could recall was that the man sat with his face buried deep in the high collar of his overcoat, so he could not catch even a glimpse of it. He marveled how in desolate wintry nights a perfect stranger shared a tonga with you and then hopped down at some turn or another and dropped out of sight—never to be seen again. Try hard as you might, you would never know whence he had come and where he had gone. "Saiyid Sahib, how do you know who I am and how do I know who you are?" "Strange, even when we think we know each other, we really don't."

As he was wondering about all this, a gentle current of doubt arose and carried his mind to the woman who stood under the streetlight and who wanted to go to Icchra: who was she? And who was the man who walked along the side of the road in darkness? He thought about Yasin's doubts, those stories he had told him. Yasin is a queer fellow. Tells such weird tales. Always says "I am *from over there*." From where? He thought about his own carelessness in never actually asking Yasin when and from what city he had come. "And since when has he become so informal with me that he waits for me in front of the restaurant precisely at quitting time and doesn't let me engage any other tonga?" He could not figure it out and wondered, "How did he get to know me? How did I get to know him?" . . . "How do you know who I am and how do I know who you are?" . . . He stopped dead in his tracks. Who am *I*?

Who am I? He felt very confused. He tried hard to determine who he was but could not. And then he suspected that he was entertaining the same sort of doubts about himself that had occurred to him about Yasin and that had occurred to Yasin about the others. In a single stroke he dispelled this doubt. He yawned and said to himself, "I am what I am! I really am!" Suddenly he realized he was making a tall claim, and just as suddenly the claim changed into a doubt-filled question, "Am I really?" This question turned another somersault and popped up, "Or am I not? Am I or am I not? If I am, why; and if no, why not? Is it possible for a man to be and not to be at the same time?" Surrounded by these questions his mind sailed back to the moment a year ago when he was thrown off his scooter on the very same street. On coming to and being told that he had fallen off the scooter, he felt very surprised for he could not remember when and how this had happened. He could not understand how one could fall off and yet not know that he had fallen off. Once again he tried hard to recall that moment shortly after his fall when upon peoples' urging, he was trying to remember how he had fallen down. Try as hard as he could to bring his fallen state to mind, not a single detail returned. It seemed, simply, that during those few moments he was not there at all, as if at first he existed and then no longer did. "But," standing in the midst of that sympathetic crowd, he thought, "but now I am!" and felt that he was, but then again, he was not. Thinking this, he feared that perhaps he wouldn't exist any more, and he summoned all his memories, his resolve, to his aid and with all his concentration tried to experience his own being. "We," he thought, "by our own thoughts experience our beings. I think; therefore, I am." How in that moment of pain he had forced himself to recollect, to bring back those memories that had taken off and flown away like birds. And he did bring them back like a coach who, catching a whimpering child, brings him back and stands him in the field, then coaxes another into submission, and then another, until all are gathered—some willingly, others by force—for the game to start. Lying in the hospital ward among the other patients, he noted with satisfaction, "Because I remember, therefore, I am." And now, walking down the half-dark, silent street, he thought, "What if I should stop thinking and suspend my memories?" And he imagined he was not thinking and that he did not exist. "Because I do not think, I do not exist."

Liberating himself from his ego, his *I-ness*, he wandered far and wide and set foot upon an unknown island and thought to himself, "The sons of Adam do not dwell here." First he saw a herd of hogs, then herds of goats came into view. He found himself in the midst of a pack of dogs. A deer, upon seeing him, wept and said in human speech, "O, ill-fated one, you've come to an island ruled over by a sorceress who has turned all men into animals. These animals you see were all human beings once, before being turned into pigs, dogs, and goats. She was especially kind to me, so she turned me into a deer."

Walking among the pigs and goats and dogs in the private chamber of the enchantress, he thought uneasily, "How long will I be able to retain my human form?"

Upon which Job said, "I swear by the Everlasting God who deprived me of my right, and by the Omnipotent Lord who changed my form, that I became a brother to serpents and an associate of the ostrich." And then Job cursed, "Let the day perish when I was born and the night in which it is said a boy was conceived." And that night Chuang Tzu dreamt that he had become a fly. When he woke up in the morning he was greatly amazed to see that he had, in fact, become a fly. And throughout the rest of his life he could not determine whether he was a man or a fly . . .

"And all those bastards out there have goat-legs."

At this recollection he returned to his *I-ness*. He remembered the man who had asked Yasin about *action* and despaired, and the man who hopped in the tonga just so it would take him *anywhere* and who then, cursing, got down. "How long," he then thought with a sadness mingled with a sense of superiority, "how long will I be able to retain my own form among them?"

That sadness, filled with superiority, comforted him greatly. Then, like someone victimized who is nevertheless able to maintain his dignity, he began to think about the mysterious travelers of the night, about those who revealed themselves in the broad day, about Yasin, about the fellow from Jullunder. And he thought about some of them with feelings of hatred and contempt, and about some others with those of compassion and fondness. And he also thought, "Because I am able to feel, therefore, I am." And then he cursed the day he was born, the living gods who had wronged him, who had changed his human form, and the serpent and the ostrich who became his brothers and his associates. And he took pity on that pathetic deer who had wept for him. "I am able to feel all this; therefore, I am!" But at that very instant his own words began to echo in his head, and also those which Yasin had spoken.

Yasin's image, staring hard at him in shock and disbelief, sailed right back to him. "No, Saiyid Sahib." He thought confusedly whether he had uttered those words, and with that thought his feelings of having been oppressed began to diminish. But he'd said all that in jest—hadn't he? In jest? But what is jest? That question confounded him totally. He could not figure out whether he had, in fact, uttered those words or not.

He kept walking along in a state of mental confusion. All this confusion was caused by that one single question: whether he had uttered those words in seriousness or in jest. Time and again he decided the words had been spoken in pure jest, but no sooner was that settled than the second, inevitable question arose: what is jest? And when do we reveal ourselves—when we are being serious or when we joke? He recalled Yasin with great envy. How in no time at all the wretch decided about things! By looking at a woman's feet or a man's legs! His questions were so simple that they became their own answers.

A dog lolling on the ground nearby stared at him with its glassy eyes. Then it got up, growled, and seemed ready to charge at him. Frightened, he backed off. Wasn't that his very own street? He got off the main road and headed for his house. He was first astounded and then angered by the fact that the mongrel saw him return home every day at the same time but suddenly today had started barking at him. He sharply reprimanded the dog and made his way toward the front door of his house. The dog backed off but then, barking, lunged forward swiftly to grab him. He stood still and rebuked the dog again. The dog retreated. He pressed forward and knocked on the door.

He went into his room and switched on the light. Several letters that had arrived that day were lying about. He opened them and began reading. The door of the room opened slowly and, startled greatly, he turned around and looked. A cat had crept in but now it stood cowering by the door, gazing intently at him with its deep blue eyes. He chased the cat away with a hiss. The cat slipped away as if it had never even been there at all. Feeling at ease, he picked up a newspaper and began to read. This morning he had only glanced at the newspaper; now that he had begun reading it, he could not be stopped. He felt drowsy and it occurred to him that after such an extraordinary day, he should get some sleep. He folded the newspaper, threw it aside, and went into the back room to change.

As he was changing in the dim light of the back room, he looked down at his bare legs and was startled. He looked down a second time. He became suspicious. But it remained merely a suspicion for he could not decide whether the legs were his own or a goat's.

Translated by Nancy D. Gross

Notes

1. Data Sahib: refers to the tomb-sanctuary of ᶜAlī Ibn ᶜU̱smān Jullābī—also Hujvīrī—commonly known as Dātā Ganj Bakhsh in South Asia, who lived in the tenth or eleventh century. The tomb is located in Lahore.

2. *Kashf al-Maḥjūb* (Uncovering of the Veiled) is a seminal Ṣūfī work by Hujvīrī, available in English translation by the famous British orientalist R. A. Nicholson.

3. Special train: See note 1 in "Comrades," p. 136.

4. "*The lover who has remained unloved,* . . .": The original Urdu couplet is: *ᶜĀshiq-e nā-murād kō lāzim hai ye duᶜā karē / jisnē diyā hai dard-e dil uskā khudā bhalā karē.*

5. Lata Mangeshkar: a celebrated female vocalist of popular Indian Hindi and Urdu movies.

6. "O man, this is the city of Kufa . . .": The allusion is to the Shīᶜite belief that the people of Kūfa (Iraq) practiced treachery vis-à-vis Imām Ḥusain, which resulted in his tragic martyrdom in 680.

The Yellow Cur

"Something like a baby fox was thrown out of his mouth. He looked at it and placed it under his foot and began to trample on it. The more he trampled, the bigger the young fox grew."

When the Shaikh concluded this holy narrative, I enquired, "O Shaikh! What is the mystery of this young fox and what secret hides behind this trampling and growing bigger?"

Shaikh Usman Kabootar then spoke, "Your headstrong, pleasure-seeking self is the young fox. The more it is trampled, the fatter that self will grow."

I then said, "O Shaikh! Do I have your permission to depart now?"

He spoke, "The permission is given." The venerable Shaikh then made a flight to the top of the tamarind tree and perched on a branch.

I then made ablutions and sat down with a pen-stand before me and some paper. "O readers! I am employing my left hand to write this account, for my right hand became a confederate with my foe and felt like writing that from which I seek refuge. The Shaikh sought refuge from his hand and called it man's enemy, though the hand is man's comrade and helper." Having listened to the Shaikh's remarks in that vein one day, I respectfully said, "O Shaikh! Interpret this fully." At this point he recounted a story of Shaikh Abu Saᶜeed, mercy of Allah on him. Here I reproduce that story:

"It was the third day of starvation in the house of Shaikh Abu Saᶜeed, mercy of Allah on him. His wife could not restrain herself any more and complained. Then Shaikh Abu Saᶜeed went out and turned to begging. As he was resolving to return home with what he had received, the police arrested him for pickpocketing and severed one of his hands as punishment. He carried that severed hand home. Thereafter he used to cry with that hand placed before him saying, 'O hand! Out of greed you begged. So you saw the end that came upon you.'"

Having listened to this story, I spoke respectfully, "O Shaikh! Do I have your permission?"

At this he became silent for a while and then said, "O Abul Qasim Khizari! Words are the *Confession of Faith* and writing is devotion. So make the ablution and kneel and sit on your heels and write what you hear." Then he recited this verse from the Holy Word:

> *So woe to them for that which they wrote with their hands and woe to them for that which they earn thereby.*

I enquired, "O Shaikh! Why did you recite this verse and why did you become sad after reciting?" At this he drew a deep sigh and recounted the story of Ahmad Hajari, which I reproduce exactly as I heard it:

"Ahmad Hajari was a great poet of his times. However, at a certain time poets in his town became too many. The distinction of the meritorious and the meritless among them vanished. Every poet began to brag that he was a peer of Anwari and Khaqani.[1] Finding things this way, Ahmad Hajari gave up composing verse and took to selling wine. He bought a donkey on which to carry the wine jars to the bazaar for sale. Wherever he passed, people lifted their fingers at him saying, 'Ahmad went astray. He has become a trader of wine and has walked out on the sanctuary of verse.' He paid no heed to people's criticism and clung to his new occupation. However, one day it so happened that the donkey turned to look at the Shaikh and recited a couplet employing the rhetorical artifice of concurrence of words with similar consonantal arrangement. The theme of the verse was this: 'Ahmad says to me, "Go," and Ahmad says to me, "Don't go."' Hearing this, Ahmad Hajari tore his collar and, heaving a sigh, said, 'Woe to these times in which donkeys extemporize poetry.' With this utterance Ahmad Hajari became tongue-tied and, freeing the donkey, he drove him off toward the town and himself withdrew into the mountains. There in a state of insanity he addressed trees and made inscriptions on the rocks with his nails."

After narrating this story the Shaikh became silent and sat with his head downcast. Then I spoke respectfully, "O Shaikh! Do the trees have the ability to speak while they are in fact helpless creatures?"

He lifted his head to look at me and said, "The tongue is never without utterance. The utterance is never without listeners. The listener of utterance is man. But when man loses his ability to hear, the faculty of hearing is bestowed upon those creatures who are initially created without that faculty. For utterance is never left without listeners." Then the Shaikh narrated the story of Saiyid Ali al-Jazaʾiri. Here it is:

"Saiyid Ali al-Jazaʾiri was a fiery orator of great renown in his time. However, there came a time when he renounced his oratory completely and locked his tongue. This spread unrest among people and when this unrest grew, they came to him and respectfully petitioned thus: 'For God's sake, address us.' He said, 'All right. Set up my pulpit in the cemetery.' People were surprised at this wish. Anyway, the pulpit was placed in the cemetery.

He went there and, ascending the pulpit, he gave an eloquent sermon. This caused an amazing phenomenon: voices arose from the graves sending benediction on the Prophet. Thereupon Saiyid Ali al-Jazaʾiri spoke with a choked voice, facing the town, 'O town! Mercy of God on you. The living ones abiding in you have become deaf and the dead ones have received the gift of the ability to hear.' Having said this, he wept so much that his beard dripped with his tears. After that, he withdrew from men and began to live in the graveyard where he started giving sermons to the community of the deceased."

Having heard this story I enquired, "O Shaikh! When does the hearing faculty become lost to the living ones and when do the dead ones receive the gift of ears?"

At this he heaved a deep sigh and said, "These are matters that God wishes to keep secret. His servants are not permitted by Him to divulge them." Then with a flutter of his wings the Shaikh flew to the top of the tamarind tree and perched there. May it be known that Shaikh Usman Kabootar used to fly like a bird, and in the compound of the house where he lived there stood a tamarind tree. Whether winter, summer, or the monsoon months, the Shaikh held his assembly of holy remembrance right under this tree. He abstained from sitting under a constructed roof. He used to say, "I am being suffocated under one roof already. Where is the strength to bear the oppression of a second roof?" One day the Shaikh's speech brought such ecstasy on Saiyid Razi that he demolished his own dwelling, and wearing a cloak of sackcloth he came to live under the tamarind tree. Saiyid Razi, Abu Muslim Baghdadi, Shaikh Hamza, Abu Jaᶜfar Shirazi, Habib Ibn Yahya Tirmizi, and this humble servant were the poor disciples of the Shaikh. Excepting myself, these disciples were men of clean hearts, and renunciation and poverty were their cherished path. Shaikh Hamza lived as a celibate and dwelled in a house with no roof. The Shaikh's way had made a deep impression on him and he used to say, "There is only one roof and that belongs to the Sovereign God who is without partner. It does not behoove his servants to construct another roof to screen us away from the first roof."

Abu Muslim Baghdadi's father was a man of prominent social position. But the son left the home severing his relations with his father and settled here under the tree. He used to say, "Social position is a curtain that hides away reality."

One day Abu Jaᶜfar Shirazi in the course of holy remembrance tore his dress and reduced it to tatters and burnt his mat saying, "The mat is a wall between clay and clay and dress involves preference of clay over clay." From that day on he dwelt on roofless ground in the nude. Our Shaikh, whose divan was bare earth itself and whose pillow was a brick, sat always reclining against the tamarind tree. He had risen above this lower world.

While making holy remembrance he often flew and perched on the wall of the tamarind tree. Sometimes he soared high and disappeared in the atmosphere.

One day I enquired, "O Shaikh! How did you acquire this ability to fly?"

He replied, "The self-seeker in you is worldly greed."

I said respectfully, "What is the self-seeker?" At this he recounted the following story:

"One day Shaikh Abul Abbas Ashqani entered his home and was surprised to find a yellow cur asleep in his bed. He reckoned that this was some neighborhood dog that had strayed into the house. He tried to drive it out, but the dog vanished, penetrating into the Shaikh's garments."

Having listened to this story, I said respectfully, "Oh Shaikh! What is the truth about the yellow cur?"

He answered, "The yellow cur is the self-seeker in you."

I enquired, "O Shaikh! What is the self-seeker?"

He replied, "The self-seeker is worldly greed."

I asked, "What is worldly greed, O Shaikh?"

He replied, "Worldly greed is degradation."

I asked, "What is degradation, O Shaikh?"

He answered, "Degradation is the dearth of knowledge."

I said, "O Shaikh! This calls for exegesis." The venerable Shaikh accordingly narrated a story, which I reproduce:

"A very long time ago there was a king who was widely reputed for his generosity. One day a man known as a wise man presented himself at the court and respectfully made the petition, 'Your Majesty! Wise men too deserve being appreciated.' The king gave him robes of honor and sixty gold *dinars* and allowed him to depart with all dignity. The news of this spread. Another man who reckoned himself wise made his way to the court and returned with his wishes fulfilled. Then a third man who believed himself to be of the class of wise men went to the court and returned with robes of honor. And then it became a regular chain of men considering themselves wise until the court swarmed with them and all of them left with gifts.

"The vizier of this king was a very prudent man. Watching this crowd of wise men, one day he drew a deep sigh in the presence of the king, who was holding court. The king looked at him and asked, 'Why did you sigh deeply?' With folded hands the vizier said respectfully, 'Your Majesty! I shall talk but first grant me immunity of life.' The king said, 'Immunity is granted.' Then the vizier submitted respectfully, 'O Master of Favors! Your Kingdom is devoid of wise men.' The king said, 'How extremely amazing! You see wise men pouring in here every day and receiving gifts. And yet you say that.' The prudent vizier then spoke thus, 'O Master of Favors! It is the same with donkeys and wise men: wherever without exception all assembled are donkeys, none of them is considered a donkey. And wherever all men come forward as wise men, no wise man remains.'"

After listening to this story I asked, "When do all men come forward as wise men so that no wise man remains?"

The Shaikh revealed, "When ignorant ones are accepted as learned men and learned men are considered ignorant."

I enquired, "When are ignorant ones accepted as learned and the learned considered ignorant?" The Shaikh answered this by telling a story, which is as follows:

"A reputed scholar was oppressed much by poverty. Hence he decided to migrate to another town. A venerable citizen lived in this other town. He gave the news to the dignitaries of his town that on such-and-such a day, at such-and-such an hour, a scholar would arrive in the town who should be offered hospitality. Having announced this, the venerable citizen himself departed on a journey. The dignitaries of the town came to the harbor at the stated hour. Promptly a ship arrived and anchored. The scholar already mentioned was a passenger on it. However, a cobbler had shared the voyage with the scholar. This cobbler was dishonest and lazy. Finding the scholar to be gullible, the cobbler loaded him with all his professional baggage and the cobbler himself assumed a burdenless air. When both of them disembarked, one of them was clad in sackcloth, the cobbler's paraphernalia loaded upon him. No one took any notice of the scholar, and all received the other one with honor and escorted him.

"When the venerable citizen who had gone away returned from his journey, he saw a man by the roadside with the radiance of learning and wisdom on his face, occupied in mending torn shoes. At some distance ahead he saw an impressive assembly of the leading people of the town being addressed by a senseless fool on important questions. The venerable citizen trembled from head to foot at this sight and spoke thus: 'Woe to you, O city! You turn the learned men into cobblers and cobblers into learned men.' Then he went and purchased the tools of a cobbler and squatted in an alley close to where the learned man sat and, like him, began to mend shoes."

I listened to this story and enquired, "O Shaikh! What are the credentials of a true scholar?"

The Shaikh replied, "He should be without greed."

I respectfully asked, "When is worldly greed born?"

He enlightened me, "When knowledge becomes scant."

I respectfully said, "When does knowledge become scant?"

He answered, "When the dervish spreads the hand of beggary, the poet conceives worldly motives, the man of ecstasy turns sober, the scholar becomes a merchant, the wise man starts profiteering." Right then a man passed chanting this verse:

In Damascus such a famine befell.
Dismissed was every romantic spell.

The Shaikh shouted, saying to the man, "Whoever you are, will you recite this verse again?" The man recited the verse again. This brought a state of inspired meditation on the Shaikh. At last when he lifted his head, he narrated the following story:

"In a certain town there was a benefactor much celebrated for his generous giving. In the same town lived four individuals, one of them a dervish, another a poet, the third a scholar, and the fourth a wise man. At one time poverty so befell the dervish that for three consecutive days he starved. He went then to the benefactor and begged. The benefactor filled the beggar's bag with abundant gifts. The scholar's wife, finding the dervish prosperous, began to taunt her husband, 'What good is your learning? That dervish is better off. The benefactor has filled his bag with riches.' Then the scholar also went and begged at the benefactor's door. The latter bestowed plenty of gifts on this man too. The wise man was under heavy debts in those days. When he saw the dervish and scholar return with gifts from the benefactor he too arrived there and stated his exigency. The benefactor bestowed rich robes on him and let him depart honorably. When the poet heard these accounts, he complained against the times saying that appreciation of poetry had died. He went and recited his verses to the benefactor and sought a reward. The benefactor was pleased by the poetry and filled the poet's mouth with pearls.

"The dervish, holding with frugality whatever he had received to avoid the recurrence of starvation, became a miser. The scholar saved part of the riches he had received and with it purchased some camels and a little merchandise, and headed in the company of merchants for *Isfahan nisf-e jahan.*[2] He made profits from the trip. So he purchased more camels and more merchandise, and started toward Khurasan. The wise man gained much experience in the skill of money lending and began to lend money usuriously. The poet turned out to be very lazy. He didn't do any more than write some more verses, some in praise of benefactors and some by way of complaint to them. And so he got more rewards. In this way the dervish, the scholar, the wise man, and the poet, all four, became well-to-do. However, after this, the dignity of the dervish, the learning of the scholar, the wisdom of the wise man, and the ecstasy of the poet's poetry were lost."

After narrating this story the Shaikh paused and then resumed, saying, "The venerable Shaikh Sa^cdi as well as I, Shaikh Usman Kabootar, was right in saying that amorous romance was dismissed in Damascus just the same during prosperity as during famine." Then he just hummed Shaikh Sa^cdi's verse and did not talk any more that day. Let it be known that our Shaikh's disposition was tender and his heart filled with sympathetic grief.

Hearing a verse always gave him religious transport. When deeply touched, he cried from emotion and tore the side of the garment he wore. Now I shall tell you about the last time in his life he heard a verse:

That day he was in a state of restlessness that had started during the night. Vigil was his established habit. This particular night he had not slept even a moment. When I entreated, he spoke the worthy words, "Sleep is not for journeymen." Then he became immersed in uttering the rosary for the glory of Allah and professing His exclusive Divinity. While the day had not yet fully dawned and he had completed the obligatory part of the dawn prayer, a fakir went by chanting in a touching voice:

Before the givers the palm of greed I cannot spread.
That hand, the pillow, had gone to sleep beneath my head.

Choking emotion took hold of the Shaikh and he spoke these worthy words: "Whoever you are, O reciter, recite this verse again." The man recited the verse again. The Shaikh's heart was seized with grief and in a voice filled with anguish he spoke, "Woe to these hands for what they sought and woe to these hands for what they bought." Then he looked at his hand and addressed it, saying, "O my hand! Be witness that Shaikh Usman Kabootar preserved you from dishonor."

The fakir, whom we had never before seen nor heard mentioned, came inside and spoke thus to the Shaikh, "O Usman! Now death should come, for the hands have become beggars."

The holy Shaikh wept at this and spoke with worthy words, "I am dead." Then he placed his head on the brick and pulling the sheet over himself became motionless.

The fakir went away in the direction whence he had come and I sat by the side of the Shaikh, confused and anxious. I lifted a corner of the sheet. Suddenly a white pigeon fluttered and emerged from beneath the sheet and in a twinkling soared high into the sky and vanished. Lifting a corner of the sheet, I cast a glance at the blessed face of the Shaikh. On it at this time was wonderfully holy splendor. He seemed asleep. I was overcome by choking grief and burst into such weeping that in the end I fainted.

The blessed union of the Shaikh's soul with the Divine affected me strangely; I shut myself in my cell. My heart felt repulsed by the world and the desire for the company of fellow men was gone without a trace. I cannot even recall how many days I remained confined in the cell. One night in a dream I saw the Shaikh's ennobling presence approach me, may God fill his grave with light. The holy Shaikh lifted his head to look above and I saw the ceiling of the cell subside and the sky begin to show through. I believed this dream to be a guidance and next morning quit the cell to come out in the open.

Heaven knows how many days I had remained in the cell. Now outside, I felt that the whole world had changed. I went to the bazaar and found splendor there that I had never seen before. All kinds of shops, orderly and spotless; moneychangers in an endless row; transactions of commodities in the hundreds of rupees made every minute; merchants the veritable lords of the place; a whole river of wealth flowing. I rubbed my eyes for certitude of vision wondering if it were a world of dreams or wakefulness, if it were the same old town or some new one. Then it occurred to me to visit my co-disciples and investigate with their help the truth of these incredible developments. First I secured the address of the home-destroyer and renouncer Saiyid Razi. After much searching I came to a street filled with fragrance and beheld a palace erect and grand. People said this flourishing mansion indeed belongs to Saiyid Razi. I looked at the palace and shouted, "I swear by God, O people! You lie to me. Saiyid Razi cannot build a home." I left the place and went on. I acquired the address of Abu Muslim Baghdadi. A man in the street led me to the palatial mansion that was the residence of the Qazi of the town and told me that this was where Abu Muslim Baghdadi lived. I looked at this grand mansion and was startled by the thought that Abu Muslim Baghdadi had accepted an office in the government. I went ahead and got Shaikh Hamza's address. And lo! Again I found myself standing in front of a mansion. I said to myself, "By God! Shaikh Hamza has shut himself under a ceiling and has become distant from me." I proceeded further and enquired about the address of Abu Ja^{c}far Shirazi. At this a man escorted me to a jeweller's shop where, clad in a silken costume, Abu Ja^{c}far Shirazi sat reclining against a huge pillow with a comely lad waving a fan over his head. Seeing this I shouted, "O Abu Ja^{c}far! Clay parted from clay." Without waiting for a reply from him I turned away and left. As I walked in the street, I encountered Saiyid Razi, who was clad in silk, walking with pomp surrounded by his retinue of slaves. I lost my patience. I advanced toward him and lifted the heavy skirt of his splendid cloak and said, "O the one who is a memorial to the revered ancestors! O chief of the holy descendants of the Prophet! You clad yourself in silk, forsaking the sackcloth." This embarrassed him and I started on my way back to my cell, weeping. And I wept for a long time and said to myself, "By God! I am left alone."

The next day I went to the holy shrine of the Shaikh as a devotee. There I found Habib Ibn Yahya Tirmizi sitting on sackcloth wearing only the coarse wool of dervishes. I sat near him and said, "O Habib! You saw how the world has changed, and how the friends have forgotten the teachings of the Shaikh, and how they have strayed from their disciplined path!"

Hearing my words he showed signs of sorrow on his face and, heaving a deep sigh, replied, "No doubt the world has changed, and the friends have forgotten the teachings of the Shaikh, and have strayed from the disciplined path."

I then spoke, "Death to the slave of *dinar* and death to the slave of *dirham*."

The same day a messenger of Abu Muslim Baghdadi came to me to say, "Come. Your old friend is calling you." I went there and found Habib Ibn Yahya Tirmizi in the company of Abu Muslim.

With a frown on his face, Abu Muslim said to me, "O Abul Qasim Khizari! You declared us to be deviators from the path of the Shaikh! And you shouted the slogans of death to this man and death to that man!"

At this I cast an angry glance at Habib Ibn Yahya and then, looking straight into the eyes of Abu Muslim Baghdadi, I said, "O Abu Muslim! Will you keep me from declaring that which the Prophet himself declared and that which the Shaikh repeated in his devotions?" Then I recited the full text of the holy tradition transmitted from the Prophet, "Death to the slave of *dinar* and death to the slave of *dirham* and death to the slave of black wool and to the slave of torn garments." And in the meantime a dining-cloth was spread on the floor and a whole variety of foods was arrayed.

Abu Muslim Baghdadi said, "O friend! Take some nourishment from the food."

I contented myself with a drink of cold water and said, "O Abu Muslim Baghdadi! The world is day and we must fast in it until sunset."

Abu Muslim wept hearing this and said, "You spoke the truth, O Abul Qasim." Then he took nourishment from the meal. Habib Ibn Yahya Tirmizi too wept at my words and he too ate to the point of perfect satiation. When the dining-cloth was folded up, the floor was taken over by a dancing girl appearing in the midst of a troop of slave girls.

I got up to depart. Abu Muslim Baghdadi said with insistence, "Stay on, O companion."

I answered, "O Abu Muslim Baghdadi! The world is day and we must fast in it until sunset." I came away from there. The rhythmic thump of the dancing girl's footsteps and the jingling of her anklets chased me, but I stuck my fingers in my ears and went on in my flight from her.

When I stepped into my cell, something clammy leapt out of my gullet and then out of my mouth and into the open. I lit the lamp and searched every corner of the cell. But I found nothing. I said to myself, "Surely it was my fancy," and I lay on the mat and went to sleep.

Next morning when I got up I went first to Habib Ibn Yahya Tirmizi and found a yellow cur asleep on his mat. I said, "O son of Yahya! You gave yourself up to greed and lust and have turned into a hypocrite."

At this he wept and said, "By God! I am still a fellow journeyman of yours and I go to the friends to remind them of the path of our Shaikh." Thereupon I saw believers of the Shaikh's spiritual powers placing offerings of gold and silver on his grave—may God fill that grave with light.

I warned, "O son of Yahya! Woe to you! You make the Shaikh a money-man after his union with the Divine. What do you do with this gold and silver?"

At this Habib Ibn Yahya Tirmizi wept again and answered, "By God! These offerings of gold and silver are divided equally among Saiyid Razi, Abu Ja^cfar Shirazi, Shaikh Hamza, and myself. As for my own share, I distribute it among humble destitutes and consider the sackcloth my share."

I got up and left and proceeded until I came in front of the palace of Saiyid Razi. I saw a big yellow dog standing at the gate: the same yellow dog I saw standing in front of the mansion occupied by Shaikh Hamza and later asleep on the wide couch of Abu Ja^cfar Shirazi. I was to see it once again, this time before the palatial residence of Abu Muslim Baghdadi where it stood with an upright tail, and I said, "O Shaikh! Your disciples have accepted the protection of the yellow dog." That night again I went into the mansion of Abu Muslim Baghdadi and when inside I asked myself, "O Abul Qasim! Why have you come here?" Abul Qasim said to me, "To invite Abu Muslim Baghdadi to the path of the Shaikh."

That night too I found Habib Ibn Yahya Tirmizi at the meal laid out in the house of Abu Muslim Baghdadi. Abu Muslim Baghdadi said to me, "O fellow journeyman! Partake of the food."

I contented myself with a drink of cold water and said, "O Abu Muslim, the world is day and we must fast in it until sunset."

Abu Muslim Baghdadi wept and replied, "You speak the truth, my companion!" Then he partook of the repast and Habib Ibn Yahya Tirmizi also ate to the point of full satiation. Then, as the dancing girl came, I repeated my words of excuse and got up. The rhythmic thump of her feet and the jingle of the anklets chased me into the distance. But I stopped my ears with my fingers and went on.

The third day I strolled again around the town and there was not the slightest change in the spectacles of the previous two days. At nightfall I found myself standing again at the door of Abu Muslim Baghdadi. I knew that I had come to remind Abu Muslim Baghdadi of the Shaikh's teachings. So I did not ask myself why I was there and went inside. As before, Habib Ibn Yahya Tirmizi was there at the meal. Abu Muslim Baghdadi said to me, "O fellow journeyman! Have some food." This was my third day of fasting and among the dishes on the dining-cloth was saffroned pilaf, that had been my relished dish at one time.

I took a morsel from it and withdrew drinking cold water after it and said, "The world is day and we must fast in it until sunset."

That night Abu Muslim Baghdadi did not weep at my remark: rather he heaved a sigh of relief and said, "O fellow journeyman! You spoke the truth." Then the dancing girl came. I took a glimpse of her; there she was, her face blazing red, her eyes little cups of wine, her breasts taut and her thighs full and plump, her belly a chiseled plate made of sandalwood, her navel looking like a miniature cup, the thin fabric of her costume readily disclosing the sandalwood plate, the miniature cup, and the silvery thighs. I felt as if I had taken another morsel of saffroned pilaf, and all the joints of my body began to moan under the sensation, and my hands were on the verge of losing control. At this juncture I recalled the worthy words of the Shaikh about hands, and in a state of alarm I got up. Abu Muslim Baghdadi did not persist in asking me to stay for dinner and the rhythmic thump of the concubine's feet and the jingle of her anklets chased me into the distance giving me a sweet sensation.

When I got home and stepped into my cell, I saw a yellow dog asleep on my mat of sackcloth. One look at the dog and I became petrified, and I broke out into a sweat. I hit the dog then, but instead of fleeing it plunged into the side of my garment and disappeared. At this, fears and evil doubts took me into their fold. My sleep vanished and my peace of mind was banished. I cried, "Mercy on me, my God! For my heart has become afflicted by contamination and the yellow dog has gotten inside me." I wept and made supplication, but my heart remained restless. Suddenly I recalled Abu Ali Rudbari, may God be pleased with him; he too had at one time suffered from the illness of evil doubts. Early one day he went to the river bank and stayed there until sunrise. In this while his heart became sad and troubled. He prayed: "O my God! Comfort me." The angel of inspiration called out from the river: "Comfort is in knowledge." At the recollection of this I said to myself, "O Abul Qasim Khizari! Depart from here, for inside you and outside you dogs have appeared and your comfort is wrested from you."

I looked at my cell for the last time and at the rare books of logic and jurisprudence which I had collected by hard efforts of many years. I abandoned all of it and left the town carrying under my arm only the written record of the worthy discourses of the Shaikh. The soil of the town withheld my feet and the alleys which had kissed the feet of my Shaikh beckoned me. Hearing these summons, I wept, saying, "O Shaikh! Your town is all shut away by ceilings. The sky has become remote and your fellow journeymen have become fugitives who turn away from you. Opposite the peerless and partnerless ceiling of the heavens, they have raised ceilings of their own, and they have separated clay from clay. The yellow dog has received honors and has become the most superior clay. Your town has shrunk for me, so I am quitting it." Having said this, I strengthened my heart and went on my way.

I walked ceaselessly until I was far, far away from my town and was breathless, my feet all blistered. But then all of a sudden something rushed from my gullet and fell forth through my mouth down at my feet. I looked at my feet and was astonished to see a baby fox rolling over my feet. I tried to crush the animal by trampling it, but it swelled and became fat. Again I trampled it over and over again, and it got fat and swelled until it turned into the yellow dog. I kicked the yellow dog with all the force I could muster and trampled it with a frenzy and then went on. And then I said, "By God! I have trampled *my* yellow dog." And I went on until my blisters were shredded and bruised and turned into sores, and my toes became wounded, and my soles blood-drenched. But then it so happened that the yellow dog I had trampled emerged from God knows where and blocked my way. I fought with it and exerted heavily to drive it off, but it did not budge an inch. I became exhausted and shrunken, while the yellow dog became swollen and enlarged. I cried for help at the door of the heavenly resort of the Lord Almighty: "O Sustainer! Man shrank while the yellow dog swelled." Once more I tried to trample the dog, but clinging to the folds of my dress it disappeared. I looked at my torn toes, my blood-smeared soles, and the blisters there that had turned into wounds. I wept at my plight, wishing I had not quit the town of the Shaikh to migrate. At this time my thoughts drifted in another direction; I recalled saffroned pilaf with its inviting aroma, and entertained a reverie filled with images of the sandalwood plate and the miniature cup and the showers of gold and silver on the holy grave of the Shaikh. I felt convinced that the disciples of the Shaikh had indeed strayed from his teachings while Habib Ibn Yahya Tirmizi had adopted the path of hypocrisy. My thoughts turned then to my possession of the written record of the Shaikh's discourses and it occurred to me that I should return to the town and revise the written record and polish the versions to make them cherished by people and loved by friends and take steps to have the book printed; in short, I should write a biography of the Shaikh in a form both acceptable and pleasing to the fellow journeymen. But suddenly I recalled the worthy words of the Shaikh about hands being the foes of man and I thought that my hands would act with hostility toward me. That night, when I decided to retire for sleep, lo, the yellow dog appeared again asleep on my mat. I hit the yellow dog then and scuffled with it to drive it off my mat. All night long the yellow dog and I fought. Now I would trample it making it shrink while I grew bigger and now it would get up and swell while I shrank. This went on until dawn and the strength of the dog declined and it plunged into the folds of my garment and disappeared.

From that time until now the battle between the yellow dog and myself has been incessant. The various phases and subtle details of this struggle are countless, and I omit them for fear of unduly lengthening this narrative. Sometimes the yellow dog subdues me, and sometimes I subdue it.

Sometimes I grow large, and the yellow dog gets ground by my feet and is reduced to the semblance of a baby fox. Sometimes the dog goes on swelling while I go on shrinking and I am disturbed by the thoughts of the aroma of saffroned pilaf, the sandalwood plate, and the miniature cup. The yellow dog declares that when all men become yellow dogs, to remain men is worse than being dogs. I cry aloud for help at such times, "O Sustainer! How long shall I wander far from the descendants of Adam, taking shelter under trees and having no more than half-ripe fruits to eat and a coarse mat of sackcloth to rest on!" My feet start moving in the direction of the town, but the enlightening words of the Shaikh come back to my mind, "The retreating feet are the foes of the devotee." I then punish my feet by walking with my back toward the town until my feet welter in blood. Then I punish my hands by picking rugged stones off the path. "O Lord of Might! I have punished my foes so much that my soles have become smeared in blood, and my fingertips have become bruised and blistered while picking rough stones, my skin has turned black from the burning sun, and my bones have begun to melt. O Lord of Might! My sleep has been reduced to ashes, and my days have become ruins; the world has become a scorching day for me, and I am there in it as an observer of fast, and the fast is growing longer and longer. The fast has emaciated me, while the yellow dog is stronger and stout, and at night it rests on my mat. My repose is gone, and my mat has passed into the possession of an alien; the yellow dog has grown in status while man has become degraded." At this time I again recalled Abu Ali Rudbari, may God be pleased with him. I knelt and sat on my heels on the riverbank. My heart was flooding with unreleased emotion of grief. I wept, crying, "Great God! Comfort me, comfort me, comfort me, comfort me." All night I wept and kept looking at the river, and all night a strong dusty wind blew amid yellow leaves, and leaves fell from the trees all night. Turning my eyes from the river, I looked at my dust-covered body and the heaps of yellow leaves surrounding me and I said, "These are my appetites and unfulfilled desires. By God I have been cleansed of pollutions and I have become a nude autumn tree." But when the dawn came, I felt some sweet sap circulating in my finger joints, as if they had come into touch with the sandalwood plate, the golden miniature cup, and the soft moonlike thighs, as if my fingers were fondling gold and silver and *dirhams* and *dinars* were jingling in their midst. I opened my eyes and beheld a horrid spectacle: the yellow dog stood with its raised tail in such a posture that its rear legs were planted on the town and its front legs on my mat, while its wet twitching nostrils touched the fingers of my right hand. I looked at my right hand as if it were lying there severed from me like the hands of Abu Saᶜeed, mercy of God on him. I addressed it saying, "O my hand! O my comrade! You became an ally of my foe." I shut my eyes and beseechingly prayed once again, "Great God! Comfort me, comfort me, comfort me!"

Translated by Daud Rahbar

Notes

1. Anvarī and Khāqānī: two celebrated masters of Persian panegyric verse; they flourished in the second half of the twelfth century.

2. "*Iṣfahān niṣf-e jahān*": "Isfahan is half the world"—one who has seen it has seen half of the world.

The Lost Ones

His wounded head resting against the tree trunk, the man opened his eyes slightly and asked, "Have we come out of it?"

"God be praised! We *have*. Safe and sound," the bearded man answered in a perfectly calm voice.

The man with a bag hanging around his neck nodded, "Yes, at last we've saved ourselves." He looked at the bandaged head of his wounded companion and inquired, "How's your wound now?"

"Oh, I guess it's still bleeding a bit," replied the wounded man.

"Don't worry, my dear," consoled the bearded man, his voice maintaining its earlier calm. "God willing, the wound'll heal up soon."

The wounded man opened his eyes wide and looked at them one by one. Then, as if assailed by a sudden doubt, he raised his finger and began counting each one of them—the bearded man, the man with the bag, and the youth. He became confused and asked, "Where is the other?"

"What?" the youth started, "you mean we're short one man?"

The bearded man gave the youth an angry look, then turned to the wounded man and chided him gently, "Friend! We are already too few. How is it that you counted wrong?"

The man with the bag appeared to endorse what the bearded man had just said, and with great confidence proceeded to count himself. He counted the bearded man, the wounded man, and the youth; then he too was taken aback. "There's a man missing. Where is he?" he asked.

The youth looked apprehensively at the man with the bag and decided to count again to make sure. He counted the bearded man, the man with the bag, and the wounded man. He too was perplexed. He began all over again. No luck. He counted the lot of them a third time, very carefully indeed, only to feel helpless and mystified yet again. "Strange . . ." he spoke under his breath.

All four looked at each other in disbelief; they were visibly upset and, by now, rather frightened. A single word, "strange," simultaneously escaped their lips in a whisper. Then they fell silent.

There was a long silence, which was broken only when they heard the sound of a dog barking somewhere in the distance. The youth looked up at the others with foreboding. "Where's that dog barking?" he asked in a low voice.

The bearded man summoned his strength and declared, "There has to be someone around. Why else would the dog bark so?"

"Who could that be?" the man with the wounded head asked indifferently.

"Him—of course. Who else?" replied the bearded man confidently and in a louder voice. "He can't be too far away. He must have gotten separated from us somewhere near here."

The wounded man straightened up, grabbed his club that lay in front of him, and said, "I'll go look around. If it really is him and the dog's holding him up, I'll help him return."

With club in hand, the wounded man disappeared in the direction of the barking. The three men sat behind him in perfect silence until the man with the bag spoke up, "Could it really be him?"

"Of course!" the bearded man affirmed. "Who else if not him—at such an odd time and place."

"Yes, it must be him," the man with the bag agreed. His voice had by now become a bit calmer. "He's scared of dogs. Many times before, if a dog appeared in his path, he'd just freeze."

"Did you notice," asked the youth as a fresh doubt began inching its way into his consciousness, "the dog isn't barking anymore?"

The man with the bag strained to hear for a while, then said, "Yes. That's strange! The dog isn't barking anymore. God knows what's the matter."

"The two of them together have probably chased the dog away," the bearded man tried to reassure them. "They'll be here any minute."

Once again the three lapsed into silence, peering into the space in which the wounded man had earlier disappeared. The eyes of the man with the bag were almost lost in the distance. Suddenly, as if he'd seen something, he said, "What—he's coming back alone!"

"Alone?" asked the bearded man.

"Yes, alone."

Their eyes rose to the wounded man as he wended his way back to them. He came up to them, tossed his club on the ground, and said as he began to sit down, "Absolutely nobody there."

"Then who was the dog barking at?" asked the man with the bag, looking shocked.

"Yes, yes—dogs don't bark for nothing," observed the youth.

"But there isn't anybody there, believe me," repeated the man with the wounded head.

"That's truly strange!" the man with the bag remarked.

The youth suddenly cocked his ear, trying to hear something. "Is that," he said, "more barking?"

All four of them tried to hear with keenly alert ears. After a while the bearded man asked the man with the wounded head, "Where did you go? The dog's barking in that direction."

The man with the bag grabbed the club lying near the wounded man and said, "I'll go and take a look."

"Why not all of us?" the bearded man suggested, slowly rising.

The other two also stood up, and the four of them began walking toward where they had just heard the dog's barking. They went quite a distance but saw nothing, which made the man with the bag mutter, "Not a soul."

But the bearded man urged him, "Call for him. He has to be around here somewhere. He isn't a ghost to've disappeared just like that."

"Yes, yes," began the wounded man, "you might as well try that too. Yes, call for him." But his voice lacked conviction; he was already feeling very weary and disappointed.

But the man with the bag was enthusiastic. He was just about to call for the missing man when he stopped short. "I just can't seem to remember his name," he said. "What was his name?"

"Name?" The man with the wounded head tried hard to recollect. "Name? I guess I can't remember it either."

"Young man," the man with the bag addressed the youth, "now I'd have thought you'd remember his name."

"Name? What name?" the youth blurted out. "I can't even remember his face."

"Can't remember his face," the man with the bag reflected. "It's odd. Come to think of it, I can't remember his face either." He then turned to the bearded man and asked, "Why, surely, you must remember his face, and his name too?"

The bearded man pondered, then tried hard to remember, then concluded thoughtfully, "Friends, let's go back. It would be risky to go on looking for him."

"Risky? Why?"

"Because we don't remember his name or his face. Suppose we run into somebody else and mistake him for our lost man, at this strange time and place . . . Wouldn't you say that's risky?"

All of them turned on their heels. Soon they were back where they had started from. They built a fire. The man with the bag yanked their meager supply of food out of the bag and started cooking. They ate and, with the meal over, sat warming their hands by the fire, tearfully remembering those they had left behind.

"Who was that man, anyway?" asked the youth, still thinking of the missing man.

"What man?" the others asked blankly.

"The one who was with us earlier, the one who got separated from us."

"Oh, that man . . . that's right. We nearly forgot all about him. Yes, who was he?"

"It's odd, isn't it, that we remember neither his name nor his face?" said the man with the bag.

"Should we then think he wasn't one of us?"

The youth's blunt question threw everybody into a state of shock. After a while, the man with the bag reasoned, "If he wasn't one of us, then who was he with? And why did he hang around with us all the time? The way he disappeared, just like that . . . just like that . . ." He choked over his words and could not finish what he wanted to say.

They began to stare at one another, appearing to think hard about what it all led up to: the way he had gotten in with them, come along, and then dropped out of sight without a trace. Yes, what did it all mean?

Finally the bearded man gathered his ebbing courage and reassured them, "Friends, let's not give in to doubt, for it will destroy us. He certainly was one of us. Just think of the hellish circumstances which led us to flee our homes. Who had the heart to recognize anyone then, or to count . . ."

"Can't we even remember," interrupted the youth with a question, "just how many we were when we started?"

"When we started . . ." the man with the bag repeated after the youth, astonished. He then tossed out a question of his own, "When did we start?"

"And from where?" added the youth.

The bearded man tried hard to recollect; after a while he said, "All I can remember is that as I was leaving Granada . . ."

"Granada!" The rest looked up at the bearded man with a start. The man with the bag broke into resounding laughter. And the poor old bearded man, already shocked at their mocking disbelief, felt utterly distraught at the laughter.

Bemused and still laughing, the man with the bag bantered, "Granada! Wow—it's as if I were raving, 'When I was leaving Jahanabad . . .'"

"Jahanabad?" They were once again startled. The man with the bag, who was still laughing at the bearded man, himself became quite upset and shut up.

A bitter, sad smile broke out on the lips of the wounded man. "I've been uprooted," he remarked dolefully, "and that's what matters. What difference does it make now for me to remember whether it's Granada that I've been thrown out of, or Bait al-Maqdis, or Jahanabad, or Kashmir . . .?"

The depth of sadness in his voice had an intensely melancholy effect on all the men. They drifted into silence. After a while the bearded man said tearfully, "Friends, we left behind all that was once ours, and now it seems we've even left behind our memories."

"All I can remember now," began the youth, his heart overflowing with sadness, "is this: At that fateful hour my father sat on his prayer rug; his lips moved gently as his fingers moved over his beads as he prayed; and a terrible smoke filled the whole house."

"And your father, poor man, lived to see all that happen!" said the bearded man in a choking voice.

The youth did not reply. Tears surged up in his eyes.

The man with the bag strained his memory and then said, "All I can remember now is that houses burned everywhere around us as we stamped-ed through a corridor of crashing, flying debris—confused and scared out of our wits."

None of this seemed to make any impression at all on the man with the wounded head. He could only say, "Friends, what is there in memories? Whether it was a javelin that pierced my head, a club that smashed it, or a sword that split it in two—what's to be gained by remembering that? What does matter is that right now my head hurts a lot and it's still bleeding."

The rest looked up at him in commiseration. After he had stared at him for quite a while, the bearded man remarked, "I've a deadlier wound in my chest than you've got in your head! Ah, what a place!" he sighed, "What a place it was, that was razed to the ground!"

And the man with the bag sighed along, "What fine men who were dri-ven out and dispersed!"

"And what faces that were smothered!" said the youth full of melan-choly, going deeper into his memory to the moment when he had kissed a pair of lips for the first time, amid promises and declarations worthy of such an occasion—a moment when neither time nor society matters much, only the path of love seems to be eternally real. He remembered that time with sadness, then muttered, "If only she were with us today, we'd be com-plete!"

"She?" the bearded man looked at the youth in amazement. "Who is she?"

"She!"

"She who?"

The youth did not care to reply and looked away listlessly into space. The bearded man and the man with the bag stared a long time at the youth, while their wounded companion just rested his head against the tree trunk and closed his eyes, as if he had had enough of that nonsense.

The man with the bag, still looking intently at the youth, asked in a hushed voice, "Was it a woman?"

The bearded man sat up with a start; so did the wounded man, who threw open his eyes.

"If it were a woman," began the man with the bag, "then, by God, we've been deprived of pleasant company."

The bearded man glowered at him and snapped, "If it really were a woman then, by God, her presence would have been the ruin of us."

The last words of the bearded man caught the wounded man as he was just closing his drowsy eyes. Suddenly opening his eyes wide, he laughed bitterly, full of irony, and remarked, "As if our condition weren't bad enough already!"

"But, surely, her company would have meant going from bad to worse."

Then and there the wounded man told the bearded man off: "Mind you, old man, better to be ruined on account of a woman than wander around in the wilderness for no sane reason." He closed his eyes again and threw his head backward against the trunk.

A long silence ensued. The man with the bag got up, collected some firewood, and tossed it into the fire. They sat warming their hands, silent, lost in their thoughts, each sunk in his own doubt and misgivings, until they were jolted out of their musings by the quaking voice of their old, bearded companion, who was muttering, "A truly mind-boggling thing. One doesn't even remember the name or the face or even whether it was a man or a woman."

The man with the bag became perplexed. "God knows who it was. Who could it have been?"

"Someone we know nothing about," proceeded the bearded man, "could be anybody—just anybody."

"And quite possibly no one at all." The man with the bag voiced his doubt.

"No one at all?" The youth was nonplussed.

After some hesitation, the bearded man finally conceded, "Yes. That is possible."

Silence prevailed. The youth, assailed by a fresh doubt, said, "All right. It wasn't a man. So who was it?"

As the bearded man and the man with the bag puzzled over the question, their wounded companion opened his eyes, gave a look at the youth, and snapped, "If it wasn't a woman, then let it be a she-devil for all I care." He closed his eyes again and dozed off.

"A she-devil?" All three looked up aghast.

The bearded man reflected for a moment and then admonished his wounded companion thoughtfully, "Friend! don't say that. Don't ever say that—unless we lose our last shred of trust in mankind."

The wounded man opened his eyes again, probed the bearded man for a long moment, and burst into laughter, bitter as before. "Old man," he said between spasms of laughter, "you still seem to trust man!" and let his eyes close again and his head roll backward against the trunk.

The bearded man looked at him with deep concern, then asked, "Friend, is your head still hurting much?"

The wounded man didn't care to open his eyes; he just shook his head and became motionless. The bearded man, dissatisfied with the answer, went on, "Can you remember who it was that hit you on the head, and what he hit you with, and how you managed to escape them once they had surrounded you?"

The wounded man, his eyes still closed, replied painfully, "I don't. I don't remember anything."

"That's truly bizarre!" exclaimed the youth.

"Not really," the bearded man volunteered. "If the blow is heavy, the head is paralyzed and one temporarily lapses into amnesia."

"I wasn't hit on my head," demurred the man with the bag. "All the same, I felt as though I had blacked out for a while."

"Well," the bearded man ventured an explanation, "this can happen. Under extreme conditions a man gets rattled." Then he started, sitting motionless for a few moments, as if concentrating hard to catch some elusive sound. Then, looking straight up at the man with the bag, he queried, "Isn't that the barking again?"

The man with the bag sat up, his ears keenly alert. A moment later he confirmed, "You're right, it is."

The three men sat up and raised their heads. Overwhelmed by the advent of some inexplicable fear, each looked at the other and kept on looking. Then the bearded man stood up. The man with the bag and the youth followed. It was not until they had actually taken a few steps that the wounded man, his eyes still tightly shut, managed to get up too with difficulty—he seemed to be in pain—and shuffled along behind the rest.

They went far, first in one then in another direction, then became confused. The man with the bag remarked, "Nobody."

"There has to be somebody," the bearded man insisted. "Why else would the dog bark?"

The question surprised them. It had occurred to none of them that, after all, no one had ever actually seen the dog.

"Now this wretched dog's become a puzzle too!" exclaimed the man with the bag.

"Puzzle!" began the old man. "Friend, man is a puzzle himself! Why blame dogs?"

"Provided one is able to keep the two apart," the man with the wounded head added indifferently.

The bearded man paid no attention to that remark. It seemed a more urgent fear was squeezing his heart. He spun around and said, "Let's go back!"

"Why?"

"It just isn't safe to go on."

So they gave up their search, trekked back to the place they had started from, and sprawled out on the ground. The youth, who seemed to be quite frightened, spoke of his fear. "Who is tailing whom? Are we tailing him, or is he tailing us?"

"He's tailing us, of course," the man with the bag answered decisively but fearfully. "But tell me, how did you come up with that question, anyway?"

"How? Well, you see it is like this: as we were backtracking, I sensed we were being shadowed; I heard footsteps behind us . . ."

"Didn't you look back to see who it was?"

"No. I didn't."

"You did the right thing, young man," the bearded man complimented the youth. "One mustn't look back—ever."

The wounded man, who had lain down in the meantime, sat up with a start, stared at the youth with wide-open eyes, and said, "The same thing happened to me. When I went out to look for this missing man, on the way back I had the very same feeling. I felt I was being followed."

"What?" the bearded man reacted with alarm. "Friend, you should have told us about this then."

"I forgot. Now hearing the youth I suddenly remember it." He stopped short and fell back into thought again.

"What's the matter?"

"Wait. Let me think." He tried hard to recollect, but seemed not to be able to. "Friends," he asked, "do you recall whether I'd included myself while I was counting us?"

"You mean yourself?" asked the man with the bag, stupefied.

The wounded man went on thinking. "Perhaps I didn't count myself," he concluded. "Yes, that's right. I forgot to count myself."

The statement stunned the rest. "So what?" they asked, feeling more confused than ever.

"So what? Well, you see, I am the missing man."

"You?"

"Yes, me."

That seemed to send the other three into a state of shock. They began to gaze at the wounded man in disbelief. All of a sudden the youth started, as it occurred to him that he too had failed to include himself when it was his turn to count. "I am the one who is missing," he concluded.

That reminded the man with the bag of his own mistake. He too had erred. He too had failed to include himself. So now he thought that, indeed, he was the missing man. The bearded man in turn sank deep into thought. When he emerged he confessed, "Friends! At least I shouldn't have made such a terrible mistake. But I did. I counted all of you but somehow left myself out. Well, I—the humblest of creatures—am the missing man."

Mystified, exasperated—they wondered who in fact was the missing man among them. "At that moment," began the wounded man as the memory came back to him of the time when he was returning after his unavailing search for the missing man, "at that moment I felt as if the missing man were certainly around somewhere, though I was not. I didn't exist, I was nowhere."

The bearded man thought for a while. "Friend," he tried to assure his wounded companion, "you are! Don't think otherwise."

The wounded man suddenly tore his gaze from the bearded man and fixed it on the other two, as if he didn't trust the bearded man and needed the others to back up his testimony. The other two men consoled him. They told him that, indeed, he did exist. Only then could the wounded man be convinced of his being. "Since you bear witness to my *being*," he sighed, "therefore, *I am*. And what a pity! I exist because others think that I do."

Whereupon the bearded man upbraided him, "Be thankful, friend. At least you've got three men who are ready to bear witness to your *being*. Just think of those who really were but ceased to be only because there weren't men around to testify to their being."

"Which means that if you suddenly decided to withhold your testimony, I too would immediately cease to be," said the wounded man.

That muddled their brains further. Am I not the lost man?—each thought to himself apprehensively, only to fall into a fresh quandary: if he really were the lost man, did that mean he no longer existed? The misgiving, the fear that tore at their hearts, surfaced in their eyes. Each looked the others straight in the eyes and spoke hesitantly about his suspicion, and not only testified to the existence of the others in a loud and clear voice but also elicited a similar testimony about his own being from the others—all of which somehow made the three feel better, reassured, and satisfied.

Not so with the youth. In the throes of fresh doubt, he mercilessly tore the thin fabric of their assurance, saying, "It's bizarre, isn't it, to think that *we are*, not because we are but because we're mutually able to substantiate each other's being?"

The wounded man broke into wild, ringing laughter. When his companions asked him what it was that made him laugh so, he replied, "You want to know why I laughed? Because while I can testify that another man exists, I cannot testify that I exist."

Once more they found themselves wallowing in a bog of confusion. Misgivings arose and filled their hearts. They started to count themselves anew. This time each began with himself but before he had finished counting, he got confused and asked the others whether he had counted himself.

Thus each managed to confuse the other. Finally the youth demurred, "How many were we in the first place?"

The question found a willing place in each heart: "Yes, how many?"

The bearded man heard each one of them out, then proceeded, "Friends, all I know is this. None of us was missing when we started. Then our number began to decrease. We could be counted on fingertips now. Soon we couldn't believe what our own fingers had counted. So we counted all of us, one after the other, and found one of us missing. Then each of us realized his mistake in counting, only to find himself missing."

"Surely you don't mean to say we are all missing?" blurted out the youth, a fresh doubt making inroads into his heart.

The bearded man gave a sullen angry look at the youth, who had again upset the pieces of the puzzle after he had barely managed to put them together. "No. No one is missing. We are complete."

"And just how do we know that?" the youth objected, again rudely. "How many were we in the first place?"

"How many—when?" the bearded man lost patience.

"When we started, that's when."

"Just when did we start?" The wounded man glowered at the youth. The youth gazed blankly at the wounded man. Slowly, very slowly, tears began to well up in his eyes. "I can't remember when, I just can't," he replied hoarsely, choking on the painful memory. "All I can recollect now is that the house was filled with smoke and my father was sitting on his prayer rug. His eyes were closed, his lips moving, his fingers on his beads."

His gaze still relentlessly fixed on the youth, the wounded man exclaimed regretfully, "Young man, that's already quite a bit. I . . . I for one don't remember anything at all."

"That's not enough," the youth protested in a sorrowful voice. "I have no memory of where she was at *that* moment."

"If only," began the bearded man with tears in his eyes, "if only we could somehow remember how, when, and from where we've fled."

"And for what reason?" added the youth.

"Yes, and for what reason?" the bearded man endorsed enthusiastically, as if it were something that had slipped from his mind and the youth had reminded him of it.

The youth was presently immersed in another dear memory. After some time he said, "If I really had fled from Jahanabad, then I seem to remember only this: the days of *Savan* were long gone. The cuckoo too had departed from the mango groves. And the swing that hung from the *neem* tree in our backyard had also been taken down and stored away." The youth was lost in his thoughts, his voice gradually becoming inaudible, as if he were talking to himself. "But she'd still come. She kept visiting our house long after the swing had been removed." He reminisced, going farther back into memory, all the way back to those moist days during the rains when he would stand in the backyard under the foliage of the *neem*. The ground would be covered with those tiny pale drops, the bitter *neem* fruit, while she would swing high in the air, singing:

Teeny-weeny raindrops!
And I—high on my swing in Savan.

"She also came to our house after the rains, much after the rains. Yes, she did. But that day—where was she that day?" The youth worked harder with his elusive memory, then gave up, exhausted. "Oh," he sighed, "I can't remember. I just can't."

All the while the wounded man kept watching the youth intently.

"Suppose it wasn't Jahanabad that you'd fled from but some other place—then what?" asked the man with the bag.

"What do you mean?"

"Like, say, it was Granada—surely you heard our honorable old man say that—then what?" The man with the bag said this in a way to show that it was a totally ridiculous thing and that he wanted to make fun of the bearded man for bringing it up.

Not so with the youth. He took it seriously. He thought and thought, then got even more confused. "From Granada?" He thought still more, then added remorsefully, "If it really was Granada, then I don't remember anything."

"If it really was Granada . . ." the bearded man repeated in a subdued voice as his mind busily combed through his memory; then, a little later, he added, "Then I do seem to remember that dawn had just broken; a dim light still hung everywhere, and the minarets of the Aqsa Mosque . . ."

"Minarets of the Aqsa—what? In Granada?" the man with the bag burst out laughing.

The bearded man was confounded and fell silent. The youth stared at the bearded man uncomprehendingly. "Aqsa Mosque . . ." he muttered to himself, then fell silent.

The wounded man again felt very irritated. "Damn it!" he proceeded bitterly. "I'm uprooted. And that's all there is to it. What difference does it make to remember now what time it was then, what season, what place?"

"That's absolutely right. Now it really won't make any difference," sighed the bearded man. "Even so, it'd be better if we remembered when and from where we have fled."

"And for what reason?"

"Yes, that too."

"Also how many of us were there when we were fleeing?" added the youth.

"We were complete at that time," said the bearded man, making one last desperate effort to convince the youth.

The youth listened to the bearded man patiently, then asked, "Was he with us then?"

"Who?"

"The one who's missing from us."

"Him—oh. He was nobody."

"Nobody? Is that so?" All of them were perplexed. "It's strange that he was nobody."

Each looked at the next man, as if he understood nothing. Their four pairs of eyes were full with wonderment . . . and dread, as they sat dazed in immobility, their lips sealed as if they would never speak again.

The youth moved his body uneasily about and cocked his ears as if trying to hear something, which made the others do the same.

"There is somebody," whispered the youth.

"Yes, maybe there really is," the man with the bag said in a barely audible voice, "that's why the dog's barking."

The four men stared at one another. Then the youth said in a very low voice, "Maybe it's him."

"Who?"

"Him!"

The bearded man gave the youth a long, lingering look, then drifted off into thought. Finally he stood up with a start. The others followed suit. Once again they were chasing after the sound.

Translated by Muhammad Umar Memon

Metamorphosis

And so it happened that Prince Azad Bakht saw that morning in the guise of a fly. It was a morning utterly cruel, for what had been apparent disappeared and what was hidden within came into the open—one appeared unblushingly naked. And Prince Azad Bakht was turned into a fly.

At first, the prince thought he was dreaming; however, when morning came, he forgot the dream. He remembered very little. Later, when it grew dark and the giant returned to the fort, thundering and roaring, the prince began to shrink. He grew smaller and smaller—so small that he couldn't recall afterward what had happened. Then he forgot even the beginning, for he was full of love for the fair princess whom he had come to rescue from the giant's fort. Yet again in the evening, the same thing happened. The giant entered the fort roaring, "I smell a human! I smell a human!" And the prince began to shrink. In the morning he found himself confused and frightened, as on the previous day. He seemed to have had a nightmare. He tried to remember the details, but nothing came to mind.

After three nights had gone by in that fashion, the prince became very anxious: "*Ya Allah!* What's happening here? As soon as it's evening, I lose all awareness of myself. Does someone put a spell on me?" He reproached himself: "You lazy fool! You came here to rescue the fair princess from the clutches of the white giant. Now you yourself are caught in the web of his magic!" Then, at the hour of darkness, he saw the fair princess turn toward him and cast a spell that made him begin to shrink. He struggled to retain his true shape, but he kept on shrinking, as on the previous evenings.

Next morning, the prince felt as if he had come out of some terrible dream; again, he couldn't recall much of what had happened. But he could remember seeing the princess move her lips. His suspicions were aroused: "Something terrible is going on here," he thought. He angrily turned to the princess and exclaimed, "You wretched person! I'm only trying to rescue you from the white giant. Is this how you reward me? By casting a spell on me?"

The princess tried to make some excuses, but the prince would have none of it. He kept asking her for the truth. Finally the princess retorted: "You fool! What I do is only for your own good. This white giant is an enemy of humankind. If he were to see you he would devour you in the twinkling of an eye. And he would also torture me. That's why I turn you into a fly every evening and put you on the wall. Even then the monster keeps shouting all night long, 'I smell a human! I smell a human!' I manage to mollify him only by saying, 'Eat me! I'm a human.' Then, in the morning when he is gone, I return you to your human form."

When the prince learned that at nights he was turned into a fly and that a woman brought about this change in order to save his life, his pride was badly hurt. He found the situation intolerable. Filled with indignation, he reflected: "Azad Bakht, you were so proud of your noble blood, of your manly deeds and courage. You thought you possessed all skills and all knowledge. But today your pride lies in dust. A monster tyrannizes a human being while you—for the sake of your precious life—turn into the most lowly of things!"

He frowned in anger, first at himself and then at the princess. The princess was dismayed. (It must be mentioned here that the fair princess had all the time kept herself physically at a distance from the prince, promising him the wine of union only after their escape from the tyrant's den. For that reason the prince had all along felt himself consumed by the fire of separation even though he was quite close to his beloved.) Today, after the prince's reproach, the princess was unusually upset. Her eyes brimmed with tears. She came close to the prince and, putting her head on his chest, began to cry. The prince's heart melted. He put his arms around her. Their bodies met in an embrace and clung to each other. Their reserve and fear were gone. Though it was day, it felt like the night of nuptials. The prince lost himself in that warm embrace, and raised his head only when the walls of the fort began to shake with the giant's approach. He began to shrink and, despite a struggle, kept shrinking until he was naught but a dark speck—a fly.

Next morning the prince awoke, filled with misgivings. Had he really become a fly? For that matter, can a man be turned into a fly? His heart overflowed with sorrow at these thoughts. He was a fine man, well initiated into all the necessary arts and sciences, and unmatched in bravery. He was of noble birth and possessed great dignity. He had conquered every country he had attacked. But in the white giant's fort, he, that noble and victorious prince, had become a fly. "So, Azad Bakht, deep down, you were only a fly!" Then he thought of his glorious past, his adventures and conquests, and he thought of his ancestors who were renowned throughout the world. Everything seemed so distant, so removed. And when it was evening, he began to shrink again until he became a fly.

Every evening the giant returned to the fort, shouting, "I smell a human! I smell a human!" Every evening the princess, full of coquetry, gave him the reply, "Eat me! I'm a human." The giant would then turn to the pleasures of night and the prince would remain stuck to the wall in the shape of a fly until morning would come again. Then the princess would turn him back into a man. Man at dawn, fly at dusk, such was the prince's life, and it left him disgusted. The princess tried to console him. She took him around the garden and offered him gifts of fruit and flowers, for there were plenty of both in the white giant's fort. There was also a feast of delicious dishes spread on the white giant's table. The prince saw this bounty and hovered over it. In his life of adventures, he had never seen such abundance before.

So, during the day, the prince hovered like a fly over the delicacies on the table, and at night turned into a fly to sleep on the wall. And the days were like nights of love, for the fair princess would be in his arms to help him forget the discomforts of the nights. Then the nights grew longer, and the days shortened. The prince had to stay longer in the shape of a fly. Soon it developed that even during the day he would suddenly feel as if he were turning into a fly. At first it would be just a momentary feeling; he would immediately be reminded of the fact that it was not yet night and that he was still in the form of a man. But slowly these lapses increased in duration. Even in the sweet embrace of the princess's arms there would suddenly be moments when he would think of himself as a fly; and the fair princess would shift under him and he would be as suddenly reminded of the bright sunlight and his manhood. Soon he began to have these lapses even when he was fully conscious of himself. Picking flowers in the garden or collecting fruit, or sitting down to a luxurious meal from the giant's kitchens, the prince would find himself wondering, "Am I still a man?" The waves of doubts and apprehensions would overwhelm him.

The prince struggled to break out from under those doubts and apprehensions; he sought some opportunity to challenge the giant. But the princess stopped him: "Look, it's of no use to fight with the giant, for his life isn't inside him. His life is in a parrot, and the parrot is in a cage, and the cage is hung in a tree, and the tree is on an island across the seven seas. In that parrot is the white giant's life."

Prince Azad Bakht was astounded. "How can it be? How can the giant live here, yet his life be in a parrot across the seven seas?" He found it hard to believe that life could exist separate from body. Then he started to wonder about his own life: Was his life somewhere else? Was it perhaps in the fly?

For days on end he was lost in thought: How was he going to get out of the fort? How was he going to make it across the seven seas and kill that parrot? When the princess saw him so absorbed, she complained: "Your love is dead. You are planning to deceive me." The prince, madly in love with her, was only too anxious to convince her of his fidelity. And between her complaints and his declarations, the subject of escape was totally forgotten.

Prince Azad Bakht was now virtually a slave to the princess's whims. He couldn't pluck a leaf without her express permission. He would turn into a fly at her command, then return to his human form when she so desired. Many a time it so happened that the prince would begin to shrink even before the princess cast her spell, or, in the morning, he would lie worn out and helpless even after receiving his human form. It would seem as if he had come out of the fly form but not fully back into the human—it was as if he lacked something. And that period of uncertainty kept increasing day after day, as did his fatigue and discomfort. In the evening he would swiftly turn into a fly, but in the morning, there would be a long and miserable interval before he would start functioning as a human being. And the memory of this period of misery would long linger on even after it was over. Finally one day, in that miserable state of mind, the prince asked himself a question: "Am I a fly or a man?"

It was the first time he had looked at the problem in that way. He became nervous with apprehension and hurried to reassure himself. "I'm a man first, then a fly. My days are my real life. My nights are only an illusion." He felt satisfied, but not for long. The doubt returned: "Perhaps my nights are real, and the days are merely a masquerade?" And once again, Prince Azad Bakht was caught in a web of fears and misgivings. He agonized: "What is my true being? Am I, in fact, a man who, only for the sake of prudence, is turned into a fly? Or is it that I was, in fact, a fly and became human only for a short time? Isn't that possible? Mustn't everything return to its origin—and thus I, to my fly form?" (This thought so nauseated him that he rejected it outright.) "But then, am I really a man?" He struggled but could not convince himself one way or the other. Finally he settled for a compromise: he was a man as well as a fly.

Now Prince Azad Bakht was a man as well as a fly. And the fly said to the man: "I protect you during the night. You should, therefore, share your day with me."

The man was very prudent. He said, "I've heard you, and I'll include you in my days."

Thus the prince's days gained a dual color. In the morning after a long and miserable interval, he would regain his human form; then, like a fly, he would pounce upon the delicious dishes laid out on the giant's table. His ecstasy would make him forget everything. But eventually the shadow of the white giant would darken his thoughts, and he would feel himself shrinking. Shut in the fort, fearful of the giant, and afraid of the princess's anger, he would shrink into himself—as if he were always turning into a fly. He would recover himself only with much difficulty. The prince felt as if he were walking at the edge of some dark abyss, that any moment he might take a false step and turn into a fly.

Prince Azad Bakht, now that he was a fly as well as a man, was disgusted by his dual life. The terrified man, walking along the edge of the abyss, thought: "I must somehow kill the giant. Then this duality will end and I'll again become a free man." But he no longer possessed the courage to fight the white giant. He made scores of plans: how he would fight the giant, how he would escape from the fort and sail across the seven seas, how he would wring the parrot's neck, only to reject all of them. He glanced up at the towering walls of the fort and considered his wretched condition; when he recalled the thundering noise of the giant, his heart began to quiver. "Why shouldn't I completely change into a fly? The fort would then become meaningless, and there would be no fear of the giant. After all, giants don't seem to bother with flies." But the prince still had some qualms about the idea; he remained suspended between his doubts and his fears, and the fly inside him kept gaining in strength. The shadow of night increased its spread over the light of day.

One day the prince felt that somewhere deep inside him there was a tiny fly, buzzing ever so eagerly. He rejected the feeling, calling it merely a trick of his imagination. But the feeling grew within him. He felt nauseated. He felt as if he were rolling in his own excrement. His being, once pure as milk and sweet as honey, was now contaminated by a fly.

And so the days flew by, and the masquerade of darkness and light continued. The prince never left the fort, for the fort became a spider's web for his fly. The fly fluttered its tiny wings and waved its needle-thin legs; it gave up all hope and hung upside down in the web. The web began to penetrate into the prince. His links with the outside world grew weaker day by day. Some cobweb dimmed the prince's memory, and the world around him began to fade away. His home, the people of his land—they were like dreams, slowly dissolving into oblivion. He used to think of his father, a conqueror of conquerors, with hopes of being rescued by him. But now the prince was confused; his mind was covered with a cobweb. "Who was my father?" the prince asked himself. And to his amazement, he could not remember his own father's name. "What is my father' name? What is my name?" he cried. "Name," he said, "is the key to reality. Where is the key to my reality?"

Once upon a time there was a fly. She was busy cleaning her house when suddenly she could no longer recall her name. She dropped what she was doing and flew from door to door, from place to place, asking people to tell her her name. And everywhere she was cursed and shooed away. She went to a mosquito and said, "Mosquy, Mosquy, what is my name?"

The mosquito said, "Go away! How should I know your name?"

Then the fly went to a buffalo and said, "Buffy, Buffy, tell me my name."

But the buffalo was very proud of herself; she did not reply. She kept on chewing her cud, her eyes closed in contentment, and haughtily swished her tail.

Prince Azad Bakht tried very hard to remember his name, but could not. It was as if his life as a prince had been in some previous birth, as if this was a new birth in which he was merely a creature, true and simple. As he reflected on the matter his apprehension increased. He asked himself, "How should I distinguish myself from other creatures?" He searched his mind for an answer, but only encountered more questions. What was his name? What was his father's name? Who were the people around him? Where was his home? But he could remember nothing. The cobweb sank deep and spread inside him. He declared: "What I was is no more than my past: I am what I now am."

So now the prince was what he now was. And the fly inside him was stronger than ever, and more compelling. The man within him was fast fading into the dim past. The prince's daily return to human form was now a painful experience. As he would wake up, he would feel himself terribly tired and filthy. His body would ache as if it had been torn apart the night before, and never healed. With his eyes closed, he would lie in a trance for a long time; only with great reluctance would he get up and, feeling himself covered with filth, go to the pool in the garden and bathe in its pearl-pure water. But afterward, he would be reminded of the night before and feel sick all over again. It seemed to him that there was something constantly buzzing behind the portals of his mind. He would take another bath, yet feel dirty as ever. His nausea never stopped.

That nausea became a part of his being. He was constantly feeling sick. After spending a night as a fly, he would, after an arduous struggle, regain his human form, but lie weak and numb beyond any help. Everything seemed to him to have been touched by something filthy: the walls of the fort, the leaves of the trees, the water in the pool, even the princess herself. He felt he was being buried under a pile of dead flies. He was now too weak to fight against the fly inside him; the fly seemed to have penetrated even into his soul. Some mornings he couldn't be sure if the princess had in fact removed her spell; he would wonder if he were still stuck to the wall. Sometimes the fly seemed to come out and overwhelm his entire being, and he would change even before the princess could finish casting her spell. The next morning, after regaining his human form, he would lie unconscious for many hours. He couldn't believe, rather he couldn't be certain that he was a man again. The act of transformation became ever more painful with each passing day. He would suffer from his uncertainty all day long. And in the evening, when the giant would return roaring as usual, the prince would breathe a sigh of relief. He felt safe and happy in the guise of a fly.

Now Prince Azad Bakht felt happier as a fly, and found it painful to return to his human form. Leaving the guise of the fly felt to him like being abandoned by his soul. One day, after a spell of excruciating pain, he was able to leave his fly form, but did not fully return to being a man. He was in a kind of limbo and felt aged by centuries. All that day, he was pursued by doubts. Had he not changed into a man? Was he in some indeterminate state? Again and again he went and stood before a mirror, and asked: "If I am not a man, am I a fly?" (But he didn't seem like a fly either.) "If I am neither a fly nor a man, then what am I? Am I nothing?" And sweat poured from him in anxiety, for it was better to be a fly than be nothing. Then he couldn't think any longer.

The fair princess trembled with apprehension when she saw his sorry condition. She blamed herself for everything. She decided never to turn him into a fly again. When it was evening she merely locked him in his human form in the cellar.

So that evening the princess did not turn the prince into a fly; instead, she locked him in the cellar. Nevertheless, when darkness spread and the walls began to shake with the fury of the giant's arrival, the prince felt scared as usual and shrank into himself.

That evening, the giant did not shout: "I smell a human! I smell a human!" The princess was perplexed: earlier when she used to turn the prince into a fly, the giant could still smell his human odor; yet today, when she had not changed him, the giant had found nothing amiss. "What has happened," she wondered, "to the human odor of Prince Azad Bakht?"

And so the night passed, in perplexity and confusion, and finally the day broke. After the giant had left, the princess opened the cellar door and was dumbfounded. There was no prince in the cellar; there was only a huge, fat fly on the wall. The princess stood, hesitant and confused, unable to understand how the prince had turned into a fly without her help. Then she chanted the magic words to transform him back into a man, but the words failed to produce any effect. That morning Prince Azad Bakht remained a fly. And thus it happened that Prince Azad Bakht saw morning in the guise of a fly.

Translated by C. M. Naim

The Last Man

Alyasef was the last man in that town. Born by God's will in a human body, he had vowed to die in a human body. And he tried to his last to stay in a human body.

Now three days ago the monkeys vanished from the town. At first the people were surprised; then they rejoiced that the monkeys who had destroyed the crops and ruined the gardens were no more. But the one who had forbidden them to go fishing on the Sabbath said, "The monkeys are present among you, although you don't see them."

Annoyed at this, people said, "Are you making fun of us?"

And he replied, "Verily, you have made fun of God, for He forbade fishing on the Sabbath and you were fishing on the Sabbath. But I tell you, He is a greater fun-maker than you are."

Three days later it happened that Alyezer's maid entered his bedchamber at the crack of dawn, then quickly ran out to his wife. Alyezer's wife then went into the bedchamber and came back surprised and frightened. Then the news spread everywhere, and people came to Alyezer's house from all over. Going up to his bedchamber, they stopped in amazement, for instead of Alyezer, a large monkey lay sleeping there. The previous Sabbath Alyezer had caught the most fish.

Then it happened that one person told another, "O friend, Alyezer has turned into a monkey."

The other burst out laughing and said, "You're making fun of me." He went on laughing until his face turned red and his teeth grew; his features became pinched, and he turned into a monkey. Amazed, the first one stood there open-mouthed, his eyes wide with astonishment; then he too turned into a monkey.

Seeing Ibn Zablun, Alyab was frightened, and he said, "O son of Zablun, what has made your face change so?" Annoyed at this, Ibn Zablun began to gnash his teeth in anger. Then Alyab became even more frightened, and he cried, "May your mother mourn for you, O son of Zablun, for something has surely happened to you." Ibn Zablun's face blazed with anger at this, and he clenched his teeth and sprang at Alyab. Alyab was overcome with fear and began to tremble. And both of their faces were changed, Ibn Zablun's with anger and Alyab's with fear. Ibn Zablun was bursting with anger, while Alyab had drawn into himself with fear. The two of them, one the embodiment of anger, the other a bundle of fear, began to fight. Their faces changed. Their bodies changed. Their voices changed, so that the words ran together and became indistinguishable noises. The indistinguishable noises then became animal-like shrieks, and the two turned into monkeys.

Alyasef, the wisest among them and the one who had remained a human being to the last, addressed them anxiously: "O people, something has definitely happened to us. Come, we must appeal to the person who forbids us to catch fish on the Sabbath." Leading the people to that person's house, Alyasef knocked on the door and called out for a long time. Then, turning back in disappointment, he shouted, "O people, the person who forbade us to catch fish on the Sabbath has today gone off and left us. And I fear we are doomed." Hearing this, the people became frightened. A great wave of fear took hold of them, and their faces shrank in terror and became disfigured. Turning around, Alyasef collapsed, for the people behind him had turned into monkeys. He looked ahead of him and saw nothing but monkeys. When he cast his eyes to the left and to the right, he saw monkeys in every direction. Afraid, he pressed on ahead, deftly avoiding them. He went across the whole settlement, but found no human being. Now, one should know that this was a seaside town, with high towers and mansions with massive doors. Its population had been large and its bazaars had always been very crowded. In a split second, though, the bazaars and the high entrances had become deserted, and on the high towers and splendid rooftops there were nothing but monkeys. With dread Alyasef cast his eyes everywhere, wondering if he were the only human being. And he was so terrified at this thought that his blood froze. He remembered Alyab, how when his face had changed with fear he had turned into a monkey. Alyasef overcame his fear and vowed that, having been born by God's will in a human body, he would die in a human body. With a feeling of superiority, he looked at his fellows with their disfigured faces and said, "Surely I am not one of them, for they are monkeys, while I am a human being." And Alyasef hated his fellows. Seeing their blazing red faces and hairy bodies, his face filled with anger. But thinking suddenly of Ibn Zablun and how the intensity of his hatred had disfigured his face, he said, "O Alyasef, don't hate, for hatred changes a man's body." And Alyasef turned away from hatred.

Alyasef turned away from hatred saying, "I certainly was one of them once," and the thought of the days when he was one of them and the feeling of love flooded his heart. And he remembered Bint al-Akhzar, who was like one of the milk-white mares of Pharaoh's chariot, and whose big house had doors of cypress and beams of cedar. Alyasef remembered bygone days: he had entered that house with the cypress doors and cedar beams from the back, caressing there in a canopied bed the one whom his heart loved. And he saw her long hair wet with the evening dew, her breasts trembling like fawns, her belly like a heap of wheat with a tiny sandalwood cup in the center. And Alyasef remembered Bint al-Akhzar, and, with the fawns, the heap of wheat, and the cup in his thoughts, he went to the house with the cypress doors and cedar beams. He saw the empty house and looked for her on the canopied bed, she whom his heart desired, and he called out, "Where are you, O daughter of Akhzar? O you whom my heart desires, see, the winter has passed and the flowerbeds are in bloom again and the turtle-doves flutter on the high branches. Where are you, O daughter of Akhzar? O you lying on the canopied bed spread out on the high roof, I beseech you in the name of does running in the forests and doves hiding in the clefts of the rocks, come down and embrace me, for my heart loves you." Alyasef called again and again, until his heart was filled with sadness and he wept thinking of Bint al-Akhzar.

Alyasef wept thinking of the daughter of Akhzar. But suddenly he remembered Alyezer's wife and how she had cried and burst into a fit of tears seeing Alyezer in a monkey's body, and how her tears had gradually distorted her beautiful features and disfigured her, and how her weeping voice became animal-like, and how, finally, her whole body had changed. Alyasef thought, "Bint al-Akhzar has gone to those with whom she belongs, for one shall be raised along with those with whom one belongs." And Alyasef said to himself, "O Alyasef, don't love them, lest you become one of them." And Alyasef turned away from love and cut himself off from his fellow creatures, considering them strangers. And Alyasef put out of his mind fawns, the heap of wheat, and the round sandalwood cup.

Alyasef turned away from love and he laughed when he saw the blazing red faces and upright tails of his fellow creatures. Alyasef remembered Alyezer's wife who had been one of the town's beautiful women. She had been tall and straight like a palmyra tree, with breasts like clusters of grapes. And Alyezer told her, "I tell you, I'll pick the clusters of grapes. And trembling, she with the clusters of grapes went off toward the seashore. Alyezer followed her, picked the fruit, and took the palmyra tree home. But now she would sit up on a high tower plucking out Alyezer's lice. Alyezer would shiver and stand up, and, righting her tail, she would sit up on her dirty, grimy paws, with Alyezer's front feet resting on her ugly hairy back. When he saw this, Alyasef laughed and laughed, until the sound of his laughing became so loud that the whole town seemed to echo with it. And he was amazed that he had laughed so forcefully. But suddenly he thought of the person who had turned into a monkey by laughing. And Alyasef said to himself, "O Alyasef, don't laugh, lest you become a member of that laughing race." And Alyasef turned away from laughing.

Alyasef turned away from laughing. And Alyasef avoided love and hatred, anger and sympathy, crying and laughing—all feelings—and, considering his fellow creatures strangers, he cut himself off from them. Their leaping on trees, their teeth-grinding, their chattering, fighting over half-ripe fruit, bloodying each other—all of this sometimes made him cry over his fellow creatures, other times made him laugh, and sometimes so angered him that he ground his teeth and looked at them scornfully. Once it happened that he got angry seeing them fight and loudly scolded them, only to feel himself amazed at the sound of his voice. A few of the monkeys looked at him indifferently and then started fighting again. And the words lost all their worth in Alyasef's eyes for he realized that they were no longer a means of communication between him and his fellow creatures. And he felt sorry at this. He felt sorry for his fellow creatures, for himself, and for language. He felt sorry for them because they were deprived of language. He felt sorry for himself because language was now like an empty vessel in his hands. And he felt that language had died and that it was a day of great sorrow. Mourning the death of language, Alyasef fell silent.

Alyasef fell silent, ignoring love and hatred, anger and sympathy, laughter and tears. And looking on his fellow creatures as strangers, Alyasef turned away from them and took refuge in his own self. Having found refuge in himself, he became like an island. Cut off from all, he was a tiny speck of dry land surrounded by deep waters. And the island said, "In the midst of the deep waters, I will raise the standard of land."

Alyasef, who considered himself an island of humanity, started to defend himself against the deep waters. He built a dike around himself so that neither love nor hatred, anger nor sympathy, sorrow nor happiness might suddenly overpower him, so that no emotion of any kind could carry him off. And Alyasef was afraid of his feelings. But then, after he had finished the dike, he had a stony feeling in his chest. Worried, he said, "O God, am I changing inside?" Then, looking at himself on the outside, he had the dreadful suspicion that the stony feeling was spreading outward, and that his body was becoming dry, his skin colorless, and his blood cold. When he looked even more closely at himself, he was even more overcome with dread. He felt as if his body were being covered with hair and that the hair was stiff and ugly. Afraid of his body, he closed his eyes and began to shrink into himself in fear. He felt as if his arms and legs were becoming shorter and his head smaller. Then he became even more afraid and his body contracted in fear even more. And he wondered if he would vanish altogether.

And Alyasef thought of Alyab who had turned into a monkey when his body had contracted with fear. He said, "I must overcome this inner fear just as I did the outer fear." And Alyasef overcame his inner fear and his contracted body began to expand again. His body relaxed, his fingers lengthened, his hair grew, the palms of his hands and soles of his feet became flat and moist, and his joints loosened. And Alyasef feared that his whole body would come apart. Making up his mind, he clenched his teeth, tightened his fists, and drew himself together again.

No longer able to bear his ugly body, Alyasef closed his eyes, but with his eyes closed, he felt as if the shape of his body were changing. Finally, very much afraid, he asked himself, "Am I not still myself?" This thought nearly crushed his heart. Still very much afraid, after a while he opened one eye and stole a glance at his body. He took heart that his body was still the same as it had been. Then he opened his eyes all the way, looked with satisfaction at his body, and said, "I am certainly still in my own human body." But then all by itself a suspicion again entered his mind that his body might be changing into something worse and once more he closed his eyes.

Alyasef closed his eyes. With his eyes closed, his mind turned inward and he felt himself sinking down into a dark well. He cried out in pain: "O my God, I feel hell both inside and outside myself!" As Alyasef sank further into the dark well, the former faces of his fellow creatures pursued him and memories of the past besieged him. Alyasef remembered how his fellow men had gone fishing on the Sabbath, and how as their hands filled with fish the sea became empty of fish, and how, when their greed increased, they started to go fishing even on the Sabbath.

And then the person who had forbidden them to go fishing on the Sabbath said, "It was the Word of God that created the deep waters of the sea and gave the deep waters to the fish for refuge. Now the sea seeks protection from your greedy hands. Therefore, you must refrain from destroying fish on the Sabbath, lest you find yourselves destroying your own lives."

And Alyasef said, "By God, I shall refrain from fishing on the Sabbath." And as Alyasef was a clever man, he dug a pool a little way in from the sea, then dug a canal from it, leading back to the sea. On the Sabbath, when the fish came up to the surface, they swam into the canal and then into the pool, and the day after the Sabbath Alyasef caught many fish in the pool.

When the person who had forbidden catching fish on the Sabbath saw this, he said, "Verily, God will deceive anyone who deceives Him. And God is surely the greater deceiver."

Thinking of this, Alyasef was ashamed of it, and he felt with dread that he was surrounded by deception. He felt at this moment his whole life was nothing but deception. He prostrated himself in God's presence, saying, "O Creator, You created me as only You can. You fashioned me according to the best standard and cast me in Your image. Would you, therefore, O Creator, now deceive me and make me into a vile monkey?" And Alyasef wept over his state. There was a breach in the dike he had made and seawater was coming onto the island.

Alyasef wept over his state, and turning his face away from the monkey-filled town, he went toward the forest, for now the town seemed even more terrifying to him than the forest; and, like language, the houses, with their walls and roofs, had totally lost any meaning. He spent the night hidden in the branches of a tree.

When he awoke in the morning, his whole body hurt and there was a pain in his back. He glanced at his body which now seemed even more changed. He was afraid and wondered if he were still himself. He desperately wished there were someone in the town who could tell him which body he was in. This led him to wonder whether it was necessary to be among men to remain a man. He answered his own question: "Man is surely incomplete by himself, for man is bound to man, and one shall be raised along with those with whom he belongs." With this thought, his soul was deeply troubled, and he called out, "O daughter of Akhzar, where are you, for I am incomplete without you." Immediately the memory of quivering fawns, and a heap of wheat, and a round sandalwood cup rushed in on him. As the seawater flooded the island, Alyasef cried out in pain, "O daughter of Akhzar, O you for whom my heart longs, I shall reach for you on a canopied bed spread out on a high roof, in the dense foliage of tall trees and in high towers! I beseech you in the name of galloping milk-white mares, of doves winging their way to the heights, of the dew-filled night, of the darkness when it seeps into bodies, I beseech you in the name of darkness, and sleep and sleep-heavy eyelids—to come and embrace me, for my heart longs for you!" And as he cried this, many of the words became jumbled, as if the thread of them were tangled, as if some of the words were being erased, as if his voice were changing. And Alyasef noticed his changing voice and remembered Ibn Zablun and Alyab and the way their voices had changed. Afraid that his voice had changed, Alyasef wondered, "O God, have I really changed?" He had the strange thought that perhaps there was some kind of device by which he could actually see his face. But this seemed very unlikely, and he groaned, "O God, how can I know that I haven't changed?"

Alyasef first thought of going back to the town, but this idea struck terror in him and his heart began to thump at the thought of the great empty houses of the town, and the tall forest trees continued to draw him toward them. As his terror rose at the thought of returning to the town, he went deeper into the forest. When he had gone a long way, he came to a lake with still water. He sat down at the edge of the lake, drank some water, and rested. Just then, staring at the pearl-like water, he was startled. "Is this me?" he cried, seeing his face in the water. Then he screamed. And his scream took hold of him and he started to run.

Alyasef's scream took hold of him. And he ran and ran, heedlessly, as if the lake were pursuing him. After a while, the soles of his feet began to hurt and a terrible pain shot forth through his spine. Still he ran, although the pain in his back grew even greater. And then he felt the impulse to bend over and he put his hands on the ground very naturally. Alyasef bent down and put his hand on the ground, and, smelling the daughter of Akhzar, took off like a shot on all fours.

Translated by Leslie A. Flemming

The Prisoner(s)

"Now *you* tell me what happened here."

"Here? What can I tell you?"

The fact was Anwar had not expected the question. If not consciously, certainly subconsciously, he had convinced himself that whatever had happened, had happened only over there. Consequently, all this time he had been showering Javed with questions. Now, asked about what happened here at home, he was caught unawares.

"So, what did happen here?" Javed persisted.

"Here?" Anwar had to think for a moment. "Nothing happened here."

"Nothing?"

"That's a fact. Nothing at all. Compared to what you saw over there, nothing whatsoever happened here."

"I see—over there we thought a whole lot was going on here too!"

"No, my friend, nothing at all." Anwar sounded a bit abashed.

"But the war was here too, wasn't it?"

"Yes," Anwar replied, somewhat crestfallen, "the war was also here."

Their conversation dragged to a halt. The passion Anwar had earlier shown asking questions was now gone. Javed too didn't display further curiosity about the matter, as if he had asked the question just in passing.

After a while Anwar continued on his own. "Actually, nothing happened here from the outside. Whatever occurred had its sources within."

"Nothing ever happens from outside," Javed remarked quietly. "It always happens from within."

"That's not true," Anwar responded with some heat. "Certainly over there most of it was done from outside. Here, though, more was done from within. That's why very little happened here during the war, but much more occurred afterward."

"Really?"

"Yes."

"Like what?"

"Strikes, lockouts, demonstrations, student unrest, riots, arrests . . ."

Javed had picked up an illustrated magazine from the table and was flipping the pages. He had seen it lying on the table all day long but had neither found a moment of leisure to look through it nor felt a strong urge to do so. Right now, however, it had drawn his attention. He seemed to find its pictures most attractive.

"There was nearly a civil war at the university," Anwar continued. "Barricades were put up. Stenguns were brought in. There was an exchange of fire all day long."

"This's quite good," Javed remarked with a smile.

"What is?"

"This cartoon." Javed passed the magazine to Anwar.

Anwar glanced at the cartoon, not quite seeing it. "Yeah," he said half-heartedly, "it's all right," and fell silent.

"Why don't we go out for a while," Javed suggested.

"Yes, let's."

"You know, if we stayed at home this would just go on. They'll just keep coming, these well-wishers. The same questions—the same talk. This is another prison. Let's get out of here." He quickly stepped over to the door leading inside and called in a loud voice, "I'm going out with Anwar for a while."

The two walked out of the room and left the house.

"Did you hear over there about the riots in Sind?"

It had suddenly occurred to Anwar that that had been a tragic and terrible event and that Javed should be informed about it.

"Yes, we heard the news on the radio."

"You couldn't have learned much from radio bulletins. Some real horrible things happened then. Quite a few people got killed. Many more made homeless. You saw the Liaquat Market before you went away—remember how big it was?—well, the whole complex was burned down. No one was spared . . ."

"Hey, what are those checker marks on her belly?" Javed had suddenly stopped, staring at something.

Anwar left his sentence unfinished and turned to look in the direction Javed was staring. It was a huge poster outside a movie house showing a half-nude woman in a reclining pose. There were squares drawn across her plump thighs and undulating belly. Anwar used to pass that way every day, always making a point of ogling the picture, but today it displeased him very much.

"Yech—never mind," and moved on.

"Want some ice cream?" Anwar asked, stopping in front of a booth.

"All right."

As they were eating the ice cream, Javed's eyes pursued a girl in flappers and oversized sunglasses till she disappeared into a store.

"Anwar, old pal, it seems like bellbottoms disappeared while I was gone."

"And tight pants too."

"Yes, both the tight pants and the tight shirts. But, Anwar, you never told me what happened here."

"You just saw what happened," Anwar replied with sarcasm, gulping his ice cream. "Bellbottoms bade us farewell; flappers joined us."

"You think that's a simple matter?"

"No, it's a big event," Anwar became more sarcastic. "And what do you think," he added, after a pause, "of this major event?"

"Frankly, I have yet to get accustomed to these flappers." Javed finished the ice cream and threw the paper cup into the wastebasket. "Shall we go?"

They moved on.

Anwar was no longer in that serious mood. Still, when he noticed Javed's inquisitiveness about even very small things, he ventured to ask a question again.

"Tell me, how did you react when you first got back?"

"What do you mean?"

"I mean, how did you feel when you came back here after your long imprisonment?"

"That's fantastic!" Javed had again come to a sudden stop.

"What? What happened?"

"Just look at that fellow. He's wearing pink *shalwars*! I think they're made of silk!"

"So what?"

"So what! I see . . ." Javed fell silent for a while, then continued, "These colorful silk *shalwars* are very popular with the boys, aren't they? I've seen so many of them, wearing red or yellow silk *shalwars* and shirts."

"Yes, they're quite common now. Listen, would you like to try some pan-fried meat?"

"Pan-fried meat?"

"That's right, pan-fried. It's time for supper anyway. There's no rush to go home. We'll have some meat, then take a long walk."

The place was crowded. Lines of cars were parked on both sides of the road. Over the entire spread of the grass and even on the sidewalk there were tables and chairs, row after row. It seemed every table was occupied. Further away, beneath a huge sign that had a goat painted on it, hung whole legs of meat. The hearths were ablaze, their flames leaping upward.

"The place is full."

"Doesn't matter. We'll soon get a seat."

Just then Anwar saw a table at a distance being vacated. He rushed over and claimed it. It was on the sidewalk, and right near it stood a car, whose hood was at the moment serving as a dining table for a bunch of boys and girls dipping into a pot brimful of meat.

"This," remarked Javed, surveying the busy diners around him, "this too is something from after my days."

"What thing?"

"This pan-fried meat."

"You're right. This is the newest dish in the city."

Javed looked at his surroundings again—at the lines of cars, at the endless rows of chairs and tables, at the throngs of people busily eating.

"This used to be a quiet area," he remarked. Then added, "It's amazing how all this crowd is just for *tikka kabab* and *karhai gosht*. I don't think previously there were so many kabab shops either."

Anwar was not being attentive; his eyes were fixed on the flaming hearths. "He's taking a long time to bring the meat," he remarked.

Javed settled down to look around more carefully. Young and old, men and women, delicate ladies and rotund gents—they were completely engrossed in eating. At one table nearby sat a hefty man eating away, not bothering even to look up, while sweat gushed out of every pore of his body. At another was a couple—the man in a fine suit and the lady, quite slim, in a finely draped sari. Their pan was nearly empty. The plate in front of the lady was piled with bones, and she was busy pulling the last shreds of meat from a shinbone. Beyond that table there were so many more tables, each with a pot of meat, flying hands stuffing morsels into mouths and dully munching jaws surrounding it. Amazed, he wondered how many jaws were opening and shutting around him. Jaws that kept growing large in his imagination till the wonder turned into terror.

"Anwar!" he said anxiously, "People seem to eat a lot more these days!"

Anwar only half-heard him, for a pan of meat had been placed on their table. "Come on, my friend, let's eat."

Javed put a morsel in his mouth. He wondered how big his jaws were.

"You're not eating."

"I am."

"No, you're not. Don't worry about table manners here. This is *karhai gosht*, my friend; to eat it one must become a bit of a barbarian."

For Anwar's sake he took a few quick bites, then let his hand slacken again. His mind wandered away. "How is Khalid? I haven't met any of the old gang yet."

"Khalid?" Anwar stopped, a morsel of meat in his fingers. "Didn't I tell you about Khalid?"

"No."

Anwar remained silent a few moments, then, swallowing the morsel he had been chewing, said, "Khalid passed away."

"Really? Him too?" His brows puckering in a frown, Javed asked, "How many deaths have you told me about, Anwar? Did so many die in just two years?"

"Yes, quite a lot of people seem to have died in the past two years."

"And they all died in their beds!" Javed remarked softly, his voice so full of wonder.

"What do you mean?" Anwar felt himself at a loss.

"It's like this. Over there death came differently. Over there we came to be estranged from the old, familiar ways of death." Javed paused, then added, "That's why we felt so strange when Rashid died."

"Rashid! Rashid is dead? But he was in Rajshahi, wasn't he?"

"Yes, he was in Rajshahi earlier, but in the last days he fled and came to Dhaka. Stayed with me for a few days, then died—but in his bed."

"So Rashid's dead too." Anwar muttered—more to himself—in grief.

"But we did manage to give him not only a shroud but also a proper burial."

Anwar couldn't comprehend Javed's words; he kept staring at his face.

"Rashid's death," Javed added as an explanation, "was perhaps the last conventional death in that country," and fell silent.

For some time they kept eating quietly—or at least pretended to eat—then drank some water and pushed the pot away. Javed again surveyed his surroundings. Many faces were new. There were fresh pots on the tables and new diners surrounding them—new jaws that munched and chewed and grew large just the same. He turned away from them and spoke to Anwar.

"Didn't you ask me how I felt when I first got back here?"

"Yes, I did."

"Well, my friend, at first I felt everything had changed. I was quite shocked. Then gradually I realized that nothing at all had changed. That was again a tremendous shock."

"And how do you reconcile these two impressions?" asked Anwar with a frown.

"I don't even try to. It doesn't matter, really," said Javed, and changed the subject. "Now it's your turn."

"If only I had something worth telling." Anwar felt too depressed to talk.

"Who were you talking about yesterday?"

"Who? What? I don't remember."

"The one who got shot."

"Oh! You mean Mirza?"

"Mirza was shot? How did that happen?"

"It was like this. He was coming out of the public meeting. The meeting had just ended and the road was filled with people."

"That's the trouble with these public meetings—afterward there are always crowds milling around. Anyway, what happened then?"

"He started to cross the road, then somebody shot at him and he died on the spot."

"Shot at him? But why?"

"Just like that."

"Oh . . .! That's amazing. Then what happened?"

"What could have?"

"You mean nothing happened?" Javed sounded a bit scared.

"No. What could have happened?"

"A man got shot; still nothing happened! That's amazing! That *is* amazing!"

"You're right. I never thought of that before."

"You never gave it a thought?" Javed sounded more terrified than amazed.

"That's true, my friend," Anwar replied, somewhat abashed. He then glanced at Javed with a look of surprise on his face.

"Javed!"

"Yes?"

"You . . . you must have seen worse things over there?—didn't you?"

Javed hesitated a moment before answering. "Yes," he said, in a voice full of sorrow, "you're right. But at least we knew why things were happening—we were at least aware of what was going on . . ."

Translated by C. M. Naim

Note

Translator's Note: The Urdu title *"Asır"* allows both singular and plural references; the author seems to want to be deliberately ambiguous as to who was/is a prisoner.

The Turtles

Vidyasagar fell silent. He listened to the loud voices of the monks as they were talking; he watched them argue and he became silent. He kept listening, he kept watching, and he remained silent. Then he got up from their midst and went outside the town, far from the town dwellers, and sat beneath a *shal* tree in contemplation. He focused his gaze upon a lotus flower which bloomed and then wilted. After the first flower a second, and after the second a third. Whichever flower he cast his glance upon blossomed, unfolded, and then faded. He grieved when he saw this and closed his eyes. He sat for a long time with his eyes shut.

After many days his old associates Sundar Samudr and Gopal approached him and said, "O Vidyasagar, we are sad."

Vidyasagar just sat there—peace personified—and didn't so much as open his mouth. Gopal said in a disheartened voice, "How unjust it is that those who should rather not speak are talking too much and the one who should really be talking has fallen silent."

And Sundar Samudr spoke, "Subhadra spoke and he acted. Subhadra said that Tathagat is no longer in our midst. He always kept us in check by saying, 'Do this; don't do that!' Now we just do whatever we feel like doing. O Vidyasagar, now all the monks are doing whatever their hearts desire and their hearts are in the grip of lust. They have abandoned their mattresses of straw. Now they sleep on cots and sit upon carpets. O virtuous one, O wise one, why do you not speak?"

Vidyasagar finally opened his eyes. He stared intently at Sundar Samudr and Gopal. He asked, "Friends, have you heard the *Jataka* story of the parrot?"

"No."

"Then listen." Vidyasagar began to tell the fable. "Once upon a time long ago King Brahmadatt ruled in Banaras, and our Lord Buddha had taken birth in the form of a parrot. He had a baby brother. Both of them were young when a birdcatcher caught them and sold them to a Brahman from Banaras. The Brahman cared for both parrots as if he were bringing up his own children. One day the Brahman had to go abroad. At the time of his departure he told the birds, 'Pollies, be sure to mind your mother.'

"The Brahman gone, his wife began to cheat on him. The younger parrot tried to stop her, but the older parrot said, 'O friend, don't butt in.' But the younger one paid no attention to him and tried to stop the woman anyway. The sly woman, pretending to be sincere, said, 'All right now, I won't commit any more sins; you did well to stop me. Come out of the cage that I may show my affection.' The poor, innocent bird came out and the woman immediately wrung his neck.

"When the Brahman returned home after some time he asked the elder parrot, 'Polly, what did your mother do behind my back?' The parrot replied, 'Your honor, where there is sin the wise remain silent, because in such a situation one's life may be endangered by speaking.'

"As the parrot said this, he thought to himself, 'Where it is impossible to speak freely, it is hard to live. I should go where I may speak.' Flapping his wings, the parrot said, 'Most exalted highness, let me leave.' The Brahman asked, 'Polly, where would you go?' The parrot answered, 'Somewhere I can speak freely.' Saying this, Lord Buddha left the bustling city of Banaras and flew toward the jungle."

The story recited, Vidyasagar got up from beneath the *shal* tree and stepped forward. He kept walking and walking. After walking a great distance, he took up residence in an uninhabited forest. Sundar Samudr and Gopal, following close behind him, also made it to the forest with great hardship and facing many obstacles.

Vidyasagar sat in the hero-posture for three days and three nights, his eyes closed, without eating or drinking. On the fourth day Sundar Samudr and Gopal each took their begging bowls and went out of the forest. They returned in the evening with their bowls. Sitting down by Vidyasagar they said, "O Vidyasagar, did not Tathagat say one should take food only to fill the stomach and drink water only to slake the thirst?"

Vidyasagar opened his eyes upon hearing this. He ate whatever was placed before him as if there were no taste in it at all. And he drank the clear, cool water of the river as if it were boiling hot. Then he said that he had only mixed dust with dust.

Sundar Samudr seized the occasion to say, "O Vidyasagar, the monks have strayed away from the true principles. They are not fulfilling the rules established by Tathagat. They have forsaken the shade of trees and lounge around under roofs on high cots. How many groups have been made out of one brotherhood! And how many sects have arisen! And every sect is the mortal enemy of all the others. Return and instruct them because you are the most virtuous and wisest among us."

Vidyasagar said, "O Sundar Samudr, have you heard the *Jataka* story of the mynah bird?"

"No."

"Then listen. A long time ago when King Brahmadatt ruled over

Banaras, our Lord Buddha was living in the jungle in the form of a mynah bird. He built himself a beautiful nest in the dense branches of a tree and began to live there. One day there was a heavy rainstorm. A sopping-wet monkey came out of nowhere and sat down next to the mynah's nest in that very same tree. But even there he was still getting wet from the raindrops. The mynah said, 'O monkey, you always imitate man so much. Why don't you imitate him in building houses? If you had a house of your own today, you wouldn't be so miserable on account of a little rain.' The monkey replied, 'Dear mynah, I just imitate, I don't have any brains.' But after saying that, the monkey thought to himself, 'It's easy for the mynah to talk as he sits comfortably in his house; but would he still talk smart if he didn't have a house and were soaked like me?' Thinking this, he tore up the mynah's nest. Lord Buddha became homeless in that pelting rain. He recited a hymn, expounding how when one gives advice to everyone and anyone, one asks for trouble for nothing. Chanting that hymn, he fled from the jungle to another one soaked to the skin."

After telling that story Vidyasagar sighed deeply and said, "What did Lord Buddha do for the monkeys and what did the monkeys do to him?" He then told this tale.

"Brahmadatt presided on the royal throne of Banaras when Lord Buddha, taking birth as a monkey, was living in the jungle. He grew up to be a healthy, strapping monkey and became king of all the monkeys who lived in the king's mango grove. One day during mango season the king came into the grove and felt terribly irritated seeing that the monkeys were damaging the fruit. He called for his archers and instructed them, 'Surround the grove and shoot your arrows so that not a single monkey is spared.'

"The monkeys heard all this. They approached Lord Buddha and implored, 'O king of monkeys, tell us what we should do now.' Lord Buddha said, 'Don't worry at all. I am devising a plan at this very moment.' So saying, he climbed a tree whose branches extended far across the breadth of the Ganges. Leaping to the opposite bank from the last branch, he measured the distance and broke off a piece of bamboo of the same length which he then tied to a bush on the other bank. He then tried to bring the bamboo piece back to the branch of the tree. But he had miscalculated the distance; a small space, about the length of his own body, still remained between the end of the bamboo and the branch. What did Lord Buddha do but tie one of his legs to the end of the bamboo pole and grasp the mango branch with his hands. He then said to the monkeys, 'Look, I have made myself into a bridge. Go over me to the bamboo pole. From the pole jump across the Ganges.'

"Eighty thousand monkeys, besieged in the mango orchard, all passed slowly and carefully over Lord Buddha's back so as not to cause him pain. But, as luck would have it, Devdatt was also among the monkeys. He too had taken birth as a monkey at that same time. He thought, 'Why don't I finish off Buddha once and for all in this birth?' He jumped on Lord Buddha's back with such force that he almost killed him.

"The king, who had been watching all this, quickly brought Lord Buddha down from above and, bathing him in the Ganges, wrapped him in a yellow shawl, anointed him with perfume, and administered medicine to him. Then he sat at his feet and said, 'O monkey-king, you made yourself a bridge for your subjects but look what they do to you.' Lord Buddha replied, 'O king, there is a lesson in this for you. A king must never allow his subjects to be in distress, even if he must lose his life because of it.' So saying, Lord Buddha breathed his last and left his monkey incarnation for another birth."

That *Jataka* tale made all three of them—Vidyasagar, Sundar Samudr, and Gopal—very sad. They lamented that Tathagat had taken so many births to save the world and had suffered all kinds of pain. But in every rebirth, demons such as Devdatt were also born who kept on creating troubles for Tathagat. Sundar Samudr asked, "O Vidyasagar, wasn't Devdatt Lord Buddha's brother?"

"He was indeed his brother." Saying this, Vidyasagar laughed at first and then cried.

"O wise one, why do you laugh and why do you cry?" asked Gopal.

"If a nanny goat can laugh and cry, why can't I—human being that I am—laugh and cry as well?"

Sundar Samudr's curiosity was peaked. "Why did the nanny goat laugh and why did she cry?"

Vidyasagar replied by telling a *Jataka* story: "Friends, once upon a time when King Brahmadatt ruled in Banaras, there was a Brahman who was well versed in the knowledge of the Vedas. He bought a nanny goat with the intention of performing a sacrifice for the dead. He bathed the nanny goat and placed a wreath around her neck. The nanny goat, upon seeing the preparations for her own sacrifice, first laughed and then cried. The Brahman asked, 'O nanny goat, why did you laugh and why did you cry?' The nanny goat replied, 'O Brahman, in my previous birth I, too, was a Brahman and a great authority in the learning of the Vedas. One day I also bought a nanny goat to offer to the dead and I cut its throat. But in return for having cut the nanny goat's throat once, my own throat has been cut five hundred times. Today the knife will pass across my throat for the five hundred and first time. When I realized this, I laughed because today is the very last time my throat will be slit. After this I will be liberated from my troubles. And I cried when I realized that in exchange for cutting my throat, you will have your throat cut five hundred times.'

"The Brahman said, 'O nanny goat, don't be afraid. I will not cut your throat.'

"The nanny goat laughed out loud and said, 'I'm a goat, and my throat is to be cut, if not by your hands, then by someone else's.'

"The Brahman pretended not to hear the nanny goat. He freed her and told his students to look after her. The students took very good care of her but that which was ordained came to pass. The nanny goat tugged on the branch of a tree while grazing. The tree fell over her and she dropped dead.

"Now listen, O friends. Next to that tree stood a beautiful tree. This was Lord Buddha, who had taken birth in the form of a tree. He immediately left his tree incarnation and, striking a posture, sat in the middle of the sky. The people were astounded to see this and began to gather together. At that instant Lord Buddha recited an auspicious hymn whose import is this: see what comes of slaughtering; he who slits another's throat will one day have his own throat cut."

Sundar Samudr and Gopal listened intently to the *Jataka* story and nodded their heads in reverence. But then Sundar Samudr said, "My question still remains: was not Devdatt Lord Buddha's brother?"

"O Sundar Samudr," said Vidyasagar, "don't ask this question. If you do, then I'll just laugh and then I'll cry."

"O wise one, why will you laugh and why will you cry?"

"After telling you that Devdatt was the brother of our Lord Buddha, I will laugh. And I will cry when I will recall that Devdatt was also a monk."

Sundar Samudr also cried upon hearing this and said, "Master, what has become of these monks?"

Vidyasagar looked at Sundar Samudr angrily. "O Sundar Samudr, do not ask *this*."

"Why should I not ask?"

"Do not ask because it so happens that, searching for evil we often end up beholding ourselves."

"How is this so?"

"Like this: the wife of King Brahmadatt of Banaras was having an affair with another man. When the king questioned her, she said, 'If I have been consorting with another man, then may I turn into a witch after I die and may I have a mare's head.' It came to pass that after dying the queen did actually turn into a witch with a mare's head. She went into the woods and took up living in a cave. She used to catch passersby and eat them. One day a Brahman, on his way back from studying in Taxila, passed by. The witch hoisted him upon her back and carried him to her cave. But the Brahman was young, and when their bodies touched the witch became impassioned. Once in the cave, she began to sport with him. The Brahman was learned, but he was young too; learning has its proper time and place, but youth has its as well! So he also became aroused. They kissed and caressed and made love. The witch became pregnant from this encounter. After nine months she gave birth to a son. This son was in reality our great

Lord Buddha, who this time had taken birth in the form of a witch's son. When he grew up, he resolved to free his father from the witch's yoke and to live in the midst of human beings. The witch said, 'My beloved, now that you have made up your mind to go among people, at least listen to the words of your poor mother. You will find it much easier to get along among witches. It is hard work to get along with men. I will tell you a spell that will be of use to you in that world. By the power of this spell you will be able to see a man's footprints for up to twelve miles.'

"Taking the spell from his mother, the son reached Banaras along with his father. He secured employment at the court of the king after telling him of his power. Seeing this, the courtiers whispered among themselves. They said to the king, 'O Great King, shouldn't we perhaps find out whether the man has this power or not?' So in order to test him, the king stole some valuables from the royal treasury and, carrying them to a distant pond, threw them in. The next day there was a great uproar because the royal treasury had been robbed. The king ordered Lord Buddha to find out about the robbery. Lord Buddha immediately saw the footprints and recovered the treasure from the pond.

"The king said, 'You did well in finding the stolen goods but you did not tell me who the thief was.' Lord Buddha said, 'Great King, you have gotten your treasure back. What good will asking the name of the thief do you?' The king did not heed him and persisted, 'Tell me the name of the thief.' Lord Buddha said, 'O king, let me tell you a story. You are intelligent. You will understand its meaning. A dancer began to drown while bathing in the Ganges. His wife saw this and screamed, "Swami, you are drowning. Pray, play your flute and teach me a tune so that I may acquire some skill to support myself after you are gone." The dancer, as he was sinking, shouted, "Hey, lucky one, how can I play my flute or teach you a tune? That very water which gives sustenance to all creatures and brings life to the soil is killing me!" Then he recited a hymn which means, "He who was once my protector has now become my destroyer."'

"After recounting this tale, Lord Buddha remarked, 'Great King, a king too is like water unto his subjects. If that very protector becomes a life-taker, what will become of the subjects?'

"The king listened to the story but remained restless. 'Friend,' he said, 'your story was good. But I ask about the thief. Tell me his name.'

"Lord Buddha said, 'O Great King, listen very carefully to what I say.' And then he told this story: 'In Banaras there lived a potter. Every day he used to leave town and go into the jungle to dig clay for his pots. Because he kept digging clay from the same spot, a pit was formed there. One day he went down into the pit and was digging when a dust storm blew over and a great heap of dirt fell on him. The poor man's head was broken. He screamed and recited a hymn: "That very earth from which buds sprout and from which living things get their food has crushed me. That very thing which was my protector has become my murderer."' And then Lord Buddha added, 'O Great King, a king is like the earth unto his subjects. He takes care of them. But if he starts to oppress his subjects, what will become of them?'

"The king heard the story and said, 'That story was no answer to my question. Go catch the thief and bring him before me.' Lord Buddha said, 'There was a man in that very city of Banaras. One day he ate a huge amount of rice. He became so ill that he was about to die. He screamed, "That same rice from which countless Brahmans have gained strength has snatched mine away." So, O Great King, a king too is like rice unto his subjects. He satisfies their hunger and gives them strength. But if he himself saps the strength of his subjects, then what will become of them?'

"This story also went in the king's one ear and out the other. He said, 'Friend, don't stall me with any more stories. Tell me about the thief.' Lord Buddha said, 'O Great King, there was a tree upon a mountain in the Himalayas. It had many branches and a great many birds dwelt among them. One day two stout branches rubbed against each other and sparks began to fly. A bird saw this and yelled, "O birds, fly away from here! The same tree which gave us shelter is now roasting us. That which was our protector has become our destroyer." And O Great King, just as a tree gives shelter to birds, so a king gives shelter to his subjects. But if the shelter-giver becomes a thief, what will become of the birds?'

"That foolish king still did not grasp the meaning of that story and kept asking the name of the thief. Lord Buddha, finally, gave in. 'Alright,' he said, 'gather all your subjects together. Then I will tell you the name of the thief.' So the king had the drums sounded and his subjects assembled. Then Lord Buddha said in a loud voice, 'O citizens of Banaras, listen carefully and pay attention to me. The same earth in which you have buried your treasures has robbed you of those riches.'

"The people were astonished when they heard this. They right away knew what Lord Buddha was driving at. They fell upon the king. After they had dispensed with him, they seated Lord Buddha upon the royal throne and hailed him."

As they listened both Sundar Samudr and Gopal hailed Tathagat too with enthusiasm. Vidyasagar looked at them both in order to determine whether they would pursue the question. Then he said, "O monks, he who explained everything to you and me has passed on to the next world. So now do not ask anyone else but become your own light unto yourself, for this is precisely the advice Amitabh had given to Anand when he passed on."

Both Sundar Samudr and Gopal recalled the passing on of Tathagat with sadness and said, "That light which illuminated the entire world and showed us the way has gone out. Now the universe is in darkness. Now we wander astray in the dim light of our own lamps. The darkness keeps spreading and our flickering lamps grow fainter and fainter."

Vidyasagar stopped them and said, "Friends, you misunderstand the point of Amitabh. He is an eternal flame, how can he be extinguished?"

Upon hearing this, both Sundar Samudr and Gopal repented their error. They regarded Amitabh with reverence and they saw a light spreading from the earth to the heavens. Their bodies trembled and tears poured forth from their eyes. And together with Vidyasagar they prayed, "We monks beseech you, Tathagat Amitabh, who dwells in heaven, upon whom fragrant blossoms rain continually. O Atmarupi, O Sage of the Shakya Clan, O Ocean of Knowledge, O Amitabh, we call upon you with veneration. Come and inhabit our beings and rekindle the light within us."

They fell silent but the torrent of tears continued to flow. They called to mind the days when Amitabh was present among them and a radiance spread everywhere—from city to city, through towns and jungles, and along roads and highways. "In those days," began Vidyasagar, "we would travel all through the night with Amitabh. In the dark nights we passed through dense forests, but it never seemed to me that I was walking in darkness. The path was always as clear and visible as if it were the night of the full moon. Trees and plants, flowers and leaves . . . it was as if the whole earth and sky were luminous and were paying homage to Amitabh."

As he listened, Gopal recalled those days. "Friends, how much we used to walk in those days. We kept on walking, sometimes through dense jungles, sometimes across desolate plains, and sometimes from city to city, from alleyway to alleyway, carrying our begging bowls."

Sundar Samudr abruptly returned from the past to the present. He said sadly, "Now the monks have ceased to wander about. Their feet have become tired, their bodies have grown flabby, and their stomachs have swelled."

Vidyasagar said on this point, "Friends, Tathagat has said that he who grows fat by eating a great deal and sleeps will remain trapped in the cycle of rebirth. Like a pig, he will be born again and again and he will die again and again."

Sundar Samudr said, "O sage, the monks do eat a lot, sleep on cots, and flirt with women."

"They flirt with women?" said Vidyasagar in an alarmed voice.

"Yes, master, they flirt with women. And I have also seen nuns of our own order smile and talk with them and wear ankle bracelets."

Vidyasagar closed his eyes and muttered in a sad voice, "O Tathagat, your monks have strayed from you. I am alone in this ocean of worldly illusion."

Sundar Samudr and Gopal also shut their eyes and murmured, "O

Tathagat, we are alone and are sad and the ocean of illusion and transmigration is raging about us."

They remained seated with their eyes closed. Then Sundar Samudr opened his eyes and said, "Gopal, do you realize that today we roamed through the whole town and received all kinds of alms except rice pudding?" Gopal agreed. "You have spoken the truth. We did not get rice pudding from anyone. Only once in a great while now do we get any."

Sundar Samudr posed a question: "Why is rice pudding no longer being cooked in the homes? Have the people forgotten Tathagat or have the cows started to give less milk?"

Gopal, remembering bygone days, said, "In those days all men and women used to say their rosary in Tathagat's name and the cows' udders were always full of milk. So much rice pudding used to be cooked in the houses that even outsiders ate to their hearts' content and there were still leftovers."

"And we used to enjoy eating rice pudding so much." Sundar Samudr's mouth began to water.

Vidyasagar became angry and looked at him. "Enjoyed it? Fool, do you eat for enjoyment?"

"No, master," Sundar Samudr said contritely. "I never took pleasure in eating a single meal. I always ate with the thought in mind that I was merely mingling dust with dust and simply filling my stomach. But when there used to be rice pudding, I remembered the rice pudding which Sujata fed Tathagat and something strange would happen to my palate and tongue."

Vidyasagar explained to both of them, "Friends, do not recall forgotten pleasures and tastes lest you should be caught again in the outspread snare of the senses."

Both of them pulled at their ears in repentance and said, "O master, we have already renounced every form of pleasure; now we take pleasure only in the memory of Tathagat."

Once again they recalled the Shakyamuni, who unceasingly imparted to the monks the teaching that this world is illusory and its pleasures are hollow. Gopal said, "Sundar Samudr, do you remember that time Tathagat snatched you from the net of lust for women?"

"From the net of lust?" Sundar Samudr tried hard to recall.

"Foolish man, you forgot, but I remember it to this very day: Tathagat was sitting with his eyes in tranquil meditation. We were gazing upon him with love and reverence. We noticed a slight smile upon his lips. Anand asked, 'O Tathagat, what makes you smile?' He answered, 'Right now a monk is having an encounter with a woman.' 'Who will win this confrontation?' Anand asked. 'The contest is most vigorous,' replied Tathagat. 'And the woman is clever. Now she embraces him and then withdraws, sulking and coy. She reveals her body and then covers it up again. She shows off the splendor of her full, voluptuous breasts and then conceals them. She begins to lower her skirt and then pulls it back up.'"

Sundar Samudr kept listening. Memories of that time came flooding back to him like an ocean. And then he said, "What a time you have reminded me of. Yes, the test was very severe. What a woman she was . . . like a lotus flower. When I first went to that town, I would roam from neighborhood to neighborhood, from street to street, from house to house begging for alms. But her beauty so enchanted me that I forgot all other paths and remained glued to her threshold alone. Every day I went up to her door and called, 'O beautiful lady, give a monk his alms!' That lovely woman took a liking to me and gave me a lot of food. I took great pleasure in it. And one day her bounty exceeded all limits; I felt that was my day. She brought me inside her house and fastened the door and then fell into my lap like a flower. Gopal, don't ask what a soft, tender body it was, what voluptuous breasts she had, and what full, round buttocks. And her stomach was creamy white and soft. No sooner had our bodies met than the image of Tathagat sailed before my eyes." Sundar Samudr took a deep sigh and fell silent.

"Then what happened?" Gopal asked. Sundar Samudr replied in a dull, lifeless voice, "What did you expect to happen? I suppressed my desire and came away thirsty from that sweet, cool river."

Sundar Samudr became quiet and closed his eyes as if he were lost in faraway thoughts. Then he opened them and said softly, "I wonder where she would now be."

"Who?" Gopal looked at him in bewilderment.

"That beautiful woman."

"Who knows where."

Sundar Samudr stood up. Gopal saw, with some amazement, that his feet were directed toward the city. Gopal called, "O friend, come back!" But Sundar Samudr kept on walking as if lost in a daze and went farther and farther away. Gopal called loudly, "Friend, come back!"

"Sundar Samudr is not going to return," observed Vidyasagar in a dry, matter-of-fact voice, "because he is now firmly in the grip of desire."

"O Vidyasagar," shouted Gopal, "pray, do something that he may escape the clutches of desire and come back."

In the same dry voice Vidyasagar said, "O Gopal, forget him. Save yourself, if you can."

"Master, don't worry about me. I am already saved."

Vidyasagar said nothing in reply to that. He kept quiet. Then he let forth a venomous laugh and remarked, "The one who talked here the most was the first to go. Desire carried him away as a flood does a sleeping village."

Gopal gazed intently at Vidyasagar's face for a while and then said, "O wise and virtuous one, what evil is there in talking?"

Vidyasagar replied, "Friend, perhaps you haven't heard the *Jataka* of the man who talked too much. Well then, listen: Our Great King, Lord Buddha, was once born into the household of a courtier. When he grew up he became the king's minister. That king, however, talked too much. Lord Buddha thought to himself that somehow it should be pointed out to him that a king's greatness lay not in talking too much but in listening a great deal.

"Now listen. In the foothills of the Himalayas there was a pond. In it lived a turtle. Two ducks flew over and came to live there also. In time they all became good, caring friends. One day it so happened that the water in the pond began to dry up. The ducks said to the turtle, 'Friend, our home is in the Himalayan mountains. There is plenty of water there, so you come along with us and spend your days in comfort and ease.' The turtle replied, 'Friends, I am an animal that crawls upon the earth. How can I, after all, attain such heights?' 'But if you promise,' said the ducks, 'not to open your mouth, we shall take you there.' The turtle promised to keep quiet. The ducks brought a stick, placed it before the turtle, and said, 'Grab this in the middle with your teeth and see that you don't open your mouth to speak.' Then one duck took one end of the stick in his beak, the other duck took the other end, and they flew away. When they flew over a city some children saw this strange spectacle and raised a ruckus. That made the turtle very angry. He started to say, 'Why are you jealous if my friends have come to my aid?' But as soon as he opened his mouth, he immediately fell to the ground.

"And where did this turtle fall but into the palace of the king! A tumult arose in the palace because a turtle, while flying through the air, had fallen to the ground. The king arrived at the scene in the company of Lord Buddha. Seeing the plight of the turtle, he asked Lord Buddha, 'Learned One, tell me how the turtle has been reduced to this miserable state.' Lord Buddha replied without hesitation, 'This is the result of talking too much.' He then related the whole story of the turtle and the ducks, concluding it with the remark: 'O king, those who talk too much come to grief like this.'

"The king thought hard about the words of Lord Buddha. And he took them to heart. From that day forward it came to pass that the king talked a great deal less and listened a great deal more."

After relating this *Jataka*, Vidyasagar observed, "Friend, we monks are turtles and we are in the midst of our journey. The monk who speaks at inappropriate times will fall and be left behind. You saw yourself how Sundar Samudr fell and was left behind."

Those words went straight to Gopal's heart. He said, "There were so many monks in mid-journey who fell and were left behind." And a little later, "From now on I'll remain quiet."

And Gopal did indeed become quiet. He would meditate, go to the city to beg, and return without talking with anyone. But one day his countryman and childhood friend Prabhakar caught up with him in the city. "Friend," he accosted him, "I have brought you a message. Listen: your father has passed away. The royal throne stands empty. Your mother calls you and your beautiful wife, adorned in all her glory, anxiously awaits your return."

Gopal said, "Friend, this world is an abode of sadness and pain; the royal throne is the net of temptation; and mother, father, and wife are all but the play of illusion. We monks are the children of Tathagat—only."

Having said this, Gopal turned away. Prabhakar called after him: "Friend, I heard your words. Even so, I shall stay in this town for three days and I'll sit on this very spot and await your return."

Although Gopal had walked away from his friend, he could not stop feeling greatly disturbed. Prabhakar's voice kept echoing in his ears. He approached Vidyasagar and, like a leaf falling from a tree, sat down next to him, and then he said, "O Wise one, I keep silent, still I feel I am falling. The stick is slipping from my teeth. Tell me what I should do."

Vidyasagar said, "Look at the flower."

Gopal, striking a posture, sat down in front of a nearby flower bush and began to gaze at a flower that had just blossomed. He kept staring. The flower continued to open. But then the color gradually faded and the flower wilted. He felt he had finally attained peace. "The world is insubstantial," he said to himself, closing his eyes. Early next morning, when he opened his eyes again, he saw another flower slowly opening on that same branch. Seeing it in its state of full bloom, Gopal's concentration was broken and he perceived a strange restlessness in himself. His eyes wandered thither and yon as he suddenly remembered that this was the third day. He stood up with a start. And his feet, of their own will, turned toward the city.

Vidyasagar watched him go but remained silent. When Gopal disappeared from sight, he laughed a venomous laugh. Then he remembered the words of Tathagat: "If during a journey the seeker is unable to find a wise companion, it is better then that he walk alone—like an elephant that walks alone through the jungle."

He found much solace remembering these words. He pondered over them and found them to contain profound meaning. "I first heard it from Tathagat and know from experience now that he who travels with a fool comes to endure great grief. It is better for a man to live and walk alone than to be in the company of fools." He recalled how much the company of Sundar Samudr and Gopal had taxed his contemplation and wisdom. They just kept on talking and time after time interrupted his meditation. It seemed to him that a heavy burden had been lifted from his shoulders by their departure. He felt himself strangely at ease and began to roam in the jungle as he pleased. Sometimes he walked through tall, tall grass; sometimes he set off down a narrow path; sometimes down a winding road. He looked at every branch and every leaf. He watched the flowers bloom and branches sway. He listened to the gurgle of the cool, refreshing stream as he walked along the riverbank. It seemed to him that the whole world had become filled with blissful music and the scent of the flowers pervaded the land and water and then he knew that he was attaining true wisdom. He thought, "Self-knowledge has its place but man must also obtain absolute wisdom."

He walked along many roads, full of the joy and bliss of absolute knowledge; he kept looking, kept listening, kept touching, kept smelling. In his wanderings he came upon a tree. "Hey, this is a tamarind tree!" He stopped short. He was amazed that he had lived in this jungle for so long and neglected to notice that there was a tamarind tree here. He was again amazed when he recalled how many forests he had wandered through after leaving the city and how many trees beneath whose shade he had camped and still had not spotted a single tamarind tree. "Well, I perhaps wasn't paying attention or maybe there just weren't any tamarind trees in those forests." Thinking these thoughts his mind traveled backward in time: the tall, dense tamarind; its long, arched fruit; the floating, descending flocks of parrots. Early at dawn in winter long lines of parrots arrived noisily and alighted on that tree. "I've seen many forests after that, but I've never seen such a lush tree and I've never seen so many parrots perched on a single tree." Little by little many more memories came back to him along with that of *that* tree: the winding, dusty roads stretching out on all sides, upon them the speeding chariots raising dust; squirrels racing up and down trees; and the chameleon, and how he would pick up a stick and run after a squirrel; how the squirrel ran off and climbed the tree and, standing on its hind legs on a branch, looked back at him and then hid itself in the foliage; and how a deep red mouth with a tongue like two threads suddenly appeared from out of a lair and then vanished, sending a wave of fear all through his body; and yes—Kaushambhi. Under the shade of the same tamarind tree she had met him at dusk, as a river meets the sea. First their lips met, then her supple arms went round his like slender branches. In an instant they had both gone off from the dusk of evening into the darkness of night. A sweetness flowed within him as he remembered this, as if he had drunk nectar. "Absolute knowledge," he said in his heart of hearts and sank into an ocean of bliss.

He remained in this state only a short while. Then uneasiness stirred within him. He thought that all other monks had left the shade of trees and gone under roofs where they slept on cots and flirted with women; only he is still wandering, lost in the forest. "Everyone else has gone back to their own homes. Why only am I far away from my own tree?" The memory of the tree became a summons to him. His feet set off on the path which led out of the jungle to his hometown.

As he was leaving the jungle, he abruptly stopped short. The train of his thoughts had been broken by a celestial figure and by the teaching which he had forgotten: "O monks, be mindful of your thoughts! And if you should stumble onto the path of evil, extricate yourself as an elephant extricates himself from a swamp!"

He returned remorsefully and, striking the hero-posture, sat down beneath a *peepul* tree. He repented when he remembered how happy he had become upon seeing the blossoming flowers and the flowing river. Did not Tathagat say: "O monks, what reason is there to smile and laugh and what is there to be happy about when this world is furiously blazing?" He looked around him. He realized that this world is a fire pit. Each and everything in it is burning up: flowers, leaves, trees, the flowing river, and his own sight. He closed his eyes.

For many days he sat still and silent in the hero-posture with his eyes firmly closed. But he did not obtain peace. His mind wandered and turned over and over again toward that tamarind tree. He became disheartened, arose, and began a long pilgrimage in search of peace.

He walked from jungle to jungle; his soles became bloody and his feet swelled and his legs began to ache. At last he entered the jungle of Uruvela and slowly, very slowly approached the *bodhivaram*. He looked at the tall, dense banyan which stood amid the other trees like a god. He sat beneath that tree, striking the hero-posture and joining his hands. He prayed: "O Shakyamuni, O Tathagat, O Amitabh, this monk is your turtle and is in the middle of his journey." Then he closed his eyes and murmured: "Peace, peace, peace."

He continued sitting for a long time. Days came and went and he sat there stone-still. Then the sorrow was gradually washed from his soul. A bud of bliss sprouted in his mind and in his consciousness a luxuriant tree sprang up. It was that very same tamarind tree. He got up suddenly. He knew that he had discovered the secret: every person has his own jungle and his own tree. The seeker will find nothing in the jungle of another person and whatever he is fated to find will come to him in his own jungle and in the shade of his own tree.

Discovering this secret, Vidyasagar intuitively realized that he had at last found the treasure of knowledge. He started off in the direction of his own tree. But as he was emerging from the forest of Uruvela, he was seized by a doubt: "O Vidyasagar, have you truly found the secret or have you been deceived by evil?"

Vidyasagar became uncertain whether the stick was still between his teeth or it had already slipped away. One of his feet remained in the forest of Uruvela and the other was pointed toward his tree, while a fire was raging everywhere around in the fire pit.

Translated by Nancy D. Gross

Glossary

alam (ᶜ*alam*): a banner; here, the spear-headed black banner of Imām Ḥusain which is carried out in procession during the Muḥarram festival.

Allahu Akbar (*Allāhu Akbar*): "Great(er) is God!"—a Muslim proclamation in war and peace.

Ammanji (Ammāṅjī): a respectful form of address for one's mother.

Apaji *(Āpājī)*: an elder sister.

Babu (*Bābū*): a white-collar worker.

Bait al-Maqdis: Jerusalem.

banaut (*banauṭ*): the art of club-fighting.

bigha (*bīgha*): a measure of land, about five-eighths of an acre.

bodhivaram (*bōdhīvaram*): the tree of knowledge and wisdom, under which, as the tradition has it, Lord Buddha received enlightenment.

biri (*bīṛī*): a cheroot or cigar common in the countries of South Asia.

chauki (*čaukī*): a small square stool with very short legs.

Chihlam (*Čehlam*): the fortieth day of mourning following the death of a relative; here, following the anniversary of the martyrdom of Imām Ḥusain; observed especially among the Shīᶜite Muslims.

chilam (*čilam*): a clay bowl that holds tobacco and fire, and is fitted to the shorter of the two pipes of a hookah or hubble-bubble.

CID: abbreviation of Central Investigation Department—the Indian intelligence-gathering bureau, which may be likened to the FBI in the United States.

Collector: the chief revenue officer of a district.

Data Darbar (Dātā Darbār): see note 2 under "Comrades," p. 136.

Data Sahib (Dātā Ṣāḥib): see note 1 under "The Legs," p. 163.

dhoti (*dhōtī*): a garment for the lower half of the body, worn around the waist, threaded between the legs, and tucked in behind; worn mostly by South Asian Hindus.

dinar (*dīnār*): an ancient gold coin.

dirham: a coin; drachma.

Doab (*Dōāb*): literally, two waters; a stretch of land lying between two rivers that unite after running some distance; here, the plain between the Ganges and Jamna.

Farangi (*Faraṅgī*): a Frank; a European; but mostly an Englishman in South Asian parlance.

ghadar: the Indian war of independence fought against the British in 1857; also known as the Sepoy Mutiny.

ghazal: a form of poetry dealing with the theme of love, whether human or divine.

gulal (*gulāl*): a red powder with which the Hindus smear each other during the spring festival of Hōlī.

Haji (Ḥājī): a Muslim who has performed the pilgrimage (*ḥajj*) to Mecca; a title of respect.

haveli (*ḥavēlī*): a large brick or stone building; a mansion or manor-house.

ᶜId (*ᶜĪd*): stands for either of the two major Muslim festivals, *ᶜĪd al-aẓḥā* or *ᶜĪd al-fiṭr*.

ᶜidgah (*ᶜīdgāh*): a large space (may or may not be enclosed) where the congregational prayer on the two major Muslim festivals of *ᶜĪd* (see item directly above) takes place.

imam-bara (*imām*; Arabic): a spiritual and religious leader, and (*bāṛa*; Urdu): an abode or enclosure: the house or abode of the *imāms*—a building in which the Muḥarram festival is celebrated.

imli (*imlī*): the tamarind tree or its fruit.

Jahanabad (Jahānābād): contraction of Shāhjahānābād; a city founded by the Mughal emperor Shāhjahāṅ (1592–1666); present-day Delhi.

Jataka (*Jātaka*): stories of the successive births of Lord Buddha.

ji (*jī*): a suffix indicating respect for the addressee to whose name it is connected.

Jumhurnama (*Jumhūrnāma*): an epic or story of the common people.

Karbala-e Muᶜalla (Karbalāʾ-e Muᶜallā): a place about 40 kilometers north of Kufa in Iraq where Imām Ḥusain received martyrdom.

karhai (*kaṛhāʾī* or *kaṛāhī*): a frying-pan; *gosht* (*gōsht*): meat; *kaṛhāʾī gōsht*: pan-fried meat.

Madina Munawwara: Madīna (a city in Saudi Arabia to which the

Prophet Muḥammad migrated in 622 C.E. and where he lies buried); Munavvara: the radiant.

Maharaj (*Mahārāj*): a form of address indicative of extreme respect, as "Your Majesty."

maund (for Urdu *man*): a measure of weight used in South Asia, usually 40 *sēr* or about 80 pounds.

Miyan (*Miyāṅ*): an address of respect; "sir."

Muharram (Muḥarram): the first month in the Muslim calendar. The first ten days of this month are spent in mourning by Shīᶜite Muslims—mourning, that is, the martyrdom of Imām Ḥusain on October 10th, 680 C.E., at Karbalāʾ.

Nawab (*navāb* or *navvāb*): a feudal lord.

neem (*nīm*): a tree with bitter fruit.

paisa: a unit of currency; formerly, one sixty-fourth, and currently, one-hundredth, of a rupee; a coin of such denomination.

pan (*pān*): a betel leaf; a chewing mixture prepared with betel leaf, grated betel nut, and *catechu* and cured lime pastes, with or without chewing tobacco and cardamom pods.

panja: literally, an aggregate of five; here it refers to a hand with five fingers extended, attached to the staff of the *ᶜalam*, signifying the Prophet Muḥammad, his daughter Fāṭima, his cousin and son-in-law ᶜAlī Ibn Abī Ṭālib, and his grandsons Ḥasan and Ḥusain.

peepul (*pīpal*): according to John T. Platts, "the holy fig tree, *Ficus religiosa*."

pera (*pēṛā*): a ball or lump of leavened dough; here, a kind of sweet meat.

Qul: see note 2 under "The Shadow," p. 147.

roti (*rōṭī*): a round, flat bread, much thinner but considerably bigger than a pancake, baked on a convex iron griddle; also can signify a whole meal.

Sab (vulgarization of *ṣāḥib* or *ṣāḥab*): Mister.

Ṣāḥib or *Ṣāḥab*: a respected man, gentleman, sir; appended to Muslim names.

salamalaikum (vulgarized form of the Arabic phrase "*as-salāmu ᶜalaikum*"): "peace be on you"; a form of greeting and salutation common among Muslims.

Savan (*Sāvan*): fourth month of the Hindu calendar (July–August); the rainy season; in poetry, the season of love and romance; also a time when women swing on swings while awaiting the arrival of their lovers.

ser (*sēr*): a measure of weight, about 2 pounds.

Shahnama (*Shāhnāma*): an epic or story of the kings.

shal (*shāl*): a kind of tree; according to John T. Platts, "The tree *Shorea robusta*."

shalwar (*shalvār*): a kind of baggy trousers worn mostly by women in South Asia and by men in the areas of Sind and the Punjab (Pakistan).

shisham (*shīsham*): according to John T. Platts, "The tree *Dalbergia sisu*, and its wood"; the wood of this tree is very hard and is considered excellent for making furniture.

"sooted-booted gentulman" (*sūṭeḍ būṭeḍ janṭalmēn*): a gentleman in suit and tie, and wearing dress shoes.

tonga (ṭāṅgā): a light two-wheeled horse-drawn carriage.

taziya (*ta*ᶜ*ziya*): to express one's sympathy, to offer one's condolences; to mourn. Among South Asian Muslims, however, a *ta*ᶜ*ziya* stands for the replica of the mausolea of Ḥasan and Ḥusain, sons of ᶜAlī and Fāṭima, and grandsons of the Prophet Muḥammad, at Karbalāᵓ in Iraq. The *ta*ᶜ*ziyas* are constructed from wood, bamboo, and paper mâché. On the tenth day of the month of Muḥarram, they are carried in procession along city streets, followed by crowds of devoted Shīᶜites reciting elegies and engaged in passion plays and self-flagellation. At the day's end the *ta*ᶜ*ziyas* are buried into the river.

tikka: a piece of meat about an inch thick; *kabab* (*kabāb*): small pieces of meat roasted on a skewer or charcoal broiled; *tikka kabāb*: pan-fried inch-thick pieces of meat.

ustad (*ustād*): a master or boss; a gang leader.

Ya Allah (*Yā Allāh*): "Oh, God!"; "O Lord!"

Ya Ali (*Yā* ᶜ*Alī*): "Oh, ᶜAlī!"

zamindar (*zamīṅdār*): a feudal lord or landholder.

Notes on the Translators

Caroline J. Beeson studied Urdu at Cornell University and the University of Minnesota at Minneapolis and in Hyderabad, India.

Leslie A. Flemming is Dean of the College of Arts and Sciences at Ohio University, Athens. She has written extensively on Saᶜadat Hasan Manto (d. 1955), one of Urdu's foremost short-story writers. Her monograph, *Another Lonely Voice: The Urdu Short Stories of Saadat Hasan Manto*, was published by the Center for South and Southeast Asia Studies, University of California, Berkeley, in 1979.

Nancy D. Gross studied Urdu at Cornell University and the University of Wisconsin. She spent a year in Lahore as a participant in the Berkeley Urdu Language Program in Pakistan. After graduating with a master's in South Asian Studies, she worked as an editor for Dover Publications, New York.

Muhammad Umar Memon was born in 1939 at Aligarh (India) and migrated to Pakistan in 1954. He was educated at Karachi University and, later, in the United States, where he took a master's in Near Eastern Languages and Literatures from Harvard University and a Ph.D. in Islamic Studies from the University of California at Los Angeles. He is now Professor of Urdu, Persian, and Islamic Studies at the University of Wisconsin, Madison. He writes fiction and criticism in Urdu and English and has also translated widely from modern Urdu fiction, of which he has published six volumes, the three most recent ones being: *The Tale of the Old Fisherman* (1991), *The Colour of Nothingness* (1991), and *Domains of Fear and Desire* (1992). He also edited *Studies in the Urdu Ghazal and Prose Fiction*, and his book on religious polemics, *Ibn Taimīya's Struggle Against Popular Religion*, appeared in 1976.

C. M. Naim hails from Barabanki (India), where he was born in 1936. He was educated in India and the United States and has been teaching Urdu humanities at the University of Chicago for nearly thirty years. He has written several major articles on Urdu literature and political and human issues in South Asia, besides translating many works of Urdu poetry and prose fiction and editing *Iqbal, Jinnah, and Pakistan: The Vision and the Reality*, which appeared in 1979. A cofounder and a former editor of the *Journal of South Asian Literature*, he also edited and published, between 1980 and 1990, seven issues of the *Annual of Urdu Studies*.

Javaid Qazi was born in Pakistan in 1947. He came to the United States in 1968 to study. He finished a doctorate in English literature at Arizona State University in 1978. He writes fiction and his work has appeared in *Kansas Quarterly, Sequoia, Chelsea,* the *Toronto South Asian Review, Massachusetts Review, Living in America: Poetry and Fiction by South Asian American Writers*, and the *Anaïs Nin: International Journal*. He lives and works in California.

(Muhammad) Daud Rahbar received his Ph.D. in Oriental Studies from Cambridge University in 1953 and taught at McGill University, Hartford Seminary Foundation, the University of Wisconsin, Northwestern University, and Boston University, which he joined in 1968. He has written numerous articles on Indian Islam and a highly regarded book called *God of Justice: Ethical Doctrine of the Quran*, besides translating a selection from the Urdu letters of the nineteenth-century Urdu and Persian poet Mirzā Asadu 'l-Lāh Khān Ghālib. He is a vocalist of classical Indian music and writes poetry in Urdu; in the *Cup of Jamshid* (1974) he has translated some of his own lyrical poems.

Richard R. Smith was at one time Assistant Professor of Urdu at Kansas State University. He later moved to Nepal to work there.

About the Book

These complex stories powerfully chart the painful course of Pakistan's odyssey from hope and visionary creativity to steady social, political, and moral decline.

The stories were written roughly between 1947, when Pakistan was created, and 1971, when it was fragmented by the establishment of Bangladesh as an independent nation. But they are equally meaningful today. Steeped in an unmistakable Shīᶜite ambiance and informed by the Shīᶜite vision of time, history, and redemptive suffering, they also draw freely on memoirs and memories, dreams and visions, Middle Eastern oral traditions, and Hindu and Buddhist mythology.

Intiẓār Ḥusain (b. 1925) is one of the most prolific and talented of today's Pakistani writers. Best known to his Urdu readership as a master of the short story, he has also experimented with novels, novellas, biographies, and plays, and he has won numerous literary awards in both India and Pakistan. He is a columnist for *Dawn,* Pakistan's largest-circulation English-language daily. **Muhammad Umar Memon** is professor of Islamic studies, Urdu, and Persian at the University of Wisconsin, Madison. Himself a well-known Urdu writer, he has also translated six collections of Urdu stories into English. He is editor of *The Annual of Urdu Studies.*